LUCKY RIDE

LUCKY O'TOOLE VEGAS ADVENTURE

BOOK EIGHT

A NOVEL BY

DEBORAH COONTS

Book published by Austin Brown, CheapEbookFormatting.com

Cover Design by Andrew Brown, ClickTwiceDesign.com

Paperback ISBN-13: 978-1-944831-75-2

Hardcover ISBN-13: 978-1-944831-76-9

V072517

PRAISE FOR DEBORAH COONTS' NOVELS

"Deliciously raunchy, with humorous takes on sexual proclivities, Vegas glitz and love, though Agatha Christie is probably spinning in her grave."

—Kirkus Reviews

"Complete with designer duds, porn conventions, partner-swapping parties, and clever repartee, this is chick-lit gone wild and sexy, lightly wrapped in mystery and tied up with a brilliantly flashing neon bow. As the first in a series, *Wanna Get Lucky?* hits the proverbial jackpot."

—Booklist

"*Wanna Get Lucky?* is a winner on every level. Deborah Coonts has crafted a first-class murder mystery coupled with a touching and unexpected love story. Against a flawlessly-rendered Las Vegas backdrop, Lucky's story is funny, fast-paced, exuberant and brilliantly realized."

—Susan Wiggs, *New York Times* bestselling author

"Get ready to win big--with a novel that will keep you glued to the pages all the way to the end. *Wanna Get Lucky?* is as entertaining as the city in which it's set."

—Brenda Novak, *New York Times* bestselling author of *Trust me, Stop Me, and Watch Me*

Wanna Get Lucky goes down faster than an ice-cold Bombay martini—very dry, of course, and with a twist.

—Douglas Preston, New York times bestselling author of Impact.

Wanna Get Lucky? Is an amazing debut novel, a mile-a-minute read, with fantastic characters, dry wit, and the gritty neon feel of Las Vegas. Bravo to Deborah Coonts—I see a great future ahead.

—Heather Graham, New York Times bestselling author of Night of the Wolves.

Novels in The Lucky Series

WANNA GET LUCKY?
(Book 1)

LUCKY STIFF
(Book 2)

SO DAMN LUCKY
(Book 3)

LUCKY BASTARD
(Book 4)

LUCKY CATCH
(Book 5)

LUCKY BREAK
(Book 6)

LUCKY THE HARD WAY
(Book 7)

LUCKY RIDE
(Book 8)

Lucky Novellas

LUCKY IN LOVE

LUCKY BANG

LUCKY NOW AND THEN
(PARTS 1 AND 2)

LUCKY FLASH

Other books by Deborah Coonts

AFTER ME

DEEP WATER

CRUSHED

CHAPTER ONE

"**A**RE you my mother?"

The girl standing in front of my desk could've been me—half a lifetime ago. Fresh-faced, a bit pale, and scared, she was tall to the point her shoulders stooped in teenage mortification. Her jeans had that designer distressed look, but without the designer price—a hard life, hard-earned. I pegged her at fifteen or a young sixteen. The raw scrape on her forehead overlying a blooming bruise made her look older.

With trouble written all over her, she needed a hug, but I didn't think that was what she was looking for, although I'd willingly comply. Something about tired children wandering into my office in the deepest, darkest part of the night hit every raw nerve of righteous indignation I had.

With that opening line and her straight-man delivery, I was sure she was kidding, so I kept my tone light. "You could do far better than me." I thought maybe I'd get a hint of a smile, or something. I was wrong. Dead serious stared back at me. "Okay, I'll play it straight, but that's not a question I'm used to getting in the middle of the night. Well, not ever. First time, really. But as an opener, it's a killer." I refocused on my preparations to leave—after a very long day, home called. Actually, a bed and a hot French chef called and I had no strength left to resist.

"Not a question I use on everybody," the girl monotoned it, her expression serious to the point of pinched pain.

The idea was ludicrous, so I gave serious its due. "Your *mother? Me?*" Each word laden with sarcasm, I hoped she got my point—she wasn't so much barking up the wrong tree as in the wrong forest altogether.

Heck, I wasn't even close to abandoning my childish ways. And that whole maternal thing...not even a tick-tock of the biological clock. No one who knew me would use parental as an adjective to describe me unless they were going for a cheap laugh.

Thankfully, I kept those shortcomings to myself. Running on fumes, with a short fuse and a penchant for semi-mixing metaphors when tired, I considered my silence an epic win.

The girl looked hungry and scared.

Been there myself; I knew the signs.

If she wanted a meal and a soft bed, all she had to do was give me a hint. To her, asking for it would be impossible. I knew that, too.

Her strong voice and the tilt to her chin were straight out of my playbook under the chapter "Offense is the Best Defense," which made me feel a kinship. Though had she asked, I could've told her it was rarely the best approach—except when dealing with my mother, Mona.

Mona was the exception to every rule.

I weighed how to handle the young woman in front of me. She seemed determined to make me work for what she wanted. Not the way to my soft underbelly. But her waifish act was clanging every rescuer bell I had.

Which always got me into trouble.

What can I say? I'm my mother's daughter—but don't ever expect me to admit it, like out loud or anything. When I'd finally admitted it to myself, I'd felt like leaping from a tall building. If I had to admit it to someone else, I'd take a running start.

With a sigh, I leaned back in my desk chair and gave her my full attention. "I would've remembered had I had a child. I'm sorry."

She absorbed that without a flinch. "Doesn't mean you

wouldn't lie about it." She tilted her chin higher.

That rankled—it shouldn't, she didn't know me. Clearly, this wasn't about me; it was about her. But her insinuation felt personal. I squeezed my eyes shut, reaching for perspective and my ever-elusive self-control. I opened my eyes—she hadn't disappeared. "A decent person wouldn't lie about a thing like that."

She gave a snort. "Right. Don't know any of those decent types." She looked me over. "You one?"

"Most days, or I'd like to think so at least." Decency was a dying art, along with civility. I owed her both. My name is Lucky O'Toole, and as the Vice President of Customer Relations for the Babylon Group, the holding company for a couple of major Vegas Strip properties as well as satellite properties as close as downtown Vegas and as far away as Macau, solving problems was not only the beating heart of my being but also of my job. The girl clearly had a problem.

"But perhaps I'm a bit delusional and decency eludes me. Anyway, you came here for a reason. Want to tell me about it?" Curiosity had a bad rap. But I wasn't a cat, so it probably wouldn't be lethal. Yes, she had me at the "mother" line; I admit it. "You do know I'm not your mother, right?" Why did I need her to believe me? There was something about her... "You want to tell me why you're here?"

She met my eyes for a moment then stared at the ground as if wishing a hole would open and swallow her. A hint of pink rose in her cheeks. "No." She shifted as if moving the load that rested on her shoulders. "I mean, yes, I want to tell you about it; but no, I know you're not my mother. Sometimes you just want something so bad..." As her voice hitched, she looked at me through too-big eyes. Then she shook her head as if shaking away a dream.

I knew all about that, too.

She dropped the combative posture but retained the attitude—a teenager to the core. "Maybe you're not my mother, but you know her."

A different tack; a broader gene pool. "I know a lot of people." Even some who would abandon a kid—not something that gave me a warm fuzzy. They say you are the average of the five people you hang out with the most. That didn't give me a warm fuzzy either.

Vegas was full of folks who would do the less-than-honorable things for honorable reasons...or less than honorable reasons...and the trick was figuring out who would do which. My job description included rubbing shoulders with both types all day, every day. This being Vegas, where the game was paramount and winning essential, I probably handled more of the less-than-honorable types than the other, although I didn't keep score. Some of their situational ethics were bound to rub off and damage my delicate psyche. Would that be a workplace injury?

As I pondered the limits of Worker's Comp, I motioned to a chair in front of the desk. "Why don't you sit?"

She ignored me.

A kid. Alone. In need of a good meal...or several...and desperate enough to play the mother card. She was so not what I needed. Not now. Not today—a very young New Year's Day, but growing older by the second.

Jet-lagged and over-amped from chasing a couple of killers in China. Still reeling from too much birthday. A hotel, my own for once, so new, and a punch list so long. All of it made me feel like moving and not leaving a forwarding address, so I wasn't in the market for another problem, another dose of the downside of life.

But she was what I got. "What's your mother's name?"

The kid pulled her shoulders back and stood tall. "I don't know."

"You don't know." Of course she didn't. At an impasse, I stared at her, cataloging our situation. Well, actually, my situation. Of all the places she could've gone to for help, she wandered far to find me.

Why me?

And, here in my new office, I wasn't easy to find. The space still looked Spartan—I'd yet to put my personal stamp on it. What was that about?

Truth be told, while I reveled in having my own hotel, Cielo, I missed my old office in the Babylon. I missed my staff—my chosen family. Hell, I even missed my foul-mouthed bird, Newton. Well, okay, the bird, not so much.

Such is change: something lost for something gained. Sometimes I wondered if it was worth the price.

Nervousness roiled my stomach as my question lingered: *Why me?*

"I think you know more than you're telling me; otherwise, why would you work so hard to find me?" She looked so heartbroken I took the sting out of my tone. "Stories and dreams are dangerous things. Once you let them out, they aren't yours alone anymore," I said, apropos of everything. "I get that. But you've got to give me something if you want me to help you."

My words jarred something loose inside her. Her face cleared as she pulled out one fist that had been stuffed in a pocket. In her hand, she clutched a scrap of paper, which she thrust at me. "I'm telling you the truth. I don't know my mother's name, but here's a picture of her. She looks like you but...smaller." The girl colored at the not-so-subtle slight.

At a fully fleshed-out six feet, I didn't think I needed to point out that everyone was smaller than me.

Finally, she lowered herself to perch on the edge of the chair in front of my desk.

I wanted to help her. Hell, I wanted to help everybody. Like limp flesh, my personality hung on the steel framework of a hero complex. Give me a problem, someone in need, and I'd dive in without looking. The results were consistently spectacular if not always successful.

What was that definition of stupidity? Doing the same thing but expecting a different result?

I was living proof...although right now, dead on my feet, the living part was in question.

As I took the photo from her outstretched hand, I didn't look at it. I kept my eyes on the girl's face and tried to shake a nervous feeling.

Why me?

Still afraid to meet my eye—disappointment was a devastating fear—she stuffed her hand back in her pocket and glared over my shoulder with the teenage I-don't-give-a-fuck-but-actually-I-do-but-I-don't-want-you-to-know-it look. Of course, most days I lived in the same headspace, so I got it, although lack of character, not age, was my excuse.

I took a deep breath and stepped off the ledge.

The photo had been torn in half. The tear looked old, the edges yellowed. Only one person showed. A young woman, short shorts and a halter top, hands on tiny hips, legs a mile long, and sunglasses that I'd bet hid a come-hither look.

I knew that look.

"Wow." The word escaped on all the breath I had.

You know her.

No shit.

Mona.

My mother.

CHAPTER TWO

YOU *do* know her." Disappointment fled from the girl's face, replaced by hope...and fear.

The hope of a dream, the fear of it shattering—I knew that, too.

Genetic bonding could explain the whole *sympatica* thing. Stars whirled in front of my eyes. I felt a little woozy.

Mona.

I struggled to find enough air to inflate words. "Know her?" At this moment, that struck me as odd. *Did* I know her? All of her or just the part I'd experienced? I would've carried that thought further, asking myself if we could ever really know someone, but that sounded like a lame excuse Judge Judy would eviscerate. Was she still on TV belittling those who came to her for help? I didn't know, so I let it lie.

Give it a dose of panic and my brain does weird things.

The girl's posture had gone rigid—paralyzed with too many emotions to catalog or counter.

Memories blindsided me as I stared at the younger version of my mother. She'd been fifteen when she'd had me. Was the photo before or after? Hard to tell, but my first memory of her mirrored the version in the photo.

"Who is she?" The girl's voice wavered. "You know her, I can tell."

I snorted at the incongruity of all of it—my day, my life, this moment...all of it. "Yeah, I know her. Most days I want to kill her." Today was one of them, but I left that part out. I put the photo on the desk between us and pushed it back across toward her with a forefinger, as far away from me as I could get it.

She vibrated with need like a puppy. "Who—"

I cut her off. "My turn." She started to argue. "If you want my help, I get to ask the questions." I sounded in control, proving once again that bullshit artist should be the top skill listed on my résumé. Emotions surged. Logical thought shattered. Yet, my voice remained calm, surprising the hell out of me.

Her shoulders came up around her ears. She lowered her chin. But that was all the fight I got. Good thing because I was loaded for bear. If she was playing me, attacking my family...

Since my brain had gone offline, flooded with all kinds of neurotransmitters all shouting for flight rather than fight, I started with the obvious. "Where did you get this picture?" Photos of my mother as a kid weren't easy to come by. Mona was really picky about that. I'd never understood why. Oh, she had her limitations, but vanity wasn't one of them. A fault, yes. A limitation? Not so much.

The girl shifted, leaning all the way back in the chair, which almost swallowed her. Her chin rested on her chest. "I've had it forever."

"Define forever."

"Long as I can remember."

"Who gave it to you?"

"My grandmother." She softened a bit when she mentioned her grandmother.

"She raised you?"

The girl nodded.

"What did she tell you?"

"That the girl in the photo was my mother."

"Curiously, I got that. I'll admit to foolish, but not stupid." Snark threatened to override civility—for me a constant struggle. "Anything else?"

The girl looked as out to sea as I felt. "Only to look for her in Vegas and that she wouldn't be as bad as she seemed."

I had to chuckle at that. "Oh, I think your grandmother was a tad optimistic." But she'd pegged Mona all right. Maybe she really had known my mother. And, if so, maybe she could shed some light. "Does your grandmother know where you are?"

"She...died." Sadness tugged at the corners of her mouth, turning them down.

"When?"

"Two weeks? I'm not sure." Her eyes glistened when she looked at me—a quick look, just enough to see the hurt there. "Life's been..."

Her pain sucker-punched me, taking my breath. I didn't have much family but the ones I had were all still here, although the Big Boss wasn't recovering from the gunshot as quickly as we all had expected. A shadow of worry drifted across my heart. Loss scared me. To lose the Big Boss... I cleared my throat, constricted by emotion. "Do you have anyone else?"

"Only the lady in the photograph, *if* you tell me who she is." The girl clung to the frayed end of a short rope.

At least she held on. My rope shredded, dropping me into an emotional free fall.

The girl looked tired and worried, a bit angry, and a lot lonely, but she also radiated scared. I couldn't shake that. She was afraid of something. I knew it like I knew so much else about the road she'd walked. Everything about her pulled me back to a place in time where I walked in her shoes and I didn't like having to relive the whole uncertainty of it all.

For a young woman alone, danger lurked in every shadow. I knew exactly where she was coming from—I didn't like that either. Too bad the past was the only immutable in life—I'd love to rewrite mine...and hers. But aren't we the product of our pasts, tempered and molded through experience?

Damn.

Maybe, just maybe, the girl was afraid of being alone and I was reading too much into all of this. She'd said two weeks since her grandmother had passed. Perhaps all this was as straightforward as it seemed and she was reeling rather than calculating.

"I need to know whether you're telling the truth or not. Look at it from my point of view. It wouldn't be too hard for someone to get hold of a photo and come waltzing in here with a grand story." A bit of an overstatement since it was Mona we were talking about, but the girl didn't know that. I moved from behind the desk to sit in the chair next to her. As I did so, I caught my reflection in a mirror someone had hung on the wall despite my best intentions to avoid decorating. Limp brown hair, wan skin taut with worry, high cheekbones—as Mona said, my only real asset—and blue eyes bloodshot and saucered with emotion. Curiously, I looked normal...at least for me.

I probably should worry about that, but, right now, larger worries demanded my attention.

Had Mona really walked away from this girl...her daughter?

Why? What would make a mother do that?

Actually, I knew the answer to that.

Mona had abandoned me when I'd become a burden. How she'd bungled it had left deep scars, but this wasn't about me. And at least I had answers about my past if not complete understanding.

But what about this one?

So many questions—paths in a forest that led nowhere.

Reaching across, I squeezed the girl's arm. "I know you're scared and a bit out of your element. I get that. Been there myself. Curiously, at about your age."

"Not like this." The myopia of youth. Each one convinced they were the only ones ever to experience the pain of their existence.

"I'll help you, but you've got to be straight with me. If you don't tell me all that you know, this whole thing is going to be hard to piece together."

Her lower lip started to quiver, which made her mad. She pinched her mouth into a thin line of control then gave me a curt nod.

Or at least I thought the nod was for me, but perhaps not—her eyes had an unfocused, faraway look. "Do you know where the picture was taken?"

"On my Gram's farm."

All the questions I wanted answered punctured my fear like shrapnel perforated skin. How to find the seeds of truth in her story? "Did your Gram own the farm?" There'd be deeds and all, easily findable—pieces to the puzzle.

"Not outright. She was paying Dr. Dean off, she'd said."

A privately financed sale. The deed wouldn't be generated until she'd paid off the farm. Okay, scratch the deed trail.

"And your name? You haven't told me your name." Jesus! How had I forgotten the most obvious question of all?

The girl licked her lips as her gaze darted around my office like a trapped fly searching for an open window. "Tawny. Tawny Rose."

Tawny Rose. She'd named herself after a color of lipstick or a kindhearted stripper.

Looked like the girl had an on-again, off-again affair with the truth.

But where did she get that photo?

"Okay...Tawny." I didn't try to hide my skepticism and slight amusement. "How old are you?"

"Sixteen." Too young to be by herself in Vegas, wandering casinos in the wee hours looking for her mother. A bad modern take on a Dickens novel.

I'd lived that life. I knew the empty heart feeling.

Thanks to my mother.

Mona.

What had she done?

If the present mimicked the past, in a nutshell, she'd abandoned me—then justified it by leaving me in the care of someone...sort of. A man—my boss—who I found out later...much later...was my father. Of course, she'd left me in the dark about that little factoid—I'd thought I was alone. And now here we were, a happy little family with a past threatening to blow it apart at the seams.

What were the legal boundaries of justifiable matricide?

And here I thought I had finally gotten my personal baggage down to a carry-on. Silly me.

My mother was a skilled emotional surgeon, slicing, dicing, leaving pencil-thin scars to crisscross one's heart.

And that girl I used to be was still a part of me. And her pain gnawed, a tiny beast that could cripple one bite at a time.

Mona had cut and run once. She could've done it again.

Funny, but that possibility had never entered my reality—not until tonight when it walked through my door.

If Mother had walked away from this young woman, I'd kill her myself.

No one deserves that, especially not a kid.

No one should have to live through what I did.

Trying to focus, I leaned forward to stare again at the picture on the edge of the desk. The photo was old, Mona very young, but I'd recognize her before I would myself. For as long as I could remember—except for those years where it had seemed she'd abandoned me in Vegas—Mona and I had been the Two Musketeers. Now she was married to my father—normal for most but an interesting turn of events for me. I hadn't known about our family ties until recently. My newfound father, Albert Rothstein, aka the Big Boss, was the majority shareholder in the Babylon Group and a major player in Vegas. As such, he and my mother were targets for every grifter and con who could get this far.

Did Miss Tawny Rose have an angle? Was she pulling a con? Or did someone send her to undermine Mona's political aspirations? I immediately eliminated the latter. Mona was the proof to the old adage that if you gave someone enough rope, they would hang themselves. With Mother, political suicide was nothing more than a timing issue. Anybody who would care knew that already.

"You want to know who she is?" I asked the girl as I paused and took a deep breath.

This was Mona's fight. I couldn't protect her from this one.

No, this was a crack that would swallow her tiny, perfect, taut little ass. I know I sounded like I'd like to see her get her comeuppance, but not really. Although, there was a part of me that enjoyed seeing Mona swing over the abyss holding on for her life. Yes, shallow is my middle name. Not something I was proud of, but something I could live with.

God knew she had a myriad of faults—up to this point, the most important of which was being irritating as hell. But she was, above all, my mother, and that counted for everything.

Family, the ties that bind. What I wouldn't do for a knife.

As if sensing the answer to her question, the girl leaned forward, hanging on expectation.

I delivered the one-two punch. "She's my mother, Mona." I lifted my chin toward the photo that still lay on the desk like an accusation. "But I think you knew that."

"Mona," the girl whispered with hushed reverence.

Misplaced reverence, but I wasn't going to be the one to burst that bubble.

A flood of emotions widened her eyes. "I didn't know."

They were blue. Like mine. Like Mona's.

"Mona." This time her voice held a bit less reverence. "Your mother." She angled her head as if seeing me anew. "And that makes us—"

"—still trying to figure this out." The words should've been sufficient to shut down that line of thinking, but I breathed a bit of cool into them for extra clarity. I do tend to overdo, but adjusting to the Big Boss as my father was hard enough. Then with the recent birth of twin siblings (you'd think after years in the bordello business, my mother would know what causes that), I was having a hard time getting my pea brain around my burgeoning family.

Now, this.

"How did you happen to get to my office?" Of all the gin joints...I knew how Humphrey Bogart felt. "Who put me together with that photo?"

"I like your name." Enigmatic to a fault, the girl gave me a half smile, surprising me and, from the look on her face, herself as well. There was more there, but the steely look in those baby blues told me I'd need a pickaxe.

But she had more to gain than I did, so that meant I held the cards. "Always play the odds, kid. You want your shot with Mona, then tell me why you like my name." My voice went low, riding on a hard demand.

The girl gave it a moment's hesitation, then wilted. Smart girl. "My grandfather, he drank. I didn't know him well. He died when I was young. Of a broken heart, my Gram said. But there were times just before he'd pass out when he'd talk to himself. I don't know why but I got the impression he was talking to someone he knew, someone who was no longer there. He called her Lucky Bean."

"And that led you to me?"

"How many Luckys do you know? Your name is all over everything at the rodeo."

"A long shot." *With a big payoff.*

"Sometimes you play a hunch rather than the odds." To her credit, she didn't rub my nose in it. Instead, she focused on the photo. "Are you sure that girl in my photo is your mother? It's not that clear and was taken a long time ago." Emotion thinned her voice, but she looked like some of the pieces to a puzzle she wasn't sharing completely had fallen into place.

"That's Mona. Even then she was distinctive." I wondered what she'd been like back then. Carefree, young, the future open and bright. How had she ended up a hooker in Pahrump? Why had I never asked?

"You favor her," the girl said.

She did, too, but I couldn't bring myself to say the words. "Flattery will get you everywhere." The angels on my shoulders whispered in my ears. Should I believe her? Should I not?

Whether she was telling the truth or not, that didn't alter the fact that she really looked like she needed help. And if what she said was true...

The good angel won.

I so wouldn't like myself if I didn't get to the bottom of her story.

Compassion, the upside to bad decisions.

At least there was one.

The girl glanced toward the doorway then gave me the eye. No, not the eye, but more of a calculated once-over with the wariness and savvy of a youngster who had seen too much. But some of the kid peeked through in the hope and fear she tried to hide. Yeah, the girl was still in there—she didn't have the tough shell and dead eyes of a kid who lived on the streets.

She smelled of horses. The shavings that clung to her fleece jacket told me I wasn't crazy. The rodeo was in town—the Western Finals to be exact.

"What'd you do? Run away with the rodeo? I thought kids ran away to join the circus. Guess I'm hopelessly out of date."

What little color she had left her face. "What?"

"You're here with the rodeo?" I pressed.

She flinched like I'd hit her with a cattle prod. "How'd you know?"

I pointed to the shavings on her jacket.

Some of the tough melted away. "Yeah." She brushed them off and they fluttered to the floor. She didn't pick them up. "You got a cleaning crew."

An explanation but hardly an excuse.

What was it they said about teenagers? Purposefully irritating so their parents would be ready to see them take wing and fly on their own? What, so they could fly around and poop on the rest of us? Or, worse, land in our laps?

I wouldn't go back to being a teenager on a bet—a child trying to navigate a grown-up, bad-guy world without a map. "Yeah, I have a cleaning crew. I'm a big cheese, don't ya' know?" All I really wanted to do was fold her in a hug and tell her life would be okay, that she'd get to be a kid a while longer. But I couldn't promise that, which made me sad and mad at the same time.

I glanced at the clock. Still too early, or not late enough, to get off the Strip—on New Year's Eve it was shut down to traffic until morning. "Have you eaten?"

Surprise flickered across her face. "No. Why?"

"Hungry, then?"

She wilted into the truth. "Starved." Her eyes flicked to the doorway again.

"Are you expecting someone?" I narrowed my eyes. "Or maybe someone is following you, hassling you?" The streets were mean for a full-grown badass like me. They'd be hell for the wisp of a kid scared out of her shoes but determined to pretend otherwise.

She met my eyes and held them. "No. No one."

I didn't believe her, but I let it go. If she had someone coming to shake me down, this was the wrong place to do it—security in Vegas hotels is unsurpassed. Well, other than letting sixteen-year-olds in without question. "You have a story, and I want to hear it—all of it. I thought we could do it over some food."

Tears sprung to her eyes. She gathered her fleece over the heel of one hand and swiped at a drop that had the audacity to trickle down her cheek. Without meeting my eyes, she nodded once.

Leaning forward, I raked together my phone and other minor detritus of my life, stuffing them in my Birkin. Then I thought better of it and pulled out my phone, pausing before I dialed. "Will the best hamburger in the world suffice? And maybe a milkshake?"

She looked like I'd offered her a king's repast, which, considering Jean-Charles Bouclet, world-renowned chef would be doing the cooking, wasn't shading the truth too much.

"Good, then." I hastily texted my chef and got an immediate, affirmative response, no questions asked. Gotta love a guy who was willing to open what I knew to be an almost closed kitchen for the asking. And I did love him. More than I knew and probably as much as he hoped.

The whole fiancé thing was so new I often blew by it when thinking of Jean-Charles Bouclet—my French chef. And, yes, my fiancé. Of course, when thinking about him, rational thought was a wish but rarely a reality.

Warmth rushed through me. I'd stopped trying to control my body's involuntary reaction at the mere thought of my chef.

Degrading, so I ignored it.

He'd be waiting. I flipped around the big sparkler on my left ring finger a few times as I tried to figure how to play this whole thing—an impossible task, considering I was running on barely one cylinder, and that was misfiring. Maybe I, too, needed food.

Or maybe I just needed a hug.

"Come on, it's just upstairs." I gathered her up and, with my hand in the small of her back, escorted her through the outer vestibule of my office and into the hall. I took an immediate right to push through a set of double doors.

"Aren't the elevators that way?" she asked with a nod down the hall.

"Yep, but you're getting the VIP tour." After shoving my card in the slot, I punched the button for the top floor and the machine whirred to life. Too bad my card wouldn't shock my heart back to a normal rhythm.

We'd settled in for the ride in the service elevator, me staring at our reflections, the girl studiously avoiding them. Once the doors closed, she stopped doing her imitation of a rabbit ready to bolt.

"Mona is a hooker...or was." I'm not sure why I stated it so harshly, maybe wanting to cut through the whitewash of the girl's fantasy.

"Was? You mean she's dead?" The girl looked stricken. The hooker part didn't seem to faze her.

"No. Sorry, I thought I'd made that clear. She's mean enough to outlive all of us. At present, she's retired from her former profession." And contemplating a political career, I thought. An abandoned child would surely derail Mona's ambition train.

Life was like ice—one hard blow and the consequences radiated outward in unanticipated cracks.

"So, you really think the lady in the photo is your mother?" I asked the girl the same question she'd asked me, both of us wanting to be sure of the answer.

The girl was half my age. Even though I was a bit thrown, I

worked through the simple math. She would have been born while I was living in Vegas, working for the man I didn't yet know was my father and attending UNLV. Mother was still working in Pahrump at her eponymous whorehouse. We didn't see each other often back then—I'd been pissed that she'd dumped me in Vegas. I hadn't known she'd dumped me with my father—I felt like I'd been abandoned and my mother had become my least favorite person. We both weathered it, but the hurts ran deep.

The girl squared her shoulders. "There's only one way to find out. Where is she? My mother...Mona."

As the elevator slowed, I pulled my phone out of my bag and squinted at the screen. I didn't wear a watch for obvious reasons—in a casino the time of day, or night, didn't matter. It was later than I'd feared. "Probably asleep."

No matter the personal cost, I wanted a happy ending for the girl—even though I doubted Mona qualified. But, she was better than no mother at all...some of the time.

The elevator whirred to a soft stop, and the doors slid open. Neither of us moved, even though I could smell the luring aroma of charcoaling beef all the way out here.

As the doors started to glide shut, I thrust a hand out, stopping them. "Come on. Let's get that food. I'm sure you have a lot more to tell me."

The girl gave me the side-eye as she stepped by me. "I can find Mona without your help."

Jesus, did dealing with a teenager earn one a special place in Heaven?

"No doubt. But getting to her might prove a challenge." I figured the photo would get Mona's attention, and probably an audience with her as well, but with Mother, one never knew. But the girl didn't know that. "Besides, the person leading the charge usually takes the first bullet." That shut down any further argument, at least for the moment.

Jean-Charles's restaurant was at the end of a short hallway. After serious, prolonged negotiations, we'd settled on JCB Prime as a name. He'd wanted just JC, but to me, that held a hint of blasphemy—not that many of us in Vegas knelt before an altar, but still. Jean-Charles had dug in his heels saying he wasn't going to apologize for his initials, nor shy away from any implication of a Divine blessing. I sorta got his point but, I'd countered with, no matter the deity you prayed to, she probably wasn't into having her name emblazoned over a restaurant in Vegas. That argument, and concurrence from his mother had carried the day. Yes, I called in the heavy reinforcements—all's fair in love and war, and this was both. Such folly mixing business with pleasure. Even I knew that. But even I didn't listen to me.

Jean-Charles had left the back door open a crack for us. A bit prophetic, I thought—the back door was the only way I'd be getting into Heaven. Anxious for a hug, I went first and dove straight into his arms almost before he had a chance to turn away from the stove.

Burying my face in the crook where neck met shoulder, I breathed him in as he held me tight. "Who knew hamburgers could be an aphrodisiac?" My lips moved against his warm skin.

He chuckled, a rumbling I felt before the sound registered on my heart. "I said that out loud, didn't I?" Given we had an audience, I should've been embarrassed. But at my last birthday, I'd vowed to give up worrying about what other people thought of me.

That was all of twenty-four hours ago, so that head trip was a bit new.

I leaned back in his embrace so I could take the kiss I wanted. He didn't disappoint, and I drank deeply.

Before I was ready, Jean-Charles pulled back. "Are you going to introduce us or are you going to let your friend stand there in her discomfort?"

What was it about Jean-Charles that made conscious thought flee? Just a scant millimeter taller than me in reasonable heels, Jean-Charles looked resplendent in his chef's whites, which hid a body that would drive Adonis to envy and me to distraction. How I would love to... I chewed on my lip as I let my mind wander.

Sex wouldn't make this all go away, but it sure would make

me feel better.

"Are you going to introduce us?" Amusement lit in his blue eyes. He knew what I was thinking.

Perhaps I should have blushed, but blushing was beneath the me I wanted to be, and, if anything, I was all about fake-it-until-you-make-it.

I wanted him. We both knew it. He reciprocated. Everyone was happy, albeit a bit frustrated at the moment.

"I'm sorry. Where are my manners?" I was usually so good at introductions and all the Emily Post stuff. Mona had seen to that. A hooker with refined sensibilities.

Mona.

Mona was never quite what one expected.

I figured hormones and an emotional hand grenade excused a momentary lapse in manners so I gave myself a pass. "Jean-Charles Bouclet, may I present..." A momentary blank—I'd forgotten more than my manners—"Miss Tawny Rose." I kept a straight face, another epic win in a night filled with odd games.

Jean-Charles raised an eyebrow, but that was it.

"Miss Rose, may I present Jean-Charles Bouclet, my fiancé and a rather good chef who has a way with hamburgers and milkshakes."

"And a way with you." Tawny gave me a knowing look.

Maybe she'd been on the streets longer than I thought. "I don't deny it. Jean-Charles, this is Tawny Rose."

He bent over her hand, making her blush. "*Enchanté.*" Then he invited us further inside before any awkwardness could get a foothold. "Come." Turning back to his work, he scooped the patties off the coals, setting them on a rack to the side to rest. "I'll be back in a moment." Wiping his hands on a rag, he asked Tawny, "Chocolate or vanilla?"

She gave a derisive huff.

"Chocolate it is. I had you pinned as a chocolate girl." With a circling motion, he indicated a high-top table with three stools next to the stove. "You sit." Then he disappeared into the restaurant, heading toward the bar.

To the side, Champagne chilled in a bucket of ice water. I chose a stool next to the Champagne.

The girl picked the one on the opposite side from me and nearest the door. "Pinned?" she asked after boosting herself onto the stool.

"Pegged." I pulled out two flutes that Jean-Charles had upended into the ice as well, drying them with a bar towel looped through the handle of the bucket. I placed one in front of his stool and one in front of me, then I filled the flutes with Laurent-Perrier rosé—the good stuff. "English vernacular. He gets close most of the time." Frankly, I found his struggle with idioms to be charming.

Apparently, Tawny did as well. Color remained in her cheeks as she looked at me from under lowered lashes. "He's..."

I detected a hint of reverence bordering on adulation. "Indeed."

Somehow, my manners returning, I resisted the overwhelming urge to bolt the Champagne until Jean-Charles returned with an extra-thick chocolate shake. He handed it to Tawny with a bow, making her giggle. He raised his flute in a toast. "To friends."

"To family," I said.

The girl looked surprised as we clinked glasses. Underneath my Pollyanna shell lurked a solid pragmatist. If Mona had done something stupid, which was totally within her probabilities, we'd do what we always did: bitch and moan, and probably panic just a bit, then do the right thing.

Jean-Charles plated the food, one burger for each of us, two for the girl, then joined us, straddling the last stool. Silence reigned as we fell to eating like ravenous wolves. I couldn't remember my last meal. Last night? A birthday celebration? Then Jean-Charles had taken his son, Christophe, home and I'd gone to work. And I was still there. Tonight, Jean-Charles had been consumed by preparing food for his clientele and probably hadn't taken time to eat. And Tawny, or whatever her real name was, had the feral look of someone for whom food was hunted rather than provided.

Despite my hunger, I managed only a few bites before

giving up.

"Is the food not to your liking?" Jean-Charles's question rode on an undercurrent of concern. He knew my aptitude for gluttony.

"I don't seem to have the energy," I lied. Frankly, I just wasn't hungry. Had that ever happened? I couldn't remember. But, I still thirsted for a liquid diet. I peered at the bottom of my Champagne flute. The rosé had evaporated—that was happening to me more and more lately.

"You have had no sleep, yes?" Jean-Charles asked. "And the adrenaline, it is gone now, no?"

How did anyone ever figure out how to answer those kinds of questions? Yes, I've had no sleep. Or no, I haven't had any sleep. They were like the thing with the air conditioner. If you turned it up, did that mean you made it colder? Or was it the other way around? Clearly higher thought was beyond my current competence, so I simply nodded, letting him jump to whatever conclusion he wanted.

Without being asked, he refilled my flute. I didn't complain. Normally, Champagne brought clarity. Of course, tonight would be the night that formula failed.

Jean-Charles finished his burger and the girl ate her two, telling me I'd figured her situation accurately, at least as far as sustenance went.

I pushed my plate toward her. "Here, finish mine." Her milkshake mustache made me smile. She nodded and kept eating. I sipped my Champagne, trying to restrain myself with a modicum of success, while I waited for her to finish.

Finally, she looked up from her food, her plate clean, her milkshake a memory. She cocked one eyebrow at Jean-Charles. "Dessert?"

"As you wish." He gave me a wink as he backed off his stool then disappeared into the walk-in cooler. Jean-Charles was playing to every chef's dream, a ravenous, appreciative customer.

The food had softened the girl's feral look, so I decided the time was ripe for more questions. "Can you tell me where you're from?"

"Outside of Reno."

"Your grandmother's ranch?"

She nodded.

"Her name?"

This was where the rubber met the road. That's the thing about lies, so hard to keep straight. I felt like adding "The truth will set you free," but somehow, I didn't think she'd get the reference—she hadn't enough years to have amassed enough worthless references. And I really didn't feel like being that self-righteous. No matter our age, we each had our own coping mechanisms. Lying wasn't the best, but it was the one most often tried first.

"Sara Pickford."

"Pickford?" Between Pickford and O'Toole there were far too many movie references in this family. You'd think that if fantasy was a family heirloom, someone would've created a better one.

"Her fourth husband. Long story. But she kept trying."

"Your gram's ranch is where the photo was taken?"

"Yes, but long before I arrived." Folding her napkin crease by crease absorbed her attention. She flicked her gaze to mine then back to her napkin.

That math I could do for myself. I wanted to jerk her napkin away. "And the place is yours now?"

Surprise flickered. "A lawyer is figuring it out. He said it would take a while."

"Do you live there?"

"I did. Right now, I'm traveling with the rodeo, as you guessed."

"In what capacity?"

This time she looked at me a fraction of a second longer, then her face started to close. "Just a helper." Her need to tell the truth warred with self-preservation.

"To whom?"

She eyed me like my IQ had suddenly plummeted. "The horses."

I raised one eyebrow.

"I muck out the stalls and shit." She rewarded me with an eye roll.

Rule Number One in the Amateur Interrogation Handbook: get under their skin. One and done. I resisted gloating as bad form—and ignored the fact I was barely holding my own in a contest with a sixteen-year-old. "Are you in school?"

"I finished early."

"Finished? You mean graduated or left?" I'd keep pushing until I got stonewalled.

"Graduated."

"And?"

Her hands dropped in a knot to her lap. "I left."

"Why?"

Pale replaced the pink in her cheeks. Her shoulders dropped as the attitude faded.

The truth. So very close, I could almost taste it. I leaned forward slightly. Grabbing her and shaking would probably not get the result I wanted, but it would feel really good. Instead, I summoned my last bit of self-control and waited. The need to tell me shimmered off her in waves.

I held my breath until I saw stars.

She pulled in a deep lungful of air. Her gaze locked onto mine. She opened her mouth to speak.

Jean-Charles breezed back to the table.

Tawny clamped her mouth shut and painted on a smile.

He slid a tray in front of us with a flourish. "A most excellent *mille-feuilles*. My pastry chef," he put his fingers to his lips then made a kissing motion, "she is to kill for."

The look I threw him flew by my pastry-enraptured chef like a knife in a circus act.

Good thing there weren't any sharp knives within reach—this might be my circus, but it was not an act. A few more moments and I would've had...something, maybe even a hint at the whole truth.

"To kill for?" Tawny, her chin still tucked, glanced at me.

"To die for." I settled back, letting the rancor go. I'd shake the truth out of her somehow.

"Yes, this," Jean-Charles said, completely unaware of just how close death was. He dealt each of us clean plates, then gave me a small piece per my usual request and a whopper for our young guest.

The kid was from Nevada. That surprised me—I was expecting someplace further away. Don't know why other than folks who blindsided me in the past had tended to travel a great distance for the privilege.

Teddie had been born in Boston.

Teddie. Why was he first to spring to mind? And why did first loves hurt so much?

Jean-Charles hailed from Provence.

"Both your grandparents are gone. Do you have any other family?" I asked. Mona had never mentioned any family, and I'd assumed she would've had she had any. Right now, life rubbed my nose in the fallacy of that assumption—or at least the very real possibility that Mona had kept secrets. Oh, sure, I'd known she was famous for skirting the truth, but not from me. Not from her own flesh and blood, her own *daughter*.

How could I have been so naïve? So arrogant in my place in her life?

But hiding secrets? That never dawned on me. Stupid, in retrospect. Secrets were so a part of my mother's way of dealing with reality.

"No one. Just the lady in the photograph. Like I said."

"Mona," I said to Jean-Charles to bring him into the conversation at least somewhat.

Jean-Charles's eyebrows shot toward his hairline as he cocked his head toward the girl and gave me a questioning glance. I gave him a little shrug. He knew how to interpret it—if he was looking for more, that's all I had.

"Other than your grandmother's story, is there any other reason you believe she's your mother?" I asked Tawny. I kept looking for a more solid answer, even though I knew she didn't have one—or not one she would share with me anyway. Maybe she was holding the heavy artillery for Mona.

She paused with a forkful of pastry halfway to her mouth. "Like what? A letter or something?"

If I got the teenage nuance right, her tone told me she thought I was being lame. "A birth certificate?"

Her façade crumpled, letting the scared come through. "I don't have anything. No papers. Nothing to prove who I am or where I came from. My grandmother is gone. There's no one else. All I have is that photo and a story."

"Your school?"

"It was pretty casual." She gave a shrug that implied a casualness not reflected in her tight, hard stare. "We lived in the country."

What secrets had her grandmother been hiding? And why? And why tell the girl Mona was her mother? Was Mona just a random kid in an old picture that the grandmother used to give the girl a story, a family?

But where did she get the photo?

Random thoughts swirled around in my head—bats in my belfry. Clearly, I was losing it. "Any idea who else was in that picture? Why they were torn away and discarded?"

"No. My gram didn't tell me much." She looked over my right shoulder as if the tile wall behind me and above the stove was fascinating.

Liars look up and to the left. I read that somewhere. Or maybe my bud, Detective Romeo, with the Metropolitan Police Department taught me that. Lately, he'd been teaching me more than I had him—a reversal in our relationship. Not sure I liked it, but that never stopped the Fates from interfering in my status quo.

Jean-Charles opened his mouth to speak.

I quieted him with a hand on his arm and a gentle squeeze. "Well, perhaps Mona can shed some light, but not now. It's too late." I ignored the crestfallen look. No way was I going to play my ace until I saw a few more of her cards. "We need to find you a place to stay."

"I'm good. I'm staying with a friend from the rodeo. What I'd really like to do is find Mona. That's what I came here for."

"I know. We both need to hear what she has to say. But haven't you accomplished a lot for one day?"

Family. Weren't they like the Fifth Level of Purgatory or something?

Tawny looked terrified yet excited—that mix of adrenaline and fear the second before you leap with only a bungee attached to an ankle.

"I'll go see her myself." The girl was like a tick on a dog.

"Be my guest. Your funeral." Mona was my one ace, and I wasn't above playing it.

Jean-Charles laughed, God bless him. Wise to my tricks, he played along. "Mona." He gave a low whistle. "She's got a nip, that one."

"Bite," I corrected with a side-eye at the girl.

"Yes, this." Jean-Charles patted the girl's hand. "And she is married to a very important man in this town. A man with many friends and many enemies."

Okay, he was starting to overplay. "She's not easy to get to," I said, cutting off Jean-Charles, or making his point, as I preferred to look at it.

"Yes, this." He leaned back and folded his arms across his chest.

"She can't be mad at me," the girl whined. "I didn't do anything!"

"She'll certainly be surprised." I wasn't feeling the normal delight I had when I one-upped my mother, which was rare indeed. This drama had a human heart element to it that was tragic no matter how it turned out or what the truth was. I quit overplaying my own hand. In my gut, I knew that even though this was my problem, it wasn't my fight. "But mad? I don't think so."

The sight of her. The plaintive unhappiness in her voice. I wilted. And I went with my instinct and wrapped her in a hug. She stiffened for a moment then relaxed into me. "It'll be okay," I whispered against her hair. "We'll figure it out. You're here now, and, family or not, we'll take care of you."

The girl needed a friend, a champion. Playing that role was in my wheelhouse. I released her but kept an arm looped around her shoulders. "Let's go. We've prevailed upon Chef Bouclet's kindness long enough. Let's get you a shower and some shut-eye, then we can handle all of this tomorrow when our strength is at full throttle."

"I've got a place; I told you that." The girl backed off her stool.

"Well, if you're with me, then whoever is looking for you won't be able to find you."

She froze, still as a statue. "I don't know what you mean."

"In my office, you were as twitchy as a rabbit in a greyhound race. Once we got into the elevators and came up here where no one else can come and no one would think to look, you calmed down. That tells me you're running from someone."

She opened her mouth, then clamped it shut, her eyes bugging as she looked over my shoulder.

"She's running from me."

I whirled around. Detective Romeo.

Standing in the doorway, he looked stern. Well, actually he looked only slightly older than twelve, his sandy hair a trifle long—something my youngest assistant, Brandy, probably had a hand in. His boyish face unmarred by the shadow of a beard, his overcoat shrouded his thin frame, while his cowlick stood at attention from the crown of his head, a flag waving in surrender.

When we'd first met over a woman who was pushed out of a tour helicopter at a very inconvenient time and altitude, he'd been a greenhorn. I'd taken him under my wing, shown him the ropes. While he still didn't have the connections a Vegas brat like me had, he'd worked his way up the food chain to where he had the audacity to consider himself my equal. Although it galled, he was probably right. Either way, we had each other's backs.

Regardless, somehow I'd been left off the invitation list to his graduation, so his new attitude still took me by surprise.

"Well, don't you sound officious and dull?" I put myself between him and the girl. I wasn't aware of it until I'd done it.

Romeo looked nonplussed, tilting his head in an invitation to get out of his way.

Seriously? That was as effective as chiseling stone with a chopstick.

While I appreciated his competence, I missed his happiness. "You do know you can do your job and still actually like it, don't you?"

His bluster melted a bit when he ran into the heat of my glare, which deepened when I saw who was with him.

Paxton Dane muscled in beside the young detective looking lean, luscious, and less than trustworthy, all traits that, unfortunately, I'd discovered the hard way. A long, tall Texan who had wooed me while he was still married, managed to get his estranged wife killed, then left.

Recently, he'd returned acting as if all was forgiven. I was still struggling with the distinction between forgiving and forgetting.

Thankfully, I hadn't fallen for Dane's act, nor succumbed to his charm. So, I wasn't struggling with forgiving myself...for once.

My history with handsome men would flesh out an entire line of Harlequin romances without the happy endings, but Dane wouldn't be a chapter.

"Why is she running from you?" I asked the young detective.

Romeo waved my question aside, which usually meant he was committed to the wind-up before throwing the pitch.

Surprisingly, I found one last erg of patience.

"That girl, there." He lifted his chin toward the girl who now cowered behind me. "We tailed her here, then Dane got Security to trace where she'd gone in the hotel."

"We got to your office, but you weren't there," Dane added.

I gave him a look intended to wither steel. "Brilliant deduction, Watson. Am I supposed to be impressed?"

"That'd be the day," Romeo said out of the side of his mouth. "I'm really sorry, Lucky, but she needs to come with me."

"Why?"

"She's wanted for murder."

CHAPTER THREE

"**M**URDER?" My brain freewheeled as my mouth went slack. Romeo didn't normally embrace hyperbole, so I took him at his word.

Murder!

"She's a kid for Chrissake! And so thin, if she was a twig she'd snap. Who do you think she killed?"

Dane stared at the ceiling while Romeo looked like he would've dug his toe into the cement floor if he thought that wouldn't be undignified for someone on his lofty rung of the detective ladder.

"Somebody grow a pair and tell me." I reached behind me and grabbed the girl's arm, pulling her closer.

Finally, Romeo met my eyes. "We don't know if she killed anybody. If you'd stand down from the Mother Bear act, maybe we could find out."

Parsing words scratched at the thin veneer of my patience. "Who died?"

"One of the bull riding support staff. This girl played a part in that."

My eyes went slitty. I hated it when Romeo played fast and loose with me...especially when murder was involved. I would've said murder is a serious business, but I didn't think I could do it and keep a straight face. "Allegedly. No matter what you think, it's still only an allegation."

"Whatever."

He was begging for it. "Do I have to give you the innocent-before-proven-guilty speech?" He looked so unhappy that I softened. "What has happened to you?"

He rubbed a hand over his eyes. His shoulders slumped as he lost all of the badass. "You work with ugliness all day and that becomes all you see."

"Attitude, Grasshopper. Haven't I taught you anything?" He started to answer. I stopped him with a raised finger. "Wait. Let me rephrase. Haven't you learned anything?"

"Yes, but probably not the lessons you intended." The Romeo I knew and loved peeked through in his tired smile. "Have you gotten any sleep?" He'd been with me in China, and we'd flown home on the same plane. Just thirty hours or so ago he was riding herd on a jewel thief in Macau and I was running on fumes trying to catch a killer.

Same life, different location.

The synchronicity pointed to me as the commonality. An upsetting thought. So I did what I always do with serious problems—I ignored it. If you can't fix it, why worry about it? A fitting epitaph.

"Sleep?" I gave a little snort of derision and stifled the urge to hug him, too. What was it with me lately, going all squishy? "You either from the looks of you."

"Not a wink." A little haunt widened his eyes. "I still keep seeing..."

"I know." I shivered then I yanked myself back. "Wait. Since when do bull riders have support staff?"

"The clown. They think I killed the clown." Tawny blurted from behind my back. She stepped into view but still stayed close enough that I'd take the first bullet. Where our shoulders touched, her nervousness vibrated through me.

I grabbed her arm. Squeezing tight, I held her close. "Don't say another word. Not one." I squeezed until she flinched. "You got that?"

She ducked her head like the kid she really was. "Yessum."

"How do you know I'm here about a clown?" Romeo asked, leaning around to get a look at her.

I felt her start to answer. "Don't."

He gave me a look of exaggerated patience. "If she cooperates, that will help us both."

"But I don't think our needs are the important ones right now." I lasered him with a stare. "Do you?"

He completely wilted. "Of course not."

"Good. Get her to the station, put her lawyer next to her, then have at it. This is too important to push the boundaries, Romeo."

"His name is Romeo?"

I heard the smile in the girl's voice. "It's Detective to you." I pulled her around next to me so I could give her the slitty-eye. "Even when I'm not there. Not. One. Word. It's life or death critical."

"Yessum."

Drawing a deep breath, I stood tall—swine that I am, I am rarely above using my height to intimidate. Of course, Dane still had me by a few inches, but Romeo was somewhat responsive to intimidation. I closed the space between us until it was slightly uncomfortable. To his credit, he didn't retreat. "Is that right? You think she had something to do with the clown's demise?" I stepped on a grin. Maybe it was the jet lag, or the Champagne, or just the incredible oddness of the whole evening, but I felt an almost uncontrollable need to laugh welling up inside me.

"Clowns are people, too, Lucky." Romeo bit his lip when he said it. Even though he fancied himself all grown, he still had a streak of juvenile humor, and he knew exactly which buttons to push.

I swallowed the laugh. It didn't help that Romeo was feeding me lines like a Vaudeville straight man. "Stop that." I turned to Dane. "So, what about the clown?"

"He was trussed like a baby calf," Dane said, ignoring Romeo's daggered look. "And that girl's rope was the murder weapon."

She started to say something.

I pulled her arm. "Don't. Not until your lawyer is present

and he says you can open your mouth. Until then, keep it shut. How many times do I have to say that?" I stared at Dane. "That's redundant."

"What," he said, momentarily derailed.

"Baby calf. A calf is a baby and therefore baby calf is redundant." Everyone stared at me as if I'd lost my mind. They were more than half right.

"I didn't do it."

"Stop!" I got control of myself, then gave her a fleeting smile and waited until I had her attention. "I know. But you did know the clown was dead. We just have to go through the formalities. Work with me. Romeo's a good guy—he'll help you." I looked at Dane, then decided not to say a word. Trust, once broken... "I've done this a time or two."

Curiously, that seemed to calm her. I don't know why—it scared the hell out of me.

"I don't have a lawyer." Her voice didn't waver.

I took that as a good sign—at least she'd been hearing if not listening. "You will. I know just who to call." I returned my attention to Dane. "Trussing the clown wouldn't kill him." As she sidled in as close as she could get, the girl pressed something into my hand. The photo.

She didn't want the police to see it. Curious.

I kept my eyes on Dane as I slipped the one connection to my mother into my pocket. Neither of the men acted as if they'd seen anything.

"She threw an extra loop around his neck, apparently," Dane continued. "The prelim is the guy suffocated, but the coroner will let us know when he reaches a conclusion."

"Us? Do you have an official role here?"

He leveled his emerald green eyes on me. "As official as yours."

A high-schooler trying to muscle into the Bigs. I found that oddly irritating. "*Apparently*, she threw an extra loop?" Unlike my friends, I was hearing *and* listening. I looked to Romeo for an answer...an official answer.

"I haven't been to the crime scene yet. Reynolds is working

it."

Reynolds.

Romeo shrugged off the opinion written all over my face.

Detective Reynolds and his boorish bravado actually had been the catalyst to bring Romeo and me into a working relationship. When it came to Reynolds, I was grateful for that, but little else.

"You're telling me that a sixteen-year-old *girl* threw a loop around a fully-grown man's neck and strangled him? She must have some superpowers we are unaware of."

"She could've been on a horse and drug him a while," Dane said, sounding like the smart kid trying to earn points with the teacher.

I lowered my gaze at the Texan. "Don't go making up things without evidence to support them." I turned to Romeo. "Anything to support that theory?"

"You'll have to talk to Reynolds. He's working the scene."

"Terrific."

"Look, step aside. Let me talk to the girl." Romeo held up a hand, cutting me off. "We'll wait until her attorney is present before questioning her. It's late, but I don't go *all* stupid after midnight. Then let me get to the scene and I'll fill you in as to what we've found." He could see my hesitation. "Get the girl a lawyer. It'll all come out. If she's innocent, that'll come out, too."

I didn't share his confidence; Justice was blind and all of that—but it would only scare the girl if I said so. "Are you arresting her?"

"Detaining."

"Semantics." I stepped in close to Romeo, using my height and my current lack of self-control. "She's a kid. Sixteen."

Romeo straightened but still couldn't meet me eye-to-eye.

Score one for the home team. I pressed my advantage. "I'm the only adult around—no parents, no family, at least not close. So, I'll take responsibility for her."

Romeo gave an I-hope-you-know-what-the-hell-you're-doing look, which I ignored.

He pulled a piece of paper out of his pocket and gave me an I'm-sorry look. I stepped to the side, giving him the floor to read the girl her Miranda rights. Those words always dropped the floor out from under me—a reminder that this shit was real.

Last time had been with Teddie.

When the detective had finished, the girl was pale with the cold slap of reality.

I felt the control I so desperately needed slipping away. "Dane, you make sure she says nothing until her attorney shows up, you got that?"

He flinched at the bite in my tone.

"You can do that without screwing it up, right?"

He nodded, but I'd seen his enormous talent for incompetence.

"Keep her in your sight. Don't let her go for even one minute. Send the bill to me. Can you do that?"

"Full fee plus expenses?"

"Full refund if you fuck up."

He extended a hand. We had our deal.

"Where are you going?" Tawny asked, a tremor in her voice. "I want you to come with me."

I put my hands on her shoulders and waited until she looked at me without wavering. "I'll be there, but I need to go roust your attorney out of bed. Go with them. But remember what I said."

"Don't say anything." Her voice was a little stronger, but not much. She gave me a quick hug. "Thank you."

I held her longer than necessary, squeezing hard. Then I turned and jabbed a finger in Romeo's chest. "By the book, Detective. You do one thing to coerce a statement out of her and I'll have your head on a pike."

His Adam's apple bobbed as he nodded.

I was overplaying—we both knew it. Romeo understood what it meant. We were a good team.

A tiny stick of a girl between the two men, Tawny disappeared through the door. She didn't look back.

Silence wrapped around me like an itchy wet wool blanket. When the girl left, the air had left too and I struggled to breathe.

"I can say, without hesitation, that you are quite likely the most interesting woman I have ever met."

Jean-Charles! I hadn't forgotten, not really, but he'd faded in light of the murder thing. I turned and met his half-amused, half-worried-as-hell look—I'd seen a lot of that look recently.

I opened my arms in supplication. "This stuff finds me. What can I say? There I was, sitting in my office, signing like a million pointless papers, and she walks in with a story."

"You don't have to fall for every pretty face with a sad tale."

I sidled in close to him. He took the not-so-subtle hint and encircled me in a hug.

"I fell for yours."

"But I have no sad story." Neither of us mentioned his wife who had died in childbirth. The one his family had loved and he still called to in his dreams.

"No, but you are mercurial."

He didn't deny it. "You do like the drama, no?"

"No." The lie slipped out. "What, I should stop helping people?"

"You cannot stop being you. Drama comes with problems." He was arguing both sides, so I stepped out of the conflict.

He released me, then grabbed my hand, tugging me with him. "Come. I am not trying to change you, merely keep you safe."

"You can't."

"This, I know." Sadness and a hint of vulnerability crept in—he'd lost a love before.

How could the heart stay open in the face of such devastation?

Mona had left.

Teddie had left.

One day he might decide my life held a bit too much downside, and he would leave.

Could I trust Jean-Charles not to? Could I handle it if he did? Was the possibility of happiness worth the price of potential pain?

Would the Almighty please send a God-O-Gram with the answers?

Even though I asked, I knew that one would be a "no." This one was on me. But, to be honest, I never did like the whole risk/reward thing. If I ruled the world, we'd all get just the reward part. Mona used to tell me that without the bad, we wouldn't appreciate the good.

I wondered how she'd feel about that now.

"I will be here for you," Jean-Charles said as if he could read my mind.

I didn't much like being so transparent to him either, but the fact was as immutable as the cost/benefit paradigm I railed against. "You amaze me."

"This is a good thing," he said with a little laugh...a very little laugh. "You scare the hell out of me."

"This, too, is a good thing."

He treated that as a joke as he handed me my purse. "You must go. The girl..." His eyebrows came together—the harbinger of a question. "Why did you not go with her?"

"She's holding back, playing me. Thought perhaps I needed to show her she's in the Big Leagues now. Romeo will take care of her."

"You want to shake her, yes?"

"Yes. And now it's time to roust an attorney out of bed." I hoped he was alone or things could get testy. "Then, perhaps, it's time to talk to my mother."

Tonight, I rode the slippery slope from bad to worse.

SQUASH TRENTON lived in a small house in what I liked to call a suburb of downtown on the outskirts of Naked City. A formerly decent part of town, Naked City, where the showgirls used to sun topless on the roofs of their apartment buildings, had been claimed by unsavories but was now going through a bit of a resurgence. Caught between the old and the new, it had a fighting chance of the renewal sticking.

The apartment buildings were a thing of the past, leaving small streets of comfortable cottages, most of which now sported bars on the windows and peeling paint. But Old Vegas charm still lurked in the detailing—a frescoed stucco, filigreed window casements, date palms stunted by the desert and the unrelenting sun, but fighting for a foothold—a visual metaphor for the city itself.

The old Andre's, one of the restaurant institutions of a classier Vegas and the scene of much of the important history of my life, had occupied one of the small homes that now sat dark and abandoned as I slipped past.

Nostalgia arrowed through me, leaving a sense of loss but the warm comfort of memories. Of course, with change, the tangible talismans were disappearing, leaving only the hope of remembering.

Change. The more I had, the more I struggled with it...or maybe against it. Is that what age does? Or maybe it's that the past is the only immutable thing in life, a constant that creates a comfort.

Either way, sometimes a drift down memory lane did the heart good.

Even though I doubted Squash Trenton had a sentimental bone in his body, I could see why he'd chosen to live here. Near the courthouse and the bail bondsmen, but far enough away to avoid having the desperate crawling through his windows at night—present company excluded, of course. Unless to escape a fire or a potential homicide, I drew the line at crawling through windows.

The large gaps in streetlights gave the neighborhood an eerie feel, as if it had been designed to hide things in the darkness. Or maybe it was simply a throwback to a different time when kids played in the streets and neighbors looked out for each other so lights weren't to hold back the darkness. Now, despite an uptick in respectability, many of the bungalows had bubbled stucco, curled trim, and bars on the windows.

Progress.

That whole reality thing again. I tried not to let it bother me.

And I tried not to let it bother me that once again I was calling on Squash Trenton, hat in hand.

Squash wasn't, of course, his real name. At least I didn't think so. I had no idea where Squash, both as a name and as a man, came from, not that it mattered. He came highly recommended by my father. Come to think of it, I had no idea how my father came to appreciate the skills of a criminal defense attorney, not that that mattered either. But I was seeing a trend here that was a bit upsetting. While not in the top five, being out of the loop was on my Top Ten Most Hated Things list.

Squash's windows were dark when I eased to the curb and killed the engine. They wouldn't remain so long—as I'd made my way down the street, I'd seen lights in the houses pop on. My arrival wasn't particularly stealthy—with over seven hundred horses and an exhaust system designed to attract attention, the Ferrari was more of a look-at-me-car than a fly-under-the-radar one. Not that I cared. The Ferrari was a loaner—my classic Porsche had met a fiery end and I had yet to replace it. Italian or German? The decision was impossible. But lately, I had the sneaking suspicion I might have outgrown the Ferrari. Maybe even the Porsche. But Porsche made an SUV now.

Progress. Was age nothing more than hope shifting to resignation?

Again, I tried not to let it bother me.

In front of Squash's house, I flipped the car into neutral, then gunned the engine a time or two before killing it. After the day I'd had, any interest in playing nice had long since evaporated.

A light flicked on in a window to the far right as I eased the car door shut. Although not worried about making a racket, I couldn't bring myself to abuse the car by slamming the door.

The circle of weak light cast by the nearest streetlamp did little to illuminate the path to the front door. As I muttered an epithet and hoped I wouldn't sprain an ankle, the light over the front door flipped on with the brightness of an interrogation beam. Appropriate, in a way, and I appreciated the irony.

Needing time to adjust, my eyes watered a bit. The brick of the sidewalk looked new, the grout still clean. In fact in the light, the house looked well cared for. The front door, painted a fire engine red, made me smile.

People constantly surprised me. Squash Trenton, über lawyer, badass, and macho male was no exception.

A red door. A port in a storm.

Squash opened the door as I lifted my hand to knock. "Working hard to endear me to my neighbors?"

His smile looked genuine, which went with the rest of him.

His hair stood straight up at the crown but was smashed on one side. He hadn't bothered to throw a robe on. In fact, he hadn't donned anything other than a pair of boxers. He had that thick, muscled physique of a wrestler, which somehow fit. And he didn't mind showing it off—or using it to his advantage.

If I knew him like I thought I did, his attire, or lack thereof, was carefully calculated to put me off-guard, an ingrained lawyer trick to give him the initial advantage. Although not a lawyer, I was wise to the game. And the fact he thought it'd work on me? Not a chance—on a good day. But today had been so far from good I couldn't see it from here. And, given my weakened state, his ploy had a fair chance of success.

I stopped on the stoop feeling a bit bedraggled. "Knowing you, I doubt you care what your neighbors think."

He leaned around me. "On the contrary. Mrs. Perino who lives in the house over there," he pointed to a house hiding in the darkness across the street, "she gave me the most incredible apple pie recipe. And Mrs. Buell," again he pointed at a house, this time one further up the street. "She taught me how to make the most incredible Hollandaise, from scratch...in the microwave."

"Offending every true French man and woman alike, but point made. Apologies offered."

"It's okay. They both are deaf as posts, wouldn't hear a bomb if it went off on their front porch. I check on them regularly. They don't have anybody."

"What? A softie hiding under that shark exterior?"

"Yin and yang are immutables in life, but you won't tell my secrets."

"Really? Why not?"

"You need me."

I hadn't even gotten an invitation inside and I was already down in this game. My energy was low as my stomach growled—I should've eaten that hamburger. "Did you ever get Mrs. Morales's recipe for green chili?"

"Oh, man. That woman." His tone dripped with respect. "If she went to law school, she'd run this town." Squash shook his head. "I'd hate to run up against her in court."

"What'd she make you do?"

He looked like he'd paid dearly. "I had to fix Freddy's tickets." Freddy was her son and the object of our mutual dislike. "At first, I thought I'd gotten the best of her."

"Never underestimate a woman who holds the cards. Don't you know better than that?"

Men, even the enlightened ones, assumed a woman would be an easy adversary. For some reason, I thought Squash Trenton would have been a bit more educated by now.

"How many tickets did Freddy have?"

"Two hundred. The Magistrate wanted to shoot me."

"One of these days, you'll listen to me. I told you you'd met your match."

"Yeah, but that recipe..."

"Was it worth it?"

"I would've taken care of two *thousand* tickets."

"That good?" Men and their recipes. "Well, I'm glad death wasn't the price you had to pay, as I have need of your services."

"The middle of the night, it must be important. I'm all ears. You want a cup of coffee?" He opened the door wider. Stepping back, he motioned me inside.

He wasn't *all* ears. Even in my diminished state I could appreciate that. "A cup won't even get my starter to turn over. Do you have an intravenous setup? That would be far easier." My body vibrated with need...for caffeine. I stepped into the front hall, blinking against the light and trying to ignore his lack of appropriate attire. But, of course, what would be considered appropriate when a woman shows up in the dead of night...inappropriately? A question requiring far more nuance than I could muster.

Squash looked a bit owl-eyed in the light as well. "An enema does the trick even better."

"Please, I'm very visual and it's too early in the morning for that kind of trauma." A shiver chased through me and suddenly I was cold, very cold, my body in shutdown mode. When I was twenty, I could run on fumes forever. I wasn't twenty anymore, and my body felt I needed a reminder. "An enema. Shit. I'm not even going to think about that, much less think about how you know that."

He shut the door, then threw three deadbolts before turning his back and charging toward the back of the house, motioning me to follow. "This way."

I fell into trail, trying not to stare at his ass and the way the muscles clenched under the thin fabric as he walked. I failed.

"Law school. Drinking. You do what you need to do."

"An enema?"

"As drunk as I was, I wasn't going to let one of my buddies perforate my arm with a needle looking for a vein. An enema was the next most expedient hangover cure. You'd be surprised."

He got that right. "More information than I needed." I took refuge behind the center island.

"You asked."

One of those shimmering silver devices with all the tubes and water vessels and knobs and dials that one needed a six-week course in how to operate squatted on the sideboard that sagged under the machine's weight.

"Espresso?" he asked, demitasse in hand.

On my heels, I caved. "Sure. The higher the octane, the better." I stared at the back of his head. "And, for the record, counselor, I did *not* ask."

He set to work making us tiny cups of coffee tar. I wouldn't have minded a bit of white stuff to improve the viscosity, but I thought perhaps that might offend some java juju or something, so I kept my desires to myself—all of them.

Finally, he turned, setting a cup in front of me while keeping one for himself. "But you did ask. Maybe not in so many words, but that's what you do. You say you're not going to ask, but it's really what you want to know. And, for the record, espresso has less caffeine per cup than regular drip coffee."

"Couldn't you have left me happy in my ignorance?" I sipped at the brew, finding it surprisingly good.

"I'm a lawyer. Truth, justice, and all that."

With the cup almost to my lips, I paused and looked at him over the rim. "That's a joke, right?"

He shrugged but didn't argue. "Tough crowd."

I took another sip and savored the hit, minimal as it was. "I'm that easy to read?"

"No. But reading people is my job, or a big part of it anyway."

With my courage flagging, I considered having him run interference with Mona. I could use someone adept to get a bead on her, especially now. Our next visit would be a doozy. But with Mona, a handsome man would just gum up the works, so I abandoned my plan. I wrapped my hands around the warm cup as a shiver chased through me. "Aren't you cold?"

He glanced down, then turned and grabbed an apron hanging from a hook on the side of the refrigerator. Slipping it over his head, he tied the string in the back, then turned, arms wide, expecting my appreciation. "Better?"

A Superman apron, stained from use. Red from tomato sauce, I bet. The yellow one could be Hollandaise. "Hey, it's your superhero fantasy, not mine." I tried for nonplussed. From the slight widening of his eyes, I knew I achieved it.

But his grin told me he could tell I was at least half lying.

Okay, I admit it. He was the stuff dreams are made of—assuming I went for incredibly handsome, yet irritatingly obnoxious hired guns, who are too smart for my own good, which I didn't...well, not for longer than a weekend in Tahoe, anyway. But that sort of romantic gymnastics was part of my past youthful indiscretion. Kids had weekends; adults had...what? I chalked up my lack of character at the moment to the whole grass-is-greener thing.

Who wasn't attracted to bad boys at least a little bit?

He even cooked—and everyone knew about my love affair with food.

But I had a good man at home. Boys, even bad boys, were things of my past. At least that's what I kept telling myself—and I took a lot of convincing. One of my biggest faults is that I find the status quo boring. Yeah, Mona wasn't the only one waiting for me to grow up.

Even though I'd adopted a no-touch rule when it came to bad boys, that didn't mean I didn't like to look. But, this being business and considering my weakened state, I was glad he'd put on the apron. Even if it didn't add any dignity, at least it added a touch of class...and modesty. Not much of a touch, but at this point, I'd take anything.

Squash watched me as if he could read the thoughts pinging around in my hollow skull. I hated it when men did that—so smug. Worse, they were almost always wrong but never believed it.

"You show up at my place in the middle of..." he glanced at the clock above the sink—a cat, its tail moving in tick-tock time—then gave a low whistle. "Way past the middle of the night." He gave me an appreciative glance. "This late, my place, I get to pick the attire."

"Deal, but I get to pick the topic of conversation."

"Was that ever in doubt?"

I sipped the last of my espresso—a meager amount of

caffeine, barely enough to get my heart rate's attention. "Enough of the sissy cups; make my next one a quadruple."

"That bad?" His expression sobered as business knifed through the banter.

"Better make a quad for yourself, too. But we can't linger. We need to get a move on."

He did as I suggested, except he didn't hurry. The wheels of justice move slowly and all of that.

I worried about the girl, picturing her in the sterile environment of the Detention Center, scared, without a friend—Dane didn't count—and I wondered if I'd done the right thing. The cops wouldn't abuse her, Romeo would see to that, but giving her a peek through the door at real world consequences would do me good.

Scare the truth out of her.

Squash and I gathered around a tiny table in the corner. The space was small, the squeeze tight, but we did it—two adults of some size around a kid's coloring table. Somehow, that seemed to fit the circumstances.

"I'd suggest the dining room, but there are no drapes on the window, and Ms. Pence across the street is up all night and obsessively curious about my sex life."

"Do you have a lot of sex on the dining room table?" I said that with a straight face and a steady heart rate. Women of the world take note and be impressed.

"I do have an obligation to keep my octogenarian neighbor's fantasies intact."

"Self-imposed obligation."

He gave me that point. "So, what do you have?"

I filled him in, leaving out the darkest family secrets. Of course, the only ones I knew were my own, and, unfortunately, this wasn't all about me. On second thought, strike that. For once, I was glad it wasn't about me.

"This kid, she thinks Mona is her mother?" Squash's voice had gone soft and quiet.

I tried to read his emotion, but I couldn't. "So she says."

"Have you talked to your parents about this yet?"

"No, I haven't had the time."

Leaning back, he stared over my shoulder as he chewed on his lip. Then he gave a soft snort and shook his head.

"What?"

"Just interesting. You never know when the past is going to walk through your door, do you?" His gaze flicked to mine and held it.

"What do you mean by that exactly?"

He gave me the innocent-eye. "You haven't spoken with your father?"

"No, why?"

"Considering the length of his relationship with your mother, and this girl claiming Mona is her mother, your father might be able to add the flip side of that."

I'd thought of it but didn't want to admit it. "Undying fealty and all that implies?"

"Wouldn't hurt to give him a couple of single malts and see what you can get out of him."

He knew my father well enough to know his whiskey preferences. I wasn't sure what to make of that.

Squash moved on, maneuvering the conversation with a lawyer's skill. "What do you know about the guy who was killed?"

A bit at sea, for once I didn't mind being maneuvered. "Not a thing other than he was dressed up like a rodeo clown and had a rope around his neck. Allegedly, it belonged to the girl."

"You got a name?"

"No. That's all I got. Romeo hasn't been to the scene. When he gets there, then I'll know more." As I worked on my coffee, I felt the caffeine raising a pulse. "Right now, I'd like to find out if the girl really is Mona's daughter."

"If she is?"

There was something in his tone I couldn't place. His flat expression didn't offer even a hint. "I hope you have time for a Murder One client."

"Yin and yang, Lucky. There's always two sides, remember that."

"They teach you that in law school?"

"University of Nevada was progressive but not quite that into Eastern philosophy."

"You picked that up all on your own?"

"Life. The best teacher." He had a comeback for every whine.

"What are you saying?"

"Get all the facts before you jump off the conclusion cliff."

He was right, of course. For once, I didn't fight just to fight. Acceptance, like retreat, was often part of winning the war. "It's just that..."

"Takes you back, doesn't it?"

Everyone knew my story, but few thought beyond the sensational aspects. Squash surprised me with his insight. "Yeah."

"Maybe the girl has a better story. If she had that photo for as long as she says, she could've started looking years ago. She didn't. Makes me think there was a reason."

"Her grandmother just died."

"There you go. Try to see there might have been some good in all of this."

I raised one eyebrow but didn't bother arguing the esoterics. Facts would show the truth, assuming we could uncover any.

"But, between you and me, if you want to kill Mona, based on past experience alone, we could make a strong case for justifiable homicide. You would make my career."

"I'll give that some thought. You know how I like to help." Even though he was a lawyer, I was starting to like him a lot. Of course, it could be just that bad judgment/handsome man thing. "Are you aware Mona is campaigning hard to get appointed to the Paradise Town Advisory Board?"

"How could I not know? She doesn't miss a sound bite. How's her act playing with the Clark County Commission?"

"My mother has a Don Quixote complex, a champion of the underdog. But a political office, more so an appointment, will be an uphill battle for a former prostitute and the wife of one of the most influential casino owners in town, which is too bad. She actually would be pretty good on the Advisory Board. When she was a lobbyist for the prostitution industry, she turned Carson City upside down."

That got a smile out of both of us.

Squash joined in my Greek chorus. "I admire her work educating hookers who want to get out. To a one, they speak almost reverently about her."

"That's probably pushing it a tad."

"Your mother and I fight on the same side in that war. We need folks to challenge the status quo in government."

"True. Just, could that monkey wrench not be my mother? Not right now. Maybe she could take a sabbatical?"

Neither one of us took that seriously. Mona carried a big stick and had a penchant for finding beehives. For her, pushing boundaries and testing limits was as Pavlovian as my need to solve problems.

"This could force her hand." Squash didn't seem to be bothered by that. Odd, since he'd just been singing her praises and all.

"I wouldn't bet against Mona's backbone. Once she plots a course, it's better to get out of the way, then trail behind to pick up the pieces when the whole thing implodes. Do you think the girl could be part of a political angle?"

To be honest, Mona's political aspirations seemed inconsequential. But politics was an ugly business—Vegas had a long and storied history of bloody power plays. Mona was vying for a spot on the Paradise Town Advisory Board, which sounded innocuous. But the money part of the Strip—the part south of Sahara—didn't lie in the City of Las Vegas, as most people assumed. No, as a result of a money power-play back when the folks who ran Vegas were a bit less law-abiding, the power brokers put their money smack in the middle of Paradise—a loosely incorporated part of Clark County. And now the Paradise Advisory Board made feast-or-famine decisions that impacted the most lucrative part of the Las Vegas Strip.

That kind of power could attract the wrong kind of

attention.

While I envisioned men with baseball bats skulking through the night intent on doing harm to my mother, Squash remained curiously unaffected by the possibility. "We'll turn over rocks like always, and we'll see which snakes crawl out. Been in this business long enough not to rule out any possibility."

I leaned forward, which, given the tiny space, put me nose to nose with the lawyer—he smelled as good as he looked. "What I'm telling you is subject to attorney-client privilege, right?"

"As long as you're not admitting to a future crime."

"That's always a possibility, but I'd never admit to it."

"Then our conversation exists only in this room. The press doesn't sniff around me anymore. I know this is hard to believe, but I can be nasty when provoked."

"It's not you I'm worried about. What about the girl?"

"I'll keep her quiet. But I better get a move on." He pushed his chair back, then came up short against the wall. He angled a look at me as if the jolt had closed a few synapses and a question formed. "How come you came to get me and you didn't go with her? You could've just called."

"I trust Romeo; he wouldn't cross the line with the kid." I'd overplayed my hand a bit with the young detective, but he'd kept pace—he knew what I wanted. "I wanted to scare her a little, soften her up."

"You think she's telling a whopper," Squash pressed.

"What I think doesn't matter and who the kid belongs to doesn't make a bit of difference in a murder investigation. Can we leave it there for now? If Mona gets caught in the crossfire, I'll run damage control, but that's the best I can do. At some point, truth comes calling."

Squash nodded, then gave a low chuckle as if laughing at a private joke, although he didn't sound amused.

"What?"

"Nothing."

"The girl is the key. I need you to get her out."

"After she's sweated for a while." The hint of a grin lifted one corner of his mouth and sparked in his eyes. "You do know this is a murder investigation?"

"My father always said, if he found his ass in a crack, you'd be his first dime." I felt the skin between my eyebrows wrinkle into a frown—normally I ignored that sort of thing, but lately Mona had made it her mission to see that I didn't need Botox before my thirtieth birthday. With thirty firmly in my rearview, she'd clearly lost count of the years, but I didn't correct her. And I left the frown in place. "How is it you became all tight with my father?"

Squash glanced at the clock. "Would you look at the time? I better put a hustle on." He slurped the last of his huge espresso and I could see the wheels turning. "You still got that in with Lovato?"

Daniel Lovato was the District Attorney. I'd done him several huge favors, one that kept him out of jail—wouldn't have been pretty being incarcerated with all those angry men he'd helped put there. "I can give it a shot." My leverage and Squash's magic had worked for Teddie. Could we be as lucky the second time around?

"Has she been charged?" Squash peered into my mug. "Drink up."

"No, at least not when Detective Romeo took her. He said she was being detained for questioning." I grabbed Squash's arm, spilling his coffee that he cradled in his hands. "She's just a kid."

"Sixteen?" He wiped the coffee off his forearm.

"How'd you know?"

"You told me." He seemed sure.

I was sure I hadn't. Well, as sure as I could be with my brains muddled and scrambled with emotion.

"Well, in Nevada, kids who commit crimes like murder are treated as adults for the purpose of adjudication. That means custody, bail hearings, all that sort of thing."

My hope fled, riding a long sigh. Why couldn't I catch a break, just once? Okay, I was whining. Tired beyond belief and not seeing any significant rack time in my future, I was a bit pissy. So, bite me. And since I was coming clean and all, breaks often broke my way. I hoped for a bit of that magic this time, too. "So, how should we attack this?"

"I'll go get the kid, scare her a bit, then see what I can do. That usually amounts to throwing my weight around and then being reduced to using my considerable charm." He shot me a smile. "Buck up, O'Toole. You're looking positively down-in-the-mouth, which is not at all like you. We got this."

I wasn't so sure, but lest I tempt the Fates, I kept that tidbit to myself. "And me?"

"I would say, go get some sleep. You look like hell. In fact, you look like someone who just chased down two killers, rescued the world as we know it from the forces of evil, is jet-lagged beyond compare, and is trying to get a fancy hotel opened while trying to celebrate or, more precisely because it's you, ignore your birthday."

"You've been reading the gossip column again."

"One of the few sources of truth these days."

"A sorry state." As I eased out of the tight space, my ego momentarily faltered. "I look that bad, huh?"

"If you can't count on your friends." He didn't even wince when I punched him in the arm. He was smart enough to let go of his coffee before I landed the blow, though.

"I need to go talk with my mother."

Squash shook his head as he drained his mug. "No, not yet. Your mother and father will wait. As you said yourself, where this girl came from, who her people are, none of that matters right now. We need to get her legal troubles under control or she'll disappear inside the system. And when it spits her out the other side, *if* it spits her out, you won't recognize her."

I shut my mind to that possibility. "Okay, that's fair. What do you want from me?"

"I want you to do that thing that you seem to have a knack for. Get to the crime scene. Snoop around. Talk to people. Win them over, turn over a few stones—you know, work your magic. I've never seen anyone better. Get me something to cast a shadow of a doubt as to her culpability—that'll help me at least get her home detention with an ankle bracelet. And find out who the hell the dead guy is."

He was slathering so much butter they couldn't have caught me in a greased pig contest at the fair, but I wasn't above reveling in my feel-good moment. "May I remind you, she doesn't have a home?"

"Aren't you the one always taking in the strays? I'm sure you'll think of something."

CHAPTER FOUR

THROUGH the years, a faction of the population had been trying to revitalize Vegas. Not so much as a tourist mecca, that was easy. Take out the family theme, throw the naughty back in, and bingo, forty-five million visitors a year.

But those of us who called Vegas home wanted a "real" city, fully realized with cultural activities besides the concerts on the Strip and the occasional pared-down Broadway touring company. For decades, Vegas was nothing more than a playland for adults, all lights and painted facades, but no substance.

So we'd built the Smith Center for Performing Arts, a world-renowned venue attracting the very best performers. The Jazz Cabaret alone was worth the price of admission. An intimate room, bar tables, food and libations, and singers so close you felt like they were singing to you. When Clint Holmes, one of Vegas's treasured crooners, performed, I always had a table.

And now with professional sports finally admitting reality and sullying themselves in the betting capital of the universe, Vegas was coming up in the world—maybe even being taken seriously and recognized as more than a playground. Okay, still a bit of a reach.

Vegas, the perpetual joke everyone wanted in on.

But, when it came to venues for monster truck shows and the tour of the former gold medal ice-skating champions...and the rodeo...we still looked to the Thomas and Mack—the basketball arena at UNLV. Of course, we now have the newly minted T-Mobile Arena, but the Thomas and Mack and the rodeo were synonymous.

I liked it that way. Change happened overnight in Vegas. So, when something stayed the same, it evoked a sense of nostalgia and belonging. At least in silly, sentimental types like me.

The fact that I could find my way there, blindfolded in the dark and stupid tired didn't hurt.

At this time of night, the parking lots were dotted with stray cars and trucks, most likely abandoned by owners who had overindulged, but essentially empty.

The security guard patrolling in his golf cart slumped in boredom as he silently scooted around with nothing to do. He motored in to check me out. As he came closer and a hint of light illuminated him, I smiled.

"Forrest!" He was the guard at my apartment building—the one I used to live in before Teddie, who lived above me, took a powder, then Irv Gittings reduced the place to cinders.

The big man perked up when he saw me unfold myself from the Ferrari.

"Hey, Ms. O'Toole. I thought that might be you. Nobody else got the balls to show up here at this time of morning in that kind of ride."

I had no idea how to respond.

Sensing his blunder, Forrest rushed on. "Man, we sure miss you at the Presidio."

I didn't lie and offer him some platitude about missing the Presidio as well. Another life. Another happiness. One that was vaporized along with all the talismans of the me I used to be.

Forced reinvention. I felt like a refugee from my life. But that pity party was done. "So great to see you!" That wasn't a lie. "How's law school going for your son?"

"He's working his ass off." Forrest shook his head—I could barely see him in the dim light from the open car door. "Does me proud, he does. Wouldn't have had the opportunity if it weren't for you."

I waved that away. "And a lot of other folks." We'd taken up a collection at the Presidio. "Gotta educate the youngsters. Who's going to take care of us in our old age?"

A very large black man, and one of the truest men I knew, Forrest extricated himself from the golf cart he was wearing, and I gave him a hug. A former NFL lineman, he was one of the few men I knew who made me feel dainty, and I loved him for it. "You always do that, brush off the compliments," he said when he set me back on my feet.

"They're embarrassing. Now quit messing with me and go pick on somebody your own size." I saw the wisecrack forming—he loved to razz me about being the only woman he could see eye-to-eye with. I wasn't sure how to take that, so I usually took it with a smile. "Don't say it."

He backed down. It was a rare man who could tell when a woman didn't want to play without her kicking him in the shin or elsewhere.

"What are you doing here?" I asked. "I know what we pay you and I doubt you need to moonlight."

He hung his head a tad. "I love the rodeo. And the job has some perks—I get free passes, can go behind the scenes."

I poked him in the ribs. "You just like the pretty women."

"I actually like the horses. And, since you're ribbing me, I don't need no women. They're nothing but trouble. Present company excluded, of course."

That last part was a vestige of his Southern gentility. I happened to know he thought I was the High Priestess of the Nothing But Trouble Tribe. I mean, how many women get their place blown up, then their car for good measure? And my car was a peach, a rare antique Porsche that had few equals in the world. "Please, you wound me. Present company is the leader of the pack."

He rewarded me with a grin, then he sobered. "I bet you're here about the murder," he whispered, sounding as if speaking of murder would conjure the murderer.

If only it was that simple.

"You know me, I never could resist a good felony." Whether referring to committing one or solving one, I didn't elaborate. Making a big, bad, mountain of a man squirm was one of life's pleasures.

"I heard a kid did it."

"Hell, Forrest, you know how unreliable scuttlebutt is," I lied.

"Maybe, but like those sayings of yours, there's a kernel of truth in there somewhere."

"Fine, but one kernel is not indicative of the whole cob, and that's what we're after." God, now I sounded like Perry Mason if he'd been from Arkansas.

"You and Mr. Teddie coming home anytime soon? His place is almost done and they've been hammering away on yours. How's it coming?"

I thought about lying, but, in a weak moment I'd bartered with the Fates and promised to give it up for New Year's. "I'm not privy to Teddie's plans." Hard for me to admit—once upon a time I knew when he drew each breath. "As to my place, I don't really know. Just can't bring myself to go back."

"I understand," he said with the all-knowing tone of a sage. "PTSD."

"No, TPO."

He cocked an eyebrow in question.

"Terminally Pissed Off. Besides, I'm not quite ready to rub my own nose in what I've lost." That included Teddie, but I didn't say that. I hadn't lost Teddie as much as he'd just wandered off, and I couldn't forgive him for that. He'd wandered back wanting to pick up the threads. I couldn't forgive him for that either.

"Reinvention can be healthy."

I skewered Forrest with a look. "Forced reinvention, not so much."

"Lucky, all reinvention is forced."

Why did everyone sound so much wiser than me lately? Life was bitch-slapping me upside the head, shattering my self-delusion. Hadn't life been better when its hurt had been hidden? That sounded really appealing right now, but I doubted it was true, even if it was life forcing my hand. Maybe that irritated me even more. I wasn't much of a believer in predestination—the Powers That Be gave me a brain and intended I use it to chart my course. That's my plan, anyway.

Regardless of whether I was the cart or the horse, I wasn't going to grouse about it. A grown-up life had a lot more shoulds associated with it than any of us liked. I nodded toward the door taped off with the yellow crime scene stuff. "Inside?"

"Yeah. Just duck under the tape. Since it's you, nobody will care."

I thought about Detective Reynolds. He would care. Oh, he would care very much. The thought delighted me. Nothing more fun than jerking with a dick, not literally, of course. Well, not here. And not Detective Reynolds. A shiver of revulsion snaked through me. I shook my head, trying to rattle my thoughts into some semblance of propriety. It didn't work.

"Has Romeo been through here?" I pinched the bridge of my nose and squeezed my eyes shut for a moment, hoping all of this would go away.

"Not that I've seen."

I blinked back tears of exhaustion when I refocused on Forrest. "In that case, if some weenie with a badge comes out here with a serious case of red ass, tell him you didn't see me, okay? That you were on the other side of the building."

"Why?"

"So I don't have to carry the weight of your losing your moonlighting gig. Since it's all about me, of course."

"If it's not, it should be. And no worries, I can handle that pansy-assed detective. Already had a run-in with him. I got your back, Miss Lucky."

"You always have, and for that, there is a special place in Heaven for you, at least if I have to say anything about it, which might be tough as it will be a long-distance call from where I'm going to spend eternity." A run-on thought if there ever was one. I was losing my grip.

Forrest looked like he wasn't counting on any stroke I might have with the Almighty, which was a good thing. I hated to raise false hopes.

"Lucky, I figure those of us with you in this life will be together in the next and we'll all just keep on like we always have."

I clung to that bit of optimism as I trudged up the stairs, ducked under the tape, and pushed through the double glass doors.

The first doorway put me mid-level, between the lower tier and the upper tier of seats. The food stalls and retail kiosks were closed and covered, but the hint of hotdogs and beer drifted in the stale air.

From the inside, the arena was almost indistinguishable from the other venues salted along the Strip. A good size, holding twenty thousand or so depending on the setup for the show, with bright lights and a ring of programmable LEDs to flash come-ons at the captive crowd. Most of the lights were dark now, the LEDs black. Only a few spots circled the huddle of people on the floor of the arena in light. Above the lights laced a latticework of crow's nests and catwalks. Two cages, pulled high, were empty now. This was Vegas—we had dancing girls at every venue in town.

Dirt had been brought in for the rodeo. The changes the crew could make to the arena were fantastic sleights of hand—from a wooden basketball court, to cement floor for concerts, to ice for skating, to dirt for the rodeo. Scanning, I worked to picture what might have happened. If the murder had happened in the arena... The place was huge, with multiple entrances...and dark shadows that could hide a witness.

Techs crouched around the body shrouded in a yellow tarp. One carefully disengaged the rope. Coiling it in one hand, she then secured it in a plastic bag. No doubt, if that was the girl's rope, her trace would be all over the thing. Not having a law degree or a functioning neuron, I wasn't sure which way that would cut.

Other than a small circle around the crime scene, the dirt had been raked. I didn't have to wonder whose bright idea *that* was. I hoped he'd been smart enough to canvas the whole arena before doing that, but I doubted it. The whole thing should've been taped off, but what did I know?

I took the steps down toward the arena slowly as I memorized details as best I could. Without a lot of information, I concentrated on everything, which was a bit much for my limited gray matter. At the bottom step that deposited me in front of the railing, I stared at the arena floor. Footprints led from some steps about midway down the south side of the arena toward the body but stopped at the last raked bit.

A young man swept the steps off to my right. He leaned on his broom as I approached. He looked as tired as I felt. Maybe exhaustion was contagious. If so, I hoped the CDC was working on it.

"When do you guys rake the dirt?"

"Once the place has cleared out. The cops stopped us until about half an hour ago. Rico just finished, in fact."

"What time did the show end tonight?"

"It finished early on account of the dead guy."

"He was killed *during* the rodeo? In front of twenty thousand people?"

"If he was killed, it was by a ghost. One of the bulls got into the arena. The clown jumped in." He pointed to the body. "That was as far as that guy got, then he dropped."

"And the rope?"

"I thought that part was weird. It was around his neck and trailing behind him."

"Nobody trussed him up like a calf in the team roping?"

The kid snorted. "Who told you that?"

"Scuttlebutt." I'd love to track down the origin of the scuttlebutt. Someone pointed a finger at the girl, and I wanted to know why.

Killing the guy in front of thousands was a stroke of genius. Too many witnesses. Too many versions of the truth as they saw it. A detective's nightmare.

"Did you see the arena before he raked it?"

"Sure. It takes a while to sweep all of this. Especially after half the crew got tired of waiting and lit out."

"What did the dirt look like?"

He reared back a bit, tucking in his chin as if I'd asked a stupid question. "I don't know, like dirt."

I reached for patience, but it was beyond my grasp. But I had no energy to muster an attitude. "I get that, but I was wondering if it looked like that body had been dragged around before being left there. Were there like any flat, smooth, trough-like marks in the dirt that would lead you to believe that might have happened?"

He pursed his lips as if thinking might be happening. I was hopeful but not sure. "Naw. It all looked just messed up like it always does at the end of the day. How could the guy be dragged with all of us watching?"

"I don't know. Stupid question, maybe. But you weren't looking at him; you were watching the bull. And maybe folks could've thought it was part of the show. How about you? What were you looking at?"

"The bull and wishing they'd catch him and wrap it up so I could go home."

"Precisely. Did you see anybody come near the dead guy before he fell?"

"No, but you just established I am an unreliable witness." The kid seemed happy about it. I didn't blame him.

"Who gave the nod to finally rake the arena?"

"Toby Sinclair. Among other things, he manhandles the cleaning crew, like somehow dealing with us is beneath him."

"Any idea who he works for?"

The kid shrugged. "He came in with the rodeo people. They're sorta like a circus, all self-contained. They roll into town and set up shop, then they break it down and are gone before the dust settles, leaving only a whisper."

"Pretty poetic for a guy with a broom." I gave him a half-smile. "You work for the circus, too?"

"There is no more circus."

"What?" I couldn't imagine a world without the Ringling

Brothers—my port in a real-world tempest. And my backup plan. The idea of running away with the circus had gotten me through many a dark moment.

"Yeah. Another one of life's certainties that bit the dust. Like the wind coming up before a changing sea."

"Way more than sorta." Change—that little wet fart of life was cropping up so often even I couldn't ignore it. But I had no idea what to make of it. "You've been reading too much Hemingway."

"English lit major. Nobody's invited me into the Ivory Tower, so I do what I can." He started sweeping again. "You watch out for Toby. He's in charge of the bulls. Used to be a rider until he got gored after a bad fall. Walks with a limp and a frown. Has a badass buckle which says he used to be somebody." The kid paused for a moment to telegraph his pointed stare.

Yeah, the used-to-bes were a special breed. "A badass named Toby—that's a first." Of course, far be it from me to judge a man, or anyone, by a name given them by someone else. Lucky wasn't exactly all badass either. Of course, Lucky Luciano had been a bit of a bully. Not exactly my namesake, but I owned him when convenient. I felt conflicted about that.

"First time for everything." The kid shrugged. Bending down, he dug out an empty beer cup from under the seat and tossed it in the pile of dirt growing in front of his broom with each pass.

"You there?" An angry shout from below.

The kid jumped but ignored the voice. "Sinclair," he said out of the side of his mouth.

I looked down and could just make out an angry scowl and mile-wide shoulders that could carry the weight of the anger and attitude that tapered to a thin waist and long legs.

He glared up at me. "Who the hell are you?"

"What do you care?"

He seemed surprised that someone would dare give him some push back. "You're slowing my crew down. Move on and let them finish."

The kid and I watched him move into the shadows, then disappear through one of the tunnels leading to the mezzanine area.

"He's either in a hurry to go home, or he doesn't want anyone talking to you." The kid didn't offer an answer. "Tell me about the guy who raked the arena? Rico?" I didn't pause for confirmation—I knew I had that name right. "Where can I find him?"

The kid lifted his chin toward the main gate at the far end of the arena, the one where the performers and competitors entered. "Head back there. You'll see a stall for the tractor off to the left. Rico won't be far. He finished not too long ago, and he likes to make his rig shine before its next circuit."

A man and his tractor. "Thanks."

As I made my way around to find Rico, I stayed to the shadows several rows above the floor and I watched the cops and the coroner. Reynolds wasn't happy about something. The coroner was pretty hot as well, and he was doing all the talking. I couldn't hear what they were saying, but if I showed myself and edged closer. I had no doubt Reynolds would throw his guard up.

Nobody noticed me at the far end of the arena as I filtered down to the floor then around to where Rico stabled his steed. As promised, he was tending to his tractor.

"Excuse me?" Not wanting to startle him, I tried for a soft tone.

It didn't work. He bolted upright, banging his head on some sort of strut or something.

"I'm sorry. I didn't mean to startle you."

A young guy, blond, with an easy smile, Rico wasn't what I'd expected. He doffed his hat and rubbed his head where it had met metal. "It's been a night." He looked a little pale. "Sorta spooked, you know?"

"Your first dead guy?" A little more calloused than my normal approach. The dead guy was a clown, after all. Didn't that at least give him a presumption of being one of the good guys? Then there was the flip side: who would kill a friggin' clown? Of course, the creepy clown thing going around on the

Internet had everyone a bit hatchet-happy.

Bug-eyed, Rico looked at me like a second head had sprouted from my shoulders. "First? Shit. Hope it's my only." Then he squinted at me. "How many for you?"

"Mmmm..." I stalled. Barely through the first full day of the New Year and already that whole no-lying resolution was tripping me up at every turn. I probably should be worried about that, but, instead I blew by it, lying to myself. Oh the irony! But lying to myself wasn't a resolution breaker. With me, it was a given.

I arranged the emotion out of my expression. "To be honest, I stopped counting awhile ago." That wasn't a lie.

"You with the cops?"

There was no way to answer that, keep my New Year's hope alive, and get what I wanted. "Yes, I'm with the cops."

Resolutions—easy come, easy go. Just another way I set myself up for personal disappointment—as if I needed more. I adopted one of those brusque, TV-cop tones. "What's your take on the...death? Did you see anything, anyone, that might help us understand what happened?"

"We were all watching the bull."

That wasn't really an answer. "I understand the bull got loose. Were there a bunch of people in the arena?"

"Yeah. The cleaning crew was picking up stuff, rearranging things to get ready for the slate of events, you know what I mean?"

If I slapped him, it would be justifiable assault. Was there such a thing? I focused, willing my mental train to stay on the main line and avoid the sidetracks. Yeah, right. "The cleaning crew?"

"All the folks who sweep up the stands, keep the aisles in the barn clean. You know, pooper-scoopers."

Considering the size of some of the animals, the only way I'd do that was with a backhoe and a HAZMAT suit. "Does the bull get loose often?"

"If it does, you couldn't prove it by me. Pretty dangerous. The rodeos I've worked on go to a lot of trouble to keep the bulls where they can't hurt anybody. Well, at least not until it's their time, you know—?"

"I can imagine." I had to cut him off or I'd end the night getting my picture taken holding a number across my chest. "Nothing unusual until the bull got loose?" Normally, a kid with an irritating speech pattern wouldn't be a blip on my radar.

"Nope." He rubbed his head one more time, then resituated his cap. "I did see the girl, though, hanging around, which, I guess, was unusual." He went a bit starry-eyed.

Another hormonally handicapped male, to the extent that wasn't redundant.

"The girl? Which girl?" I tried to keep my tone impassive, but my heart hammered.

"The Rodeo Queen."

Not the answer I expected, thank God. "Not unusual, I shouldn't think. It's the rodeo. She's the Queen."

"She's young; it was late. Her father is a rodeo dad."

"If that's anything like a stage mom..."

"Worse. He had her on a short rope. Never saw her without him sweeping up for her, know what I mean?"

I squeezed my eyes shut and counted to ten before I opened them again. Knowing what anyone meant beyond what they said was out of my reach—I needed a Rosetta stone to translate subtext. But the kid's anger pinked his cheeks. "He made decisions as to who was acceptable for his daughter, is that it? Separated the wheat from the chaff?"

"He didn't even care what Poppy thought." Hurt...and anger...slithered through his words.

Nothing like a young lover scorned.

It hurt. Bad. I remembered. While the memory of the boy had faded, the hurt remained. "He was with her, then? The father?"

"No, that's what struck me as odd. She was alone, but she looked all agitated, you know—"

"I know."

"Anyway, she was yelling at some guy in the stands. I

couldn't make him out. At first, I thought maybe it was her sidekick, but I didn't see her, which was odd."

"Sidekick?" This time I braced for the verbal impact that seemed inevitable.

"Yeah, cute girl, but total jailbait. She hangs out helping out and all. Really has a way with the animals. And she loves to throw a rope. Just learning. Darrin's teaching her."

"Darrin?"

"Darrin Cole, one of the clowns."

"The girl have a name?"

"Bethany, I think."

Bethany. I described the girl who called herself Tawny Rose.

"Yeah, sounds like her."

"She wasn't with our Rodeo Queen. You're sure?" If I could hazard a guess, the kid had been on her way to find me.

"I'm sure."

A young man would keep track of the young women within his reach, I figured, so I leaned toward believing him. "Could you tell what Poppy was yelling at the man?"

"No. I tried to get to her. She looked freaked, know what..." He stopped himself. "Sorry."

Guess he'd picked up on my near-homicidal state. Being half unhinged had its advantages for a member of the grammar police.

He ducked his head as he smiled—a shy smile that seemed to say he was trying to jettison the trappings of youth but it was hard.

I knew that, too.

"You never got a chance to ask her what had her so hot and bothered?"

"All hell broke loose when the guy dropped. I lost her in the chaos. Haven't seen her since."

I couldn't tell whether he was shining me on, protecting her, or telling the truth. Clearly, my detective super powers needed sleep. "When did you rake the arena?"

"Just now." He placed his hand on the machine. "Engine's still warm if you don't believe me."

"I believe you. Who gave you permission to rake?"

He leaned around the enclosure then pointed toward the small crowd gathered around the body. "The guy in the fancy suit."

"Detective Reynolds?" Even I knew how to do his job better than he did, which said more about him than it did about me.

"Yeah, that's the guy. Pompous prick."

"The more they pose, the less they got. Remember that."

"Ain't that the truth." He grinned, telegraphing the joke. "You know what I mean?"

"Got it. Now stop it. Tell me how the rest of tonight went down, after the show was over."

"I was almost done raking when the guy in the white jumpsuit showed up. I thought he was going to stroke out."

"The Coroner?"

"If you say so." Pointing out that his jumpsuit had CORONER in block letters across his shoulders seemed salt to a wound, so I let it lie.

"When did the Coroner get here?"

"It took him a bit. He's only been here thirty minutes maybe."

I guessed, this late at night, it might take a little longer to pull together a team. But, then again, this was Vegas. The nasties came out to do their business under the cover of darkness. "Can you show me what you raked up?"

He blinked at me a few times, then shrugged. "Sure. We get all kinds of stuff. You wouldn't believe."

"Oh, I believe. People throw stuff out of the stands, performers drop things, even competitors lose stuff—their lucky rabbit's foot, that kind of thing."

"Exactly." He looked at me with new appreciation.

I had a new fan. Well, a faux fan as I'd been lying my ass off, making it up as I went. Give up lying for New Year's? What had I been thinking? Lying was essential to my job. No, it was essential to my life.

I wondered if it was too late to make a substitute resolution. Could I give up Mona for New Year's? Was I confusing New Year's with Lent? All the self-deprivation events of the year tended to meld in my psyche into one long *noooooo*. Confusion was inevitable.

"What did you rake up today? Anything interesting?"

"You know, I quit looking." He shook his head. "You wouldn't believe what some folks carry as good luck charms."

"I'm sure you're right, and from your tone, I don't think I want to know."

"Dead stuff, parts of people and animals, and all."

Okay, not exactly what I was expecting.

"Parts of people?" Even though I wanted to, I couldn't resist.

"Vials of blood. Fingers. Ears. I hate it when they do that. I have to turn it all in to the police. Just a lot of trouble, you know..."

I shut him down with a slitty-eye.

He smiled.

The twit was playing me. My admiration for him grew like the Grinch's heart at Christmas. "I was right; I didn't want to know."

"Sorry. It just haunts you, you know what I mean?" He jammed his hands in his pockets and shivered.

Guess my slitty-eye needed work. If he asked me that one more time, even though he was playing me, I couldn't promise I wouldn't slap him, so I stepped out of reach. "Now, I know." So stop asking me, I silently shouted.

Sarcasm—a spear that bounced off his shield of youth.

Yeah, he'd won this round.

"Do you still have today's take separated from what you gathered before?"

The top half of him disappeared into a barrel off to the side. He shimmied back out, then tilted the barrel onto its side. "Yeah, barrel was clean when I added tonight's rake." He started to pour the contents onto the floor.

"Wait!" I grabbed a brush and swept a small area clean. "Okay, now."

He dumped the contents and I squatted to sort through them. He was right, all manner of things: wilted flowers, bits of leather, a belt buckle, which I pulled aside with the eraser end of a pencil I'd found at the bottom of my bag. A comb, beer cans...what one would expect. Nothing dead—guess my luck was turning.

And then I saw it, a square elongated tube—the end of it jutting up at me. With my pencil, I pushed at it until I'd maneuvered it to the side.

A tube of lipstick.

I couldn't read the color, but given three guesses, I'd give back two. "Can you read the color on the end there?" I asked Rico. Younger eyes.

He squatted next to me, his hands on his knees. Leaning forward, he squinted. "Tawny something."

"Rose?"

He gave it another squint. "Yeah."

I sat back on my haunches. Given that Detective Reynolds had ensured we couldn't prove where the lipstick was found, as a clue the tube carried little weight. But as a question? It was huge. "Do you have an unused plastic bag or something?" I asked Rico.

He thought for a moment, then nodded. "Gimme a sec." He disappeared around the corner into the barn.

I focused on my treasure trove, trying to envision who had lost what when. Hard to know. Easy to do some willful speculation.

"What are you doing there?" The voice was hard, mean.

Rico crab walked backward into a corner.

I flinched then regained my bluff. "My job." I rose and turned to face the man who had addressed me. Amazingly, I didn't cringe.

He was huge. And angry.

How I didn't falter, I don't know. Stupid tired had something to do with it, I'm sure. Self-preservation was the first thing to go. "And you are?"

"Homer Beckham." He stuffed his hands in his pockets and hunched his shoulders.

Too big to be a cowboy; too fat to do much heavy lifting.

"What do you do around here?"

"Around here?" His brows crinkled in confusion. "Just pray. My kid is a barrel racer. Poppy, she's the best there is." He looked over my shoulder as his eyes grew distant. "They voted her Queen, but what we really need is a win."

Ah, the rodeo dad, and I felt sympathy for his daughter. And Rico. He'd braved old man Beckham for a chance with his daughter. The kid had balls. "I'm sure being the Western Champion comes with perks."

He snorted at my understatement. "Life-changing, that's what it would be. Endorsements, paid appearances." On closer inspection, Homer looked tired...and haunted.

"I get that. But it's late, the show long over for the night. What are you doing here?"

He rubbed his hand over his eyes.

I couldn't tell whether he was stalling or just tired. My job kept flipping my cynical switch. The girl and the dead guy hadn't helped.

The girl and the dead guy—now there was a name for a Clark Gable movie. Or was it John Wayne I was thinking of? Or Humphrey Bogart?

Teddie would know.

"Couldn't sleep. Thought I'd check on the horse. Do you know how much these horses cost?"

"Sorry, not my world."

"A friggin' fortune, that's what. Horse was off his feed. Doc Latham, the vet, is here. Horse is having a hard time breathing."

"Sorry to hear that."

He glanced out into the arena. "Weird stuff has been happening."

"Weird stuff?" That was an interesting way to frame murder.

"Yeah, horses foundering, some just dropping dead." He shot me a side-eye, then clammed up as his gaze drifted over my shoulder.

"Dead, like the clown out there?"

He gave me a hard stare. "Who *are* you?"

"My name is Lucky, and I'm trying to help."

He huffed in derision. "If you're with the cops, you guys need to do your homework. That wasn't a clown they offed."

"Who was it then?"

"Another father, like me. Turnbull. A man trying to make his way, you know, and do something for his kids." There was pride there, and anger.

"You know his name?"

"Sure. Rodeo's a tight community...or was." He shook off a thought and had the wall back in place before I could ask him about it. "His name's Trevor Turnbull. Around here, he's known as T-squared. From Wikieup, Arizona. His boys competed in the team roping."

"Why would anyone want to kill him?"

"Your guess is as good as mine."

I thought not. Like he said, the rodeo is a tight-knit community.

CHAPTER FIVE

DETECTIVE REYNOLDS was as excited to see me as I had been to find him handling the scene. Reynolds slouched under his Burberry overcoat, proving the old adage that the clothes didn't make the man. Twenty years on the force and still pegged on clueless, although he had become much more adept at arrogance. He eyed me with the look of a man who had a better place to be. "Who let you in here?"

"You haven't shut any of this down. Jesus, they didn't even sign me in to this tiny crime scene. It should've been the whole arena. Jesus, Reynolds, you're as much of an inept ass as the day I met you."

The Coroner didn't look up but I could see his shoulders shaking.

I shrugged off Reynolds, focusing on the coroner who I knew well. "Hey, Doc. Whatcha got?"

Reynolds tried to push me aside. "Don't talk to her. She's not part of the investigation."

One of the few perks of being large was being immovable. The cop might as well have been shoving at Mount Rushmore.

Doc glanced up. "Hey, Lucky. This one's interesting." He peeled back the tarp.

A blue face, contorted in a grimace.

I recoiled a bit, but not enough to embarrass myself. Although, I really didn't aspire to being a seasoned veteran in the Murder Game.

One resume line item I decided not to pursue.

"Tell me." I leaned over the coroner who was on his knees next to the body.

"Well, it looks like the guy suffocated. See his blue fingernails, the blue around his lips?" Doc pointed out each of these things.

"Even though there's a rope around his neck," I said, thinking out loud, "there are no ligature marks, which rules out strangulation, at least using that rope."

Doc rocked back on his heels then turned and looked up at me. "You want my job?"

"Not on a bet. Besides, you couldn't afford me."

"I get you for free now."

"Like I said, you couldn't afford me."

"You're right. Why change when it's working so well?"

"It's my civic duty to help rid my city of the down-and-dirties." My help got me access, and that was worth almost any price. A large part of my job was keeping my family and our hotels out of the news. Murder tended to attract attention. So, if I could get in early, often I could sprinkle pixie dust, bring the parties responsible to justice, and smooth everything over. At least it had worked that way so far, but I had the sneaking suspicion I'd used up all my beginner's luck.

Now, with all of this, whatever this actually was, I wasn't so sure my pixie dust would be enough.

Mona could be counted on to make a big, messy splash. This time, she may have outdone herself. I know, I was jumping to a guilty verdict, but cutting and running was her MO. And, as they always said, the past is a good predictor of the future. Not sure I believed that, not totally, but, like a cliché, it held that kernel of truth.

The coroner motioned to one of his techs. "Take some close-ups of his neck and the rope."

A young woman with dark hair cropped into a bob and wearing a jumpsuit that would fit someone twice her size moved in and did as her boss asked.

I bent over both of them to get a better view. "Someone

didn't want that rope to come loose."

"The knot is a cow hitch with a reserve half. Never seen them thrown together quite like that," the girl said from behind her camera as she clicked away. She must've sensed the coroner and me looking at her as she lowered the camera enough to expose one eye. "Scouts."

"The Girl Scouts teach knots? Back when my mother tried to get me involved, all they did was bake."

"This is the only country that separates Scouts based on gender. Where I come from, we were all just Scouts and we did all the same stuff."

"And we Americans think we're so progressive. I would've liked Scouts if I could've done the cool stuff, but they made the girls all wimpy." I gave the coroner a knowing look.

"I'm assuming the Girl Scouts did not teach you how to throw an elbow and break a nose?"

The coroner tossed me that hanging slider and I couldn't disappoint. "Whorehouse skills."

That got two eyes from the girl behind the camera. I didn't elaborate. Her imagination would be way better than reality. "But if someone didn't choke him, how did he suffocate?" I asked the coroner.

Doc's eyes narrowed as he looked up at me looming over him. "What do you think killed him?"

This had turned into a training lesson or a game of one-upmanship, which I would, of course, lose. I had an advanced degree, but from the School of Hard Knocks, not a medical school—I didn't think my MBA would help either. I pursed my lips as I stepped back and straightened, giving him room. "Tox screen could be interesting."

"Good thinking. There are a lot of drugs that can disrupt oxygenation." Doc put his hands on his knees and started to get up, then quit. "It'll take a while though, even if I light a fire."

"You might want to pull in all your markers. One of the dads told me weird stuff has been happening around here—horses getting sick, dropping dead, that sort of thing." I extended a hand as I lifted my chin toward the corpse.

He took my hand and let me help him to his feet. "Knees aren't happy with all the running I used to do. I'll put a rush on. I can't keep the rodeo in town for long. Ten days and they're out of here." He brushed the dirt off his jeans. "Anytime you want a job..."

"Thanks. I've got more than I can handle."

"This is easier. The targets don't move."

I gave him the sad smile he wanted.

He looked down at the body. "You know anything about him?"

"I know he died in the middle of a bull-riding event. Bull got loose; clowns came in to help. The rope was around his neck, then trailing behind. He keeled over and this is where he fell. Is there any way to tell whether he was dead when he dropped or lived a bit longer?"

"My guys are talking to the clowns," Reynolds said, sounding officious.

"I wonder if he went to school to learn how to sound that way," I whispered to the coroner.

"They were the only ones in the arena at the time," Reynolds continued.

Unable to stifle myself, I kept going. "Knowing Metro, they offered extra credit if you took it at the Academy."

"Would you quit?" Doc said, his face a bright red. "Hell of a way for a clown to die, though."

"*Detective* Reynolds, I'd double-check my facts, if I were you. The clowns weren't the only ones in the arena." I gave a special emphasis to the detective part. Was I trying to convince him or me? Who knew?

I followed the coroner's gaze and stared at the dead man at my feet. "And he's not a clown."

That got me the side-eye.

"He's the father of a couple of boys competing in the team roping."

"That explains why his clown suit isn't hooked up like it should be and the size is a bit wrong." He motioned to one of his techs. "You heard that?"

"Yessir."

"Ignore it. Process the trace with fresh eyes as always."

"Of course, sir."

He turned back to me. "Sometimes, it's too easy to reach a conclusion before you look."

"Expectations—they trip you up no matter the venue." Life and death had unexpected parallels.

Detective Reynolds had pulled out a pad and a pencil and now moved closer. "You got an ID?"

"Reynolds, you should be an extra, but you get leading man pay. You let others do your job for you while you pick up the crumbs." Dissing him only made me feel good—it didn't make him feel bad. There was a lesson in there somewhere. "Have you even talked with *anyone?*"

Embarrassment clearly wasn't in his arsenal.

In an effort to facilitate the capture of a killer, I told him what I knew...well, part of it. "His name is Trevor Turnbull, known as T-squared, from Wikieup Arizona."

The idiot made a note, then got on his phone.

Why, with such a visible murder at a high-profile venue, did we get the B-team?

Where the hell was Romeo?

WITH nothing more to add and running the real possibility that Reynolds would arrest me for something, I left the Coroner to do his job and to keep Reynolds from messing the rest up. I found the cleaning crew kid a few rows from where I'd left him.

"Takes a while to clean up the mess, huh?"

"Especially short-handed as it ran so late with the excitement and all."

"Got a question for you."

"I got an answer," he said with youthful swagger.

"After the guy fell, do you remember anyone rushing over to him?"

He didn't answer immediately; instead, he cocked his head and his eyes went distant, as if he was running a tape reel in his mind. When he refocused, he said, "Hang on." Then he turned and scanned the arena. Finding a target, he set off at a lope, taking the stairs two at a time.

A young woman stopped to speak with him. She looked around him at me as they talked. If only I could hear what they were saying.

When my young friend returned, he looked like he had an answer. "That's Poppy. She rides in some of the events, but she's cool. A friend of hers who sweeps with me had somewhere to go tonight, so she stepped in. She said you need to talk to Darrin Cole. He's one of the clowns. He also teaches roping. Bethany and Poppy are his star students."

"I'd like to talk to Poppy. I've already met her father."

"Then you know why she can't be seen talking to you. She's not even supposed to be here. Her old man would have a cow."

"He's already had a cow, and he's looking like the kind of guy who would eat his young for dinner." I glanced over his shoulder. The girl was hunched up and wary, but still not convinced her cover was blown.

"Smooth the way. I'm here to help. I promise. Her friend, the one who was supposed to be here then jackrabbited when the shit hit the fan, she's being held by the police for questioning."

He waffled—clearly torn between allegiance and a healthy disrespect for us older authoritarian types. I couldn't say I wouldn't do the same in his shoes. "Okay, but no quick movements. She scares easily."

"Movements. Anyone raise their hand to her?" I felt the Amazon in me come bubbling up.

"I don't know. It' a crazy world when parents live through their children. Things get weird."

I got that but, somehow, with my totally dysfunctional

family, that little bit of craziness I'd missed. Mona didn't want any part of my life. Well, that wasn't true—she wanted to share the business stuff with my father. She'd find a way in; I had no doubt. Anyone who stood between my mother and what she wanted usually didn't survive.

As he led me over to Poppy, who eyed me like a wary cur who'd been abused then abandoned to fend for herself, I asked the kid, "Do you know anything about the new girl?"

"Like what?'

"Her story."

"Naw, keeps to herself, but she and Poppy are tight. Only thing I know is she rides with the vet, Doc Latham."

I came to a halt in front of Poppy the Rodeo Queen masquerading as a lowly member of the cleanup crew, and I tried to work through a strategy for getting past the wariness I saw in her eyes and her posture. Although she was rodeo royalty, she looked like a kid to me with a gap between her front teeth, her auburn hair braided down her back, and a splash of freckles...well, more than a splash. Her nose had a slight upturn to it, as if testing the scents, that made her appear younger than she probably was. Her skin was flawless and sported nary a trace of makeup—rather unbefitting of a queen.

I extended a hand. "I'm Lucky."

She kept her hands nested on the top of the broom. "Yeah. So."

"I'm a friend of Bethany's."

I saw a hint of softening, of curiosity. "But I think you knew she was coming to see me."

"Where is she?"

"Police have her." That hit with the force of the bomb to end all wars, obliterating resistance but causing panic and worse.

"What?" Poppy's posture collapsed. "That's like the WORST thing that could happen! She was counting on you."

"The police will keep her safe. Why don't you tell me what's going on?"

"Right." She punctuated the word with the appropriate teenage eye-roll. "Grown-ups. You guys are so not cool."

"Tell me about it. But Bethany came to me for help. I let her down. Maybe you could help me fix that?"

She cocked her head as if sizing me up.

What did a kid know about life and how it hammers away at you, then takes a knife, carving off chunks...a slow evisceration until you cave or become who you're supposed to be?

Life, the surgical suite where character was built.

Even if Poppy wasn't yet wise, she looked like she was pretty smart, and I was the only help in sight.

She let out one big sigh as she leaned on her broom. The show was over. As the bravado leaked out of her, the scared kid surfaced. "That's the thing—we don't know what's going on. Well—" she flicked her gaze to the kid that had brought me over.

He caught her drift and moved out of earshot. I thanked him with a smile.

Poppy leaned in, her voice riding on a whisper. "We know what's going on. We just can't prove it."

"Really?" I moved closer, trapping the truth between us. "What?"

"Well, we know how it started. A simple extortion plan, maybe even a little blackmail. Happens a lot in the world of expensive horses and even more expensive competitions." Her words tumbled as they rushed out in her need to share the burden of a big secret. Grown-up words coming from a kid.

"Pay up or something happens to your horse or kid or cow or whatever?"

"Yeah. Everybody's a bit freaked."

Extortion—a game as old as Vegas. Living in Vegas, one could pick up on the nefarious plots of the criminal underground almost through osmosis, as if the air carried their secrets, transferring them with each breath. "Any idea who was behind it?"

She pressed her lips together and shook her head. "How do

I know I can trust you?" A kid caught between a murder and a bad dad.

I felt for her—when did childhood get so real?—but that couldn't stop me from applying the pressure. "You don't."

"My lucky day, huh?"

My self-respect would evaporate if I let myself be baited by a kid. So, adhering to the old adage that I should fight with someone my own size, I kept my inappropriate and decidedly unhelpful responses to myself.

"We thought we had things in hand, were closing in on some answers..."

And watching too much television, but I didn't say that out loud—at least I didn't think I did.

"We suspected some blackmail. Mrs. Bates was pretty much popping rivets. There was talk she'd been asking around about ways to kill her daughter's horse and make it look like natural causes."

"Mrs. Bates?"

"Yeah, her daughter rides with us. Her mother is a whack job. She works for the rodeo."

"What was her play? Insurance?"

She looked at me as if I'd already cast my lot with the swine who would kill a horse for money.

"Hey, I live in Vegas. If there's a con or a scheme or a money grab or a whatever, it's happened here. I've been here long enough to have heard about all of them...twice." To her, I bet I was as old as the Ural Mountains. Those were the oldest mountains on the planet. How I knew that, I didn't know.

My mind, a steel trap for useless information.

But I really was a huge asset in Trivial Pursuit, if anybody valued the game of knowledge anymore, which I doubted. On the flip side, I was death at a cocktail party. "And then what happened?"

"Reno happened."

"You mean like the city Reno? Not like Reno, a two-bit hood from middle school?"

She gave me a look that told me to grow up. "After the

rodeo in Reno, things got really weird. One of our friends, Josie, Josie Brown, her horse dropped dead." She gave me a pointed look. "He was only seven."

"Any idea why?"

"Doc Latham said he had a bad heart."

"Could that be true?"

She gave a shrug. "Maybe, but Josie's parents were acting all snake-bit and all before it happened." In her eyes, I saw the hate of someone much older. "Those things shouldn't happen. They were nice folks."

"Can you give me their names and phone number?"

"I don't have it. We weren't close. Last name was Brown from somewhere near Atlanta, I think. Mrs. Bates will have it, though."

"Dora Bates?"

"She works in the front office, handles the money, that sort of thing."

"I'll find her, thanks."

"She knows more than you might think." The red flush of anger faded her freckles.

"Like what?"

"I don't know, but she's got something going on."

So did Poppy, if I could read her right. "So, what changed in Reno?"

"Everything."

"Who were you shouting at while all the chaos was going on?"

"What do you mean?" She looked genuinely confused as the red flush receded.

"Someone across the arena?"

"There you are!" The angry bellow from behind me made me flinch. I stopped myself from the involuntary cower to move out of harm's way.

Poppy dropped her broom and backed away.

I didn't need to turn to know who it was. Homer Beckham, Poppy's Rodeo Dad, had found us. More worrisome, he had found her.

Headed for his daughter, he brushed by me.

Squaring my shoulders, I caught his arm and held on. "Hold on a minute, cowboy. Let's not add child endangerment to your list of legal woes."

Red-faced, walking the tightrope of control, he turned his anger on me. "*My* legal woes? Just wait until I report you to your superiors." He hooked a thumb over his shoulder. "She's a kid. You can't question her without a parent present."

Even though practically all of that was wrong, I thought it best not to poke him with the semantics stick. "We were just having a chat. She's free to go."

Every fiber of my being screamed for me to take that child and not let him touch her. But, he was her father.

And I had no proof he'd do anything to her other than yell. Even though words were our most effective weapons, yelling wasn't yet a felony. Not until it became something else.

Another one of life's lines, often impossible to draw.

Where did anger end and abuse begin? Easy to prove if there was a bruise. But how did you show a bruise on your soul?

Frozen by indecision and indignation, I stood between Homer and his daughter. What should I do? What *could* I do?

"It's okay," Poppy whispered. "He yells. It's his way to offload stress. He has never..." Her voice trailed off.

"You sure?" Where my hand gripped his arm, I could feel Mr. Beckham's anger still vibrating through him, but it was dissipating.

She nodded. At first a bit hesitant, then stronger. "We're good. I lied to him. I came here to sub for Bethany so she could go find you. Who knew Mr. Turnbull would get himself killed?"

Interesting phrasing, I thought as I watched the father lead his daughter away. Despite his anger, he leaned onto her, wrapping a protective arm around her shoulders and planting a quick kiss on the top of her head.

Relationships.

"***D***O you know you are like the most difficult person to find? You are never where I think you should be." Romeo didn't look disgruntled, although he sounded it.

Lost in thought after Poppy disappeared with her father, I hadn't wandered far. The detective and I convened at the railing just above the arena floor. "I've been doing legwork, as requested. How's the girl?"

"A tough customer. I couldn't even get her real name out of her."

"Bethany."

"Bethany?" Despite knowing better, he sounded like he didn't believe me.

I didn't dignify his skepticism with a protestation of competence. Frankly, I would have gone as far as expressing insult had I had the energy for it. "Her grandmother's last name was Pickford, her fourth husband's name, at least that's what I was told. I haven't checked that out. Not sure if the girl uses it or another."

"Your Mr. Trenton pretty much shut us down." He stared at the group clustered around the body. His hands gripped the railing. His knuckles turned white. "He could tell I was just fishing." Romeo gave me the side-eye. "What do you call him?"

"Squash."

"I can't figure his name. Does he play it or do it?"

"Do it, if I have to pick one."

Romeo swallowed hard as he turned to watch the techs and his colleague begin to clear the crime scene. "Anyway, he let me run with the line a bit before setting the drag and reeling me in. Even with his tacit complicity, we couldn't get anything out of the girl. She's either one cool customer or scared beyond belief."

"If you had to choose?"

This time he looked at me square on. "I really couldn't tell you."

"Did you get anything out of her at all?"

"No family. No home. From Reno."

Reno.

The girl hadn't told him about Mona. I wondered why.

"What did you do with her?"

"We had to let her go."

"You just let her walk out of there into the night?" My voice rose with indignation. "Guilty or not, she's a kid. And as a girl, she's a target for all kinds of nasties who lurk in the wee hours of the morning. You know that."

"Of course I know that. Squash is riding herd on her until he tracks you down. A word to the wise, I think you're paying time and a half."

"Me?"

At the look on my face, he gave a laugh. "Why are you surprised? You're the one who went all mama bear. You become what you pretend to be."

"Tossing my own platitudes back at me won't get you any points."

"Being at the top of the heap isn't all it's cracked up to be, is it?" Romeo could find the insight when he looked for it.

"You think I asked for it? I was promoted to the level of my incompetence by attrition—I was the only one left standing."

"Lucky you."

"Who put you onto the girl in the first place?"

"One of the clowns." He didn't look at me as he pulled his pad out of his pocket and flipped through the pages. "Darrin Cole. He said he saw the girl arguing with Turnbull in the barns before he staggered into the ring."

Darrin Cole. That was the second time his name had come up tonight.

"I'd sure like to know why Turnbull went into the arena with a bull. What was he after?"

Romeo, fresh out of answers, shook his head.

"Your Detective Reynolds is more of an idiot than I remembered. How does he afford those Italian suits? And how does he not get fired?"

"His wife writes romance novels. And I don't know." Romeo looked as beat as I felt.

"We've got to stop hanging out together. I don't think it's good for either of us." I don't know where that came from or why I said it.

"I've tried to let you go, but I just can't." Romeo snaked his thin body through the railing, dropped to the dirt, then turned to stand in front of me. "You coming?"

I looked at the narrow gap, the four or five feet to the dirt. "Not that way."

While I circled to the stairs, Romeo waited for me. "You look like hell."

I looped an arm through his, locking elbows. "I'd be nice if I were you. I'm about to be your best friend. Come with me."

I filled him in on what I'd gathered so far, which, while not much, was a darn sight more than anyone else had, as I led him through the main gate of the arena. I nodded when we passed Rico, who was finishing a wipe down of his tractor. I patted my pocket where I'd secured the lipstick in a plastic bag, and he smiled.

"Any idea what's with the lipstick and the Tawny Rose thing?" Romeo sounded like a typical man at sea when it came to female war paint.

"A clue, maybe. But so far, the women I've met have been young and completely fresh-faced."

Continuing straight ahead, we entered the wide main aisle of the temporary barns. Rows of stalls extended off to each side. Behind wooden walls and visible only through the thin metal slats of the top half of the stall door, animals shifted, some curious, some wary, most settling in to work on sweet coastal hay. Mona had bought me a pony when I was barely old enough to remember my name and where I lived.

"Where are we going?" Romeo hissed, as if afraid of startling the horses. He needn't have worried—the animals weren't bothered by us.

But something else had them moving and shifting at a time

of night when they should be settled. Of course, murder could do that. Man and beast, a connection that spanned eons. And horses were more sensitive than we realized. That pony had taught me that. While not a dog that would pull me out of a burning building, that pony knew my moods.

Mona hadn't wanted a pony. After a year or more of wearing her down, I finally broke her and she relented. Looking back, I think she got the last laugh. A Welsh pony, blind in one eye and mean as spit, he took me all over Pahrump with nothing but a rope and halter and a bit of moxie.

My first sense of freedom. I'd been six.

But if I let my guard drop, he'd whip around and bite me on the ass—a good introduction to the vagaries of life. I still carried the lesson with me, along with a scar or two.

That pony had saved me. He didn't whisper behind my back or say cruel things to my face. He didn't care what my mother did to put a roof over our heads and food on the table. In Pahrump, prostitution was legal but not popular with the locals.

"Stinks in here," Romeo muttered.

The sweet smell of fresh shavings. The muskiness of the animals. I thought it smelled like heaven—a little girl's heaven for sure.

"Do you ride?" he asked.

I glanced down each row of stalls as we moved past. "Been a long time."

"Is there anything you don't do?"

"I don't sing in public." At the next intersection, I saw what I was looking for to our left. I tightened my arm hooked through his and steered him down the row of stalls to our right. "This way."

Romeo disengaged his arm. "You sing in private?"

"For a price and only in the shower."

Romeo gave a low wolf whistle.

"Would you quit?"

"You asked for it."

"I did indeed," I said, referring to something else altogether. I liked his smile and his guff and was glad they'd both returned.

We found Homer Beckham nervously pacing outside a stall in the middle of the vast barn. The horses in the stalls close by seemed nervous, upset.

"Animals, they pick up on stuff we don't even begin to see. I find that interesting, don't you Mr. Beckham?"

"What?" He looked startled to see us but recovered his composure quickly.

"Where's Poppy?" I couldn't shake the nagging need to protect her. But from what? Or whom? Her father? He was the obvious choice, but the answer was rarely found in the obvious.

"I sent her back to the hotel."

"Alone?"

He shrugged off my concern as he grabbed a rope knotted tight to the bars of the stall. A halter hung from the end. "It's a block or two. She'll be fine." He lifted his chin toward Romeo. "Who's the kid?"

I felt Romeo stiffen beside me. I knew how he felt. He had to overcome his apparent youth. As a female in a man's world, I had to overcome my presumed incompetence. Nobody said the world was fair or people were smart, but that didn't mean we had to tolerate unfairness or stupidity. "This is Detective Romeo with the Metropolitan Police Department."

Beckham snorted. "Where'd he get his badge? A box of Cracker Jacks?"

He never saw my elbow. It connected with his jaw, dropping him like a stone. Romeo shouldered in next to me. I rubbed my elbow as we both stared down at the inert lump of Homer Beckham.

"Why'd you have to hit him?" Romeo asked, knowing the answer.

"Hard-wired to vigilante." I threw an arm around his shoulder. "If you get tired of chasing the bad guys, you'd make a great setup man. We could take our act on the road."

A shiver of pain flicked through his smile. "Not a bad idea."

Something was going on with him—I hadn't imagined it. Some time with a high-octane liquid lubricant was in our future.

"Beckham has been begging for me to hit him all night."

"A bit of hyperbole." Romeo looked at me from under a frown. "What's he done to you?"

"He's a bully and an idiot."

"Hardly indictable."

"Exactly. So..." I motioned to Mr. Beckham laid out at our feet. "Sometimes we have to do our own dirty work."

Romeo shook his head. Mr. Beckham hadn't moved. "A glass jaw."

"Excuse me?" I feigned indignation.

"You're going to regret that." Romeo looked at me with a glint in his eye.

"He broke one of my cardinal rules." I waved off my own assertion. "In fact, he offended me in most ways possible, but the last one put him over the edge."

"And that was?" Romeo knew it—I could see it in his smile—but he asked anyway.

"I'm fair game, but don't insult my friends. And, for the record, that one was worth it."

"You don't always have to ride to my rescue." His ego bloomed.

"Of course I do. It's what friends do." I looped an arm around Romeo's shoulder. "Besides, you know I can't resist knocking the stuffing out of a bully."

"He's twice your size."

"With men like that, even before I open my mouth, I'm ahead of the game. Underestimating women is the secret handshake of their brotherhood."

"Along with scaring children," Romeo muttered as he looked at the inert form of Homer Beckham with growing distaste. "Surprise leveled the playing field then?"

"Please. I think I'm offended. I got skills. Tilting at large human windmills is Rule Number One in the Lucky O'Toole Rules for Life."

"You sure have a lot of rules. How many are there?"

"As many as I want."

A man half stood, his head barely visible between the metal bars comprising the top half of the stall walls, giving Romeo a start.

I expected to find him here. And he looked about as I thought he would—the frown and lack of eye contact of someone more comfortable with four legs than two. Younger than I thought—not the seventy I envisioned but closer to a world-weary fifty—he had dark hair. A few streaks of gray, from what I could see, but the weathered skin and the ancient look in his eye gave away the years. A stained baseball cap tilted back on his head. A Giants fan.

"Who are you? And where is Mr. Beckham?" His voice fit him, smoothed soft by time and a life dedicated to healing, wary, as if humans couldn't be trusted.

"You must be Doc Latham?" I brushed by his question about Mr. Beckham.

"Yes, and you are?"

Romeo did the badge thing, and I rode in on the implication I was with him.

"I see." His tone remained gruff, like someone rousted out of bed in the middle of the night might have, but it lacked even a hint of wary. "And Mr. Beckham?"

Romeo and I both glanced down.

Doc Latham followed our gazes and his frown disappeared, replaced by a look of respect and a hint of satisfaction, if I read him right. "What happened?"

"He said the wrong thing," I explained.

"He's good at that," the doc said, then he disappeared.

Romeo and I stepped over the slumbering giant and leaned into the stall through the open doorway. The horse smell rose up strong and pungent.

I breathed deep, stirring happy memories, but my young detective wrinkled his nose. "City boy," I said out of the side of my mouth.

"If you could call Minneapolis a city."

"What else would it be?" In my weakened state, I was easily sidetracked.

"An outpost in the tundra."

I smiled at his involuntary shiver. That explained how Romeo ended up in the Mojave. We'd never really hit on the topic before, but I wasn't surprised to learn he was a Midwesterner—solid stock like my right-hand man, Miss P.

Doc Latham squatted next to a pretty pinto, brown and white patches with a hint of black—a striking color combination. Well, it would be striking except the poor pony's eyes were wide with fear and rolled back enough to see the whites. His nostrils flared enough to see the pink inside. A dark stain of sweat matted the hair on its neck, permeating the small space with the smell of fear.

"What's going on?" I took the lead since Romeo still hung back a bit.

The horse didn't move except to pull in labored breaths, all its energy focused on the expansion of its rib cage. The vet ran his hand down the length of the horse's neck, a gentle stroke, and murmured in a soothing tone. He had large, wide hands, strong from pulling fences and settling scared animals, I suspected. "There, there. Just relax. You'll be better in a bit."

The horse cocked an ear back as if he understood. His breathing slowed, or maybe I imagined it. My breathing rate adjusted to the horse's—a sympathetic response as I willed the horse to fight but to relax. Panic made breathing more difficult. But panic, once entrenched, was hard to shake off.

Learning to function despite the panic—that was the key. Now, how to communicate that to the horse?

"Horse is having a hard time breathing, pulse is slow, temperature has dropped, but he's stabilized."

"Any idea what caused it?" Romeo asked, leaning around me to get a better look.

"Yeah," the doc pivoted to face us. He held a syringe in a gloved hand. The syringe was huge by human standards; the needle had the diameter of a garden hose. He stroked the horse's neck again, his fingers probing. "See this here?" His fingers found a knot in the flesh. "Puncture wound and a messy one."

"Like someone was in a hurry?"

"Or surprised." He tilted his head as he fingered the lump. "Or the person doing the sticking was an amateur."

"The horse might've jumped or fought?" I looked at that needle and thought if someone approached me with that thing, I'd do a whole lot more than flinch.

"No, they're usually pretty calm about venous sticks."

"What are you saying?"

"I'm not sure how this all went down, but I'd say someone intended to kill this animal."

Weird things have been going on. That's what Beckham had said. "Go on."

Beside me, Romeo eased his pad and pencil out of an inside pocket.

"I'll know more when we test that syringe and determine what exactly is in it. But I'd hazard a guess that it's a barbiturate. We use that for euthanasia. It's a controlled substance. As a vet, I have a supply, but I have to comply with very strict documentation procedures and the medicine must be locked up at all times."

"Where do you keep yours?"

"In my truck, in the back. It's secure, I assure you." He tilted his head toward the arena.

"Did the horse get the whole dose?" The syringe was empty, so that was a good guess.

"Hard to say. I don't know how much was in it to begin with. But he didn't get enough to kill him—almost but not quite."

"Why do you think the horse got barbiturates?"

Doc Latham pursed his lips and nodded. "They suppress breathing. In large enough doses..."

"You suffocate," I finished.

"How do you know this stuff?" Romeo sounded peeved.

"My pony. Long time ago." But it still hurt like it was yesterday. The look in his eye, so trusting. Was it a betrayal to end pain? My brain said no. My heart disagreed.

"The horses suffocate, too?" The young detective asked the vet.

"Yep. Sometimes they can even know what's happening but can't change the outcome. That's why you don't use this on an animal that is awake."

"Or a human," I whispered, thinking back to Mr. Turnbull staggering into the arena, most likely fighting to breathe. A little tidbit of horror I didn't want to own.

"Do you think Mr. Turnbull could've surprised whoever was trying to kill this horse, and he got a dose of the joy juice instead?" I asked Romeo.

"It fits the facts that we know so far. Lab will confirm it." He jotted a few notes.

"The rodeo was going full-bore," I said, pointing out the obvious to make my point—another of my highly-developed skills. "Odd time to kill a horse, with everyone around." I stood and turned slowly, taking in the interior walls of the stall. They were modular units, intended as temporary housing, and, as such, these panels had seen better days. Scratched, dented, showing teeth marks and a few half-moon hoof prints, the walls wouldn't tell me what I wanted to know. "If there was a fight in here, there's no way to tell that I can see."

That piqued Romeo's attention.

"Who called you out tonight?" I asked Doc Latham while Romeo made his pass around the stall.

"My assistant."

My radar pinged. "Assistant?"

"Bethany. She's a doll. Signed on in Reno; we both did. She's been accepted at Cornell, a joint program, undergrad then vet school. Been a vet tech all through high school. She knows her way around the animals."

For a kid who claimed innocence, her name was cropping up in the thick of everything. "Bethany? Cute kid, all legs and big eyes. Just lost her grandmother?"

Both the Doc and Romeo turned on me, wide-eyed. "How'd you know?" Doc asked.

Romeo already knew the answer. "The girl."

"You know her?" Doc looked between Romeo and me.

Romeo, his pen poised over his pad, eyed the vet. "You got a last name?"

"Fiorelli." The vet looked between Romeo and me. "What's going on?"

"How's my fucking horse?" The voice, muffled, rode on an undercurrent of anger. Even half-looped the guy had a hard-on for conflict.

I gave the doc my best sardonic look. "I don't think Mr. Beckham is a good candidate for long-term animal ownership. What do you think?"

"Trust me, you don't want to know what I think."

"I'm taking it this warm and fuzzy side of his personality is normal?"

"The guy is nothing but a fight looking for a place to happen." Doc collected his things, putting them back in his satchel. "Lately though, he's been worse. Like something was eating at him. Don't know what. You might want to ask him, but I'd put something between you and him before you do."

I rubbed my elbow where it had connected with Mr. Beckham's jaw. "If I can't take him, I can outrun him."

I motioned to Romeo. "Would you mind riding herd on the guy? I just need a moment."

"As you wish." Romeo bowed low.

I ignored him, although he knew the way to my heart was through vague movie references.

"That man has been a thorn in my side," Doc Latham continued.

"Can I come in there and poke around in the shavings?"

Doc shifted to the side. "Sure, just be quiet and gentle."

"That'll be the day," Romeo muttered.

"I pay him to keep my ego in check," I said to Doc Latham with a nod to Romeo as I stepped into the stall.

"Is he worth the money?"

"Every penny and then some." I squatted next to the doc.

"You do know your assistant...Bethany, is it?" I kept hoping he'd say I made a mistake and it was one of the other girls.

He nodded. Hopes dashed.

"You do know she's under suspicion in relation to the death of Mr. Turnbull?"

"What?" The word held genuine surprise, if I was any judge. "Bethany wouldn't hurt a fly."

"Yes, well, maybe her love for all in the animal kingdom doesn't extend to the lowly humanoid cousins."

"Impossible. The kid has had some hard knocks, sure. But she has her whole life, her dreams, within her grasp."

The warmth of the horse was comforting. When I was young and life was harder than normal—it was a challenge being the child of a local whore—I'd put my hand, fingers splayed, on my pony. The strength, the power of the animal flowed through me and it was as if the planets aligned for just a moment to give me peace. Now I closed my eyes and did the same thing. I could feel a smile playing with my lips as I pressed my hand to the horse on the ground. He was afraid but fighting. Weren't we all?

"It's magic, isn't it?" Doc whispered.

"A moment of visceral connection to who we used to be."

"Exactly."

"Are you guys going all Zen in there?" Romeo sounded worried as Mr. Beckham stirred and groaned. "Stay where you are, Mr. Beckham."

The man bellowed—the primal howl of a pissed-off animal. "Where is that bitch who hit me?"

"Right here, Mr. Beckham," I called through the stall rails, happy for once to be inside the pen. "And if you don't sit tight, the Boy Detective will shoot you."

Romeo looked at me wide-eyed—he didn't carry a gun. I passed him the Glock that I'd taken to carrying in the waist of my pants. A holster would be a good idea, especially if I didn't want to accidentally shoot myself in the ass, but somehow wearing a holster seemed pretentious.

The whole concealed carry thing was a holdover from

China reminding me I had yet to fully transition from that continent to this one. Carrying a gun was illegal in China, which, of course, ensured it was a necessity. "Doc, do you have an extra pair of gloves?"

"Sure." He rooted for them in his bag.

I snapped them on, then felt across the floor, moving my hand under the shavings, sweeping near the horse, then back again. On the first pass, as I brushed some shavings out of the way, I caught a hint of color I didn't expect.

Red.

I worked back through, sifting. Then I found it—a tangle of red fibers. Using a piece of hay, I separated it out, then worked around so I could see it in the dim light. A ball. Like a little puff thing—short fibers gathered together with a thread tail, coming apart at the end. Like it had been ripped or torn, pulled from something...like a costume.

"Do the barrel racers wear costumes?"

"Some do." The doc gave me a look like he knew what I was thinking. "Couldn't tell you if Poppy does."

"Mr. Beckham?" Even though he kept quiet, I could feel him absorbing everything we said and did. Something was rattling his cage, something more than the obvious.

He'd gone still, quiet. "I don't pay much attention to that girl stuff." A stage father who micromanaged every detail? His assertion sounded like a lie. But, as a human suffering from the Y-chromosome defect, he acted consistently with my expectation, not that I was a bit disappointed. I'm always hoping for easy, but, to be honest, Teddie is the only man I knew who would have known the answer.

Teddie. I shrugged off that hope for comfort—we were long past that.

With the hay, I scraped the fluff ball into the baggie Rico had given me. After pocketing it, careful to keep the contents separate by folding the baggie, I continued my search.

On my third pass, I felt it.

After retrieving the object, I smiled.

A tube of lipstick.

"I'd be betting this is Tawny Rose."

Someone had been leaving clues. Or the bad-deed-doer was conveniently inept.

But what did they mean? Who did they point to? I retrieved my baggie and then handed it and the tube, after encasing it in the latex gloves as I peeled them off backward, to Romeo. "Evidence," I said as if he needed me to point out the obvious.

He rolled his eyes, then carefully stowed the bag in his inside pocket.

With both hands through the handle of his case, which hung across his thighs, the doc looked at Romeo. "I've done all I can."

"How's my girl's horse?" Mr. Beckham bellowed. "She'll be out of her mind if anything happens to that animal."

"He'll be fine. His breathing is normalizing. Anything else you need from me?"

"Nobody's going to do that to my girl, you got that?" Mr. Beckham's voice carried a threat.

"Not to worry, Homer. The pony's going to be okay. You're one of the lucky ones."

"What do you mean by that?" My voice sharpened.

The doc gave me a level stare. "Homer's lucky that someone interrupted what was going down in here."

"How do you know someone interrupted the horse killer?"

"If they hadn't, we'd be looking at one dead pony. Had one just like it at the last stop in Reno."

"The Browns?"

"Yeah. Real nice horse." He took off his ball cap and ran his fingers through his hair before replacing it. "One dead horse is an accident. Two is a coincidence."

"And I don't believe in coincidences, Doc."

"Not that unusual, Ms. O'Toole, is it?"

"Yeah. The horses are insured?"

"The good ones, sure. It takes a lot of money to get a horse to this level. Freak accidents can happen."

Odd phrasing for a vet. "Intentionally killing a horse isn't a freak accident. So, to ask the detective's question—do you have any idea why someone would want to hurt this horse, besides the obvious?"

"Any idea who would want to hurt this horse?" Romeo asked, circling back around. We'd covered the why, now he'd worked his way to the who, a far more interesting question.

"No."

It was hard to tell whether he did or he didn't. Regardless, he didn't feel compelled to educate me any further.

"Where were you tonight, Doc?" Romeo asked. No matter how casually he asked, it always came out sounding like an accusation.

"You really think I'd sign on as a hired horse killer?"

"Answer the question, please." Romeo used his detective voice.

"It's my job to be here during the rodeo."

"So, you were here?"

"Didn't I just say that?"

I jumped in—nothing I hate more than someone trying to be vague. "No, you said it was your job to be here. You didn't say where you were. Answer his question."

He chewed on the inside of his cheek as he rolled his gaze upward. Divine inspiration wasn't going to alter the truth, but I didn't think I needed to tell him that. "I was with Dora Bates. We had some dinner at the steak stand, then she walked me out and I left."

"You and Dora are friends?" I watched for a hint of evasion.

I got it. He stared at his feet. "You could say that."

"Did anything about what went down, as you called it, seem unusual or strike you as odd?" Romeo asked.

"You mean besides Turnbull dropping dead?" Now the good doctor adopted a testy tone.

Silence was the best antidote to sarcasm, so Romeo and I both crossed our arms and looked at him.

Beckham jumped into the fray, his voice crackling with

glee. "You and that friggin' whack job? Man, I bet she's one hell of a ride."

Doc Latham dropped his case and lunged for the big asshat. Beckham braced for impact, his feet wide, his hands fisted, a smile splitting his face.

I used my body to block Beckham, while Romeo caught Doc Latham.

"Knock it off!" Romeo shouted. He glanced at me as Doc got hold of himself and stepped back, retrieving his case.

With both hands in the center of his chest, I pushed Beckham back. He staggered a bit, then sank to his knees, falling back into a seated position. He looked a bit green around the gills. I'd smacked him pretty good, but not that hard. Hanging his head, he looked like his world was spinning.

"You okay?"

"Been under a lot of pressure. Now the horse thing, and Trevor. Shit." Capitulation rang in his words—we were getting closer to the truth.

"You've got a lot of money riding on this, don't you?" I bit down on the smile—puns...I love puns...and clichés and platitudes and all their cousins. A terrible habit but one I had no intention of abandoning.

"Money, hopes, dreams...my girl..." His sigh carried the fullness of the thought, and in it, I heard a hint of humanity. "This was our first season on this part of the rodeo swing. Poppy had been doing real well regionally, but now we're on the national stage, a big leap."

"Where were you tonight, Mr. Beckham? Were you here before Mr. Turnbull staggered into the arena?"

"No. I was at the bar down the street from the hotel. I'm sure they've got me on video or something."

"Why did you come back here?"

"Got a call. Said my horse was sick and I needed to call the vet ASAP, which I did but he was already on the way."

"Who called you?"

He didn't want to tell us, that much was obvious. "Poppy. Okay? It was Poppy. I should've been here."

"She's safe and the pony will live. It all turned out okay." Yeah, I had a mile-wide obvious streak.

"Except for poor Trevor." Emotion resonated.

But I couldn't tell which emotion.

"Mr. Beckham, you're free to go," Romeo said. "But I'm going to check out your alibi. And you stick close, no leaving town until I say so. You got that?"

Mr. Beckham didn't acknowledge that one way or the other.

"If you leave, I'll hunt you down, and you won't like what'll happen next."

Man, the kid was plagiarizing from my playbook. I liked it.

With the two men glaring at each other, I stepped in.

I turned to our bystander, who'd been awfully quiet. "Well, Doc, perhaps then you could take Detective Romeo to your truck and show him how you secure your controlled substances. Maybe he could double-check your documentation with your inventory?"

The doc stared at Beckham. Even I could read the dislike.

"I'll make sure Mr. Beckham isn't still seeing stars before I let him climb behind the wheel," I assured the vet, even though I doubted he cared overmuch.

Mr. Beckham gave me a veiled look, but he didn't move from his seated position, his legs drawn up, his arms banded around his knees, holding them to his chest. His color was normalizing, but he still looked like he might be wobbly, which pissed him off.

Romeo offered my gun back, butt first.

I pushed it back toward him. "You keep it."

His thoughts marched across his face as he glanced at Mr. Beckham.

"I got this." I cocked my elbow in a show of confidence I didn't feel. I'd rather Romeo had my gun—not that he couldn't throw a punch, but I had bulk and experience on my side.

The vet stepped around me. "I've got nothing to hide. You can check out anything you'd like." Just past me, he turned. "What's going to happen to Bethany? I swear she had nothing to do with any of this."

"How do you know?" The pony stirred, lifting its head and curling its legs underneath it.

The vet took my arm and eased me out of the stall. "He'll get up now. You know they can't lie down for long."

"A circulation thing, I know."

"You like horses?" A hint of admiration crept into his flat tone as his gaze met mine and held.

"I thought we established that. I'm female, born and raised in rural Nevada."

We stopped at the opening and both turned to watch the pony struggle to his feet—wobbly but improving. Yes, a very good sign.

"About Bethany."

I raised an eyebrow in question—I'd asked the last one and it was still hanging out there.

He tried to slip his gaze from mine, but I ducked and weaved to keep it.

"She's a good kid. Had some hard knocks, but she'd never hurt an animal, that I know."

"Why do I get the feeling everyone is spoon-feeding me a story, not the real story, only pieces? It's like being served the sides without the main course—it leaves you unsatisfied." I gave him my best stare. "And hungry."

"Take care of her. You'll see I'm telling the truth." Once out of the stall, he moved aside, ignoring me and motioning for Romeo to precede him. "Detective?"

Romeo stepped back. "No, after you, Doc."

Before Romeo moved to follow the doc, I stopped him with a hand on his arm.

He lifted one side of his mouth—it wasn't a smile but more of a grimace. "I know, don't trust anybody. I got this."

I leaned in close as I watched the doc move down the aisle. He favored his left leg. "Watch your back. I'll wait here for you," I shouted after Romeo.

CHAPTER SIX

MR. BECKHAM glared up at me as the silence amplified the fact that I'd put myself in the pen alone with the bull. And I'd given Romeo my gun.

I decided to dazzle him with my own particular brand of bullshit. "Let me hear your theories on who would want to kill your daughter's horse."

"The kid said I could go."

"True." I pursed my lips as I gave him my best serious look, which, considering my present state, was probably a bit cross-eyed. "But I'd think that, if you didn't have anything to do with any of this, and if you don't want your daughter to think you tried to kill her horse, you'd cooperate."

He weighed that for a moment. "My daughter is good, really good. To get to the top, the rider has to be decent, but the horse has to be one in a million."

"Was your daughter with you tonight?"

"At the bar?" He didn't hide his disdain at my stupid question.

No kids under twenty-one in the bar. As The First Commandment of Vegas Gaming, it was tattooed on my ass, but I wasn't going to let Beckham see it. If he thought I was just another stupid female too ignorant to know the gaming rules... Some people, all you had to do was give them the rope. Mr. Beckham struck me as the type who would eventually manage to get that rope wrapped around his neck, his feet dangling. A rather macabre analogy, all things considered, but I sorta liked it...all things considered.

"Where was she?"

"In the room." Maybe he was lying, or maybe she'd snuck by him at the bar and he was none the wiser.

"Who stands to gain if your daughter's horse is dead?"

Mr. Beckham gave a huff. "Everyone competing against her. And, being the Rodeo Queen makes her a larger target."

"Anyone in particular having a fit of jealousy?"

Looking up at me, he gave me the side-eye. "You're not with the cops, are you?"

"Not officially, but more of an outside consultant. I don't like people messing with my Vegas magic."

"That's it?" His Neanderthal was slipping.

"No, this one's personal."

"Aren't they all?" He stared into the distance for a moment.

I'd sure like to see what he was visualizing. "Who's the next best barrel racer?"

He pretended to be interested in something far down the row of stalls, his eyes holding a glazed look. "I'm not making any accusations, but Doreen Bates has been giving us a run for our money."

"Bates? Dora Bates's daughter?"

"Yeah, her mother is just crazy enough to do something like this. Lately, she's been weirder than normal."

"Someone said the same thing about you."

He gave a derisive little snort. "True." He motioned to the stall. "With this sort of stuff going on, wouldn't you be?"

Even though I didn't want to, I gave him that point.

He swung his head like a lion eyeing a meal—I wasn't sure how to interpret that. "Dora's from Tahoe. She's one of those stage moms. Batshit, you know? Does crazy-ass shit. Doesn't mean she'd poison a horse, though." Beckham pulled back from his accusation. Something in his tone got my attention.

"What?"

"Nothing. She's crazy, that's all."

"From my experience, it's usually not the crazy ones. Is that the same Dora Bates that Doc Latham is sweet on?"

"The crazies, they find each other." Mr. Beckham picked up a piece of hay and started chewing on it.

"You have no idea where that has been."

He clapped those dark eyes on me. "What?"

I watched the piece of hay bob as he chewed on the end. "Never mind."

I was cementing my stupid female status. Unintentional, but I was okay with it—I wasn't above playing any angle to help me figure out what was actually going down with all these...people.

"There's somebody for everybody." When unsure what to say, which was often, I resorted to platitudes. The man sitting at my feet threw a sliver of doubt into the truth hidden in that one—although he did have a daughter.

Beckham gave me a grin. Clearly, my IQ had plummeted enough for us to be friends. Or he was feeling more comfortable in playing me. I wasn't sure either was a good thing. "What's so crazy about Dora Bates?"

"She's always pushing people around. Trying to pave the way for her kid but making it worse."

"Did Dora try to push you around?"

He eyed me with a flat expression. "How far do you think she would get?"

I took that as a yes. The lady had balls...or was desperate. "You know Doc's assistant, Bethany?"

"She hasn't been with the rodeo that long—maybe joined around Reno? I can't remember exactly. We're new on this part of the circuit, but she hooked in with my daughter. Thick as thieves, those two." He had a soft spot for his daughter.

Yes, his humanity was leaking through the cracks in his bluster. But it didn't mean I wasn't afraid of him—just that I liked him a bit...a tiny bit.

"Do you think Bethany had anything to do with what happened to my horse tonight?"

"The police are questioning her; that's all I know."

"They're just pawing in the hay like everybody."

"Which hotel are you and your daughter staying at?"

"We scored a couple of rooms at one of those suite hotels around the corner. Don't remember the name. Some forced Vegas kitsch." He shifted, putting weight on one meaty hand to lever himself up.

Apparently, he didn't know she was sweeping out the arena with the cleaning crew, subbing for Bethany. But if Bethany was the vet's assistant, what was she doing on the cleaning crew?

"Any idea why someone wanted to hurt your kid's horse?"

"I can speculate, same as you."

I took that as a "Yes, but I'm not telling you."

"Where'd you learn to hit like that?" Beckham worked his jaw, then fingered the growing knot.

He probably could tell I felt like doing it again.

"First female to knock me on my ass." He gave me a sloppy grin that came off as a leer. "Not the first to try, though."

"Spent my formative years in a whorehouse." Watching him unfold himself to his full height made me appreciate Jack as he watched his beanstalk grow.

"A whorehouse?" He gave me a look I was used to—lewd with a hint of interest.

"My mother owned the place. She has her issues, but putting her daughter to work for her wasn't one of them."

"Oh." The interest faded, but the lewd remained.

"Be careful I can read guys like you in a glance." Too tired to pull my punches, I didn't feel the need to elaborate. "Before you go, the cops are going to want to talk to you."

He glanced toward the circle of light in the arena. "Cops? Didn't I just talk to the cops? You and Captain America?"

"Not officially. The guy in the arena there," I pointed to Reynolds but was unable to call him Detective, "he's going to want to take your statement."

"I've said all I have to say."

"Your choice, but I've found things go better with the police if you play nice."

Not that I followed my own advice or anything, but he didn't need to know that. "How long had you been here when you found me talking to the tractor kid?"

"Just getting here. I parked my truck on that side—easier to get into the barn that way."

"You didn't see anything or anyone?"

His gaze drifted from mine as he smoldered. "No."

"You want to tell me what's going on?"

His eyes locked on mine. "I'd like to know the answer to that myself."

"Maybe so. But I think you know more than you're telling me."

I watched him head off in the direction of his truck. He was stonewalling me, for sure. But why? Who was he protecting?

CONCERNED about the horse, I cooled my heels. He seemed to be breathing easier. His eyes weren't as wild, his nostrils not as flared. The scared was leaving him. Back on his feet, he was still struggling. What kind of vet left a horse *in extremis*? Okay, I was overstating, but still... Maybe the vet's behavior wasn't convicting but rather the reflection of a long day and a late night.

The pony stuck his muzzle through the partially opened stall door. Ever a sucker, I ran my hand down the horse's neck over and over, trying to give peace and find some. His head resting in the crook of my arm, he absorbed the love. If anything could bring him back, love could.

Something was nagging at me—I resisted smiling at the unintended pun. What can I say? I'm a pun magnet. No, scratch that, I'm a bad pun magnet, to the extent that's not redundant. And clichés, don't get me started. They're just so...expressive.

As Romeo had said when excusing my bad habit, a hint of truth that resonated with most of us.

Romeo. He should be back anytime.

Why would the doc leave a horse who was obviously still struggling a bit? Why would Mr. Beckham not argue with him about it?

Romeo.

What the hell was going on?

And the girl? What part did she play? Or both girls, for that matter?

So many questions. Way too many moving parts. Dora Bates. Darrin Cole. Toby Sinclair.

Romeo.

Maybe it was almost losing him in Macau, but I kept coming back to him.

Something wasn't right. My gut knew it. I'd learned to listen when my gut shouted, as it was now.

I turned and ran. At the intersection with the main aisle, I paused a half step. Reynolds was still subjecting the group in the arena to his ineptitude, but it looked like the coroner and his team were wrapping things up.

Nothing there.

Racing down the center aisle, I glanced down each row of stalls but saw no one. His truck. That's what Doc Latham had said. I burst through the open doorway at the end of the aisle and skidded to a stop.

A sea of trucks and trailers greeted me.

Terrific. I thought about shouting, then stifled myself.

He could be in trouble.

I'd just have to find Romeo the hard way. Crouching I crab-walked up and down the rows, keeping my head low and only popping up to get my bearings. The night was still, so I kept an ear cocked.

Nothing...and no one.

Despite the cold night air—the high desert cooled quickly without the sun—sweat trickled down my sides. I never realized how large the parking area was. My thighs screamed, and my body begged to be unfolded and stand upright. I alternated between feeling foolish and feeling something was wrong.

I worked through the trailers then I remembered what Mr. Beckham had said about parking on the side of the building near the tractor stall. The vet would know the convenience of that entrance as well.

God, I needed a brain transplant. *Think!*

Shuffling, struggling, forcing my legs to move, I worked myself around that way, using trucks, trailers, and commercial signage that had been taken down for the night as shelter.

About halfway there, I heard it. An engine gunning. Then one pop. Then another.

Gunfire.

I abandoned my cover and ran.

A weak light over the entrance helped push back the night. One truck, black, huge, like a pickup had mated with an eighteen-wheeler, angled into the entrance. California plates, coated in road grime. Dust hung in the air, diffusing the weak light.

Someone had left in a hurry.

Banking on it being the shooter who'd felt the need to disappear, I skidded to a stop and started shouting. "Romeo!" Silence. I stopped at the front of the truck. "Romeo!"

"Jesus, you could wake the dead." Romeo. Alive but grumpy. "Over here."

I followed his voice around to the other side of the truck. Doors on the side of the back bay winged open, exposing an array of veterinary medicines and equipment, all carefully arranged on shelves and hooks.

Booted feet attached to jeaned legs protruded from under the right door. Not Romeo's choice in footwear, so I didn't panic. I sneaked my head around for a look.

Romeo knelt by the inert form of Doc Latham. I landed on my knees next to him. The kid didn't look at me as he focused on the doc.

"Is he okay? What happened?" I didn't see any blood on either of them, so that was a good thing. My heart slipped back down where it should be.

"That asshole, Beckham, came around the corner like a bull chasing a cow in heat. Caught the doc in the back of the head with a two-by-four." Romeo reached gently around the doc's head. His fingers came back bloody. "Crushed the bone."

He didn't have to tell me what to do. "You got a phone?" Mine was in my purse, and my purse was missing at the moment. Had I left it in the car? Without looking at me, he handed me his cell, and I punched the emergency button. A few sentences to the 911 dispatcher and I'd summoned the cavalry.

When I'd finished, I dropped his phone back into his pocket. "He's breathing, right? How's his pulse?"

I pressed my fingers to the side of his neck. Closing my eyes, I shut out the world and focused, searching for a beat...something, anything. "Shallow. Thready. Hope the EMTs get a move on."

Already, sirens sounded in the distance. The comforting sound let some mad seep in where the worry had been.

I wanted to be angry with Beckham, and I was, but I was furious at myself. "This is my fault. I should've walked Beckham over to Reynolds and introduced the two of them."

"I told you he could go." Romeo puttered trying to make the vet comfortable—a futility that wouldn't be appreciated anyway—the guy was out.

I sat back on my heels. "Hell of a life."

"But we rid the world of the Forces of Evil," he said, parroting my Pollyanna act as he shrugged out of his jacket, laying it over the doc. Watching him, I smiled. Funny how kids grow up and absorb lessons when you aren't looking.

"Well, not the Forces, but perhaps their minions."

"A win. I'll take it." With nothing else to do but wait, he settled back on his heels and looked at me.

"Whoa. That's quite a shiner."

His eye was already swelling, a shadow circling underneath

dark enough to be seen in the half-light.

"He landed one, but that was it. Staggered me a bit. Gave him just enough time to grab what he wanted then he ran—he took the evidence you gathered from the stall, as well as grabbing stuff out of Doc's van. I got two shots off, but it was really more of a pissed-off reflex. He'd jumped in his truck and fishtailed out of here before I could level my gun. Might've gotten a tire, but don't think so."

"He took the tubes of lipstick and the red ball thingy?"

Romeo shrugged.

"Don't beat yourself up over it. Not much you could've done. Any idea what he took from the van?"

"Barbiturates? But that's just a guess. We'll have to do an inventory." He glanced down at the doc, who hadn't moved. "Without his help, it might be tough."

"Bethany was his helper. Maybe she can shed some light." The girl was too clever by twice. Perhaps I could figure a way to corral that intellect. Leverage. Yeah, I needed more leverage or at least the illusion of more.

The doc's hat had slipped to the side. I resisted the urge to set it back right. It might be holding his head together or a bleeder in check. Another lesson learned the hard way. Where were the pros? From the echoing sirens, I'd say they were on the opposite side of the arena, working their way around. Pale and immobile, the doc looked darn near dead.

"Maybe." Romeo's lips stretched into a thin slash across his face. His hands on his thighs, his fingers twitching, he watched the doc.

"There's nothing we can do. The EMTs are almost here."

As the words landed, the ambulance screamed around the corner, then skidded to a stop at an angle to the truck.

Romeo and I backed away, letting the pros do their thing.

With no tolerance for any more death, I couldn't watch. I stared toward the lights of the Strip, close enough to paint the west horizon—the high-beam light from the top of the Luxor had been extinguished, signaling the end of night and heralding the impending day. From where I stood, the magic of the Strip was light-years away. "Any idea how much he took?"

"We don't even know exactly what he took, but I'm willing to run with the theory that he took barbiturates and he had time to take enough."

I felt Romeo's stare, then sensed him turning to follow my gaze.

"You think he was replenishing his supply?" he asked.

"I've got nothing to base an opinion on other than a gut feeling, but no. I don't think he was part of what has been going on. If I could hazard a guess, I'd say he's more of a victim. That's why he was so angry. Men like that don't like feeling helpless."

Romeo pulled in a deep breath. "I agree. But something about tonight put him onto somebody."

"Yeah, now he has a target." I nudged the detective. "You need to get after him."

That got a response. He pulled out his phone and started punching numbers and barking orders. At one point, he covered the phone and addressed me. "Any idea what hotel?"

"One of the suite places around the corner, probably on Paradise."

He nodded and went back to his conversation.

When he'd cut the connection and repocketed his phone, I gave him my one-eyebrow-raised look, which got under his skin. "Not asking Reynolds to lead the cavalry charge?"

With no more energy to engage in repartee, he glowered at me. "I give up. You win; now stop."

"Concession is a hollow victory, but, swine that I am, I'll take it. Did the doc have any chance to look at his inventory and comment on it before Beckham swung in like an Avenging Angel of Darkness?"

"A moment of shock or uncertainty, I can't be sure, but he left me with the impression some was missing. Which makes sense."

I sat back on my heels. "Doc could be covering up something."

"Or he was surprised." Romeo leaped to the man's defense.

Was that a Y-chromosome knee-jerk thing, protecting their own? With what little I knew about men, I was unqualified to answer.

"Guess we'll never know," he said.

"Spoken like a man who has forgotten he's an ace detective." My voice turned hard. "Oh, we'll know. But not until we find the killer."

"Mr. Beckham?"

"Well, he's certainly a suspect. But, I think he's probably a better suspect in a future murder. He's after somebody, but who?" I grabbed Romeo by the arm and turned him to face me. "Are you okay?"

"I have a black eye, not a bullet to the chest."

"Then what are you doing standing around here? Go get Mr. Beckham. When you have him, call me. I'll bring the thumbscrews. We really need to know what he knows before someone else ends up short of breath."

*S*QUASH'S call caught me stalking in the general direction of where I thought I'd left my car. I'd watched the EMTs stabilize the doc, then load him and screech away, leaving me choking on dust and questions. Then I retrieved my purse from the pony's stall—he'd tucked into some oats, so I crossed him off my worry list. Now all I wanted to do was go home.

"Please tell me you have Miss Bethany with you," I said. My patience for pleasantries had expired days ago.

"Is that her name?" He didn't sound surprised I'd ferreted out that tidbit. That was as much of an attaboy as I would get from Squash Trenton.

"Bethany Fiorelli."

"News to me. She dug in her heels—wouldn't say a word. Not without you there, she said. She said you told her that."

"Not exactly. I told her to wait for you, then take your lead." Even though the girl could really push the boundaries, I gave it to her for moxie. Had to admire that. "A miscommunication, of sorts."

"Figured, but she ad-libbed. No harm, though. As you suspected, the cops were just on a treasure hunt. They don't have anything on her...or anyone far as I can tell."

"She didn't give you anything?" Who knew Squash's gamesmanship didn't extend to the younger generation? Those of us older and presumably wiser were at risk...or at least vulnerable. I'd figured it was a double-X chromosome deficiency. Shown up by a kid. Could life get any more humbling?

And here I'd been counting on the patented Trenton charm to squeeze something out of her. I didn't think it would help telling the lawyer he'd fallen short of my expectations. In my experience, men didn't respond well to that sort of thing—no matter the venue.

"Did you also sic a keeper on her?" Squash asked. His tone held certainty that I wouldn't be fool enough to think he'd do it, and he wasn't fool enough to offer.

"Yeah, I lined up Dane to keep tabs on her, but I'm not sure he's got the skills."

"Gotta think like a kid. Dane's close enough."

My sentiments exactly. But I worried I'd subbed the B-team for a pro. "You're too expensive to be a kid-sitter. Besides, I need your expertise to keep her out of the legal system and to help figure out who is the right one to be shoved through that slop-chute."

"Does she even know a lawyer can actually help her?"

"She's got trust issues." The Ferrari waited only two rows over from where I thought I had left it.

"You sure she's not your sister?"

"Cute. And no." Had everyone ganged up to point out my deficiencies? I fumbled in my bag for the keys.

"She stonewalled me at every turn. Downright unappreciative—like someone else who will remain unnamed, but I'm talking to her. I've a mind to run her over to the Child Welfare folks."

"She'd just age out before they could figure out what to do with her."

That got a laugh, even though it was the truth and, as such, not a bit funny.

"I assume she's listening to all this?" As I folded myself into the Ferrari, I waved Forrest over. Switching ears, I held the phone with my shoulder as I arranged myself in the car.

"Roger, that. Along with her shadow."

The phone slipped from its perch and I muttered a curse as I rooted around in the dark for it. Finally, I found it under my right heel. This time, I clutched it as I pressed it to my ear. "Sorry."

"Multitasking, it's not good for your brain."

"You're describing my life, Counselor. At this point, the best I can hope for is an early medical retirement."

Forrest eased his golf cart next to me. "Hang on," I said to Squash, then pressed the face of the phone against my thigh, my thumb over the microphone. "Do you happen to know who danced tonight?"

"Sure, Becky and Suzie, cute kids. They're staying in a trailer on the edge of the parking lot. I escorted them home not too long ago."

"Which trailer?"

"The blue and white one in the corner, over there?" I followed his point.

"Got it, thanks."

I waited until he'd motored out of earshot before resuming my conversation. "Can I talk to Bethany, please?"

At the push of a button, the Ferrari started with a comforting growl, and I maneuvered through the empty parking lot toward the trailer Forrest identified. A light still burned behind pulled curtains. Someone peeked through the slit as I eased the car to a stop and killed the engine.

Some fumbling and muttering I couldn't decipher came over the line before Bethany got on the phone.

"Lucky?" Her voice sounded taut to the point of breaking.

"How're you holding up?"

"Okay. Kind of. This isn't how I thought it would go. I just wanted to get to Vegas. The rodeo seemed like a good idea. That clunker of a car Gram had would never have made it. Doc offered to bring me. He's a friend of the vet who used to travel with the rodeo."

"Nice of him. Want to tell me about your friend the Rodeo Queen and über barrel racer?"

"Poppy?"

"Yeah, little Miss Poppy Beckham. Why was she sweeping out the arena when she should be getting her beauty rest?" I really should be doing this in person where I could corner her and maybe run through my intimidation repertoire.

"Subbing for me." Bethany lowered her voice, as if any of this should be a secret from her lawyer.

"You do know Squash is on your side? He works for you, and whatever you tell him or say in his presence, he is bound by law to keep to himself?"

"Folks don't always do what they should." Such cynicism in one so young must've been hard-earned.

Unimaginable. "What do you know about her dad?"

"He's not as bad as he seems. He'd do anything for Poppy."

"What would he do to anyone who stood in her way?"

"I really don't know. He's got a temper."

She sounded like the voice of experience. "Any anger he's thrown your way?"

"No, but I saw him arguing with one of the hands. Lifted the guy right off his feet. It got ugly."

"Who was he arguing with?"

"Mr. Sinclair, he's the bull guy. Used to ride, then got hurt. He also drives the bull trailer. His niece competes with us but she does the poles."

Doing the poles in Vegas conjured something entirely different. I shut my mind to that visual. "Any idea what they were arguing about?"

"I don't know. Something about one of the bulls being a killer, but Sinclair wouldn't get rid of him. They were at the end of one of the stall rows, so I wasn't real close."

"Okay. One more question. If you're Doc Latham's assistant, then why are you on the cleanup crew?"

"Money. I'm not even a vet tech. Doc told me an unskilled helper wasn't in the rodeo budget. Doc can't pay much, but he got me this far, *and* he got a room for me." For a moment, her voice brightened. "My own room. It's awesome."

"Where are you staying?"

"At one of the suite hotels on Paradise. I'm sure Doc's worried, even though he knows my nights are late. I tried to call him, but he didn't answer."

I told her what had happened. I didn't lie, and I didn't insult her by soft-selling it. I think she appreciated that. "Will he be okay?" Her concern sounded genuine but a bit resigned for someone so young.

"The paramedics thought so. I've got one more question. Did you call Mr. Beckham about his horse being sick?"

I could hear the radio in the background as she quieted.

"This isn't a game, Bethany. The police are not to be played and neither am I, nor my mother. Tell me the truth and it'll all be okay." Yep, that's me, making promises I had no idea whether I could keep. I shut up and waited.

Her call.

Finally, she pulled in a deep breath. "Yeah, I called him."

"How did you know about the horse?"

"I checked on him like I always do. I've got a little more rope to run with—no parent checking on my every move." Apparently, a love of clichés was a family thing.

"Did you see Mr. Turnbull?"

She didn't say anything.

"Bethany, did you see Mr. Turnbull?"

"Yeah, I told him about the horse. He was acting weird, staggering around. I thought he was drunk."

"Did he say anything to you?"

"He told me to run."

"Did he say who from?"

"No."

"What'd you do?"

"I ran. I came to find you. My Gram always told me if I needed help, you'd be the one to find."

Boy, I wanted to deviate down that path, but I resisted. Murder took precedence.

"What time did you talk to Mr. Turnbull?"

"About eight-thirty. They were just finishing the early classes. After that, they cleaned the arena and had everyone come in to clean it up."

"Did you call Mr. Beckham?"

"Yeah, I tried, lotsa times. He didn't answer."

"You didn't talk with him?"

"No, when Poppy and I changed places, I told her."

"You didn't run right away. You joined the cleanup crew and stayed around to watch what happened to Mr. Turnbull, didn't you?"

"Yeah."

"Why?"

"Mr. Sinclair grabbed me, told me to get to work. I need that job. I figured I could sneak out later."

"When Poppy came to sub for you?"

"Yeah, but she was late. The whole place was nuts. Took them a while to get everyone out."

"And she called her father?"

"I guess. I don't really know."

She pulled in a shaky breath. "Look, I know I haven't been totally square with you. I don't trust easy. Will it help if I promise no more skirting the truth? I promise I'm telling you all I know. I need your help. Please?"

She sounded like she meant it, but meaning it and doing it were two different things. Probably against my self-interest, I felt like giving her the benefit of the doubt. "Who do you think hurt Poppy's horse? Mrs. Bates? I've heard she's been spouting off about collecting insurance if the horses die."

"She's horrible."

"Could she have done it?"

"She's batshit crazy enough to do almost anything. But we can't prove it."

"We? Who's we?"

"Nobody. Just me." Now that lie was easy to spot.

But I didn't need an answer. The kids had ganged up on the adults; that was pretty easy to figure.

"Maybe you just have it out for Mrs. Bates—fixing your friend's problem by putting her abusive mother on ice?" A shot in the dark but a reasonable theory.

"Mothers." A lifetime of hurt filled that one word. "There's no telling what moms will do."

I didn't have a clever retort for that one, but I had enough gray matter working to hear the subtext. "Tell me about Mrs. Bates."

"You know Poppy's dad?"

"Mr. Beckham. Such a peach."

"Mrs. Bates is worse."

I gave a low whistle. "You're telling me that, when I talk to her, I need to make sure my shots are up to date."

"Won't make any difference. She's rabid." The girl sounded like she'd been bitten more than once.

"All the more reason for you to hang with me or Detective Romeo, or maybe even Dane, if I decide to forgive him, so nobody will mess with you."

"What did Dane do?"

Like I said, too clever by twice, but now was not the time to shade the truth. "He lied." I paused for dramatic effect, hoping she got my point.

"You're not to go anywhere without talking to me, you got it?"

"You're pretty bossy."

In the background, Squash let out a hyena laugh.

"Ignore him. Pay attention. This game is way above your level."

"I know."

I worked through the possible places I could stash

Bethany, keep her safe, and have a good chance she'd stay where I put her. "Would you like to go to the hospital to see Doc?"

"Yeah. He's been really good to me." Her voice hitched. "I'd just die if anything happened to him."

"Don't go tempting the Fates. I'll have Mr. Trenton take you there. Put him back on, okay?"

She fumbled the phone, then Squash's voice sounded strong through the connection. "I'm assuming I have marching orders?"

I gave him the short and sweet as I watched the trailer. The girls kept sneaking a peek through the curtains. "Take her to UMC. There'll be a uniform stationed outside the doctor's room. We don't know if he's in danger, or a suspect, or whatever, and I'm too tired to work through all of it. Make sure the uniform keeps the girl there until I show up in the morning. Tell Dane he can get some shut-eye, but I want him back at the hospital early."

"It's already early."

"Right. I just want him to make sure that girl doesn't go anywhere without him shadowing her. Whoever tried to kill that horse and who probably killed Mr. Turnbull might think Bethany saw him. Maybe she did and doesn't know it; maybe she didn't."

"And that makes her a potential target."

"Bingo. The cops thought she was interesting enough to take in for questioning, and that makes me wary. She can sleep at the hospital. Make sure they take care of that. I'm practically catatonic. Nothing productive is going to happen on my end until I get some shut-eye. I'll be there when I get there."

"You're welcome." There was a hint of humor in his voice as he rang off, but he would make me pay.

Oh, yes, he'd make me pay.

CHAPTER SEVEN

*T*HE door opened before I'd found the courage to shift my weight to the thin metal stairs of the trailer. Someone held it a few inches open as she hissed, "Come in. Make it quick."

Throwing caution to the wind, I stepped. Metal bent under my bulk, but it held and I launched myself at the door. Once inside, my back against the closed door, I faced the two young women, Becky and Suzie—identifiable by the initials strategically stitched on the triangle of cloth that served as underwear. The fake crystals pushed the decorating past overkill and all the way to uncomfortable...at least for me. They remained remarkably confident and comfortable. I averted my eyes and tried not to wonder how far they'd taken the bejazzling thing. I'd heard rumors of women decorating their...I winced in wonder and shut down that thought.

Their faces were pale, their expressions worried, their bodies exposed. With their over-waxed eyebrows, tiny Cupid-bow mouths, and cheap bottle blonde, they could be twins...or a metaphor. Goosebumps peppered the vast expanse of exposed skin. Looking at them, their youth, their tiny figures, I found myself consumed with lingerie envy—well, not the personalizing aspect—but the lace looked French. My mother believed a woman could conquer the world with French lace and an attitude. One of my goals in life was to prove her right. "Did you know that the finest lace used to be made in Calais? Now the jobs have been shipped to China, and we're all stuck with cheap knock-offs."

Both girls blinked rapidly but said nothing as they stared at me, their mouths open.

"Sorry, one of life's indignities that gets stuck in my craw. Now, about the murder?"

The girls recovered nicely. "Do you think the killer will come after us?" One of the girls breathed the words, filling them with excitement and a hint of fear.

I tried to hide a surreptitious glance at the woman's crotch. BW.

Becky. Were initials and bling part of the rodeo uniform?

"Why would you think that?"

"We were dancing, watching like we always do," the other one chimed in. Suzie. Seeing as there were only two of them, I didn't have to glance at her crotch. She grabbed my arm and pulled me close, then lowered her voice. Her breath smelled like gin. "We saw everything."

Becky nodded. "Everything," she whispered.

"What exactly did you see?"

Suzie grabbed my hand and pulled me toward one of the two queen beds filling the living area. A curtain separating the two had been pulled back and gathered against the front wall. Against the opposite wall, they'd set up a bar, row after row of the good stuff, on a folding picnic table. If there was a kitchen, I couldn't find it. I assumed the other end of the trailer housed a bathroom, but I didn't want to ask.

A loud banging on the door had the three of us practically jumping for cover. "You girls in there?"

The girls recovered before I could get my heart rate under control. I mouthed a question at them, "Who?"

Becky grabbed my arm. "Best if he doesn't find you here," she hissed in my ear as she propelled me toward the other end of the trailer. "The bathroom. Quick."

She thrust me inside, then shut the door as silently as she could in her haste, leaving me to decide whether to rifle through their medicine cabinet or use the glass beside the sink as a microphone to amplify what was being said in the other room. Turns out I didn't need to do either—the walls were as thin as parchment.

"Why, Toby, what a pleasant surprise." Becky's voice—at least I thought it was her—pierced the walls of my enclosure as if they were nonexistent.

Hidden from view but not from discovery, I didn't dare breathe for fear Toby would hear me and I'd spoil his little party.

"Whose Ferrari is that out there?" Toby didn't sound happy and he wasn't using his inside voice.

"What?" That one sounded like Suzie.

"That's Mr. Picarrelo's, you know, the geezer I told you was sweet on Suz? He got into the Sapphire. Must've been one of those recalled bottles with the booze content off the charts. We had to send him home in a limo." Becky could think on her feet. "What are you doing here, Toby?"

The floor creaked, absorbing his weight, and the spring-loaded door shut. Now the bull was in the henhouse—a tortured metaphor, but panic crossed my wires. "Just checking on you girls. With the excitement and all, I thought maybe you might need some comforting." The words oozed on a slick of meanness.

"We're good, really." Becky got her backbone up. "You need to leave. We were just getting ready for bed."

"You've read us all wrong." Underneath the honey, Becky's voice held an edge. "We're just dancers, and that's workout enough. No extracurricular activity here."

"You girls just don't get it. I take what I want."

"Ow! You're hurting me."

"You guys have been chatting up Dora Bates. I want to know why."

"Who?" The surprise sounded genuine.

"Older lady. Looking a bit worn. But she's a nosy cuss, always looking for an angle." Toby sounded like he'd had personal experience.

"Oh, I know who he means, Suz. That old bag with the tacky clothes, overdone make-up, and the shoddy bejazzling."

"Oh, yeah, the one you thought was digging for some dirt

to shake us down with."

"That's right."

"What'd you tell her?" Toby asked, his voice guarded.

"Honey, she wasn't asking about you." Suzie's Southern charm sounded as tired as I felt. "Why? You got something to hide?"

Oh, she should've stopped.

Sounds of a scuffle. A slap.

"Oww!" a female wail of pain.

Toby's voice went low and hard, demanding. "Come here."

"You're hurting me." Becky's voice rose in pain.

A sharper slap. Becky pulled in a sharp gasp.

Suzie said nothing. What was the woman doing? Of course, she was wobbly at best with a bellyful of gin. I could picture her cowering in a corner.

"You guys like to talk. Shutting up would look better on you."

Them was fighting words. I looked around for a weapon.

"Let me go!" Becky whined, the fight leaving her. Giving up was something women learned early, especially when faced with overwhelming physical odds against them. Most men would never know the terror of physical intimidation.

The incendiary cocktail of anger and adrenaline flooded through me.

"Get over there," Toby said. "And stay."

The bed creaked as it took Becky's weight.

"What'd you two see tonight? Anything you told the cops?"

Suzie mewled. Toby had turned his attention to her.

"I don't know what you're talking about. We didn't see a thing." Becky sounded calmer now. "What do you think we saw?"

Good girl. Buying time. How could there be nothing in the bathroom I could use to disable a misogynistic asshole?

"A sassy one. Looks like I need to teach you a lesson."

One more quick search of the bathroom. *Nada*. And, right now, thinking on my feet wasn't my best thing. With my hand on the knob and my shoulder against the door, I took one deep breath, then turned, opened, and hoped surprise would even the odds.

I dodged around Suzie, who indeed cowered out of the way. Toby loomed over Becky, who was sprawled on the bed. Sensing movement behind him, he whirled. He'd gotten his buckle undone, and that would be as far as he would get.

Reaching across my body, I grabbed a full bottle by the neck. Like Federer lining up a backhand, I coiled, then swung as hard as I could. The bottle broke across his forehead. As the light in his eyes went out, his surprise remained.

Slowly, he fell backward. Becky rolled out of the way as he landed on his back on the bed. His eyes rolled back in his head, leaving the whites showing, which creeped me out. The glass opened a gash in his forehead. Blood leaped to line the edges, then pooled at the end, leaking out of the corner into his short-cropped hair. That was almost as much fun as breaking his nose with an elbow. "Shut his eyes, would you?"

Becky wrinkled her nose at the idea of touching him. I didn't blame her, so we let him lie.

"Shit. That was awesome." Suzie had found her voice.

"If you girls are going to parade around in your skivvies and stay out here in a trailer all by yourself, I suggest you at least take a self-defense course. Or better yet, get a gun and be ready to use it."

They nodded. Funny how a close call could enhance receptivity. "So, what did Dora Bates want with you two?"

"She was just looking for dirt," Becky said, indignation creeping into her voice. "Everybody thinks just cuz we're dancing, we do other stuff."

"Stuff you'd pay to hide?"

"I've got one more year at UNLV, then I'm going to teach English to high-school kids," Suzie said, proving once again the book and its cover fallacy. "Being a hooker wouldn't enhance my job prospects. I'm smarter than that."

"Indeed." I struggled to keep a straight face considering her attire. "Me and Becky don't have anything to hide. The lady left."

"I bet she dug up a bunch of stuff in her job," Becky offered.

"The front office?"

"Yeah, she handled all the money for the rodeo. If someone was short or had a score, she knew it. And payroll, she wrote the checks." She glanced over my shoulder to the mirror behind me and fluffed her hair. After a quick press of her lips together and a swipe under her eyes with a forefinger, she seemed satisfied that she'd come through the tussle in fine form. "A lot one could do with that kind of information." A hint of respect crept into her tone...or larceny.

"Indeed." I couldn't tell whether she was smart or just clever, not that it mattered. Either one, unchecked by scruples, would set her up for a slippery downhill slide. "That kind of path won't lead where you want to go."

She flicked a glance at me—guilty that her thoughts were so transparent? Or guilty for another reason? Did she give the goods on anybody to Dora Bates?

Lights flashed across the wall behind me as someone pulled up in front. "More visitors?" I grabbed another bottle.

"Not that one, okay?" Suzie asked.

A fifteen-year-old single malt. I got it, so I grabbed another, this one a run-of-the-mill gin.

"Lucky? You guys okay in there?" Forrest called through the closed door.

At the familiar voice, I relaxed. "Come on in. We're fine but we could use your help with a mess."

The thin metal stairs held and he slid sideways through the narrow door. He took everything in with a glance. "How can I help?"

I knew he'd do anything I asked, even bury the body. I tossed him my phone. "Get Romeo here. He's number one on the favorites list. And then sit on this guy. Don't let him move."

"Gotcha."

I smiled when Forrest took me literally. Fumbling around, opening doors, I finally found the closet. Two jackets hung in the back—a bit short, but they would do. "Here." I handed one to each of the girls. "Cover yourselves. You ought to be able to wear what you want without getting unwanted attention, but I think you probably should stop short of underwear in public. It just sends the wrong message." I wasn't sure where that line was drawn, and, frankly, having to draw the line offended me—men ought to honor a woman's wish to express herself and remain un-groped, but what should be rarely was what was.

Sirens sounded close by. As I thought, Romeo hadn't gone far.

"So, girls, tell me quickly what you saw. Do you have any idea who killed Mr. Turnbull?"

"Mr. Turnbull?" They seemed surprised. "You mean that wasn't Darrin?"

"Darrin?" I wracked my brain. I'd heard his name, but with too many names, too much adrenaline, I couldn't place it.

"One of the clowns. He and Toby hated each other."

"Why did you think the dead guy was Darrin?"

"He was wearing Darrin's clown getup, and he went after the bull." Becky sounded sure.

"Okay, so who went after the man you thought was Darrin? The man who died?"

Both girls looked at Toby, still out cold on the bed—or dead from suffocation under Forrest's bulk. "He did," they said in unison.

*T*HE sun streamed through the open windows—I'd forgotten to pull the heavy velvet curtains closed. I'd also neglected to disrobe. Perhaps propriety had compelled me to kick off my shoes but I couldn't be sure—my feet, hanging off the bed, were numb.

Arms outstretched, I'd fallen backward on the bed, and there I had remained. One thing about memory foam is it sort of formed around you, making it an uphill climb to crawl out of the hole formed by several hours in the same spot. Lacking the conviction to fight inertia, I rolled my head to the side to angle a look at the clock.

Not several hours. Ten. Ten catatonic hours.

Noon had come and gone.

My head throbbed—major sleep coma.

My body ached with immobility—a body at rest, and all of that. Curiously, overnight, my muscles had calcified. Tentatively, I tried moving my arms and legs. After much grumbling, everything worked, creaking and groaning in protest—well, everything except my brain, which was spinning but not gaining any traction. I assumed the World As We Knew It had not ceased to exist while I'd been offline; otherwise, someone would've found me. On the third sweep across the bed, I located my phone. Squinting, I raised it so I could see it.

In a last-ditch effort toward self-preservation, the one thing I'd managed to do last night was silence my phone.

Twenty-seven text messages. After enlarging the text—why were some messages in readable type and others miniscule?—I scrolled through them, squinting to focus and closing my left eye against the pain.

One was from Jean-Charles saying he'd checked me in with the front desk, so he knew where I was and there was no need to call him unless I felt like it. If there was a rebuke in there, I chose to ignore it. Men and their delicate egos took way more energy than I had today. Besides, I sucked at that game—he'd get used to it...or not. Not that I didn't care. I did—tremendously. I just couldn't muster the energy to sound General Quarters over a phone call. Romeo's rebuke about pushing people away sounded, a distant alarm I chose to deny. I didn't push them away, my life did.

I kept scrolling.

Seventeen messages from my mother because she was lonely—none worth saving, but I wondered what she really wanted. With Mona, habitual obfuscation made communication a minefield of intentional misunderstanding.

Mona. I'd have to deal with her pretty soon. I was sitting on a keg of dynamite. She'd either light the fuse or not. If I was a betting woman...I shook that thought away. Last night it had been too late or too early, not sure which exactly, but a bad time to corner my mother. And I'd needed the sleep. But ten hours! When had I ever slept ten solid hours?

But it allowed me to live to fight another day.

I continued scrolling down through the messages. As of an hour ago, the kid was still at the hospital. Doc Latham was awake and responsive. They'd controlled the swelling. He was stable. Dane was riding shotgun. I wasn't sure how I felt about that. Was he doing it because he cared, or was he trying to get leverage with me? Would I ever trust him again? Impossible questions.

But the doc was stable. Another thing off my worry list.

One from Romeo. Ten minutes ago. I hit his number, pressed the phone to my ear, and closed my eyes. Without light, the headache lessened, starved of its fuel—or that's what it felt like.

"Where are you?" No niceties, but no hard edge to his voice either. Guess this business-as-usual was our new reality. I missed the old us. I knew change was the only constant, but, dang, right now I hated the validity of platitudes.

"Never Never Land." I closed my eyes and wished on the second star to the right, but I'd already gone straight on until morning.

"Cielo?"

I heard the accusation and immediately flipped to the defensive. "Yeah." I didn't offer any excuses about how late my night had been and Jean-Charles having been home with Christophe and not wanting to awaken anybody. Romeo didn't sound in the buying mood.

"You going to sleep all day?"

"If it'll make you like you used to be, then yes."

A moment of hesitation. "I'm sorry. This job..."

"Is like every other job...but with more blood. Balance, Grasshopper."

"Like you?" he scoffed.

"I'm getting better. I can't save anyone if I don't save

myself."

"Hence, ten hours of sleep."

"Precisely. The rightness of the world doesn't begin or end with me...or with you. Anyway, you called? Can you bring me up to date?"

"Took the girls' statements. You already know they had some interesting things to say about Dora Bates?"

"I heard. Have you talked with her?"

"No, she didn't show up for work today."

I didn't like the sound of that. "The daughter have any idea where she might be?"

"Doreen? Still can't find her. You might want to ask her little buds if they know where she's holed up."

"Will do."

The sound of pages flipping rustled through the line. "You also know they fingered Toby as Turnbull's killer."

Keeping my eyes closed, I rubbed my temples. "No, what they did was say he got all badass with Turnbull. They argued. But they couldn't say for sure he actually injected him with barbiturates."

"True. But the fact they argued makes Toby look—"

"Like a person worth talking to," I said, grabbing him before he leaped off the assumption ledge. "Have you questioned him?"

"No. You clocked him pretty good, and I couldn't say for certain, but Forrest sitting on him might have bruised several ribs. The hospital kept him overnight for observation. He's just been released and my guys are bringing him in now. I'm assuming you want in on it?"

"For sure. I'll need a shower, so leave him cooling his heels, okay?"

"I'm not far ahead of you. Had to sleep as well. So yeah, we'll cool him off until you get here."

"And Beckham? Please tell me you have him." A big man with a bad case of red-ass usually made a splash, so he wouldn't be hard to find.

"Ummm, no. He didn't show up at any of the expected

places."

Not a good sign. "I would suggest you look in the unexpected places."

"Actually, funny you should mention that. Got a call from one of your security at the Babylon. He was seen skulking around the Kasbah late last night."

"The Kasbah? Really?" The Kasbah was our secret, hidden hideaway for the high rollers and the seriously famous.

"What was he doing? How'd he get in?"

"Skulking, like I said. How he got there is your purview." Romeo pulled in a breath. "I'm thinking of getting out of this business."

"What? Just when it's getting interesting? Don't be ridiculous. So, you didn't get him." A statement, not a question. All the time I'd spent schooling the young detective had given me a Rosetta Stone for a few of his subtext dialects. "And his daughter?"

"She was where she was supposed to be. We left her there, tried not to alarm her. She couldn't tell us where he was. I kept a black-and-white on her." That meant a couple of Metro officers, which didn't exactly fill me with confidence. The ones I'd met were like Detective Reynolds, their arrogance exceeding their competence by many magnitudes.

Was the daughter, Poppy, stonewalling us? Battered-daughter syndrome? Was I letting my bias against blowhard men trump logic? "Where is she now?"

"Still in her room. No barrel-racing today."

I propped myself up on one elbow and was surprised the world came into focus. "We need to track down Dora Bates."

"We're looking."

"Aside from being a fairly adept extortionist, if public opinion holds any truth, she was Doc Latham's alibi. They were having dinner during all the fuss."

"Oh, yeah, one of my guys canvased the food vendors. One kid at the hot dog stand claims to remember them—well, her mainly. Said she was a real piece of work, and not in a nice way."

"I get it. So they were there like the doc said."

"Yeah, but the kid had them there a lot earlier, like more midafternoon or earlier. He said the lunch crowd had thinned and dinner hadn't hit. You know anything I don't?"

"It's just her name keeps cropping up. And Bethany has a particular bit of hate for Ms. Bates." I filled him in on the girl's whereabouts. "Maybe she just has a hate thing for all mothers or maybe there's something there. I want to check it out."

"I'll figure out where this Dora Bates is staying, see if I can find her."

"Her kid's one of the barrel racers. I'm curious why Beckham was wandering around the Kasbah. Did you check the guest register?"

"Yeah, Brandy pulled it. Nothing jumped out but we're running the names."

I drug in a breath, preparing to jump all over him.

He cut me off before I got started. "Discreetly, of course."

I let the breath out in a thin stream. "Thank you." Background checks and cops had a chilling effect of the *joie de vivre* in the high-roller rooms. "Give me a half hour to pull myself together. I'll meet you at the Detention Center. But, in the meantime, would you please find Mr. Beckham before he hurts somebody?" The man was an amateur on a pro's mission—collateral damage could be huge.

"We're looking. It's like the man evaporated."

"He's after someone, or he wouldn't have taken the meds from Doc Latham's van."

"Curiously, I got that far all by myself."

Now Romeo was quoting me verbatim. "Sorry. Thinking out loud. Didn't mean to..."

"I know. We both are barely hanging on."

"With some sleep, I'm doing better. Did you get any?"

"Yeah, some."

But not enough. Unspoken, but loud and clear.

"Look, I'll keep Mr. Sinclair on ice for a bit. We need to process him and all of that, which will take time. Would you go talk to your mother? I know you're avoiding it, but she might be able to shed some light, light we could really use."

I worked through all available excuses and came up empty. "Okay. I'm assuming we don't have any more rodeo-related deaths that could possibly distract me, do we?" Half-kidding, the words had the ring of inevitability to them if we didn't get Beckham first. I didn't know why. The girls had fingered Toby. But Beckham was on a mission. None of it fit together. And none of it made sense, not that murder ever did, not really. Did murderers have instant regret like the jumpers taking a suicide plunge?

"Somebody dies, you'll be the first to know."

"I can't tell you how happy that makes me. I'm over the moon. While I regain my equilibrium, I suggest you put Beckham's daughter's feet to the fire and find out who his friends are here and if he said anything that might hint at what he's planning. We'll find him. Vegas only shelters its own."

"I'm on it, Lucky. Surprisingly, the world kept spinning on its axis while you were asleep."

"So much for being important. Let me know if you find anything." Where would a guy like Beckham go? If he was looking for help committing a felony, in this town, the possibilities were endless. And why the Kasbah?

I rang off and fell back. I had to think. But first I had to move. Without much hope, I pondered the possibility.

Not optimal, but fear was a great motivator. A confrontation with my mother, then questioning a potential murderer. With that on my schedule, I felt certain today couldn't get much worse.

A small consolation.

But first a shower. I had my standards, low was they were.

"YOU'VE had sex!"

The voice came from behind me as I strode through the lobby of Cielo, fresh as a daisy and filled with purpose. My best friend, Flash Gordon. "Anybody else, and I would've shot you on sight," I said, knowing she was within earshot, even if *I* used my inside voice.

With Flash, everything she said was punctuated with an exclamation point, everything she said was usually cringe-worthy, and everything about her was overdone. So I really was feigning the whole displeasure thing. Sometimes it even worked. This little farce, or variations thereof, was part of our routine, like a secret handshake or something. Truth of it was, Flash would run through fire for me, bring the baseball bat to the party, help me bury the body...all of that. And I'd do the same for her.

Loyalty—more precious than water in the Mojave.

Heads turned. Eyebrows raised. My employees smirked. My customers looked like they were considering pumping me for advice on how to get laid in Vegas. Frankly, if you couldn't get laid in Sin City, then you had a pesky disease, non-existent social skills or a low limit on your credit card.

While I pretended not to be rocked by her observation, her verbal assault blew to smithereens the careful plotting and planning that I'd developed in the shower.

With me, organization was a delicate thing and once imploded, all was lost and the day generally careened out of control. An excuse for my normal operating procedure, but I had to blame someone. I shouldered a lot of things, but today, blame wasn't one of them. So I was a bit miffed.

But Flash had her uses—taking my offloaded bullshit was only one of them. History and experience had taught me a few things. One of them: gathering info was best delegated to the pros. And, as the best investigative reporter in Vegas, Flash was a pro.

As she skidded in beside me, I continued with my little rant. "Humiliating me in my own hotel is hardly the way to get what you came here for." I still didn't know what that was exactly, but, knowing Flash, I could narrow it down to one thing: something salacious no one else knew. Which meant the inside skinny on the rodeo murder. While I tried to figure out how much I'd give up to get the info I needed, I let her run.

"Please." She blew at the bangs that tickled her eyes. "Sex isn't humiliating."

She looked like she believed that. She also looked...predictably scary.

Flash was the Mutt to my Jeff, and she compensated by wearing the most insane heels, six inches of pain-inducing fashion. I never appreciated my height as much as when I looked at Flash's feet. I prayed for them.

If Flash was any indication, today was neon green day and I'd missed the memo. She'd captured her lush figure in a barely-there circle of nauseating green Latex, which, I must admit, offset her dark red curls cascading over her shoulders with some panache. Her makeup, as usual, was a bit overdone—if anything, Flash was consistent.

"Sex not humiliating?" I gave her a disbelieving look. "I have one word: Elliot Spitzer."

"That's two. He wasn't humiliated, just browned off at getting caught. You know guys like that. They think they deserve a wife and a mistress...or two or three."

"Bad behavior cloaked by the public trust. Well, I'm not quite that egotistical or morally corrupt, I hope. But, even though you know where all the bodies are buried, metaphorically speaking, go easy, I've a carefully constructed corporate persona. But, as to the sex charge, you should know."

She started to argue, then a shit-eating grin split her face. "Damn straight. And proud of it, too. Then again, I get your jam—I'm not corporately-constrained like you."

With Flash, offence was the best defense. Yes, I meant it that way.

At least someone pretended to appreciate the shackles I wore. "Do I really look like I had sex? If I did, it was three continents ago."

"No birthday sex?"

"We're saving up. But I get it. Even a working stiff in town deserves some nookie."

"Working stiff. Cute, but mundane. You can do better."

Not even a grin. I was insulted. "Not today."

"Besides, I'd hardly call Jean-Charles Bouclet a casual piece of ass." She fell into step beside me.

"Good to know. I have cred to protect."

"He must be some incredible working stiff. The after-orgasm glow suits you." She actually said that with a straight face. Impressive.

"This might be somewhat disappointing, but sleep actually is better for that whole youthful glow thing."

Her perfect brows crunched together. "That would be profoundly disappointing."

That was already more information than I could handle on an empty stomach. I watched her breasts bounce as she worked to keep up with my long strides. "Do those things ever escape?"

She rewarded me with the guffaw I'd been hoping for. "Only when I want them to. We all have our assets. The key is recognizing them and knowing how to put the package to its best use."

"That's what I was afraid of." I stopped in the middle of the lobby. Today, the whole Japanese Zen thing, with the soothing water features, subtle lighting, and walls of manicured grasses was lost on me...almost. Ever the corporate-type, I took a moment to catalog all the action around me. Nothing amiss.

Yes, I owned one of the few hotels on the Vegas Strip without a casino. An oasis from the over-amped Vegas vibe. We were about pampering and rejuvenation. And I counted on others paying well for the privilege. A risk. An outlier. Either succeed beyond dreams of avarice or fail miserably. A metaphor for my life lived at the edges.

Flash scurried a few steps further, then, when she realized I had stopped, she turned around to face me. "Give it up. I know you were front and center with the dead body at the rodeo."

"You know the drill. Ongoing investigation. Not free to share, despite first girlfriend status. But here's the common knowledge as I know it." I gave her my edited version of the truth.

She plucked a pencil from between her breasts and a notepad from God knew where and started taking notes.

When I'd wound down, she gave me a thoughtful look. "What do you need from me?"

That caught me a bit off guard—not her usual angle. But I knew the steps of the dance, no matter who led. "I need you to get the videos from YouTube. No security feeds inside the arena, just outside in the parking lot where everyone expects bad to happen. So the interesting stuff will have been captured on an iPhone from the crowd. You can bet the videos will be posted almost immediately to YouTube where news has a shelf life shorter than last week's tuna. The killer knew he'd go viral. So let's watch what he wants us to watch."

"Got it."

"And I want you to dig deep into Reno."

"Reno? Like the city, Reno? Nothing ever happens in Reno besides quickie divorces and air-show mishaps. Good people just stop there for gas and Ho-Hos on their way to Tahoe. They don't linger." Her face flushed with emotion.

"Really?" The vehemence was over the top, even for Flash. Like a flashing red light, it slowed me down a bit, but it didn't make me stop. I was never one to err on the side of caution—nope, I'd blow through the warnings every time. Had the scars to prove it, but I was still alive. "Something bad happened when the rodeo made their Reno stop."

Her lips clamped tight into a thin line. "I would say Reno is known for bad, but that's too whiney even for me. Got in with a black hat there." She raised a hand. "Don't ask. And yes, bad cowboy is not an oxymoron. So, if a bit of nasty went down with the rodeo, I'm your gal. Got a knife to sharpen."

"Isn't that an axe to grind?"

Her eyes narrowed. "No."

"Alrighty, then." I wasn't sure if Flash being poised on pissed off and contemplating sharp weapons was a good thing or a bad thing.

"So something happened in Reno. Like what?"

I gave her a look. "If I knew, what would I need you for?"

"Comic relief?" My look wiped her attempt at a smile. "Okay, this is serious shit. I get it. So, stop with the visual memo—I hate it when your eyes go all slitty. Makes me want to run. So, seriously, any idea?"

"Actually, I do know one thing. A healthy horse suddenly went hooves-up when the rodeo stopped there." I gave her the particulars. "I want you to see if you can find the owners and talk to them."

"What are you looking for?"

"Connections."

"Connections I can do." She tried not to smile but failed.

"Be careful. This isn't a busload of NBA players all thinking you're a worthy piece of ass and you working hard to live down to the expectation."

"Those days are in my rearview," she said with a haughty air.

"One day doesn't count." I shut down the banter. "First YouTube, then Reno."

I started to walk away to keep her attention. "And then find out what you can on a Sara Pickford. She owned a ranch outside of Reno." I thought about asking her to dig deep into Dora Bates, but I figured we'd have her soon enough and her present was way more interesting than her past, right now. I didn't specifically ask her to check into the girl's background. Maybe I was protecting Mona, or myself. With or without my help, she'd come out in the grandmother's story. Justification, I know.

"Easy-peasy." She tucked her pencil and pad away. "The normal agreement?"

"Give me what I need and you'll have the exclusive." That agreement had worked well, and I had no intention of breaking that streak.

Our dealings finished, I continued to the front of the hotel and pushed through the doors into the day. Cool and crisp, it called for a light jacket and I was glad I'd grabbed mine as an afterthought. Leather as soft as butter, it settled over my shoulders as if made just for me. Money might not be able to buy happiness, but it sure could buy exquisite Italian leather...and fine Italian iron. The growl of the Ferrari echoed from the bowels of the parking garage to the right.

Although so new he squeaked when he walked, the valet actually had found my Ferrari—or one that looked like it. Such trifles didn't hit my radar today.

Mona loomed in my near future. Questioning a potential murderer was child's play compared to the kid-glove handling my mother would require.

Grateful for my car, I handed the kid a twenty. He returned my gratitude with a smile and a shallow bow.

Flash followed me around the car, then hovered as I folded myself into the small space. "You think I could get a bow for a twenty?"

"Not the kind you're alluding to."

She thrust herself through the open window. "I'm on this. Anything else?"

"Bring me back something to help me break this open, and you can write your own ticket." I stepped on the brake and shifted into drive. Flash pulled back and I accelerated down the driveway. What if the truth steamrolled Mona? Would I let Flash run with the story? After a nanosecond, I knew I would. I'm not some holier-than-thou Holy Roller, but I do believe that one has to own up to the truth, to accept it, to pay the price. And I was no exception to that rule.

Keeping life simple, elemental—harder in the short run, but far easier as time strung itself out in an ever-thinning line toward the future.

Yeah, another lesson learned the hard way.

I'd sent Flash on what sounded like a wild goose chase. But she usually bagged her limit and then some.

This time, I was counting on it.

And dreading it.

CHAPTER EIGHT

MY mother was exactly where I expected to find her—in her apartment, the one that had been the Big Boss's alone for as long as I could remember. The hour was well into socially acceptable and cruising toward happy hour. Alcohol sounded alluring, but breakfast should probably be first on my list...if my waning self-respect was a concern.

Champagne, not just for breakfast anymore.

I should probably be made to wear that saying pinned to my shirt like a scarlet letter—not that it would change anything. Shame wasn't one of my hobgoblins...and a good thing, too.

The ride up in the elevator had done little to give enlightenment as to how to proceed with my mother and not lose blood in the process. The private elevator had deposited me in the middle of the great room, which I stopped to drink in, as usual. Its perch on the fifty-second floor of the Babylon and its wall of surrounding windows on two sides gave the space the feel of a very comfortable tree house. By day, the view of the Strip paled, muted by the ever-present sunshine, but by night it was magical—a kaleidoscope of lights that could be seen from space, or so I'd been told.

Masculine was still the overriding motif: leather upholstered walls dotted with lighted works by the lesser Masters. The more important works by the major Masters hung in the Big Boss's private museum in the Bazaar at the

Babylon, our high-end shopping corridor downstairs off the lobby. The wood floors added warmth. Clustered on bright colored rugs, the furniture made of exotic woods and the pelts of animals that had formerly found a home on the Serengeti added testosterone. Personally, I'd rather watch the animals bounding across the savannah, but the Big Boss hadn't consulted me, not that that was unusual or anything. A dead zoo offended my sensibilities—thankfully there were no desiccated heads or stuffed carcasses here in the more public area of the apartment. But in the private sections, Mona slept under the watchful eye of former carnivorous predators—stuffed heads lurking over her like vultures at a dwindling waterhole.

In life, irony abounds if you look for it.

Mona had moved into my father's space, but little had changed.

If anything, my father had a mile-wide out-of-my-way streak. From the outside, his incorporation of my mother into his world and his space seemed seamless. But, knowing my father as I did, I could see the toll it took. He loved her desperately; I knew that. But loving Mona exacted a price.

"Lucky? Is that you?" Mona's voice sounded sharp and full of purpose—unexpected and terrifying. With the birth of the twins, Mona had milked the overworked, under-slept sympathy card to the point of making most who dealt with her for any length of time desperate to stuff a sock in her mouth, then paste a couple strips of duct tape over her nose and mouth. She often had that effect—it was her special gift.

But now she sounded like she was back on her game.

And, when Mona got the bit in her teeth, all bets were off. I shuddered and blocked out the most recent fiasco—a thousand live turkeys, a public market at the holidays. But that was better than her scheme to auction a virgin...a national black-eye that proved there really is such a thing as bad PR.

My mother could sense my presence as if by osmosis, which had freaked me out as a child. Now I tried to spin it as a positive—if my mother knew I was close by, maybe, just maybe, she'd rethink whatever stupidity she was contemplating. My theory rarely worked, but hope springs eternal and all of that.

Even though I knew where she'd holed up, I followed her voice, squinting against the sunshine streaming through the ceiling-high looking-glass walls. Ignoring the bar and its myriad weird and wonderful healing waters took Herculean self-control.

The mirrored glass at the Mirage concentrated the sunlight like an aluminum panel sizzled a sunbather before SPF.

"You're going to fry sitting there."

As expected, Mona curled in her normal place in the crook of the couch, giving her a view of the Strip angling into the distance to the left and the right and the mountains directly beyond. Her feet tucked under her and behind a fortification of bright silk pillows, Mona stared out the window. "The only light I see these days is reflected."

I gave her a longer than normal look. That sort of comment was a bit circumspect for Mother's shoot-them-between-the-eyes approach. I chalked it up to a clever coincidence, but still, it put me on my guard. If she was contemplating a step into the spotlight, running for cover became a viable strategy.

She glanced at me as I took a similar spot on the opposite end of the couch. I didn't bother with the pillow wall—silk wouldn't offer any protection from my mother. For that I'd need a cross, some holy water, and a silver bullet.

"Happy birthday." Mona stared out the window like a caged animal eyeing freedom.

Frankly, being imprisoned with two tiny humans who did nothing other than eat, cry, sleep, and poop sounded worse than a life sentence to Devil's Island. I tried to stifle the pangs of sympathy welling in my chest. I needed my strength, my fortified resolve. Mona could sense weakness like a shark trailing blood. Forcing her into answers she didn't want to give, to relive a history that couldn't be pleasant no matter how I tried to spin it would take all my skills...or a two-by-four between the eyes.

"Thanks." Everyone knew how much I hated my birthday, so they were well-trained to offer only the lightest good wishes and then drop it.

Bethany's photo burned a hole in my pocket. Yes, although I wore a new outfit—the old one had seen two continents, too much Champagne, and an adrenaline overload that made it offensive even to one with diminished sensibilities such as myself—I'd managed to remember the photo in the old one before I'd stuffed it into the box for the valet. A mental level normally not associated with pre-coffee me.

"Do you have any coffee?" I decided to try subtle first and resort to force as a last resort.

"I'm off stimulants."

I stepped on an inappropriate response.

She gave me the side-eye. "Isn't it a bit late for coffee?"

"Time of day is hardly a criterion for determining appropriate beverage intake, especially in Vegas."

Mother had dressed for the day. Gone was her normal tattered robe and beleaguered air. In her tailored peach suit, hot pink shirt, double strands of South Sea pearls, and pantyhose, she looked almost like herself. A pair of Lou-bous tangled, abandoned under the side table.

"Are you going to tell me about Macau?"

Her question caught me off guard. Had I really not seen her since I'd returned from China? Of course, that had only been what? Two days ago? Two days, a murder...a lifetime.

Sympathy softened her tone. The several bodies I'd left in my wake during my recent trip to the Far East could account for that. Or, it could be another game entirely.

"No."

No wasn't a word she was used to hearing, but this time she took it in stride.

Happy to see her back in full feather, I nevertheless raised my shields as I adjusted my previous assessment. She didn't have the look of a caged animal eyeing freedom. No, she was contemplating food—a predator looking for a conquest.

Yep, the old Mona I knew and feared had donned the camouflage to throw the unwary off her scent, to lure the weak and ignorant into her web.

"What's with the battle dress?" I asked, feigning a note of casual indifference. "You look stunning, by the way." And she did, another tiny cut to my flagging ego.

She was perfect in every way that I was not. Although I was old enough to see my own skills, I wasn't yet to the point of valuing them enough.

And as a kid, I thought I'd know everything when I was a grown up. Well, I didn't. And there were only two possible explanations: as a kid, I was misinformed, or I was not yet grown-up.

I hid behind the latter—a great excuse.

Her soft brown hair was gathered in a tail that trailed down her back—she'd been letting her hair grow. A few loose tendrils curled next to her face to soften the cliffs of her cheekbones. Her eyes, a sharp blue that seemed to shine with purpose, were large and round. Doe eyes, someone had said. Baiting the trap, especially when it came to men, someone had said years ago and it had stuck. True or not, Mona had a mesmerizing effect on the Y-chromosome set bordering on the creepy...or the pathetic.

She pretended to pluck at an invisible speck of lint, then she gave me an aw-shucks bat of her eyelashes. A tactic wasted on me, but she was definitely honing her skills. Nothing like a starring position on the practice squad. "Dressed for battle, girding your loins and all of that, do you mind telling me where you're going?" I tried to infuse my voice with interest rather than letting my worry run unfettered through the simple question like a computer virus in an unprotected hard drive.

"I'm meeting with my constituency."

"Oh." Yes, panic usually rendered me monosyllabic. "Constituency?" My voice carried that strangled-ferret squeak—I couldn't help it.

"Yes, you do know I'm campaigning for a spot on the Paradise Town Advisory Board."

"It's an appointed position. Your constituency, as you call them, won't have a say." I don't know why I wasted the breath. When Mona identified a mission, she was relentless—truth would never dissuade her. Heck, it wouldn't even slow her down.

"Lucky," she adopted a pedantic tone that I found particularly irritating, "the people always have a say. They may have a vote, or not, but they always have a say."

Political pressure. Okay, she had a point. I'd give her the rope she wanted so badly. She could make a noose or a bridge, her call. Recently, I'd come to realize that I didn't rule the world...not even my little corner of it. To be trite about it, I was a pawn in the chess game of life.

Took a bit of pressure off.

Maybe it was growing up. Maybe it was being too tired to care. Did it matter?

Aware she'd lost my attention, Mona huffed. "I've called my people together today because we have a rabbit problem." She gave me a nod, her face a mask of concern.

I waited for the punch line, but none came. Some sort of odd, panic-driven emotion bubbled up inside me. "A rabbit problem?" My voice rode on a tinge of insanity—even I heard it. Words tumbled—I was helpless to stop them. "Have the rabbits finally had it with being pulled out of hats? Maybe there's been an uptick in demand for lucky rabbit's feet. Boy, someone wanting to lop off a limb would certainly get me hopping mad." I raised a hand when Mona opened her mouth. "I don't think rabbits die for the sake of pregnancy confirmation anymore, so it can't be that." I took a breath.

Mona was smart enough to stay on the sideline. She eyed me with an odd detachment that spurred me on.

"Easter! That must be it! Too many kids getting rabbits only to end up with twenty-seven of the darlings three days later. Then the rabbits end up living in poverty and procreating to pass the time, making it worse—like the Catholics in South America."

"Lucky!" Mona used her parental tone, snapping me out of it.

"Over the line. I agree. But no birth control? Are the Catholics serious?" I crossed my arms and tried not to laugh as I speared her with a look. "Mother, really. Rabbits?"

"Well, it's actually close to what you imagined and managed to articulate so poorly. And it does sort of have to do with Easter, but only tangentially." She didn't seem huffy, just impassioned—and suddenly in love with four-syllable words.

"Have you been taking those smart pills? They're unproven and risky." I made that up. Mona with a genius IQ was as dangerous as a narcissist with tons of money.

First turkeys, now rabbits.

What could possibly go wrong?

"Okay, I can see you need to get this off your chest. I'm listening." And trying not to laugh, but I didn't say that part—it would just get me a longer lecture. "So, tell me about the rabbits?"

Mona reached across to lay a hand lightly on my arm. "Not just any rabbits, Lucky," she almost whispered, her tone conspiratorial. "Feral rabbits."

I didn't quite catch the laugh in time, and something dribbled out of my nose. I wiped at it with the back of a hand as I worked to keep a straight face. "Feral rabbits?"

"They're everywhere." Mona leaned back with a self-satisfied look.

"Really? Everywhere? Are they attacking tourists on the Strip? Are they carrying off small children? Are you sure delusions aren't a sign of postpartum depression?" Tears leaked out of my eyes.

Mona gave me a withering look and waited for me to compose myself.

When I finally could pull in a lungful of air, she said, "Are you through?"

The smile fled as I remembered why I'd come. "Oh, I'm just getting started."

That serious note got her attention. "Really?" She lost some of her stuffing, wilting a bit.

"Yeah. Not a social visit. I'm sorry." And I was...for all of us.

"Your father?" If a thought could age someone ten years, that one dimmed her youthful glow considerably.

"No. He's fine, as far as I know."

She breathed deep, and youth was restored.

"Is it bad, then?" She didn't seem that worried—her man was okay; life would sort itself out.

That feeling, that importance given to another, wasn't something I knew, and that bothered me. Should it be something I waited for? Or was it something earned through a lifetime of fighting for the relationship? Another question for a different day—not that Mona was self-aware enough to give me the straight skinny. And not that I was self-aware enough to know what I didn't know. "It depends on what you have to say."

One of her hands moved to her neck where she twisted her pearls, sliding them back and forth. "Me?" She actually sounded surprised. "I haven't been important in quite a while."

She used to run a business, even lobby the state legislature for her industry—she'd been somebody in the way society decides worthiness. After marrying my father, she'd given up all of that and stayed home, having babies, keeping the home fires burning, supporting her man—a nobody under the metric that had formerly found her worthy.

When had we become a society that valued employment and denigrated heart?

And why did women buy into that?

My mother was a pain in the ass, but she led with her heart, the only thing standing between her and serious bodily harm perpetrated by those of us who kept pulling her ass out of the fire. "Keep going, Mother. You're on a roll. My news can wait. Tell me about the rabbits." I kicked off my shoes and pulled my feet up under me, settling in. Forestalling the inevitable, I know. But for a few moments longer, I wanted life to be as I knew it to be.

Mona understood—her worried look remained, but she brightened a bit, regaining some of her previous momentum. "Rabbits, right." She brushed down her skirt then tugged the hem to straighten the fabric. "Well, it's all very obvious. Kids get rabbits, like you said. They can't take care of them, so their parents release them to the wild, thinking they're doing the poor animals a favor. The problem, is they're domesticated rabbits, for one."

"For another, left to their own devices, they breed like..."

"Rabbits. I *know*." Mona breathed the last word as she gave me a serious nod and conjured Marilyn Monroe. "I dare you, walk into any park around here with food a rabbit would like. At first, it's cute; then it's scary as they keep coming out of the Yucca and tall grasses. People just trying to have a simple picnic have been terrorized! One poor family, the rabbits tried to follow them into their car."

"And you plan on getting the city fathers, not to be gender specific—just for want of a better term—to do something about these feral rabbits?" Feral rabbits. Wasn't that an oxymoron? Or the idea for a straight-to-video-overseas B movie? "Aren't these the same city fathers who decided it was illegal for people to give food to the homeless on city property?"

"Indeed." Mona sat up a bit straighter. "I changed that, didn't I?"

I'd played into her hands—that one victory launched her political ambitions. "That you did. Okay, have at it on the rabbit issue. If I can help, let me know." Ingrained, reflexive, manipulative capitulation—a survival skill in my family. Mona wasn't the only one having a fling with four-syllable words.

Not that any of it would fool my mother. She pulled the pillows tighter around her as her satisfied smile faded. "Now." She steadied herself, pulling her shoulders back and leveling an almost regal, above-the-fray look. I used to wonder where the act ended and the real began, then I realized at some point, with Mona, the act was how she'd survived. "Why don't you tell me why you came?"

I'd charged over here full of desire to eviscerate her with my limited inklings and strong suspicions, but, now that I was here, I couldn't do it.

No matter what Mona had done, I knew her, and I knew her heart. And I was sure that, whatever it was, it had been the best decision she was capable of making at the time. That was all we could do—our best given the knowledge we had.

And now, her best had come back to haunt her.

I took a deep breath. “A young girl came to my office last night.”

CHAPTER NINE

*T*HE elevator dinged. We both swiveled that direction, looking over the back of the couch. My father stepped into the room. Today, he seemed smaller than I remembered, somehow less, lacking his normal air of invincibility.

A bullet to the chest could do that.

When he caught us both looking at him, he forced a bright smile. "Well, just what a man wants to see when he comes home—his two favorite people in the world." He stopped at the bar, pouring several fingers of amber liquid into two glasses and some juice into another. "Happy birthday." He tossed the words over his shoulder.

I didn't respond—he didn't expect me to. "Do you ever wonder about the opportunities missed, the people passed, just because of a few seconds?" I asked Mona as we watched him.

Mona gave me a sideways glance. "Or the consequences missed by a few millimeters?"

Even if he didn't exude his normal force, he looked like his normal self. Salt-and-pepper hair trimmed to within a millimeter of perfection. His strong jaw tilted, a challenge to the Universe...and hopefully Death. An open-collared starched button-down in light pink, steel gray slacks creased to a razor's edge, and Ferragamo loafers worn in the Italian style with no socks—his casual-day uniform normally reserved for the weekend.

As he rounded the couch, Mona and I rotated, following

him like plants keeping their faces to the sun.

"Which third-world country are you two plotting to overthrow?" My father doled out the beverages. A Wild Turkey 101 breakfast for me. Two fingers of the single malt for my father as well—the age would give me a hint as to his day, but I didn't ask whether he'd poured the fifteen or the twenty-five. Breastfeeding kept Mona on the sidelines, and she accepted her juice with a turned-up nose but she graced him with a megawatt smile.

Mine was a little more cautious. My worst fear realized: he didn't look better; in fact, he looked worse. Pain etched the lines of his face into troughs bracketing his mouth and radiating from the corners of his eyes. Paleness dusted the rosiness from his skin until it looked translucent where his dark beard shadowed despite a close shave. The hollows in his cheeks accentuated his cheekbones, which normally mounded under the folds of a smile.

"You're not following doctor's orders," I commented as I eyed him over the top of my glass. The first sip burned a welcome trail of courage, then exploded in my empty stomach. What I'd give for the hamburger I gave away last night.

"My life, my rules."

Mother gave a nervous laugh and patted the cloth expanse between us. "Sit here, Albert. Lucky was just starting to tell me about a visitor she had last night."

"Your family, Father. You have responsibilities."

He wouldn't look at me. He knew. Maybe not what...or who. But he knew.

With a sigh and a wince he tried to hide, he settled between Mother and me. One arm he snaked around his wife's shoulders, pulling her close. But the other arm he kept curled across his stomach, abandoning his double old-fashion Steuben tumbler to his wife. She took a sip, but only one. Fortification? Did they both know?

He patted my knee. I caught his hand and gave it a squeeze. His skin was cold. Both of them looked at me, waiting.

I didn't bother with a windup. "Yes, a young woman came to my office last night with quite a story." I leaned around my father and captured Mona's gaze with mine. "She claims to be your daughter."

Mona stilled, her expression frozen between disbelief and denial.

My father reached over and captured her tiny hands in his large one and squeezed—his knuckles turning white. A look passed between them, one ripe with meaning for them but lost on me.

Mona drew in a sharp breath. "Oh." She turned a worried look to her husband. "Albert. I told you...someday." Then she looked at me and her face cleared. An air of acceptance settled over her. "What's she like?"

"What?" I tried to adjust to a question I wasn't expecting. A denial? I was prepared to field that. But a question, not really, not this question. "She's sixteen," I said as if that explained everything.

"I know how old she is." If Mona realized she'd tipped her hand, she didn't appear to care. "What's she like?"

"Like me at her age."

Mona drifted on the memories as a smile played with her lips.

Tossed into a sea of emotions, I flailed about like a two-year-old unable to swim. "Odd you haven't seen fit to tell me I had a sister. But, then again, this whole family thing has been on a need-to-know basis." Anger burbled to the surface, molten lava sizzling in a cold sea. "Are you going to tell me about her?"

Mona flicked a gaze at her husband; then something inside her seemed to steel. "No. It's none of your business."

Of all the things she could've said, she said the one thing that pegged my pissed off. "None of my business," I spluttered. "None of my business?" This time anger solidified in the words. "Since when was family not my business?"

The two people who had kept my father's paternity from me stared at me with blank looks.

"Oh, yeah, keeping me in the dark is a family tradition, I forgot. How stupid of me. Mother, is the girl yours?"

"Don't ask me that, Lucky. You can't get near this. You

have to promise me to let it go. For once, let me handle my business."

"The girl has a photo for Chrissake and a story, but a DNA test would be definitive."

"It'll show there is a very strong likelihood I'm her mother." Mona's voice was as hard as steel.

"What?" I couldn't think. Thoughts pinged like buckshot off of steel, whizzing dangerously close to soft flesh. I took a few deep breaths as I weighed my options. My father wouldn't meet my eyes. He looked paler if that was possible.

Great.

This was the sort of thing my bleeding-heart father would get lathered up over. Whatever was going on, they both were in it up to their eyeballs. No doubt divide and conquer would be a better strategy, but for now I had their united front to climb over, if I could.

"The girl...Bethany is her name...Bethany Fiorelli."

I caught another veiled look between my former family members.

"Bethany," my mother whispered. Tears welled. She didn't try to hide them.

"Bethany," I said, pressing any advantage I could find, "is a person of interest in the murder at the rodeo last night."

"What?" Mona looked like I'd plunged a spear through her heart.

"Don't," my father barked at her.

An order not to be denied and Mona clamped her mouth shut.

He softened his tone. "I've already spoken with..." With a head shake, he caught himself before he said too much. "Was she arrested?" he asked me.

"No." That cut off that advantage—if the girl was in danger maybe they would've been more forthcoming—so I tried another. "An abandoned child will torpedo your political aspirations, Mother."

She gave a little shrug and dabbed at her eyes with the monogrammed cuff of my father's shirt. He didn't go ballistic.

This was serious...way more serious than I feared.

What were they hiding? Well, besides the obvious.

"So be it," my mother whispered without even a hint of whine. The idea hurt her, but whatever she was hiding hurt her more.

"Who says she was abandoned?" my father asked.

"Aren't you the voice of reason?" Tackling them one at a time I could do. Together, I hadn't a chance. I wilted under his pragmatic stare. "Okay, no one. Why won't you tell me what's going on?"

My father turned to his wife. "I wouldn't."

Mona kept her lips clamped and gave a curt nod. When she looked at me, she deflated. "I want to, Lucky, I really do. You deserve to know, but I can't tell you." She reached across my father and grabbed my hand. "You must promise to let me handle this."

"Is she my sister?"

"I can't, Lucky. You must know I love you more than life. If I had a choice, I'd tell you." She swiped at her tears.

I didn't know who they were for—Bethany, the Big Boss, me...herself? Or the family we used to be. "And the girl?"

"Let your father and I talk, then I want to meet her."

"So, you want me to tell her that she's right, that you're her mother?"

"That should come from your mother, don't you think?" My father swung into his protective mode. He put his hand on mine. "We love you, Lucky. Give us time to sort this out. Your mother isn't playing one of her games."

That cooled my anger and lit my panic. "Why can't you tell me?"

He turned to stare out the window. He loved the lights, the magic, just as I did. But now, in the heat of the day, the sun dimmed the magic until it was barely visible. "There's no statute of limitations on murder..."

"What?" My breath left me in a whoosh, carrying that one word and my heart with it.

Mona quieted him with a hand on his arm. "Don't. Not

yet." She speared me with a look that filled me with her pain. "And Bethany's grandmother? Where is she?"

"The girl said she's dead."

Mona slumped as if her bones had turned to jelly. She looked relieved. "Albert, they're all gone. All of them."

"All but one." He stared at her pointedly. "And you're my wife."

"The girl wants to come here and meet you, Mother."

"I need to think about that." Her gaze flicked to her husband.

"Would you two let me in?"

They both whirled on me. "No!" they said in unison.

"Give us time," my father added.

"We may not have time." I took back what control I could. They both focused on me. "Like I said, Bethany is wanted in conjunction with a murder at the rodeo."

My mother tightened her grip on her husband.

He shook his head. "I heard about that. Turnbull was his name. The father of two of the competitors."

"How old was he?" Mona whispered, the color draining from her face.

"Early forties." He patted his wife's leg as she relaxed a bit. "What do the police think Bethany had to do with Mr. Turnbull's murder?"

"They don't know. They've just taken her in for questioning."

"Then it'll be all right. Does she have an attorney?"

"Squash Trenton."

A sad smile lifted one corner of my father's mouth. "He's the perfect man for the job."

"How so?" My phone jangled, making me jump. "Fuck," I said, hopefully under my breath. From my mother's scowl and my father's resigned amusement, I didn't pull it off. After snagging the device from its holster at my waist, I glanced at the caller ID. Miss P, my assistant. "This better be good," I barked as I pressed the phone to my face. She didn't deserve it, but I needed it. I'm weak that way. Something else to add to the ever-growing and already extraordinarily lengthy Lucky O'Toole Self-Improvement Program.

Now, I love a goal. But an unattainable one, especially one I set for myself, pisses me off. Which, at the moment, wasn't helping.

"Have you had your coffee yet?" She didn't seem rocked by my tone.

"No, but I've had a shot or two of cold urine to the heart, a much better jumpstart." I didn't mention the Wild Turkey. Pride cometh before a fall and all that, which I chose to ignore.

"Not from where I'm sitting. I'll put a pot on. I hope you're close."

"Upstairs."

"In that case, forget the coffee and meet me in the Kasbah. Is Detective Romeo with you?"

My breath caught. "No, but I know where he is."

"Bring him, too. I've already called Metro so the coroner ought to have been alerted."

Oh, so not good. "Where?"

"Kasbah. Bungalow Twelve. I've got all the appropriate folks *en route*, but you need to be rolled in on this one."

Just as my feet had hit the sacred soil of Sin City, bodies had started to pile up. I must've picked up an ancient curse overseas. "Are curses contagious?"

"If you are receptive."

It appeared that sympathy wasn't on the menu this morning. "On my way."

Death vs. family.

Right now, an easy choice. If I didn't leave, Romeo would have several bodies to deal with and, as overworked as he was, I'd feel really bad about adding to his workload.

I discarded Miss P's call and pulled up my favorites. First on the list, Romeo had the primo spot. If that wasn't the sign of a misspent life, I didn't know what was.

He answered on the first ring. "Are you here?"

"Yes, I'm here, but I think we have different definitions of that, and different geography since I'm not there."

"You worry me," he said with a sigh.

"Stand in line. We have a bigger problem."

"Larger." From his tone, it was easy to tell he was at his problem limit. "We have a larger problem. Bigger indicates size. Larger indicates—"

"Magnitude, I know. Ms. Filbert's English 101, had to take it twice. Sounds like a death in the Kasbah. Miss P called. Metro's *en route*. I'm on my way there now. Remind me to slap you when I see you."

"Be there in ten. Not on your life."

I tossed the phone in my bag, then gulped the rest of my breakfast and levered myself to my feet. Three strides and I was around the couch and halfway to the elevator.

"Lucky!" Mona called after me, her tone imploring, yet infused with steel, cut a gash in my heart.

I didn't look back. I didn't answer. I pressed the button. The doors didn't open immediately. Numb, for once, I didn't mash the button repeatedly in irritation. Instead, I waited patiently, staring at my shell-shocked visage in the polished metal of the doors. I looked normal—soft brown hair, big blue eyes, haunted yet hungry, dark circles underscoring them, fine lines fracturing my face in ways that made me different than the me I used to be. But inside, I still felt like the old me. An inner/outer lack of synchronicity that kept me out of sorts.

But this too was normal, a normal I was trying to change. Well, except the hair, I really liked the hair.

Caught in the trap of my own emotions, it never dawned on me that I waited because someone had called the private elevator—someone I wouldn't want to see.

The doors slid open, leaving me face-to-face with another problem with no solution.

Teddie.

He looked as shocked to see me as I felt in seeing him.

Way past playing nice, I didn't try. Yes, I was still punishing him, and myself, in the process. Someday, I'd grow up, but today wasn't that day. "Terrific." At least I could still mutter and grouse, even if complete thoughts were still out of my reach.

He stood there mute, looking like he'd been slapped.

I knew how he felt.

Why did first loves have to hurt so much and for so long?

When he regained function, he gave me a sad look, followed by what I thought was the hint of a smile, then he moved to step by me.

I caught his elbow, and, careful of his leg that had recently had a bullet tear through it, I steered him into an about-face. "Not now." My tone and vise grip on his arm didn't allow any argument. "My parents need some time alone."

Once the doors shut behind us, he gave me a look as I leaned back against the back wall of the car. Putting distance between us, he pressed himself into the opposite corner. "I come up sometimes to check on your mother," he said as if he needed to explain.

He didn't.

"How'd you get up here?" The floor was private, housing only one other apartment.

"I'm staying in your old place next door. My place..." He let the words hang.

Even though I'd been the target, not the perpetrator, I still felt responsible for the explosion that had displaced us both. "Yeah." That small apartment next door was becoming a halfway house for the brokenhearted. That would make a good title for a country-western song.

Teddie's musical genius was a bit more throwback, so I kept my thought to myself.

"I hadn't seen the twins since..." His brows furrowed as his gaze slipped to the floor.

"Now's not a good time."

This time he gave me a full appraisal. "Are they okay?"

Another question with no real answer. "I think so. No blood was shed." My attempt at humor didn't amuse either of us.

"I would ask if you want to talk about it." Uncomfortable, he shifted, looking for footing on emotional quicksand.

Even with the mess between us, I could still read him almost intuitively. "Don't." I missed the days when I could run to Teddie with the biggest secret or the most insignificant irritation. He'd always known how to make me laugh. And laughter cured most ills. Not sure about my current one, but part of me really wanted to give it a try.

"Buy you a drink?" The hope in his words stung.

Guess he could still read me as well. "I've been summoned by Miss P."

"You look like that's the last thing you need."

A whole history in unspoken words passed between us. "When did life give me what I needed?" The minute the words escaped, I regretted them. Beating Teddie up for being who he was, was a fool's errand and getting old. I held up my hand before he could jump in. "I'm sorry. Bad day."

The thing I'd realized about Teddie and me was that I was part of the whole implosion. I couldn't put it all off on Teddie. The fact that we stood on different rungs of the maturity ladder had been obvious to me from the beginning. Not that I was any guru or anything, but I had already learned the downside of indulging my ego—he had not. And he'd sacrificed us on that ego altar.

Maybe he'd learned; maybe he hadn't. Time would tell.

I could forgive but I'd never forget. Was that enough?

Teddie gave me a small laugh. "Despite your efforts to the contrary, you are as easy to read as block letters in big type in a first-grade primer. Anything I can do?"

He looked sincere. He also looked...good. A bit wan, but I was beginning to understand that getting shot could do that. Why did the men around me always seem to be getting shot? I was the common denominator. I tried to connect all those dots, but I had been given a mental piece of chalk when I needed a fine-tipped Magic Marker.

To be honest, like a wilted flower given water, he'd perked up a bit since our plane ride home. His short blond hair had been freshly gelled. The turquoise of his eyes looked enhanced—it wasn't. And the fringe of long lashes inspired envy in each woman he met—if she could get past the lust part. Most couldn't. I hadn't. And I'd lost a treasured friendship for it. The sex had been delish, but not worth the price.

He radiated the comfort of the we that we'd used to be. How I longed to dive into his arms for a big hug to make the world disappear. But I wasn't an any-port-in-a-storm kind of gal.

Morals, such a bother when the child in me longed for comfort.

Ah, well, like I said, life rarely gave me what I wanted, but I was old enough to know it generally served up what I needed, whether I liked it or not.

"How's the leg?" I asked, then realized it had been maybe a day since we'd gotten off that plane, not even.

"Same." He'd changed clothing since I last saw him. The bandage on his leg necessitated the gym pants. In keeping with comfort, he'd grabbed his Harvard sweatshirt, the one with the neck cut out...the one I used to wear. Yeah, Teddie was the whole package--Harvard, Julliard, GQ, but he'd made the fatal error of believing his own press.

The elevator whirred to a stop and the doors slid open, inviting in the cacophony of the hotel at full bore. Catapulted by my need for normalcy, I leaped into the fray. A few strides took me to the center of the lobby, where I stopped under the canopy of blown-glass hummingbirds and butterflies in sweeping flight. While I relished having my own hotel, the Babylon was still my responsibility and it would always be the home of my heart.

People schooled like tiny silver fish, flashing Vegas sparkle as they darted through the lobby, completely oblivious to the inlaid marble floors—a work of art that took millions of man-hours, not to mention a hefty pile of green to complete. In Vegas, if you don't push the limits, you're falling behind. That held true in every facet of the life experience here.

Excitement and joy permeated the air. Lines snaked from the stations at the reception desk that lined one side of the lobby under brightly hued cloth tented above. Staff clothed in miniscule gladiator uniforms worked the lines, offering complimentary flutes of Champagne. The opposite wall was a huge sheet of Lucite behind which skiers could try their hand at skiing in the Mojave on our man-made slope, complete with moguls, a rope tow, and a buff and bodacious Ski Crew ready to give comfort. I'd suggested a St. Bernard with a neck flask of medicinal spirits, but the insurance guys slammed that idea. Such killjoys.

The Big Boss loved to promote his indoor hill as the only skiing in Vegas. While he was technically accurate, he neglected to mention there was skiing in the winter months a short drive north of town at Mt. Charleston. Even folks who visited Vegas multiple times a year often didn't know they could shush through real snow in the morning, then sun by the pool in the afternoon. Of course, keeping our clientele at the tables was job number one, so I didn't feel the need to enlighten.

If you didn't keep them in the House, the House couldn't win.

And the House always wins.

A few survivors of last night's New Year's Eve pandemonium staggered through the sets of double glass front doors. A girl with smeared lipstick, a wilted dress, and sparkly stilettos clutched in her hand. Several young men, arms thrown around each other's shoulders in an effort not only to remain standing but to walk in a relatively straight line. Just inside the doors, they paused, confusion reigning over their features. One of our security guards checking hotel room keys—a New Year's requirement to get into the hotel—rushed to help them. Another young man piled in behind the others. Naked except for a clear plastic guitar filled with an amber liquid that he wore on a shoulder strap just the right length for the guitar to cover vital external organs, he sloshed when he walked, giving anyone who cared a peek. Another security guard handled him. I could tell from the young man's outstretched arms that he didn't have a key, but, boy, I bet he had a story—if he could remember. I was tempted to edge closer to practice my eavesdropping skills, but homicide goaded me with the shock of a cattle prod.

At the far corner of the lobby, the opening of the Bazaar yawned, giving a glimpse of the treasures that could be found there. Practically any tangible thing worth having could be acquired there. A gross overstatement, but it captured the goal. From a Ferrari to a quickie wedding, with stops for gourmet burgers and beautification, then add some bling and designer duds and accessories, and the Bazaar was a one-stop glam shop. I wasn't sure where weddings fit into the picture—frankly, I'd never been sure about weddings. Most I'd seen were merely the beginning of the end.

When I turned to head into the casino, I realized Teddie had disappeared. Captured in his own pain, he hadn't wished me a happy birthday.

Despite a strong desire, I didn't scan the crowd to see where he headed. Where he went and what he did no longer interested me, or so I told myself.

What did Mona always say? Be it until you become it? Yeah, that. When it came to Teddie, I was still in the fake-it stage.

With a smile pasted on, I waited impatiently at the foot of one of the small bridges over the indoor stream that meandered between the lobby and the casino—our own version of the Euphrates. The bridge provided the perfect photo op—from the apex, it was possible to catch the reed-lined water, the paddling waterfowl, and the flying birds and butterflies in the background. With the New Year's crowd, today's line was longer than usual.

The casino continued the lobby motif with carpets that swirled with bright colors, muted lighting—much of it from wall sconces that enclosed flames under glass to mimic the torches of ancient Mesopotamia. Colorful fabric looped from the ceiling, giving a warm and welcoming air.

People ringed the tables, their intensity palpable. A few cheers, fewer groans. The casino still corralled the excitement of last night and amped it, building toward tonight. While the insanity of the Strip on New Year's Eve was hard to handle for the hotels—the flow of pedestrians, progressive inebriation and commensurate chaos, the fireworks, and silly stunts were all part of the party—for me, the hardest part was being trapped on the Strip—after nine p.m. the Strip was closed to cars, ingress or egress, until the next morning. Most hotels limited entry to those who were staying there, which limited the gaming revenues. A small price to pay to keep drunken marauding at a minimum—or so they said. And, for the casinos, walking the tightrope between when a player was properly oiled versus totally tanked made the evening a nightmare. By law, we had to cut off the really drunk players, which often meant the risk of serious bodily harm. Broken bones or a chat with the Gaming Commission—guess which one usually won?

Delilah's Bar, where the feeding and lubricating of our gamblers was of paramount importance, occupied a raised platform in the middle of the room. I caught Teddie's ass as he worked his way up the steps on his bum leg. The white baby grand tucked in a corner called to him—a place where he lived, he'd told me.

In my former life, I'd often joined him there after a long day and listened to him play before we headed home.

Home.

I wasn't sure where that was anymore. My owner's suite felt like work. Jean-Charles's house felt like his home. I couldn't bear to go back to my burned–out apartment. At some point, I was going to have to commit.

Not my strong suit. Hell, I couldn't even decide on another car.

Another problem for another day.

By design, the entrance to the Kasbah was well hidden behind a couple of towering palms. A narrow-arched doorway led to a hall. Like the entrance to a secret garden, the hallway was lined with palms, the high-domed glass ceiling allowing light to keep them alive. At the end, a guard sat behind a desk to measure the entrants' worthiness...but mainly to confirm they had a key. He nodded to me as I passed.

The hall turned hard left after the guard, and the carpet changed to tile as the room opened up in front of me—a soaring atrium with a glass dome and rings of rooms stretching to the sky. As with all the Strip properties, there was a hierarchy here. The most important folks got the bungalows, then we put the next tier on the twenty-sixth floor, and the rest we salted in where they fit. Not my rules, but I was tasked with enforcing them, which, of course, was impossible. Was Cher more important than Sting? And a high-ranking Chinese diplomat who wasn't supposed to be in Vegas, where did you put him? Where he thought he deserved to be or where he wouldn't attract attention? Or somewhere lesser, more sequestered? Obvious, but try telling him that and avoid an international incident.

Those were the hard cases. For everyone else, the perks in Vegas hinged on money—how much you had and how much you kept in play. Celebrity was an afterthought.

As our high-end, home-away-from-home for the high-rollers and celebrity types, each bungalow was a self-contained small house. The bungalows came with the commensurate comforts, including a 1:1 staff-to-guest ratio and 24/7 food and comfort specialists, which included massage therapists but not hookers, at least not officially. Since one of the big names in town went on national primetime and told everyone they could get anything they wanted in his hotel, everyone had come to expect...everything. If my concierge provided more than was legal, that was on his or her back. Legality was my corporate limit.

My personal limits were a bit sketchier. Or so I told myself when I needed to feel all badass, like now.

A water feature wound through the properties, separating them. Some bungalows, like Bungalow Twelve, my destination, had private pools—more like dipping tanks, in my opinion, but I guess there's a limit to extravagance, even in Vegas.

Craning my neck to catch a glimpse of the sky, I felt like Dorothy entering Oz. I pivoted to the left toward Bungalow Twelve. Miss P paced in front, the effort not to wring her hands evident in her scowl. She brightened when she saw me—nothing like off-loading a sticky problem to brighten a day.

"There you are!" Her relief was evident in every word.

Despite the worry, she looked...happy. A much younger, hunky Aussie husband could do that, I guess. But her job was most of it—she'd been promoted and was now the me I used to be, and she was better at it than I was. I counted on her competence, even if I wasn't used to the spiky hair and beautiful clothes. "I'm really sorry I had to rope you in on this one." She winced when she said it.

I started to ask.

She shook off my question. "You'll find out soon enough. And, for the record, you're starting to rub off on me, and I'm not all that happy about it."

"Starting to? I'm wounded." Banter to buffer the ugly, Miss P's normal MO. "This isn't just any old homicide, is it?"

"No." Miss P crossed her arms, rubbing her upper arm as she glanced at the bungalow. "This one's got personal written all over it." She gave me a look—half fear, half green.

"Murder is usually personal." Thank God. The idea of joy-killing made me want to move to the moon. "I'm guessing it's not a prostitute stuffed under a bed?" Sad to say, that was our normal murder, if those two words could ever be used in the same sentence.

She shook her head.

"Or a heart attack, stroke, or OD?" All fairly common. Vegas should come with a warning label, like exercise. If it's not part of your regular routine, don't jump in the deep end.

She acted like she hadn't heard me. "Maybe you should wait for Romeo."

"He couldn't be more than a few minutes away. When I called him right after I talked with you, he was at the Thomas and Mack. What about the rest of Metro? All the minions and stuff?"

"You're the first."

"Jerry?" Jerry was our head of Security, my better half in the corporate world.

"After last night, I hope he's on an airplane to Tahiti."

Drat, no moral support. "I assume you've called Security to get them started pulling all the security tapes?"

"I was waiting for you."

I gave her a look. "You're the Head now. You got this. I'm here to back you up."

"Not with this one." She rubbed her arms, then a shiver raced through her. "You need to see it for yourself."

"Who called it in?"

"Genevieve, one of the butler staff. The do not disturb had been on the door since yesterday. No calls to room service. The staff got worried."

"A greenhorn." I let out a long sigh. "I'm sorry for that." Through years of handling the seedier side of life, I'd risen to the championship level of compartmentalizers.

Great for coping until I'd locked all of me away.

"How is she?"

"She's having a hard time." Miss P looked as sad as I felt.

"You have to keep her here. The police will want to talk with her."

"I know."

"Maybe call the doc to come talk with her?"

"Good idea." Miss P looked like she wished she'd thought of it.

"I've been doing this a lot longer than you. Is Dora Bates registered in Bungalow Twelve?"

"Yes, but not under that name." She checked her clipboard. "She used the name, Fiorelli. Mean anything to you?" She glanced up. The look on my face told her what she wanted to know. "Guess so. Anyway, she missed her checkout time—another reason for the staff's concern." She glanced at me over the top of her cheaters, which had slid to the absolute last foothold on the end of her nose.

I resisted shoving them back to a position that would make me comfortable. "To hear the rodeo crowd tell it, Ms. Bates is scrounging for cash like the rest of them. Wonder where she got the green to spring for a bungalow? How'd she pay for the room?"

Miss P opened her iPad and scrolled. While she searched the database, I worked on finding the courage to face what had put the haunt in Miss P's eyes.

"Cash. She paid cash." Miss P sounded surprised. "How'd you know?"

"Didn't know the answer, just knew the question." Cash. Now that was interesting. "I'm assuming the bungalow is booked tonight?" We didn't keep them filled as we did our rooms—they were expensive to operate. Only when someone earned that particular kind of stroking did we book them in the Kasbah.

"Yes. For a couple of weeks."

"Weeks? Really? Who..." I trailed off when I saw the look on her face.

"Jordan?"

Clutching her iPad to her chest, she nodded, the adoration of a bobbysoxer mooning after Sinatra painting her face.

Jordan! While I didn't crush on him like Miss P, a little bit of happiness burned inside. A bit of normal, a touch from the outside world to brush back the cold finger of death. Okay, overstating, but still...

A personal friend from way back, Jordan Marsh had been *the* Hollywood leading man for several decades until he grew tired of the charade and married his long-time partner, Rudy Gillespie, also a personal friend. Serendipitously, his timing had been perfect, and, while the confirmation of his sexual preference broke millions of hearts worldwide, it didn't dim the glow of his Hollywood star.

A little-known fact, but I had introduced Jordan and Rudy, then been tasked with keeping it all hush-hush...for a long, long time. Staying in the inner circle of a Hollywood A-lister was sometimes more give than receive, but I guess that's the ebb and flow of every relationship. Except with my mother—that was all give. Anger and hurt flared anew. I had no idea which emotional door to shut it behind. Maybe family betrayal didn't have a compartment. The thought terrified me.

"What's Jordan doing in town?" I was a little hurt he hadn't called me, but that had more to do with the knife blade my mother had stabbed between my shoulder blades, nicking my heart. So I let it go.

"Taking in the rodeo and getting in some rehearsal time with Teddie, at least that's what he told me," Miss P downplayed it, but a bit of gloat rounded her words.

I let her have her fun. Frankly, I'd half-forgotten Jordan and Teddie were going to do a joint drag thing in the lounge room at Cielo—a sold-out, limited-run opening in a few weeks. "I'm assuming Jordan hasn't arrived?"

She glanced at her phone, which she still clutched in a white-knuckled death grip. "His plane touched down five minutes ago."

"Let me guess, we're booked solid, right? No place else to stash him?"

"None that he'd tolerate."

My mind worked through the possibilities. "Call the limo. Reroute to Cielo. Put him in the guest suite next to mine and ply him with anything he wants."

Miss P looked happy to have something to do. She should've gotten there on her own and not waited for me, but we'd have that discussion another day.

Was that my fault? Was I still holding on when I needed to let go?

With my life such as it was, work was the only control I had.

Self-delusion, another coping strategy. Clearly, I needed an intervention or a house in the south of France with no connectivity.

It didn't take long. Once done, I tilted my head toward the door of Bungalow Twelve that stood open, a gaping maw that made me want to flee rather than fight. Not an option. Without really thinking about it anymore, I walked up the short walk.

"I'll just take a quick look before the cops and the coroner stake their claims," I called over my shoulder as I ducked inside.

A few feet inside, I smelled death—the wafting stench of the final realization riding on a silent scream. I followed it into a great room with high ceilings and large French windows to drink in the pool and riot of bordering flowers. Hand-knotted

Oriental rugs in bright hues of silk lay over polished mahogany floors. Antiques from many eras, in many styles, tucked among the overstuffed sectionals and comfortable ottomans, creating a luxurious home away from home. Along the left wall, a stocked bar beckoned, the bottles gleaming against a wall of glass behind a granite-topped counter fronted by a row of red leather stools. Tulips, in purples, reds, oranges, and yellows, sprang from a Chihuly vase in the middle of the coffee table captured in the crook of the couch.

An oasis befitting a king. I let my gaze wander, drinking it all in. For a moment, I forgot why I was there.

"Oh!" I fell back a step, staggered. A moment of confusion. Incongruity. Horror staged amid the luxury.

I hadn't been expecting a woman. And not above the grand piano where the light trained from the spot above glistened off each fake crystal of her bejazzled jeans.

Hung from the ceiling, upside-down, a rope around her ankles, a straitjacket binding her arms, she had a thick torso and spindly legs. I couldn't see her face. Her back rotated as the body spun slowly as the air circulated.

My breath stuck in my throat as her face turned into view. In keeping with my preconceived notions, her makeup was overdone: red cheeks, huge eyelashes, one set mashed down covering one eye, lipstick firmly in place.

A dusty red that looked a lot like Tawny Rose.

Purple rose underneath the skin in her forehead and pooled around her eyes. She must've taken a beating. Why hadn't anyone heard? Worse, maybe they had and hadn't reported it. If that were the case, I wasn't sure I knew how to live in that world.

Clear tape wound around her head, keeping her eyes wide in fear, her mouth open, stretched into a wide grimace. Probably the last turn of the tape covered her nose.

The killer had wanted her to know, to feel each interminable second of the creep of death.

Battling bile rising in my throat, I concentrated. The rope looked a lot like the one wrapped around Mr. Turnbull's throat—a stiffer kind used for roping rather than hanging. I pulled out my phone and started snapping photos. The knot, too, looked familiar but hard to tell from this vantage point. Something bothered me as I snapped away: I'd seen that knot before and not just around Turnbull's neck. No, I'd seen it somewhere else.

A pair of cowboy boots lay discarded, kicked to the corner. Grabbing a pencil from the side table, I squatted and inched the boots around so I could see them better.

The lady wasn't one of the competitors—her age, late forties maybe, aged her out. But she'd been wandering around the arena—dirt, dung, and shavings stuck in the creases between the soles and the upper portion of the boots.

"Whoa!" Romeo shouldered into the room, then skidded to a stop, his eyes wide. "That's like something out of Chris Angel's show."

"Except she was no magician and there was no escape. I'd say we found Dora Bates."

"Shouldn't be hard to get a note from her doctor excusing her from work."

"Any word on Beckham?" I rose and kept taking photos from every angle I could get to without disturbing any possible trace or adding any of my own.

"No, can't find him or his daughter either." Romeo approached the body, then walked slowly around it. "Ever see anything like that before?"

"Not that didn't involve a lack of clothing and auto-erotic asphyxiation." I caught his shocked glance out of the corner of my eye. "Which, by the way, is almost always accidental, unless of course it's staged, which I would doubt this was. Besides, it involves a ligature around the neck, not the ankles." Something bothered me as I stared at the woman. Some connection I should make. "There's a message in this killing. With a small window of time, it would've been easier to dispatch the woman and stuff her under the bed, so why go to all the trouble?"

"Stuff her under the bed?" He sounded shocked.

"Please, this is Vegas. Ugliness happens at the intersection of dreams and reality. Happens more than you want to know. Not generally in the higher-end properties. But the ones that rent rooms by the hour? For them, it's a bit of an issue."

"You scare me."

"My small talk can shut down even the best cocktail conversation."

"Any ideas?" Romeo looked a bit at sea.

I knew the feeling—I lived there. "The whole upside-down thing was meant to slap us in the face."

I understood the sarcasm—he'd learned it from me. "Wasn't there someone in history hung upside-down as sort of a statement thing?"

"Well, there's the crucifixion of St. Peter." At my look, Romeo shrugged. "Catholic school. In a church setting, it's a sign of the devil or the antichrist."

"I'd hardly call Las Vegas a church setting." Although I loved my city, I didn't gloss over its seedy underbelly.

Romeo gave a tight little chuckle. "True. I think now the upside-down thing is used to mock holiness."

I turned to the body once again. "But this wasn't a crucifixion."

"No, but reminiscent of one."

"And then there's the straitjacket." I lost myself in thinking out loud. "Although we pride ourselves on offering our guests all the possible amenities, I don't think that's one we stock."

Romeo pulled out his pad and started jotting notes. "No. He came prepared. And he sent a message."

"Yes, but to whom? Why here?" That's one of the things that really bothered me: why was her murder staged in my hotel?

"You're not involved in this, are you?"

"Only through the girl's assertions, which you know." My stomach clenched as I thought of my mother and father. What were they hiding?

"You sure this is Dora Bates?"

"Not sure, but it's a good guess." I pointed to the cowboy boots. Two initials in pink leather on each heel. "DB. Dora Bates."

"The doc's alibi?" Romeo gave a low whistle.

"Which would put him squarely in the suspect hot seat except he's been under your protection at the hospital."

"There is that."

"Once you guys confirm her identity, you're going to need to get to her daughter before someone else does."

"Her daughter! I forgot." He gave me a look that was easy to read.

"You find her; I'll run interference." And put the thumbscrews on these kids.

If the murders were connected—and it was easy to jump to that conclusion—was there more to the connection than a simple extortion game?

He turned his back and made a quick phone call, then turned back to me. "I've got a victim's specialist rousted to go find the daughter. This is getting a bit close to home, don't you think?" With his pencil, he pointed at the body. "Same type of rope as the one at the rodeo. Boots in the corner. The girl with familial designs on your family is traveling with the rodeo." He leveled a serious look at me.

I knew what it meant. "Yeah, too many connections to ignore." And my mother is stonewalling me. "When you guys get the body down, will you take some close-ups of the knot and send them to me? I need to talk with Bethany."

Romeo's personnel streamed in around us. I stepped out of the way while he did his thing. When the medical examiner from the Coroner's Office arrived with his staff, he gave me a disgruntled look like somehow I was responsible, then set to work.

My phone rang. A quick look at the ID and I stepped back to take the call. "Hey, Jerry. What do you have?"

"I'm knee-deep in flogging my staff. Can you handle a problem in the Hanging Gardens?"

THE HANGING GARDENS OF BABYLON were one of the Seven Wonders of the Ancient World. After extensive research, the Big Boss had done an admirable job at re-creating them in a huge atrium at the Babylon. The humidity of the only tropical climate in the Mojave Desert slapped me in the face as I pushed through the doors into our little slice of jungle. My lungs and skin, desiccated by the lack of any measurable water content in the Vegas air, sighed in relief.

Above me hung our Garden Bar. Connected to the hotel via a rope bridge, the bar resembled a tiered and terraced tree house. Today, people hugged the roped railing looking out over the gardens.

Someone had strung a latticework of rigging from one pillar on the fourth floor, across the hanging gardens with all its flora and fauna and meandering streams, to several pillars on the fifth floor on the other side. A man with a balance bar teetered in the middle of the lowest rope as he worked his way across. Above me, a man hanging by his knees from a trapeze let loose from his stand on the top tier of the bar and swung out over the small cluster of men and women I could see gazing skyward through the trees. Another launched himself from the other side of the atrium.

In the middle, high above, two women had scaled separate ropes hanging from the highest point and were now wrapping the ropes around their torso, legs, and whatnot. I didn't even want to know what came next.

I didn't have to guess. One let go, dropping as she spun toward the earth. Just above the trees, the rope caught, arresting her fall and my heart. My anger redlined, which probably didn't help my old ticker, but it was used to this sort of abuse.

Another perk of being me.

There was only one person in town who could be responsible. On my second pass, I spied Philippe LeGronde in the cluster below. I covered the ground as if I rode on a broomstick. Grabbing him on one shoulder, I pulled him around.

A small man, tight and compact, with thinning hair and

ruddy cheeks, he looked happy to see me.

My scowl solved that misplaced emotion. "What the hell are you doing?"

"Practicing, but of course." His smile never faltered.

Clearly, my bark needed work.

"The show, they would not let us practice there. Insurance, they tell me. So, since we are all staying here, it was the logical choice. I know you don't mind. We are not bothering anything." He swept his arm in a circle, taking in all the hotel customers watching in rapt attention. "We are providing a free show. You should be pleased."

As I opened my mouth, the crowd gasped then held its collective breath as one of the trapeze guys let loose, launching into a double flip. Horrified, I gazed skyward as my breath stuck in my throat.

Time stopped.

At the last minute, the man snagged the outstretched arms of his compatriot. The crowd cheered and applauded wildly.

"You see?" Sounding proud, Philippe beamed. "My students, they do good work."

My breath came back in short gasps and I was in danger of hyperventilating. "Students?" My voice squeaked.

"Yes, once a year I hold a training. They learn my special techniques to tie off the rigging. It is good, yes?"

"No, it is *not* good."

He blinked at me. "No?"

What was it about talking to the French that made simple concepts seem so difficult? "Yes, it is good you practice, but not here in my hotel. Our slip-and-fall policy wouldn't cover your high-wire act." Above me, the performers continued their show. My first instinct was to start yelling—a distraction sure to give me what I was trying to avoid: acrobats splatting all over the Hanging Gardens. "We have no insurance at all for this. Make them stop. Right now."

The man actually had the audacity to pause for a moment as if I'd given him a choice and had asked nicely. Clearly, self-preservation was not one of his strengths. Of course, he defied death every night.

A cluster of people knotted behind him stared at me with varying degrees of distaste and malice. Guess they were the students who'd have to practice elsewhere.

The crowd above booed as Philippe called to the performers to climb down.

I felt eyes bore into my back. Winning friends and influencing people, just a couple of my many talents. "Did security not try to stop you?" I eyed the rigging—they'd set it just above the cameras focused on the floor and just below the ones capturing the higher floors that jumpers found attractive. Clever.

I got Jerry back on the other end of the line. "Where were you on this one? Dear God, if someone had fallen!"

"I know. I just got here—only four hours of sleep in the last three days is not enough. My staff was a bit preoccupied with the murder. The performers rigged it so we had to know what we were looking for. We missed it. Not making excuses. I'll take care of it."

Cameras gave a picture. Experience interpreted it. "I understand. It'll be a good lesson during our next training session. Refocus everyone on your end." I almost rang off, but a thought hit me. "Wait, Jerry?"

"Still here."

"Can you call my office and ask Brandy to send you a photo of Homer Beckham? We're looking for him in conjunction with the murder at the rodeo, assault of a police officer, and anything else I can drum up to get him tossed in with men who might look at him as a plaything. I don't expect him to be wandering around here—it's a long shot, but worth a try."

"She sent one over a while ago. We identified him last night sometime in the Kasbah—he'd gone before we started looking for him. You need me to send anyone to help you?"

"No, I've got a handle on it." I eyed the Frenchman who watched me with interest. "Philippe owes me a favor."

"Tell him to pay up. With you, the interest rate can triple the cost."

I held my phone away from my ear. "Did you hear that?" I asked Philippe.

Finally, his cherubic smile dimmed. "*Oui.*"

"And, Jer," I said, returning the phone to my ear, "check in with Miss P. Make sure she's okay and your staff has her back—she's a bit freaked."

"I'm on it."

My voice dropped. "Did you see it?"

"Not yet, but sounds like Miss P isn't the only one freaked."

"You will be, too." I ended the call then pulled up my photos. "I need your help with a knotty problem," I said to the tiny acrobat still watching me with a half-bemused expression.

Philippe concentrated on the photos of the two different knots, the one around Turnbull's neck and the new one around Mrs. Bates's. I'd made sure to enlarge them so only the knots were showing.

"Go back to the first one," he said. I did as he asked. He stared at it for a moment. "Now the second." He gave that one more attention while I waited semi-patiently.

My patience ran out. "What do you think?"

He held up a hand to silence me, then brushed my hand aside and did the flipping between the photos himself.

Finally, he stepped back. "The first one, it was tied in a hurry. The person, he was not so careful. The second one is more precise, like he meant it."

"Okay." I fought a shiver. *Like he meant it.* Damn straight he meant it. "Were they tied by the same person?"

He pursed his lips. "*Oui,* I think so, but it is hard to tell. There is an extra turn of the rope, if you will."

"Something unique?"

"Yes. And the person was left-handed, I think. We work very hard to make the knots the way they should be, but sometimes the person's comfort, it comes in. The knot is still good, just different, depending on the knot."

I pocketed my phone in a bit of disgust. "Now I know how Prince Charming with the one glass slipper felt as he asked the ladies to try it on."

Philippe gave that Gallic shrug, which, on him, I didn't find so cute. "But it is something, no?"

"No." The ropes started snaking down as the crew dismantled their web. "How long did this take you?"

"We are quite fast."

As fast as we covered our ass, someone would dream up something new to keep me awake nights.

Vegas, the Mischief Capital of the World.

And it was my job to make sure it didn't become the Murder Capital of the World.

I needed help.

Flash answered on the first ring. "Nothing yet, shit; art takes time, cupcake."

"Investigating as art? Interesting, but who am I to quibble? That's a rhetorical question." I added that, lest she wanted to dismantle my character or list my shortcomings. Either would take far longer than I wanted, given that I was distracting her from her sleuthing. "We have another dead body, one Dora Bates, but this one is on the QT. Her daughter has yet to be told." I gave her a few of the personal details, but none of the grisly. "Run a background on her. I want to know everything, whether she has pimples on her ass, who she's sleeping with, has she met the police up close and personal, where she's from and where she's been, you know the drill."

"You don't know where she's from? That would help focus the search."

"I've been told she's from Reno, but I haven't confirmed it. Her daughter is competing in the barrel racing. I'm sure the rodeo would have that info. Hell, it's probably listed in the program. And she works in the front office of the rodeo."

"She handles the money?"

"Yep. So, follow the money trail, if there is one. No one has said anything about accounting anomalies, but it wouldn't hurt to ask."

"Got it." She paused and I could picture her scribbling notes.

"What about YouTube? Find any interesting footage?"

"Still working on it. We weren't quite fast enough. Ever since that nutcase in Chicago took to Facebook to post his own little real-time snuff film, they've been a lot more vigilant about taking all that kind of stuff down. I've got an inside track, though. Once it's posted, it never disappears if you know how to look for it."

I didn't want to know what laws she was breaking in the name of justice. But, if she went to the slammer, maybe we could share a cell. Although, in a small confined space with Flash, I'd last maybe fifteen minutes before doing something I'd regret.

"Are we done?"

"This getting to you?" Flash knew the answer, but she couldn't resist letting me know I sounded testy.

"Being all wound up with no one to strangle makes me a tad grumpy."

"I'll take your word for it. I do have one thing, although, I can't tie it up with anything or anyone in this farce yet."

I wanted to tell her it wasn't a farce, but she knew that. We all have our coping strategies. Flash's was to pretend life was nothing but a great scoop. "Good."

"No, not good." The taunt left her voice, which meant only one thing—I was so not going to like what came next. "You're not going to like it," she said, reading my mind.

"Nobody has told me anything I liked in I can't remember when. But, if you can help me solve this..." In the emotion of the moment, I managed to stop before I made promises I'd regret.

"Well, there was a murder in Reno about the time the rodeo was in town. An old guy, a retired doctor. Dean was his name. He owned the farm the girl's grandmother was buying. He's got a son. I'm trying to locate him now."

Murder. I hated being right.

"What kind of doctor?"

"A vet, just retired."

Must've been the one Bethany mentioned.

"There's more."

Something in Flash's tone put me on high alert. "O—kay." I stretched out the word to prolong the inevitable.

"I'll keep digging to see if any of the victims have pasts that collide. As far as the murder goes, there's one person of interest." She pulled in a deep breath.

I braced myself.

"Lucky, they're looking for your girl."

CHAPTER TEN

THERE were actually two places in town the police set up shop. The Detention Center was one of them. All the cases of mischief that happened in Clark County were handled there. And, curiously, all of the Strip, the most lucrative section of what the world considered to be Las Vegas was in Clark County, outside the confines of the City of Las Vegas, and out from under the thumb of the mayor. Personally, I liked the mayor, but this was an end-run perpetrated before Vegas became a monetary powerhouse by some casino owners disgruntled at the idea of city rule. Never one to willingly accept the yoke of government authority, I could appreciate their motivation. Back in the day, scuttlebutt had it that the power brokers owned the County Commission, or thought they did.

Politics, a dirty business, then and now. Different players. Same game.

Yes, this was the potential cesspool Mona had chosen to wade into.

Mona. We had two dead and she was sitting on the truth.

Half of me wanted to kill her. The other half wanted to kill anyone who tried to stop her. If I wanted a fight, I didn't have to look far—I could just fight with myself.

A win-lose proposition at best.

I parked the Ferrari across the street from the Detention Center where it would attract little attention. A kid slouching against the wall just out of the glow on the streetlight gave me the once-over as I got out and made sure to lock the car. I pulled out a fifty and extended it toward him. "There's another one here for you if you keep everyone off my car."

He took the bill and gave me a nod, then he resumed his former position.

As I crossed the street, Squash Trenton fell in at my shoulder, matching my stride. "You realize you just gave cash to one of the biggest dealers in town? Normally, that would get you a Go Directly to Jail card."

I'd done plenty of business with the kid, but Squash didn't need to know that. In fact, nobody needed to know that. It would be more dangerous to the kid than to me. We all had our contacts—I liked that word so much better than snitch. We'd helped each other out, me and the kid. That's how it worked on the streets. I had a high friend in a low place, and he had a low friend in a high place—worked for both of us. "Really?" I feigned ignorance with a shrug. "Who better to watch my car?"

"A C-note says your ride won't be there when you get back." Squash peeled off a hundred from the roll of cash he pulled from his pocket and held it out in front of me.

I didn't take it. "Deal, but apply it to my tab."

He held the door at the entrance to the Detention center for me. His face fell when he caught the look in my eye. "I lost the bet, didn't I?"

"I never count my chickens. Anything can happen."

"You ever think about going to law school?"

That got a smile; I couldn't help it even if I didn't feel like it. "Me? A lawyer? The possibilities for disbarment and incarceration would be endless."

He didn't argue. "Who are you here to see?"

"A bull handler from the rodeo."

"Toby Sinclair."

It wasn't a question. I whirled on him. "Oh, no, Counselor. You already have a horse in this race. You're bought and paid for."

He held up his hand—meager defense, we both knew it.

"He called the office. I passed him off to a less-than-reputable outfit around the corner. You were the first to call my name in this game of legal Red Rover, Red Rover, so you have my undying fealty." He pressed a hand to his chest in exaggerated sincerity.

"He who calls first wins?"

"No," he put a hand on my arm and squeezed. "He whose call is accepted first wins."

He won that round. "So, what are you doing here?"

"Playing Tonto, Kemosabe."

"Oh, and I'm the Lone Ranger?"

"You do prefer going it alone, except when you get your ass in a crack."

A slam-dunk rebuttal was out of my reach, so I didn't even mount a defense. "A little bird told you I was on my way?" The idea chafed. Who knew? Better yet, who knew and would tell?

Even I recognized that cynicism had become my middle name.

Mentally, I worked through the list of possibilities and couldn't think of a one. Like Squash said, I liked to run under the radar, and part of my self-delusion was that I could pull it off.

Chinks were showing in my armor, but I couldn't fathom a mole in my inner sanctum.

Squash ended my search for a Judas. "They just released Sinclair from the hospital. You didn't show up there, so I figured I'd find you here eventually."

"You waited in ambush at the hospital all this time? Why didn't you just call?"

"I did. Went right to voicemail."

"Sorry, I went down for the count. And since then..." If I'd seen that he'd called, I spaced it.

"I didn't leave a message. I wasn't worried—our worlds tend to collide."

Like highly-charged particles speeding through a vacuum at the speed of heat. "Is this soon enough?"

"Your timing is impeccable." He bit back a smile as we

arrived shoulder to shoulder at the intake desk. The female cop behind the Lucite blushed when Squash graced her with his patented grin. Her look of adulation evaporated when I spoke. "Lucky O'Toole. Detective Romeo is waiting for me."

"Yes, ma'am." Who knew those two words could hold such indifference and contempt at the same time? "And Mr. Trenton?"

"He's with me."

"Oh." Crestfallen, she buzzed us through the doors. "Down the hall to the right."

I didn't tell her I could find the interrogation rooms in the dark. "Thank you."

Shoulder-to-shoulder, Squash and I cleared a path down the hall. "One of your fan club?" I asked, then gave myself a silent talking-to for even going there. I never had been a grass-is-greener kind of gal...had I? Run at the sign of a guy with a rope? Did that have the ring of me in it?

"Jealous?" He shot me a sideways glance.

"No. Impressed."

With a folder under his arm and a sour mood I could read from where I stood, Romeo met us coming the other way. "Interrogation Room Three," he said to me, ignoring Squash. "What's he doing here?"

"Anything I need."

"Convenient. Can't wait to see how you play this one." He grabbed my elbow, slowing me down. Squash took the hint and walked on.

"You do know you have too many men in your life as it is, don't you?"

Since I knew his motivation, I wasn't offended at the insinuation. "Better than anyone."

"Good." He stepped back. Straightening, he tugged on the hem of his suit jacket, but even I could've told him those wrinkles were there to stay. "You really clocked Mr. Sinclair. Hairline fracture. Hell of a cut—took the plastic surgeon two rows of sixty sutures each. Sinclair's acting like he's lingering on the edge of a concussion, but the doc felt sure he was overplaying it."

"The bottle was all I had. He was assaulting the ladies."

"They told me." We joined Squash, who waited outside the interrogation room.

"You okay with me watching from behind the glass?" he asked Romeo.

"If we end up in court, his statement's discoverable anyway."

Squash took that as a yes and disappeared through a door to his left.

With his hand on the doorknob, Romeo asked me, "Do you think Bates was our extortionist?"

"This is starting to feel like one of those Agatha Christie novels where everyone had a motive for murder."

"Or at least a strong desire to see the deceased...deceased."

"Same difference, but your version is more eloquent. From all accounts so far, she had a sweet gig. But, as most who walk on the wrong side of the line, she pushed it too far, stepped on the wrong set of boots."

"The trick is figuring out who thinks murder is a good solution to a pesky monetary problem."

"That's why we're here, Grasshopper." He was sounding more like me than I was.

"Anything you want to add before we do our tag-team thing?"

I gave him a synopsis of what I'd overheard in the girls' trailer.

"They corroborate."

"No doubt." A bit of indignation at being lumped in with the less-than-truthful crept in. "You stop believing me and I'm implementing Plan B."

"I misstated. Your story corroborates theirs." Too little, but not too late. "You have a Plan B?"

"Please, I may be a corporate grunt, bought and paid for, but so far I've avoided the shackles."

"So you think." He said it under his breath but loud

enough for me to hear. "What's Plan B?" he added to head off my verbal parry.

"Passion on the Beach." That got the hoped-for response—not a word, just a wide-eyed stare. "It's a juice bar. I have the concept all figured out—passion fruit will be the main ingredient."

"On the beach?"

"Kauai. Maui is a bit overrun these days and I don't want to work too hard."

"You'd make it three days, max, then be bored out of your skull."

"You asked me if I had a Plan B. I didn't say it was a good one." Now that I had him back on his heels, I pressed my advantage. "Right now, before we begin, I do have one question."

He used his frown as a shield—hardly intimidating on someone who looked all of twelve. "You never ask my permission for anything."

"Truly, my bad. I'm sorry."

He blinked rapidly, not sure what to make of me.

Inconsistent was my middle name—didn't he know that?

"Okay." He sounded hesitant. "Fire away."

"Can I be the bad cop this time? You promised. Besides, you just look so nice."

With his black eye and black mood, he was morphing into the bad cop in front of my eyes, but I didn't tell him that—I'd told him that enough times already.

He rolled his eyes. "I know better than to take you seriously in situations like this. And, no, you can't." He held up a hand. "We don't do that anymore."

"What?" My air left in a deflating whoosh. "Since when?"

"Since they figured out that intimidation sucked as an interrogation technique. It gives you bad results. People start telling you what they think you want to hear because they're scared."

"Works when they use it on me," I groused as he turned his back and pushed through the door. "I shoulda known they'd take all the fun out of it."

Romeo ignored me—he didn't hold the door.

Sinclair was seated at a gray metal table that was bolted to the floor in the middle of a consistently gray room. The dark rectangle of two-way glass filled the wall behind him. A camera mounted high in the corner blinked its red eye at us.

His hands folded in front of him, his head down, Sinclair didn't look up as Romeo and I took the two chairs across from him.

Romeo put his folder in front of him. If Sinclair had any interest in what was inside, he didn't show it. "I'm Detective Romeo with the Metropolitan Police Department. This is Ms. O'Toole."

Tilting his head, Sinclair angled a look at me. His eyes were dark and carried a hint of hate. Of course, that might be his normal look. I didn't know and wasn't anxious to find out. "We've met."

Steri-Strips held the gash closed supporting the tiny black ones that ran like tracks along the contour of the cut. The smear of blood or iodine stained his forehead a light reddish brown. Some blood had pooled under the skin below his left eye and was now turning purple. If he wasn't a badass, he now looked like one.

"That's one heck of a buckle." Romeo said in an I'm-your-friend-and-just-want-to-chat amicably. "I couldn't help but notice it."

As an opening salvo, that one surprised me. And I decided I wasn't a fan of the new buddy-buddy interrogation technique. I was more of a thumbscrews and waterboard kind of gal. Not technically accurate, but not a gross overstatement either.

Apparently, the Universe wanted to prove me wrong (nothing new there)—Romeo's approach worked and Sinclair gave the young detective his undivided attention. "From another life."

"National Champion Bull Rider." Romeo gave a low whistle. "The toughest."

Like a bladder being filled with hot air, Sinclair's ego

inflated before our eyes, straightening his posture. If his head got any larger he'd need a custom cowboy hat.

The guy had to know Romeo was playing him...

"For a moment, I was on top." Sinclair's face clouded and he sagged a bit, like coal as it burns and drops into a superheated pile. "Knew it couldn't last."

"It's not supposed to," I added, desperate to poke a pin in his bubble. Male egos—at once irritating and awe-inspiring. As a female, I wished I could capture some of that overblown confidence, but the XX-chromosome rationalist always shot me down.

"I've been around. Not news to me." Sinclair stared up at the camera in the corner, weighing his words.

Romeo and I waited as if we had all the time and patience in the world. Time, I could give. Patience? Don't make me laugh.

After toting up all the pros and cons, Sinclair looked at us both straight on. "Look, I know you know my story and this is just your way of getting me to tell it. So, here it is." He leaned forward, focusing on Romeo, man-to-man.

I didn't feel left out—last thing I wanted was to be pulled into a my-dick-is-bigger-than-yours game. Winning would be too easy, but I didn't think crushing my opponent would help us get what we came for. I was beginning to understand the rationale for the kinder-and-gentler interrogation approach, not that I liked it any better.

But, if it could help us find a killer, I was all in.

Romeo held his ground.

"That fuckin' a-hole, Darrin Cole, helped me into an early retirement. Problem was, I wasn't so ready to go, seein' how my 401K wasn't fully vested." He gave a little snort of derision.

"How'd he do that?" Romeo, the awe-gee-shucks interrogator, sounded like he really wanted to know.

"By not doing his job. I took a bad ride—twisted my leg coming off of Blindside. That bull is fun to ride, has a bit of killer instinct in him." He gave a tight smile. "I went down and like he sensed I was hurt, that damn bull turned on me. Cole was right there. It was his job to keep the bull off of me."

"He didn't do it." Romeo filled in the easy blank, urging Sinclair deeper into the meat of the story.

Sinclair took the bait and warmed to his tale. "Thank you, Captain Obvious. Pansy Ass Cole cowered back. The bull got me right in the side. Got my liver and a few other important things. I damn near bled out. Also stomped my hand pretty good." He held up his left hand; the fingers were a bit mangled, the palm closed in on itself slightly. "Broke most of the bones. Shredded tendons. I've got enough Gor-Tex in there to make a fucking jacket."

"You're left-handed?" The question blurted out of me before I could help it.

Sinclair eyed me as superfluous. Romeo nodded, urging him to answer. "Was. It was my dominant hand. After the bones healed and the docs did what they could, it still was pretty useless, as you can see. Learned to do everything with my right, but it's still not natural."

I'm not sure whether his answer kept him in the pool of knot-tying suspects or not. "And now, regardless of your hand, with your other injuries the docs won't clear you to ride again."

"They say I'm a medical risk, lucky to be alive. What the fuck do they know?"

They took away what he loved, what fed his soul. A grudging respect bloomed somewhere inside. Not that I wouldn't crucify him if he'd killed Turnbull and Dora Bates, but I understood.

"I'm stuck handling the bulls rather than riding them. Gotta pay the bills."

"Yeah, the 401K thing," I said.

He gave me the dim light of his full attention. "I think you've got a bit of meanness for me like that bull." The way he said it almost sounded like a compliment.

"Only if you're hurting people. Did you let that bull into the arena? Maybe give Cole what he gave you?"

"Hell, no. There were a bunch of people in there."

"But you figured Cole would sacrifice himself to draw the

bull away from them. Not a bad idea, really, when you think about it."

He absorbed that, then leaned back in his chair, his arms open. "Look. I know how it all looks." He flicked a glance my direction. "Especially since you caught my act with the ladies."

Oh, the guy was a fast learner.

"I just wanted to give Cole a bit of what he gave me. I didn't know the guy in his suit wasn't him."

"And the rope around his neck?"

Sinclair tried to shrug away from the question. "Just to scare him a bit."

"Did you tie the knot in it?"

His eyebrows arched then fell back into place. "No, it was the girl's rope. She'd been practicing."

I stilled. "Which girl?"

"The cute kid with the freckles, Poppy."

The breath I'd been holding left me in a sigh. "She tied the knot?"

"How would I know? Why don't you ask her? Or better yet, why don't you ask her father? He does everything for the kid but wipe her ass. Wouldn't put that past him either." Sinclair gave me a leer, his tongue between his teeth.

Ah, *now* I had someone to strangle. I was feeling better.

But, instead of giving him the satisfaction of knowing he'd burrowed under my skin like a tick, I kept my expression flat, my voice hard, my manner calm. Why didn't they award Oscars to everyday people? "What else did you do to Turnbull besides threaten him?"

"Nothing. He took off like a scared rabbit. I had no idea it was him—his face was smeared with white paint like the clowns use. They weren't due up for a while, so I thought maybe I'd caught him putting on his clown face. Trevor was an okay guy, and he'd jump at his own shadow, so not exactly fun to get all lathered up."

"You two had argued in the barn. What about?"

"Who told you that?" I stared at him until he continued. "A bull; we argued over a bull. He thought he was a killer and would get out and hurt someone. Wanted me to get rid of him, but he was the hardest to ride. Separated the men from the boys." He rubbed his side and stretched, an involuntary action.

"That the same bull that hurt you?"

"Yeah."

"What happened?"

"I told Turnbull to fuck off and he did. Like I said, he wasn't one to put up much of a fight."

"Like the girls, Suzie and Becky?" My voice held a cold steel edge.

He shot me a look and wisely said nothing.

"And where were you when you encountered Turnbull?" Romeo asked.

"By the side entrance where Rico parks his tractor, but I thought he was Cole."

"So you said." I had a feeling Turnbull hadn't backed down quite as easily as Sinclair wanted us to believe.

The guy was a creep and had a habit of bullying people. Hurt and anger could warp a guy, but enough for murder?

I wondered what being scared would look like on him. "This is a great story, but it's not the one you started into with the girls," I said. In the trailer, in that fraction of a second before his lights went dark, he'd had enough time to process my presence. So I knew the truth. Couldn't wait to see how he'd spin it.

"I was pushing to see what they thought they saw and what they'd told the cops."

"You have a habit of pushing people around, don't you?" Romeo had picked up a bit of my mad.

"Only when they deserve it."

"Did Mr. Turnbull deserve it?" I leaned forward, pressing my advantage.

"Turnbull?" Sinclair spat the name like an epithet. "He was a pansy. Just cared about his kid and her stupid horse." He turned to me. "Did you know horses have brains the size of a walnut? A huge, strong animal, and stupid as all get out."

Romeo grabbed my arm, knowing I was about to draw an

obvious comparison. I resisted...barely. Life held so few perfect opportunities...

"I really didn't mean to hurt him. You have to believe that."

"But you meant to hurt someone and he was collateral damage."

Sinclair shrugged and crossed his arms, a satisfied look on his face as if he'd managed to hoodwink us. "Not hurt them. Scare them." Then he seemed to sober as if prodded by some dim chime of wisdom. "I didn't mean for the dude to stroke out."

"Where'd you get the rope?" I asked, inserting the question in his moment of comfort like a surgical blade sliding between two ribs.

"What?" The question knocked some of the arrogance out of him. "What do you mean?"

"I think the question is self-explanatory." Romeo used his grown-up voice.

"I...I...I don't know. Around."

"You're telling us a very nice, hand-braided custom lariat was just lying around?"

"Yeah, that's exactly what I'm telling you. I was back by the side entrance and saw who I thought was Cole. Lit my fuse, I can tell you. I grabbed a rope and headed after him. Got the loop around him as we ran down the side of the arena."

"So, who had the rope?" Romeo sounded confused.

I elaborated, making a point. "It was just...there?"

"Yeah." Sinclair's eyes had the wide-eyed fear thing going on.

Romeo looked at me. I knew there was another question. I reached for it. Thankfully, it appeared. "I'll ask again—the knot, did you tie it?"

A bead of sweat trickled down the side of his face. "No, that's why I grabbed it—it was already tied. I didn't have the time to stop and tie the thing. Besides, I don't know nuthin' about tying knots."

I leaned across the table, getting as much in his face as I could. "What about extortion? What do you know about that?"

He leaned back, his gaze darting as if desperate to avoid me and my question.

"What did Dora Bates have on you? She was shaking you down, right?"

"Bates?" His eyes locked on mine. "What's she got to do with this?" He swallowed hard.

"She's dead."

That wiped the smirk off his face. "Dead?" Relief, then fear. "I didn't have anything to do with that. Not that I'm sorry to see her get what was coming."

"Where'd you go last evening after the rodeo?" Romeo's voice had lost a bit of its warmth. The buddy act was over.

"This lady put me in the hospital."

"Between the show being interrupted by Mr. Turnbull's death and when you and Ms. O'Toole had your encounter."

"I stayed in the arena area."

"Did you see Mrs. Bates?"

"No."

I sure hoped Flash was getting somewhere with the YouTube videos—who was where would prove enlightening, I felt sure. "What'd she have on you?"

Romeo opened his folder. "I can answer that." He pulled out a few sheets of paper, then turned them around so Sinclair could read them. "You've got a pretty long rap sheet here. Assaults, mainly. Even did some time in Nebraska. But I bet the rodeo organizers don't know, do they?"

A bad cowboy—somehow that diminished the world as we knew it.

Sinclair did a slow burn, the red creeping up his neck then coloring his face. "No."

"And you really need that job." I turned the screw tighter.

"Yeah. Most folks these days run your background before giving you the gig. With the rodeo, my Championship got me in."

Secrets, such delicate dangerous things.

"Did you kill her?" I asked, even though he'd denied it

once.

"No." He looked at me with cold eyes. "But when you find the killer, I want to know. I'd like to shake his hand."

Either the guy had a sociopath's set of balls, or he wasn't guilty.

He pressed at the bandage covering the cut on his forehead. The anesthetic would be wearing off. "Bates was hitting a bunch of us, scraping off the cream so none of us could get ahead. Beckham was trying to rally everyone to put an end to her act. He had the most to lose, I think. That pony, his kid, they were his last hope."

"You think he finally snapped and took care of the problem?" Romeo asked.

"Possible. His temper could get away from him."

"Same could be said about you," I added, unable to resist, which got me a narrowed-eyed look. "Anybody else seem particularly hot around the collar when it came to Bates?"

He snorted. "Everyone. But Cole had something to hide. Don't know what exactly, but he was running scared."

I resisted rolling my eyes. "Two things are wrong with that statement, Mr. Sinclair. First, it holds as much weight as a spouse's accusation in divorce court, and he certainly was running scared, but not from Bates. He was running scared from you." Having heard enough, I got up and, without a word, walked out the door. Romeo wasn't far behind. The minute the door closed behind him, I whirled around. "Oh, please, tell me we can slap that guy in irons and haul him off. He's got to be guilty of some actionable offense."

"Unless Mr. Turnbull presses charges..."

"Mr. Turnbull is dead."

Romeo tucked his folder back under his arm like an officious Gestapo official or something. "I thought it safer to let you reach the obvious conclusion on your own. We all know what happens to the messenger."

I took a deep breath, then grabbed him in a bear hug. "You're back. Do you have a rap sheet on anyone else in that folder? Any more secrets someone would kill to hide?"

"Actually, yes. Beckham has a felony assault charge—old and only one, so not a huge motivator, but you never know."

"Interesting. Anything on Turnbull?"

"Clean as new snow."

"I think that's white as new snow."

"I made myself clear." Oh, a bit of an attitude—yep, he was carrying a load.

"Did you run anything on Doc Latham?"

"Didn't get a hit. He's a vet. He handles controlled substances. His fingerprints should be on file. But, I've got a new kid on it. He's screwed up before. I'm sure we'll find them. We'll keep looking. But now that you put Sinclair back on his heels—good job, by the way—I'm going to step back in there and see if he can give me a full definition of 'everyone' or if he's just casting the seeds of blame trying to obscure his own."

"Poetic."

"Poetic justice would be even better."

I'D given the kid his second fifty and made it as far as my car before Squash caught up. To be honest, I wasn't trying to get away. Lost in short straws and theories that had gone nowhere, I'd forgotten about him.

The engine purring, the car ready, and nowhere to go. I sat there at idle, my mind racing.

"You win." Squash thrust a bill through the open window.

I didn't even jump. Either I was dead or seriously distracted. "Losing is never an option."

"My kind of gal."

We'd reached that moment—that one you can't define but you just know. Either we jumped in, or the opportunity would be lost forever. I hated those kinds of absolutes. Keeping my options open was more my style.

For the first time ever, that idea bothered me.

At some point, one had to commit. I knew that.

And it terrified me.

I'd never admitted that—not even to myself in the deepest, darkest part of the night where anxiety and second-guessing assaulted me.

I eyed the bill. "Apply it to my account." Squinting against the light, I closed one eye and angled a look at him. "I may not have all the fancy degrees, but I am living proof that who you know can be as important as what you learned."

"I am clay for you to mold."

"Not a good idea, Mr. Trenton."

He stepped back. The closed look on his face told me he'd gotten all the meanings and subtext in that comment. "Understood. Where are you going now?"

"Did you know our little Miss Bethany Fiorelli is wanted for questioning in two deaths in Reno?"

"I did."

That took the bluster right out of me. "And you didn't mention it because?"

"That attorney-client thing, and I've got it covered." His flat expression told me I wouldn't get any more.

"Have you been talking with my father?" Why I said that, I don't know.

He put his hand on my shoulder. "Let me take care of this one, okay?"

"Sure," I flipped the car into gear. "I've got work to do." Everyone knew more about what was going on than I did, but they all looked to me to solve the problem.

Not that this was unusual or anything.

Darrin Cole was next on my list, a fact I didn't share with the good attorney.

I didn't tell him that I was going to corner Darrin Cole before he got the word that Sinclair would be unleashed upon the world to continue terrorizing him—Romeo could hold the guy for twenty-four hours. After that, he had to have a solid reason. Unless the ladies pressed charges...which wouldn't happen...he had nothing.

First Darrin Cole, then Mona. Then some digging into Miss Bethany Fiorelli.

As a life, mine right now could use some work.

WITH the event for tonight cancelled, I wasn't sure where to look for Darrin Cole. Luck was with me and I caught him throwing loops in the warm-up arena behind the Thomas and Mack. A plastic calf bobbed on springs thirty feet away. Catching the loop of the rope in his right hand, he weighed it, then let it slip through his fingers as he moved his arm in a circle. Slowly letting out rope, he grew the loop. Stepping into it, he let it fly. A bull's-eye—the plastic bull was captured.

My clapping caught his attention.

"It's much harder when they actually move," he said as he advanced on the bull, flipped the loop from around it, then re-coiled the rope. This time he used his left hand to pull in the rope, gathering it in his right.

"I'll take your word for it." I slid through the gap in the pole fence. "Show me how?"

"Sure."

He placed himself behind me, his arms around me, his hands guiding mine. "You're right-handed?"

"Yes. Which is easier for you?" I let the question slip out naturally.

"I'm naturally a leftie, but I can throw with either. Okay, keep the coil in your left hand. Grab the loop here at the knot." He slid the rope until the knot was across my palm.

Not wanting to pay undue attention to the knot itself, I let my fingers do the seeing for me. It wasn't the same as the knots on the ropes around Turnbull and Dora. Not the answer I was hoping for, but it didn't rule him out either.

"Start swinging it in a circle. As the pressure increases, feed more rope into it, letting out rope from your left hand and letting it slip through the knot in your right."

I did as he said as best I could. The whole left-hand-doesn't-know-what-the-right-is-doing thing always tripped me up. Back in the day, Mona had harbored dreams of me as a great pianist. Something to legitimize the illegitimate. But I'd failed at her dream.

Not the first time, not the last.

As I swung harder, the loop grew. "Like this?"

"You're doing great." As my poor flaccid loop limped around in a lazy circle, I realized that while bulls may be Toby's purview, bullshit was Darrin's. "Now, just as it comes around and you feel the weight shift forward, let it loose."

I did as he said with less than spectacular results. My loop fell harmlessly ten feet short—the plastic calf would live another day.

"A great first try. You're a natural." He had no idea.

Pretending to be devastated, I pulled the rope back in, rewinding it in my left hand. "Hardly." As I gathered the rope, I hefted it, trying to show appreciation. "Nice rope. I'd like to practice. Where would I buy one?"

"From me. I'll cut you a deal."

"Why would you do that?"

"I like you. I buy the ropes off a guy in Wichita Falls—one of the old guard. He doesn't make many. In fact, I think I buy most of his production."

"Really?" I coiled the rest of the rope, fingering it appreciatively—it looked like the others. "You lose a lot of ropes?"

He laughed at my stupidity. "No. I teach roping. I buy a bunch, then sell them for like three times the cost to my students. Sometimes the kids leave them around. Better for me, right?"

"Nice." I veiled the sarcasm.

He leaned over to look. I caught a whiff of Aramis. Did they even make the stuff anymore? "A man's got to make a living. I take my opportunities where I find them."

"The rope artist have a name?"

"Sure, but I keep it a secret. Wouldn't want anyone going

behind my back."

I thought about throwing the rope around him and tying him up, just for the satisfaction of it, but he probably wasn't the right guy. "Who do you teach?"

"Oh, mainly rodeo folks. Helps pass the time. Despite what people think, we have a lot of downtime."

"Where were you before Turnbull got killed?"

"That afternoon I was giving some lessons to the kids."

"Which ones?"

"Mainly Poppy. She's pretty keen on it. Her friend Bethany was here, too."

"You were here all afternoon?"

"I never left. Went and got some grub at the steak place upstairs with a couple of the other guys, then we came back down, and that's when all the ruckus started."

I made a note to have Romeo check out Darrin's dinner accommodations. "Did you ever cross paths with Dora Bates?"

The skin between his eyes puckered and his mouth lost its upturn. But he did sorta seem happy not to be talking about Turnbull.

"I take that as a yes."

"I hadn't talked to her much until yesterday. I'd heard the rumors, so I'd stayed out of her way. I don't have anything to hide, so I figured she'd leave me alone."

"So you knew about her extracurricular activities? Extortion being the main one?"

"Sure. The rodeo is a tight family. We usually have each other's backs."

"Even when something bad goes down?" I watched his face, his eyes, trying to read him.

"You mean like me and Sinclair?"

I nodded.

"That was some bad shit. I didn't do my job. The bull looked at me, and I knew he would kill me. I froze, not for more than a second or two, but long enough. Toby's finding it hard to forgive me, but he's got nothing on the guilt I live with."

"You think Turnbull got caught in one of Toby's anger exercises?"

"Makes sense if he thought it was me." He twirled the loop at his feet, parallel to the ground, letting it get larger. Then he stepped in and out of it as he kept it spinning and growing. A great distraction so he didn't have to face my questions...or me. "He likes to rough me up a bit to remind me, but he never goes too far. He doesn't want to kill me." Darrin let the loop drop to the ground. "Living with the guilt is much worse than being relieved of it. He just wants to make sure I never forget."

One sick cuss, but pretty normal. "What did Mrs. Bates want yesterday?"

"She wanted to know if I needed anyone to help me put Toby Sinclair in his place. At least that's how she framed it."

An offer of help, a lifetime of blackmail. The lady was a peach. "What'd you say?"

"I told her that sort of thing wasn't my jam." He slowly gathered the rope. "I'll take care of Toby in my own time, my own way."

"You think he let the bull into the arena?"

"Could've, but I doubt it."

"And then there's the whole thing with Turnbull wearing your clown suit."

"Was that not totally weird? Turnbull? He never said much to anyone. I can't imagine he pissed someone off to the point of homicide. We all keep our stuff in lockers set up by the arena gate. They're not locked. Who would've thought someone would take my clown stuff?"

Yeah, who woulda thought? "Any idea why he decided to put on your stuff?"

"Not a clue. I never talked to the guy. He kept to himself mostly. I just wished he hadn't torn up my getup. We don't make that much money as it is, and the costume is on us."

The bane of employees everywhere. "Any idea why Poppy thought I needed to talk to you about Turnbull getting killed?"

"Maybe because I talked to him right before..."

"You did? Why didn't you tell that to the cops?"

"I did."

Reynolds. "What did he say to you?"

"Huntsville."

"Huntsville? Alabama?"

"I don't know. I've been hearing that in my dreams but I don't know what to make of it."

"And Bethany? You put the cops on to her. Why?"

"I just told them she and Turnbull had a little *tête-á-tête* in the barn. He had her by the arm, then she ran away. After that, he staggered into the arena and croaked. What was I supposed to think?"

"That she went for help?"

"I'd heard the whispers."

"Whispers?"

"She'd left some dead folks behind in Reno."

"Where'd you hear that from?"

He gave me the side-eye. "Around. I've been with the rodeo a long time. Things come my way."

"I'll bet."

As he weighed the rope, he looked at me as if I was the next calf he would rope. "None of this should've happened. The bull shouldn't have been there. That bull especially."

"*That* bull?" A moment of clarity and I knew. "That bull was Blindside, right? The one that got between you and Toby Sinclair." And the one Toby Sinclair and Turnbull had argued over.

"Yeah, they should've killed that bull after he got Sinclair. Sinclair wasn't the bull's first, which made it hard to understand when he refused to get rid of the bull. Frankly, that animal's highest and best use is dog food. Some animals are just broken, you know?"

Did I ever.

As I started to leave, Darrin stopped me with a hand on my arm. "I do have one thing on Huntsville, but it makes no sense."

"What?"

"Huntsville, Texas. There's a big prison there. They used to have a famous rodeo there every year."

CHAPTER ELEVEN

AFTER I left Cole, I headed to the barns, ostensibly to check on Poppy's pony, but something kept niggling at me, something I couldn't quite remember or place. Maybe I'd find the answer in the barn. That's where it all happened and there was something I was missing. The rodeo was quiet, the pall of Mr. Turnbull's death hanging over the place like smoke from a forest fire.

Nobody was around as I approached the stall. The pony perked up at the sound of my voice. He was munching hay and looked as if his brush with death was nothing more than a forgotten memory. Having a brain the size of a walnut could be a good thing sometimes. I stuck my fingers through the slats. He nuzzled them, then, realizing they weren't carrots, went back to his hay.

I turned to go. The halter, still hanging on the rope caught my eye.

What was it about that rope I was missing?

The knot.

I knew that knot.

MY call caught Romeo in a bad mood, not that that was unusual.

"Tell me you have something, anything," he said without even a lame attempt at the niceties.

If he was going to read from my playbook, I probably needed to clean up my act, rewrite a few rules. I could get away with bad social skills. A cop, not so much.

"Toby Sinclair meant to kill someone...okay, overstating...he meant to scare someone. It could've been Trevor Turnbull. And Dora Bates cut a wide swath." I told him what I'd pieced together from Darrin Cole.

A bunch of shuffling came over the line as he shifted his phone so he could take notes.

"And the knot found on both ropes is also the one used to tie the halter rope at the Beckhams' stall."

"Who tied it?" Romeo's voice sharpened.

"Beckham would be a logical choice."

"Or his daughter. Or even the vet. I'll keep working on it and see if I can get an answer. And I'm following a lead on a prison rodeo in Hunstville, Texas. It's a long shot. The last rodeo was sometime in the 90's—a weak attempt to revive it. It had officially closed in the 80's."

"Where'd you stumble across that connection?"

"Your buddy, Detective Reynolds has a bit of a sharing problem. You might want to watch your back."

Romeo let out a huff. "He's already got one knife in. I feel like the bull staring down a skilled matador."

There was something going on with the kid. I knew it! "You need to share. I can help you."

"That's what I've been told, but not now. When all of this is over."

"Okay."

"So, what do you think about what we know so far?"

After I'd wound down, Romeo didn't say anything for a bit. "That's great about Sinclair, but a good defense attorney would rip it to shreds. Besides the DA would probably never go for it in the first place unless you used whatever amazing thing you have against him, which is truly awesome but really wouldn't be a good idea."

"Holy cow."

"I know, verbal regurgitation. I'm all better now."

"Who knew it was that easy? Could you keep him on charges of reckless endangerment? He let that bull loose into an arena full of people."

"We don't have anyone willing to say he did it. No proof means I gotta let him go. But it would be nice to keep him out of the general population until we narrow in on a suspect. I can run it past the DA. That may be good for an extra twenty-four hours or so, unless you use your stroke with Lovato."

Daniel Lovato was our DA and he owed me big time. "No, I don't want to squander my stroke with him on something like this. Toby Sinclair has a serious anger issue—he needs a shrink, not a date in court. But I really don't think he intended to kill anyone."

"Until we have more, I'm with you." Romeo had seen enough in his rapid rise to detective to know when to double down and when to let it ride.

"I'm still trying to unravel the whole knot thing to see if we have anything there. Remote at this point." Not a pun, but, in the dim light holding back the darkness, clever helped me cope.

Romeo gave an exaggerated sigh. He knew why, he just didn't appreciate it.

"What? Not even a groan? Damn." I pulled myself together for his benefit. "Anything else? What did the coroner say about Dora Bates?"

"Suffocation, but he won't know whether by the tape or whether by drugs until he runs the tox screen. He's pushing it and Turnbull's as well. Hopes to have the results tomorrow morning."

"So quick?"

"He's limiting the request to the barbiturates."

"Got it. What about time of death?"

"He said he'd try and narrow it down by the morning as well—something about it not being an exact science even though all of us non-professionals took it as gospel."

That so sounded like the coroner. "Okay, I'll check with him in the morning. Anything else?"

"You mean besides the fact we are no closer to finding who is really at fault in the deaths of Trevor Turnbull and Dora Bates and whether the two are connected or just a happy coincidence?"

"Sarcasm, Grasshopper, and in someone so young." I knew he wouldn't appreciate it, but I couldn't resist. "The rodeo connects them."

"And a million other people." He ticked them off. "We have the vengeful father, the angry former bull rider, the clown who may or may not have intended to let the bull rider get gored, the vet with access to the murder weapon, a kid on the run with access as well, and a dead guy in her recent past. Anyone else?"

"You're a real buzzkill. Not to mention you're starting to sound like Agatha Christie."

"If you're trying for an insult, you're falling short."

"Yes, falling short seems to be part of my current reality. It's getting old."

"Ah, well, even the gods fell to earth." He sounded completely unsympathetic.

"You're not helping." I wallowed in self-pity for a few seconds and decided it was beneath me.

"Are you going to tell me how the meeting with your mother went? I assume not too bad as you're still walking around a free woman."

My mother *and* my father. How to explain?

"No."

AS I stepped through the door of my office, I called Dane, dispensing with the pleasantries when he answered. "You and the girl still at the hospital?"

"She's curled up in the chair fast asleep."

"Tie her down until I get there. And the doc?"

"Holding his own. The girl in trouble?" A hint of protectiveness crept into his voice. Dane loved riding to the rescue—probably the sign of an overblown hero complex, but I couldn't even figure out my own shortcomings, so I probably should leave his well enough alone.

"Up to her eyeballs and going under fast. I'm serious, don't let her out of your sight. I'm swinging through the office, then will be on my way. And don't be surprised if one of her fellow competitors shows up." The odds were great that one, if not two, would come looking for her.

The moment I walked in the door, my old office wrapped around me like a hug. My excuse for stopping was that someone might have called, or Security might have an insight, something we could use in the investigation. A long shot, but I needed reorienting in the normal, the familiar, of my world.

Breathing deep, I followed the aroma of fresh coffee around the divider to our small break room. My hand shook as I poured myself a mug. Don Francisco's Vanilla Nut—the nectar of the gods. The night was young and I needed a caffeine hit.

"Put some Bailey's in mine," Miss P said as she rounded the corner to join me in the tiny space.

"You're still here?"

She gave me a look. "Please, it's New Year's. We're all here, and will be until tomorrow."

I knew that. Not that it made me feel good, but long hours were part of the big salaries...oh, wait...

"That poor woman," Miss P said, snapping me out of an endless mental loop of frustration. "I'll never forget that. Please tell me it will fade over time."

"Fade? No. But the memories do get filed away and aren't quite so present." I didn't tell her that sometimes, in a moment of weakness, they could ambush me and be as horrifying as the day they happened.

"At least you're honest. When I signed up for this job, I didn't realize death would be a part of it."

"Just one of the perks." I eyed her, then added a splash more Bailey's. "Doesn't the alcohol just negate the caffeine?"

"Not helping." With her mug of steaming nerve tonic in hand, she took the chair behind her old desk. In keeping with old habits that had yet to die, I settled myself in the chair opposite the desk with my back to the window that overlooked the lobby floor. Leaning back, I waited for the hit of adrenaline. My brain knew the glass would keep me from falling, but my eyes didn't get the memo; they never learned.

Today, no jolt of fight-or-flight joy juice. Not good. I was counting on some high octane to get through the day.

With a sigh, I stretched my legs in front of me, crossing them at the ankles. Settled, I took a first, tentative sip of my caffeine-delivery vehicle of choice. The warmth traced a path all the way to my stomach where it melted into a pool of comfort.

"Fuck you, nasty bitch!"

That caught me mid-swallow, and some coffee squirted out my nose.

I'd forgotten about the bird.

While I'd been fixated on my java jolt, Miss P had uncovered his cage.

I dabbed at the coffee drops on my slacks—a dark blue, they'd hide my slovenliness well. "Pretty late in the day to be unleashing Newton." A multicolored Macaw with a foul mouth and a checkered past, Newton was my bird—at least that's how he saw it. Out of the vast sea of more appreciative humans, I had been the one he chose. I liked that, in a masochistic sort of way.

With my apartment being uninhabitable, the owner's suite just barely, and Jean-Charles's house a curse-free zone due to the residency of his five-year-old son, Christophe, the office was Newton's new home. Each day he voiced his decided lack of appreciation—not that he was any less potty-mouthed when he was happy, but he did seem to relish the words a bit more these days.

Someone had told me that birds choose their humans and attach for life, which made me feel guilty. Just once, couldn't I have a guilt-free relationship? Guilt got me to my feet and I stuffed some apple slices through the bars of his cage. "I'm sorry, big guy."

"Asshole!" He gave me his best word with enthusiasm, making me laugh.

I'd come to think of it as more of an endearment. Justifying, most likely, but it worked. This time, when I plopped back down in my chair, with the caffeine coursing through my system, I took a look around, absorbing my old office.

It looked the same. I narrowed my eyes at Miss P. "Why are all your things out here? As head of the department, your place is now in my old office, not out here in the outer office."

"I like it better here."

Relishing the comfort, I knew what she meant.

"Your office is your office," she said. "Always will be."

I leaned forward and traced the name I'd had stenciled on the corner of her desk: Jeremy Whitlock. That had been when they'd just started dating and I shepherded Miss P through a serious case of waning confidence. Jeremy used to wander in all the time and park a butt cheek on that corner, so I reserved it for him. "Who says?"

"We took a vote, and, since there are only three of us and two have voted the same way, your vote is irrelevant."

"My vote carries more weight." I glanced down at my thighs with less than the full complement of self-love pop-psychology pundits screamed we all needed. My thighs were not deserving. Once, I'd made the mistake of looking at them with Miss P's reading glasses on. Double magnification spiked my blood pressure and took years off my life. Even now, I wasn't sure I'd fully recovered.

"No, one person, one vote, it's the rule of the land." Miss P rattled that off as if she made the rules.

"You're lucky I'm too tired to put up a fight." Truth of it was, I really wanted my professional life to be as it was, at least a couple of days a week.

"Brandy and I decided you need to split your time." Miss P

sounded as if she was reading my mind.

We'd known each other a long time, which bothered me a bit—familiarity breeding contempt and all of that. Maybe I should decamp to my new office to give everyone a break. The child in me revisited logic, preferring to go with emotion.

Pretty much my normal level of functioning.

As if on cue, Brandy, the youngest and most beautiful of my team, burst through the door radiating youthful enthusiasm, saving me from arguing against my self-interest simply for the sake of being disagreeable—one of my many faults. Give me a losing cause, and I'll pick up the sword.

The bird gave a piercing wolf whistle. "Pretty girl. Pretty girl." One look at my young assistant, and the bird had fallen hard.

A bit of a blow at the time, his lack of loyalty had whittled my ego down to size, at least where fowl were concerned—which, come to think of it, covered most of the two-legged Y-chromosome set. An upside to a bad bird—I'd finally found one.

Brandy handled the adulation with casual confidence. Of course, with her stripper's body, wide eyes, and a Julia Robert's grin, she attracted a lot of attention—most of it unwanted. And, with a black belt in some sort of Far Eastern Maiming and Mutilation Secret Self-Defense discipline, she was far from helpless. The sort of unexpected thing I loved.

Brandy gave me a megawatt smile. "Thank you for bringing Romeo back in one piece." Yes, the two of them were an item—one of those odd couplings that created magic.

I took pride in their happiness and not a tiny bit of responsibility, even though misplaced—I'd made the intro; they'd made the choice. Thankfully, Romeo hadn't told her how close I'd come to losing him in China, so my invisible cloak of invincibility still masked my incompetence. I could live with that, but increasingly I felt like I was wearing the emperor's new clothes.

"Your detective didn't need any help from me. In fact, he was key—I had no idea he had such capacity for theft."

"There's barely a line between virtue and vice." She gave

me a knowing look, her smile drifting away.

"Sounds like something I'd say, not that it makes me proud or anything."

"Has he talked to you?" She lowered her voice, bringing me into her life, her concern for Romeo.

Yes, someone had Romeo's nuts in a vise.

"When this is over, he said."

She recovered a hint of her smile. "Good. You do know we learned that fine-line thing from you, right?"

I started to argue, but Miss P stopped me short. "We both did."

"I don't even want to know what else I've passed along when I wasn't paying attention."

"Fresh coffee?" Brandy asked Miss P, who nodded.

Brandy stepped over my legs, following the aroma as I had done. "You've heard about our vote, then?" Her voice filtered from behind the partition. "It shouldn't be a problem for you to move back into your old office since you never moved out." She cradled the mug in both hands when she reappeared. "Sort of Freudian, don't you think?"

"More of a failure to launch sort of thing, if you ask me. I just can't seem to leave home."

Both she and Miss P seemed fine with it, so I guess I could grant them their wish. "Miss P, will you ask Jeremy to do something for me?"

The Beautiful Jeremy Whitlock, her much younger husband and Vegas's primo PI, was my go-to guy when in a pinch and needing someone who wouldn't mind sticking a toe across the line.

"Sure."

"Will you have him run the names of everyone on the suspect list through the prison database for the penitentiary in Huntsville, Texas?"

"Can you narrow it down?"

"The names, no. The time frame, yes. Start in the early 80's." She accepted that and got on the phone.

The door flew open, banging off its stops. Amazingly, I

didn't spill a drop of my coffee—I must be dead.

Flash skidded to a stop, saving herself from face-planting over my legs.

"You could've moved," she pretended to grouse.

"And spoil the fun?" I took a sip of coffee, resisting the sigh of contentment as I eyed her.

Today was neon orange, yellow, and lime green day. Normally, Flash wore one-size-fits-all Spandex, but today she had on a pair of high-waisted bell-bottoms and platform shoes. The personification of bad taste and disheveled excitement.

"Phone Peter Max, the 70's is looking for that outfit."

She fluffed at her wild red curls, then straightened her short jacket—I was pretty sure if she turned around, Elvis would stare back at me. "Haven't you heard? What's old is new again."

I eyed her over the top of my mug as I breathed in the aroma. "There's hope for us all."

"Speak for yourself."

"Don't you want to know why I'm here? You're one hell of a hard woman to find, by the way."

"That's bull—you called Jerry and he told you. Security knows everything."

At Flash's crestfallen look, Miss P stifled a smile.

"But, all kidding aside, I'm really happy to see you. I know you wouldn't come in person unless you wanted to gloat, so I know it's going to be good."

"Good," she scoffed. "Please, I do *good* in my sleep."

That was a hanging curve ball waiting for me to hit it out of the park, but I didn't need to say it for her to hear it. All I had to do was raise an eyebrow.

"Cute." She waggled her phone at me. "But, if I were you, I'd make nice. You're going to want to see this."

I pulled my feet underneath me and bolted upright. "YouTube?" This time I did spill my coffee. Miss P handed me a tissue and I dabbed at the spots on my pants—thankfully, the dark blue had been a perfect color choice today. "Anything interesting?" I motioned for my staff to gather around as Flash pulled the chair next to mine around to face me.

She perched on the edge. Miss P leaned over her, with Brandy kneeling to get a closer view.

"I broke several laws to get these." She glanced up from her phone. "Had to pay for a couple of them, so that'll show up on my expense account."

"Cheaper than bail." Unable to hide my excitement, I moved closer. "Have you looked at all the footage?"

"Yeah, I got three videos. One was a bit fuzzy; the other two were decent. Three different angles, which is good. A video guy I know edited them together to give us a pretty good pano." She glanced around the group for a moment of drama building. "You guys ready?"

"Flash!" I gave her the satisfaction of my impatience.

The video started—the quality was surprisingly good. I let her do a complete run-through before stopping it. The feed picked up just before Turnbull staggered into the arena. "Okay, let's go through it slowly. Can you do slo-mo?" Flash nodded. I brought in the other two with an encompassing glance. "If anything looks odd or jumps out at you, speak up, okay?"

The bullpen attracted my attention first. Toby Sinclair was there, advancing on Turnbull in Darrin Cole's clown suit, who staggered away from him. The pen opened, the bull charged out—a thousand pounds of pissed off looking for somebody to kill. Turnbull turned in surprise. A few moments passed before folks realized what was happening, then they started yelling. Hard to tell who released the bull—folks were crowded around in front of the gate, including Sinclair and Turnbull. Then the gate flew open, knocking several people out of the way.

Turnbull turned to climb back out of the arena.

He saw someone, someone who scared him. He backed away, then turned, and with a drunken gait moved into the arena.

He could've been looking at Sinclair, but he'd known he was there waiting—he'd been running from him. Who else? I scanned the figures.

With no easy exit, he headed for the bull, waving his arms,

trying to get the bull's attention...trying to be a clown, to save the others. My heart hurt for him.

I turned my attention back to the figures huddled by the gate the bull had burst out of. Only one leaped out at me. A figure, his face hidden by a hoodie, his clothes nondescript, watched Turnbull until he dropped. Then the figure eased back into the crowd.

"Did you see that? Can you rewind maybe ten seconds?"

Flash did as I asked and we all huddled closer, focusing as she ran the video forward again.

"Any idea who that was?" I asked, but blank faces answered me.

"I'll take a screen shot," Flash said. "See if my friend can work some video voodoo."

We watched the video through three more times. The man remained hidden, no distinguishing features. He backed away then lurched through the crowd, up the stairs, then, in a halting gait, he disappeared.

Finally, I'd seen enough and leaned back. Flash remained perched on her chair, Brandy sat cross-legged on the floor, and Miss P propped one butt cheek on the corner of her desk. They all waited for a sign from me. "Miss P, did you get any security videos from Jerry?"

"Not yet. He's waiting for a time of death so he can narrow his search."

"Let's make a list of who we saw there."

Miss P took out a pen and paper. We tossed out names then double-checked our memories for accuracy against the video. At the end, she tore off the list and handed it to me. It was short. If Sinclair killed Turnbull, he had an accomplice.

Dora Bates was conspicuously absent. The vet, too, but he'd told us they'd been together. And Beckham said he'd been drinking at a bar somewhere on Paradise.

"I still can't put Dora Bates's murder with Turnbull's." I let out a slow breath as I looked around my little band of merry men. "Brandy, you go work with Jerry. Help his staff to find Beckham or anyone else we can identify anywhere in the hotel sometime last night. Flash, you see if you can get me any more on the person who pushed Turnbull into the arena, anything that might help identify him."

"What should I do?" Miss P asked, her pen poised.

"Keep me from shooting my mother."

They all knew not to ask.

My phone jangled for my attention.

Dane. "Whatcha got?"

"Two girls now. One waking up. The other one scared out of her boots."

"On my way."

FOR once, I decided to wait for the elevator instead of taking the stairs from my mezzanine-level office to the lobby below. Maybe I needed a moment to catch my breath, to throw a rope around my thoughts, torture metaphors...whatever...but, when the doors opened, I met my father face-to-face.

"I was just coming to find you," he said. Worry had frayed him around the edges, but guilt for keeping me in the dark was still nonexistent. He looked older than he had earlier today. "I'm glad I caught you out here."

He stepped out of the elevator before I could join him. "Can we talk out here? Fewer..."

"Eavesdroppers?"

He stepped to the railing and I joined him. Normally, we loved to look out over the bustling lobby, soaking up the fun below. Today, the pall hanging over us diminished the glow of monetary enhancement. Eager to avoid each other, we both stared at the crowd anyway.

"I've got to go get Bethany and her friend and work on finding a killer...or two. If you're not going to help..."

"Do you have any leads?"

"Some suspects, but nobody who stands out at the moment. More questions than answers."

"We had another murder, didn't we?" When he turned to look at me, his skin was as gray as granite.

Curious his use of the term "we." "Yes, in the Kasbah. A woman."

"With the rodeo?"

"Yes, the mother of one of the competitors."

"Do you know her name?" His voice was almost a whisper; yet, he held my gaze with his.

"Dora. Dora Bates."

He flinched.

If I hadn't been looking at him, I would've missed it. "You know her?"

"I'm not sure. I need to talk to your mother."

"Any idea why she would register under the last name Fiorelli?"

My father's head swiveled; his pained expression meeting my questioning one. "She did?" His voice was a strained whisper.

"That's the last name Bethany uses. Who the hell are the Fiorellis?"

He swallowed hard. "Ask your mother."

"You know how far I got last time."

Pushing him, trying to manhandle him, wouldn't work. Screaming and crying might, but that wasn't part of my pissed-off personality. "Well, when you two decide how much time you're willing to do for obstruction of justice—may I remind you that you both have two very young daughters who need their parents—let me know. Right now, I have to go try to catch a killer with, what I fear, is less than the whole truth. If I die, if *anyone* else dies and you and mother could have stopped it...I hope you two can live with it."

Turning my back, I dove into the open maw of the elevator, leaving him standing there.

I didn't turn around until the doors had shut.

Yeah, my final salvo was harsh, but the stakes were beyond high. And I was disgusted. If the Big Boss and Mona were covering up an old murder to save their skins and a new one happened, I would be without a family.

Thinking of my parents in those terms, that they could do that, left a pain in my gut.

CHAPTER TWELVE

*F*ROM the chair in the corner, Bethany glared at me as I skidded into Doc Latham's room. The doc, a bandage replacing his ball cap, looked a bit haggard but alive and aware. Blood had filled the white of one of his eyes and a bruise purpled his jaw on one side, probably a result of the fall after he'd been clobbered, but just a guess.

Poppy sat on the windowsill on the opposite side of the doc's bed. Paler than I remembered, her freckles darker against porcelain skin. "My father didn't hurt anybody." Emotion jolted her to her feet, her posture stiff, her hands knotted at her sides.

"He clobbered the doc. Darn near spilled his brains."

That took the starch out of her. "But he didn't *kill* anybody."

"Not a big leap from crushing someone's skull." I advanced on her. "Who tied the halter to the slats of your stall?"

"What?" the girl looked like she had no idea what I was talking about.

"The halter. It's dragging on the ground in front of your horse's stall, the rope tied through the slats."

"I'd never do that. That's one of the first things my father drilled in my head. You leave it like that and a horse could get his foot tangled. If that happened, the horse would freak and break a leg or something."

Of course! *That's* what had been bothering me! It's been a

long time, but I'd heard that same thing only in a voice from my past.

"Any idea who tied it there?"

"Someone who doesn't care about horses."

"Not helpful. Tell me who you were yelling at and why when the bull got loose in the arena."

"The doc, here. He was heading out. I thought maybe he could do something."

"I think you're mistaken," the doc said. "I wasn't there." His eyes turned to mine. "I was upstairs on the mezzanine having dinner with Dora."

"I saw you. I couldn't see your face, but I knew it was you..." Poppy trailed off, looking unsure. "At least, I thought it was you." She looked at Bethany, who shrugged. "I guess that's why he didn't answer," she said to me.

Two against one, I couldn't argue. Trying to separate lies from not in this group was a bit of a challenge. Had neither of these girls ever read the story of the little boy who cried wolf?

Why did teenagers always think that, because of their superior intellect, they could easily manipulate all of us advancing on our dotage? Was I ever that stupid?

Ever or still? That was the more accurate question.

Bethany saved me from my awkward fence straddle. "I want to talk to Mona, now."

I whirled on her. "I'll get to you in a minute. And you're in no position to demand anything."

After pasting on a forced smile, I turned to Dane. "Having fun?"

"Shits and giggles. I thought it best to keep them apart and quiet so they couldn't gang up on me or coordinate stories."

He was thinking and trying, both of which I appreciated. After scrolling through the photos on my phone to the most recent—where others had friends, animals, or exotic destinations, I had a montage of two murders—I handed the phone to him. "I'll handle the girls if you could take a look at these and tell me if anything stands out."

"Why me?"

"Well, you *are* a PI, and you have the whole cowboy thing down pat—a world I'm not familiar with."

He nodded. "Deal." He retreated to the hall but stayed where I could see him.

I had no idea whether I'd answered the question he'd really been asking. "Okay, you two," I speared each one of the girls with my best maternal *you're dead* look. "You have to tell me what's going on."

"I told you, we don't know." Bethany crossed her arms and lowered her chin, a look Mona would use in the same situation.

My look needed work. "But you do know about the lipstick."

A surprised look passed between the two girls.

Bingo. "I've met Ms. Bates. Tawny Rose suits her, don't you think?"

"Mrs. Bates," Bethany huffed. "She's crazy as hell."

"How so?" I leaned against the wall, one hand on a hip, and gave Doc Latham, the man caught in the middle who looked like he'd run if he could, a sympathetic look.

"I can second that," the doc said. "She's erratic. Exhibits classic signs of some mental issues, bipolar if I could hazard a guess."

"I thought you were sweet on her?"

He gave a self-conscious shrug then winced. "There's all kinds of crazy."

"You and Doreen's mom?" Poppy looked like she'd smelled week-old fish that'd been left in the sun. "That's gross." Then she whirled on her friend. "You knew about this, Bethany?"

"No." She feigned indignation, but it fell flat, fooling no one.

"How could you not tell me?" Color rose in Poppy's face.

"What difference would it make?"

With the girls a bit at odds, I pressed. "What about Doreen? That's the daughter's name, right?"

"Tough being a kid with a nutcase for a mother." Bethany's attitude grated.

"Your sensitivity needs some work. Mental illness is not crazy."

"Whatever."

Ah, the word, the inflection to define a generation.

Intent on the murder, I'd momentarily forgotten that Dora Bates's murder wasn't common knowledge—and the people in this room would be profoundly affected by it. I cycled down the attitude. "Where is Doreen? Do either of you know? Was she part of this whole scheme?"

"What scheme?" Bethany still pretended superiority.

"Planting her lipstick at the scene of the murders." They had to be behind it.

Doc's head swiveled to his assistant. He sucked air in between his teeth against the pain, but he kept the mad and the hurt. "You did that? What would make you do such a thing?"

Bethany pressed her lips into a thin line.

Poppy stared at her friend. "How—"

"Shut up," Bethany hissed.

"She used the name Tawny Rose when she came to see me. I don't believe in coincidences."

"Jesus, Beth, that's so lame." Poppy looked disgusted.

"I hadn't thought she'd ask me my name." That got an eye roll from her friend.

"Poppy, where were you in the afternoon before Turnbull got killed?"

"Hanging out at the rodeo. Darrin was showing me some rope tricks."

"He was there all day?"

"I didn't pay that much attention, but yeah, I think so."

She was acting pretty complacent about the whole thing. In fact, both the girls were. I had just the dynamite to break this loose, but I felt terrible about using it. "Doc, I'm sorry to tell you this, but there was a murder at my hotel last night."

He pressed back, dodging a blow. "Dora?" he whispered, as if giving voice to the horror would make it true.

"I'm so sorry."

His face went slack with shock. "She was a good woman. Had some trouble, that's all. Her family didn't know what to do with her. Put her in a sanitarium somewhere up north. They helped her, gave her meds, stabilized her." His eyes filled with tears as he looked at me. "She was fine when she took her meds, but they were expensive. The generics didn't work, but the real stuff was ten times as expensive. You can imagine the fights with the insurance bastards. Sometimes she ran out."

The girls had lost their defiance. Both blinked at me with big eyes as they processed their part in this mess.

"Want to tell me what the deal was with the lipstick?"

I waited to see who would find their decency first.

Bethany. "Sometimes, Mrs. Bates would talk about needing money, about how the insurance company would pay if the horses died. I figured she was crazy enough to go through with it. I wanted the cops to check her out, but I didn't want to snitch."

"Now, we've gotten Mrs. Bates killed." The emotion in Poppy's voice was hard to read. Horrified, yet juiced by the power? Hard to tell, but, whatever it was, it didn't have the right ring to it.

"Maybe, but I don't think so. There's more going on here. You don't string...do what the killer did to Mrs. Bates because of money. Not emotional enough. There's something else."

"What'd he do?" Poppy's voice dropped conspiratorially.

"Crazy does some weird shit," Dane mumbled as he sauntered back into the room, his attention on my phone.

"Excuse me?"

He looked up to find us all staring. "Oh, sorry. I think you're going to want to see this." He motioned me out into the hallway.

I stayed in the doorway, my back to the room. "What?"

He leaned in and lowered his voice, "Seriously creepy shit in those last pics. Whoever did that..."

Damn, why did he have to smell so good? "I got that far on my own, thanks." I glanced back over my shoulder. The girls were now perched on either side of Doc's bed. Bethany held his hand.

Dane took the hint and stepped back, out of my space...barely.

Normally, I'd be bothered he didn't totally vacate, but when murder was close, I took comfort in holding close friends closer. And, as mad at him as I was, he was my friend—although I wasn't ready to tell him that.

"Look here." He held the phone between us where I could see. "It's really about the rope." He pointed to a photo of the rope around Mr. Turnbull's neck. "See the red and blue threads running through the rope?"

I got closer and squinted. Fine threads I'd overlooked before, wound over and under the hemp. "Yeah."

"A signature. Custom rope makers use them, and they are as identifiable as a Paul Revere stamp on the bottom of a silver tureen."

A cowboy who knew his silver. Somewhere, a Southern mother smiled. "Yeah, I'd gotten that far. I need you to chase down who made it. I'd like to ask him some questions."

I had a feeling Darrin Cole was lying to me. Screwing his fellow rodeo folks by jacking the price indicated a strong inclination to squeeze a penny so hard Lincoln screamed. Someone like that wouldn't buy the ropes from a middleman. He'd go straight to the source. The fact that Darrin Cole wouldn't share that info with me was like dangling a red cloth in front of a bull. Even though Poppy had given him an alibi, I still wasn't going to let him off the hook. He was around when Turnbull was killed. "Can you find out who made this rope?"

"Easily enough. But look here." He scrolled through to a photo of Mrs. Bates. "Same signature on this rope."

Needing a bit of support, I opted for leaning against the doorjamb, safer that way. Dane oozed his normal charm, but he looked tired and a bit off his feed. Somehow, I resisted the urge to comfort him. Falling into quicksand unawares was one thing, stepping into it on purpose a whole other thing.

"The way I see it, either the rope is a specialty item with few sales, mainly to killers, which would be awesome, or the rope is mass-produced and sold everywhere, getting us nowhere. Which bet would you place?"

"Neither. I prefer to hope for the best." He waited for a beat, but I didn't respond to the subtext. "I'll chase it for you—if that's okay?"

Was I going to let him back in the game? "You lied to me."

"I lied to myself."

Not the whole story, but a step toward...what? "Let me know what you find."

As I turned my back and stepped into the room, I speared Bethany with as sharp a look as I could muster. "You and me, we have some talking to do." I motioned for her to follow me into the hall.

"What do you want me to do right now?" Dane asked as I slipped by him in the doorway.

"Can you do some of your sleuthing from here?"

He held up his phone. "Computer in a pocket."

"Good, then sit tight for a bit, if you would?"

"Sure thing." He went back into the room, leaving Bethany and me alone in the hall.

I cut to the chase. "Want to tell me why the Reno police are looking for you?"

Again, the big-eyed blinking thing, this time coupled with a blank stare.

"Don't bother making up some tall tale. It wouldn't be in your best interest right now. You're leaving dead people in your wake and you need some serious help. The truth really is your best bet here, trust me on that." Depending on what she'd done, I wasn't a hundred percent sure of that, but I went with it.

"They want to know what happened to the doc." Her voice was flat, devoid of emotion as if fear had tamped her feelings down to empty resignation. She ran the zipper on her fleece up and down.

"Dr. Dean?" At least she wasn't trying to hide what she knew. If she was surprised I knew his name, she didn't let on. "Tell me about him."

The zipper: up and down, up and down, faster now. "He was this old guy; he owned the place. He was a vet. He's the one that got me interested. He was one of the few who cared."

"So, he kept coming around?"

"Yeah, he was nice. But my grandmother was always cool to him. There was something there, but she never told me what."

"Why'd he come around?" The grating zipper got on my nerves, but I didn't stop her.

"When the animals got sick, he'd come no matter the time. Never charged us. He always let me help him. Sometimes, he'd drop by and pick me up to make rounds with him. He always had stories about the rodeo."

"Really? Did he work on the rodeo?" I glanced over my shoulder at Doc Latham, who was talking with Poppy.

"Yeah. He was ready to retire, which surprised me because he always said he couldn't wait to get back out on the road. But I knew when he did, he'd feel guilty about leaving his patients behind. That's where Doc Latham came in."

"How so?"

"Dr. Dean hadn't been feeling all that good. He said it was his heart. Then Doc Latham showed up. Dr. Dean seemed sort of conflicted but he let Doc Latham take his truck and sub for him here. He told me it was for the best."

"You do know somebody killed him?"

Her hand stopped mid-zip. "No, they didn't," she whispered. "He had a heart attack."

"Who told you that?"

"Gram." She swallowed hard and tears swam in her eyes. "Gram..." Bethany's voice hitched, reminding me she was just a kid learning how disappointing and downright terrifying adults could be. She had lost her bellwether. When Mona abandoned me, I had thought I'd lost mine. The panic stayed with me still.

Her hands dropped to her sides, and she pulled herself up straight, but I could see what it cost her.

Being a grown-up sucked most of the time. Having to pretend to be one sucked way more. "Before she died, Gram told me some bad things happened. And if anything happened to her, I needed to find my mother. She would know how to fix it."

I saw the plea in her eyes.

When?

Something was wrong, very wrong. "She didn't just die, did she?"

Bethany's lip quivered.

"My grandmother." For a moment, the girl looked as if she was made of stone, then a crack grew into a fissure. "You're right, she didn't die. Somebody killed her." She gulped air, struggling to get the words out. "I came home, and there was so much blood...and he'd strung her up, upside down with a straitjacket on." Tears overwhelmed her and she fell into my arms.

Caught off guard, I staggered back but then steadied under her weight, such as it was. She was all bones and no meat. What kind of life would do that?

Rhetorical question—it made me feel better. At least I knew the answer.

"He killed her?" I held her tight, and her sobs reverberated through me. "Who?"

"I don't know." The words came in gasps between ragged, tortured breaths. "He...won't...stop."

"Why didn't you tell me this before?"

"Would you have believed me?" She swiped at the tears that wouldn't stop.

"I would have no reason not to. Now you've done your whole smoke and mirrors routine, and it's hard for me to figure out where the truth stops and the lies begin." The urge to take her and drop her in mother's lap overwhelmed me. It was time for the two of them to meet and the truth to come out.

Secrets. My family legacy. Why couldn't it have been a key to Fort Knox? Did they still keep the nation's gold there? Or better yet a superpower or something useful?

My vision swam. I pulled in air, but somewhere it got waylaid before it hit the gray matter. My thoughts swarmed like bees disturbed from the hive. One would alight briefly, only to buzz off to join the swarm when I reached for it.

Was this all about the girl?

No matter the angle, I couldn't make that theory fit. If he'd wanted her, he'd had plenty of opportunities to grab her...or worse. No, he was after something else...or someone else.

Mona.

"How can they be related? Mr. Turnbull? Where does he fit in with your grandmother and the doc in Reno? Is this an extortion scheme? Or an insurance scam? Or something else?"

"I don't know. I can't figure it out. I've tried. I'm so scared. That's why I came here, to find you...and Mona. Gram said you would have answers."

Gram was overstating.

I rubbed her back as she clung to me. Now I understood what she wanted. And how she found me.

But the why still eluded me.

Why her? Why the rodeo? What the fuck was going on?

A text dinged. For a moment, I thought about not reading it, but I needed answers almost as bad as Bethany did. I snaked one hand into my pocket, searching for my phone.

Romeo. *Any idea where Doreen Bates is? We talked to her. Sent a psych to help. Now she's gone.*

I raised my head and brought the others in the room in with a look. "If you needed to find Doreen, where would you look?"

"Do you think he took her?" Bethany's voice was a whisper against my neck.

"If he did, I'll kill him myself." Children were off limits in my book, and once someone crossed that line, there was no redemption. "The police are doing their best, but we could use your help. Any inside scoop?"

Bethany tugged me back into the room. "Poppy, do you know where Doreen is?"

"Sure," Poppy sounded confident. "She's with her horse. Since all this has started, she's slept in his stall and spends the days sitting in his hay bin. She's terrified something is going to happen to him."

"With her mother a bit unstable, that horse is all she has," Doc Latham added. "I used to bring her a hotdog before I left for the night."

"Anybody else know?"

"No, her mother thought she was with me," Poppy said.

Note to self: Never have kids. Not ever. "So, the three of you cover for each other and fancy yourselves modern-day Nancy Drews."

Bethany pulled herself off my neck and leaned back to give me a look. "Who?" she said, pulverizing my youth-fantasy.

"Never mind." I tried not to grump.

Having something to do, someone to save, seemed to restore Bethany's backbone. "Let me try her cell."

I don't think anyone in the room drew a breath while we waited. After multiple rings, Bethany shook her head. "Rolled to voice mail, but sometimes cell service is sketchy in the barn."

That was one of those I-know-it-isn't-true-but-let's-roll-with-it things. We all bought in—the hook of a silver lining to hang our hope on. "Can you take me to her?...quickly."

As the three of us ran down the hall, I jotted off a quick text to Romeo. *Where are you?*

Stuck at the Babylon.

Okay, I'm on Doreen. Meet up after.

I pocketed the phone and ran after the girls.

Dane was on my heels.

NIGHT had covered the city and lit its magic, but none of it brightened my mood and all of it blurred as I sped through the city at the speed of heat. I focused on driving, pushing thoughts of kids and killers out of my head. She'd be okay. She had to be. I wouldn't allow otherwise.

In the past, I thought Mona was the closest I'd come to homicide.

I was wrong.

The parking lot at the Thomas and Mack was empty. No crowds circled the building as I bounced up the rise into the lot. Bethany let out a yelp as her head hit the roof. The girls were stacked in the passenger seat, Bethany on top.

The Ferrari had a few limitations, but speed wasn't one of them, and tonight speed was what I needed. We'd lost Dane somewhere on the 15.

And maybe knocking Bethany on the head might impart some sense. Jesus, now I was subscribing to my mother's silly theories. The apocalypse was near.

The car fishtailed in the dirt, then I regained control. "Awesome," Poppy whispered. The sentiment surprised me. But Ferraris and breaking the traffic laws weren't part of her world as they were mine.

The rodeo had gone dark. Don't know why that hadn't crossed my mind. A man had died. A woman, too, but that wasn't yet common knowledge. A time to pay respects.

And to catch a killer.

The dirt clouded around us as I slid to a stop. Doc's truck hadn't moved. Dirt covered the yellow crime scene tape, which sagged in places, making the whole thing look like bad Halloween staging.

The girls piled out of the Ferrari and took off running. I was a step behind.

In Vegas, if there was no crowd, then the show was failing. Tonight, I was grateful someone had called off the crowd.

We ran, unhindered. Rounding a corner. Halfway down. We all skidded to a stop.

The stall was empty.

Well, the horse was there, but no Doreen.

"Shit." I was on the verge of apoplexy.

The girls were fine, not the least bit winded—further proof there was no God, or, if there was, she wasn't smiling on me.

Bethany lifted the latch and threw her weight against the

door, pulling it open. Poppy and I stuck our noses through the bars.

"Any sign of Doreen?" I asked, ever hopeful.

Bethany didn't answer. Instead, she spoke in soothing tones to the horse. Kneeling next to him, she stroked his neck. Something came over her, a calmness as if this was her place. The horse responded, nuzzling into her.

A friggin' sixteen-year-old horse whisperer. "What do you see?"

Poppy nudged me. "Shhhh. She's got something."

"There're letters carved in his neck," Bethany said.

"What?" I cringed back. First kids, now animals. What kind of sicko *was* this?

"Not carved." Bethany's voice never changed to angry, but I knew she vibrated with it...she had to. "Shaved."

I breathed a sigh. "He didn't hurt the horse?"

Something about my smile made the girl smile. "No."

Somehow, not hurting the horse was important to me. Like it was the very last little thread of my rope. "Okay, what does it say?"

"S. S."

I turned my back and leaned against the stall. Defeat rested heavy on my shoulders.

S.S.

I hadn't a clue.

And Doreen was gone.

"Okay, we're both assuming something bad happened to Doreen. Her mother's dead. Where would she go?"

Both girls shrugged. "Here."

"Okay, let's look for her then."

We'd traversed half the barn, calling out. No one answered.

"We need to split up," Poppy said.

"Not on your life. You two stick with me."

We'd made it through the barn and stood in the large opening in the back. I'd scanned the parking lot twice when movement caught my eye. “There? Who’s that?”

A slight figure walked toward us, head down, tucking in her shirttail.

“Doreen!” Both Bethany and Poppy shouted as they ran.

I wasn’t far behind.

Doreen, all blonde hair and chiseled features, smiled when she saw the girls. She grabbed them, one in each arm, then she looked at me over the tops of their heads. Almost my height, she looked a year or two older than the other two.

I introduced myself. “I’m sorry about your mother.”

“Thanks.” She seemed sad but not broken up.

The damage parents can do.

The girls started chattering excitedly, just happy to find their friend.

When they wound down, I used the lull to get a word in. “Where were you? You had us panicked.”

“I just was taking a shower at the trailer. Becky and Suzie let me use their facility. They’re the best.” It was clear Doreen wanted as little to do with her mother as possible. Well, she got her wish.

“You and your mother weren’t close?”

“No. I didn’t want her here. She...”

“I get it.” I felt sorry for her. Women with difficult mothers were legion. I was one of them, but Doreen Bates put my mother in a whole new light.

“And then when Doc showed up, Mother was at her worst, it seemed.”

“Really? Why?”

“I don’t know. She never was good around men, but she didn’t have the best picker either.”

I could so relate. “He wasn’t here all the time?”

“Off and on, when Dr. Dean would get sick.”

Dr. Dean.

“He joined us full-time in Reno, that’s what mother said.”

Bethany pulled away and looked at me. “We need to talk to Mona...now.” Bethany’s demand was hard to ignore, and the rationale overwhelming, but I couldn't take her to Mona.

The kid was leaving bodies in her wake. How many now? Three? Four? She had the opportunity to kill all of them as far as I could tell, the access to the barbiturates, and a motive...revenge. No way was I playing the part of the Trojan Horse, helping the killer get past all defenses.

"I've spoken with her. Not now. This is my call and I expect you to honor it. I can help you, but my first job is keeping everyone safe, including my mother. If the killer is using you..." I left it there, hoping her imagination could fill in the list of horribles I pictured. If all of this was really related. And if somehow the killer was using Bethany to get to my parents. Or if she was the killer...

Then I wasn't going to facilitate that.

Mona and the Big Boss were hiding something big, something cataclysmic; otherwise, my mother would be looking to me to solve it.

But who was Turnbull and why was he killed?

And what did Toby Sinclair have to do with any of this?

And why Dora Bates? And why in the manner she was? Which was just like Sara Pickford.

And Doc Latham coming and going.

And where the hell was Beckham?

Until I had answers, I was going to limit access to my parents. I knew my mother. If the Big Boss was threatened by the past, by what Mona knew, even a kid with a sad story couldn't force the answers out of her.

Not even her own kid.

I was living proof.

CHAPTER THIRTEEN

WITH no answers and no clear path, I stashed the two girls at the Babylon with a security detail to make sure they stayed put. Doreen wanted to stay with Becky and Suzie. At eighteen, Doreen could do what she wanted. I'd told Dane to go home and get some rest.

Romeo was still tied up, no pun intended this time—with the vision of Mrs. Bates in my head, I couldn't stomach the humor—so I'd told him to meet me at JCB Prime at Cielo. Yes, right now I needed my happy place. And more and more I was calling a barstool home. Not good. I knew that. But nothing I could or would do about it.

I was motoring south on the Strip headed to Cielo when Flash caught me.

"Got something for you." Her voice carried her own special kind of breathless, which meant she was telling the truth.

I wasn't sure how I felt about that. The truth cut both ways. Resigned to the inevitable, I said, "Besides Sara Pickford being murdered, that much I've learned. Give me what else you got."

"I hate it when you do that. That was like my best pitch."

"We both need a very long vacation from reality."

"Hey, speak for yourself. My reality is a twenty-five-year-old Italian working on a Ph.D. in Archaeology."

"Which means he will expect you to pay for everything, then leave you broke and heartbroken."

"Thanks. Sour grapes coming from someone whose reality

is murder."

She had me there. "Remind me why I keep you as a friend?"

"Blackmail. So, do you want it straight or do you want me to be entertaining?"

"I like murder served like whiskey."

"Straight it is. The doc was sort of a run-of-the-mill murder, nothing elaborate."

"You mean other than being strung up upside down in a straitjacket?"

"Damn. That was my second best pitch."

I didn't tell her I was guessing. First Dr. Dean, then Sara Pickford, now Dora Bates. "Let me guess, barbiturates."

"Bingo. That's why they want your girl—contact with the stiffs and access to the murder weapon."

"Weak but understandable. What about Dr. Dean's son?"

"They're still looking for him. I do have some skinny on Sara Pickford. She was a bit more interesting, not because of what I know, but because of what I don't. On the surface, an above-board rancher's wife. Dabbled in entertainment. Married...a lot. But here's the interesting thing: she had two daughters, twins. I can't find a trace of either. I tracked them until they were fourteen. Everything looked boringly normal, then, poof, they were gone. Disappeared."

"Any idea why?"

"Not a one. Not unless they were married off, which I doubt. We're talking Basque country up in Northern Nevada—they are staunch Catholics. I'm still digging."

"Okay, thanks. Anything on Dora Bates?"

The sound of pages flipping echoed through the line as I motored up the driveway to Cielo. I should feel like I was coming home, but I didn't. I felt oddly disconnected, like I had as a child when Mona had sent me to Vegas. What was wrong with me? It would probably take a battalion of shrinks and more money and patience than I had.

An excuse, an avoidance strategy. Even I could hear it.

"She's sort of that typical mid-American, mid-century sob

story."

"A woman with a brain born in a time and a place where subservience was her only path?"

Flash gave a low whistle. "Oh, that's even a bit cynical for you."

"Am I wrong?" The valet opened the door. I left the key and stepped out, using his proffered hand to help lever my bulk from the low machine.

"Not really. Life was so bad, apparently, she needed help from the mental-health professionals. A sanitarium upstate, just north of Sparks. She was released last year—her third extended stay. First time, she was a kid. Tough road."

"There but for the grace of the Powers That Be..."

"Amen, sister."

"Place shut down years ago, so that's all the info I got. Chasing old news articles, but there's not much. Can't find anyone who'll even talk about the place."

"Not sure it's important. Was she from the Reno area?" A connection would be nice. I crossed my fingers—stupid but I had nothing else, no lucky rabbit's foot, no dried body parts.... Rico's revelation still made me cringe.

"No, somewhere east of Bum-Fuck, Indiana."

"There is no place by that name." Why her vernacular bothered me right now, I don't know. Developing sensibilities this late in the game was remote at best.

"There is if you're a girl born in the late sixties, early seventies, and have ambitions beyond..."

"Bum-Fuck Indiana, I get it. The American Dream." Women have been shackled by that dream far too long. All opportunities, with equal pay, for everyone willing to work for them. Why was that so hard?

Vegas. I was so glad I'd landed in Sin City where everyone had a chance, although, sexism was still rampant. I was a Pollyanna but not that gullible.

Another battle...for today, tomorrow, and every other day.

So many inequities in the world...including murder. *Focus, Lucky, focus.*

"Let me know when you have something more. You've given me more pieces to the puzzle. Pretty soon it'll start to take shape."

Fantasy, always better than reality.

HUNGRY, angry, worried, and wired, I made a pass through Cielo. The lobby was full, everyone happy and well-libated. Nothing needed my attention, so I headed upstairs, taking the public elevators and using the front entrance to JCB like I was a real person.

Only ten o'clock, so the place was full, the staff sliding between tables, the vibe elegant yet happy. I eased onto a stool at the bar. The bartender didn't even ask. With a flourish, he produced a crystal flute, then filled it with pink bubbles.

"You look like you're carrying a load." The young man tried to be sympathetic, which I appreciated. But there was a huge gap of years and ugliness he couldn't begin to comprehend, much less cross.

"Jet lag." At least I could say it with a straight face.

Jean-Charles would be busy in the kitchen, so I didn't bother him. There wasn't anywhere else I'd rather be, so I nursed my bubbles. I'd exhausted the limit of my contacts; the cops were chasing the leads I'd uncovered, minimal as they were. I had no desire to be around my family—whatever had happened between us still burned.

Halfway through my second glass, a body slipped onto the empty stool next to me. I moved to give him room, but I didn't look; frankly, I didn't care and was way beyond small talk.

"Hey." Romeo.

Okay, his small talk I could do. "You look like you're wasting away." I motioned to the bartender. "A platter of sliders, please. Tell the chef it's for Lucky and Romeo. He'll know what to do."

"Yes, ma'am."

I'd resigned myself to being of Ma'am vintage, but it rankled. Couldn't they at least pretend I was still of the Miss variety?

Romeo leaned across the bar to get the bartender's attention as he focused on entering our food order into the computer. When he had it, he pointed to the shelves of bottles behind the bar. "That bottle there, third shelf, in the middle, the Wild Turkey 101."

"A glass for you, yes sir."

"And the bottle."

Romeo settled back on his stool as we both stared at him.

At the bartender's questioning look, I gave a slight nod, then I braced Romeo. "I was going to ask you if you'd found anything, but I guess I have my answer."

We both watched the bartender pour several fingers of amber liquid into a glass in front of Romeo. He left the bottle next to the glass—perfectly staged like an advertisement showing the hazards of our lifestyles.

Romeo took a long pull—he didn't even choke.

"Impressive, but you can't do that for long."

"Right." He clinked his glass against my flute. "You're the poster child for liquid sustenance. What have you had to eat today?" Point made.

"So?"

"Once we got Mrs. Bates down, I waited while the coroner and his team got the straitjacket off. Underneath, she still had on a blue jean jacket that she or someone else had done all this fancy stuff to."

"Bejazzled."

"If you say so."

"Anyway, on the underside of the sleeves from the cuffs back about halfway to the elbow..." He paused, taking another sip of his medicinal spirits.

I knew my cue. "Let me guess. Little red ball thingies."

"You get a gold star. One was missing."

"Okay, so we have Beckham lurking around the Babylon. He saw that I found the red ball thingy in the pony's stall. He had barbiturates. Things are lining up against our man with the bad temper."

"We've got all assets working on finding him," he said in answer before I could ask.

In the mirror backing the bottles behind the bar, I caught sight of my chef bringing our platter of hamburgers. Watching him work his way through the crowd, I must've smiled.

"You are going to marry him, right?" Romeo asked.

That startled me out of my lascivious thoughts. "I said yes, didn't I?"

"That's not an answer, that's avoidance. Why'd you sleep at the hotel last night?"

"It was late." Even I heard the lame in that excuse.

"You've been gone a week, and the first night you're back you sleep by yourself." He let the accusation hang between us like raw meat bleeding out, before continuing, "You know you have a habit of doing this."

"What? Sleeping by myself?" I lowered my voice as the bartender was sneaking closer for a good listen. Then I glanced back at the mirror. Jean-Charles had been waylaid by a table of four who were fawning.

"No, keeping people at bay, then letting them go when it gets uncomfortable."

"I do not." Smacked by the truth, I feigned indignity.

He threw back the rest of his drink, then poured himself another couple of fingers. "Just not with this one, not until you're sure. Okay?"

Jean-Charles's voice grew closer. Without turning, I could sense him close behind me. Of course, the aroma of the burgers helped...or that's what I told myself. I snuggled toward him as he planted a kiss on my neck.

After lingering for a moment, breathing me in, he raised the platter on one hand over our heads, setting it in front of us with a flourish. "*Voila.*"

His inhibitions buried under the booze, Romeo didn't waste any time in snagging two, which he mashed together, then took a huge bite.

I turned on my stool, capturing my chef between my legs, which had the added advantage of blocking Romeo from view. Sliding my hands down Jean-Charles's arms, I captured his hands in mine. The look on his face held a wisdom I lacked, but my heart matched the love. "I'm sorry."

He gave one of his patented Gallic shrugs that I found endearing. "My heart is sad without you close, but I know your life—"

"—is no excuse. Balance, right?" I let loose of one hand to reach up and brush back his hair where it just curled over his collar. Then I caressed his cheek with the backs of my fingers.

He leaned in to my touch and closed his eyes. When he opened them, they were a light, untroubled blue. "You have ice feet, then?"

I felt a smile start to bloom. "Cold feet?"

"Yes, this," he said, and I couldn't tell whether he was misusing the words on purpose, knowing how much I enjoyed it when he did.

Romeo cleared his throat.

I could do this on my own without his stage direction, but his concern made me smile. "Yes, a bit, I think. Marriage is not something I ever thought of for myself."

"Why not?" At my discomfort, he looked around as if remembering where we were. "Perhaps you will tell me later? We can talk about it over a bottle of the fabulous wine I have discovered from Santorini. Very dry, lots of minerals, you will love it."

"I love you. And that sounds perfect." I barely managed the words before he covered my mouth with one of his patented best-kisses-ever.

And the world disappeared.

Romeo's phone jangled for attention, jarring me back a little. I didn't let go of my chef, preferring to linger in the kiss, keeping the real world at bay a few ticks longer.

As Romeo addressed whatever minor issue was at hand, Jean Charles pulled back. "Trust your heart. Do only what it says. But, I will tell you, mine says we will be very good, you and I."

Romeo barked a few curt words that I only half-heard. After he repocketed his phone, he leaned around Jean Charles to get my attention. "Hate to break this up, but we gotta go." In addition to rising pink in his cheeks, he had a touch of Béarnaise sauce at the corner of his mouth.

"You've got something here?" I touched my mouth to show him where.

He swiped at it with his napkin, then threw it on the bar. "Come on." He backed off his stool.

Jean-Charles stepped out of the way and extended a hand to help me off the stool. He motioned to the bartender who had stayed close, a puppy eager to please. "Wrap up those hamburgers. Ms. O'Toole needs to go." He gave me a smile. "You must eat. Promise me."

"I will." A bit conflicted about diving into Romeo's world again, I turned to the detective. "What's the rush?"

"We have Beckham."

*A*S it turned out, the "we" meant me. Jerry had Beckham sequestered in our very own holding cell in the lower reaches of the hotel. Normally, we reserved it for belligerent drunks, allowing them to sleep it off, or bellow it off, their choice. But they did it far from prying eyes, which was good for everyone concerned.

Romeo followed hot on my heels as I took him into the bowels. "I've never been down here."

"We try to keep the police out."

He grabbed the back of one of my sweater sleeves as he stepped on the back of my heel. "Seriously? What do you do down here?" The kid had returned.

"Thumbscrews and waterboarding."

"Wow, seriously? Is that how you do it?"

I whirled around to give him the full force of sarcasm and

ran into a big grin, which made me laugh and made my heart happy—he was truly back.

Now, if I could hang onto me. How to do that when relationships were shifting like dunes in the desert?

Jerry met us at the elevator. Even after the craziness of New Year's Eve, he was spit and polished, pressed and creased. Was it easier for men to do that? Or was I a terrible failure to my gender and humanity in general? Of course, Jerry took a special pride in impeccable. A trim, Black man, his bald pate was shaved and polished to a rich brown shine, his face without a hint of a five-o'clock shadow, his collar open but stiff with starch, his khakis creased, his loafers polished. A flash of gold at his wrist completed the whole stepping-to-the-bridge-of-a-yacht-in-the-Med look.

He acknowledged Romeo with a nod. With me, he cut to the chase. "Brandy forwarded a photo. My staff did the rest. We found him sleeping off a serious bender—he ran up quite a tab at the Daiquiri Den."

"Where was he?"

"In one of the dumpsters behind the Bazaar. Trash guy took a look before he started the crusher. Beckham's one lucky dude."

"Is he sober now?"

"Enough. Being held for the police on a potential murder charge can do that."

Adrenaline, the antidote to inebriation, if it didn't kill you.

"You make the call," I said to Romeo, tossing the words over my shoulder.

"Why don't you do the questioning; then it's not an issue."

"It's an issue if you want to use the statement later." I stopped, forcing him to do the same. "Before we get to the holding cell and before Beckham can overhear, let's figure out how to play this. You're the boss."

The kid took that in stride and with only a slight widening of his eyes. "Why don't you ask him a few of the obvious questions and see what he says. After that, I can take him in. We can get him stone-cold and then put him under the bright light."

He really was starting to sound like me. I couldn't tell if that was progression, regression, or whether he wanted to communicate with me in my own dialect. "I like your style."

"Just a page out of your playbook."

Beckham rose from the chair in the middle of the cell and rushed toward us, his big hands grabbed the bars. "You going to let me out of here?" He shook his cage like an enraged animal desperate for freedom and willing to do anything for it.

He looked like a future homicide waiting to happen. If his unwavering stare was any indication, Jerry was his intended target.

Beckham's face was crimson. One eye was swollen shut and a gash in his lip still leaked blood.

I raised an eyebrow at Jerry. "He didn't want to come with us."

"And your men?"

"One has a broken arm, two others bruised ribs and various cuts and abrasions."

Mr. Beckham shifted his stare to me—this one had a bit less murder in it. The smell of yesterday's alcohol and cold sweat wafted off him in nauseating waves.

I expected him to start gnawing on the bars. "You've cut a rather wide swath. I doubt you'll get out of there anytime soon. You clocked Romeo and Doc Latham pretty good. Put the vet in the hospital. Not to mention our Security officers."

He let his hands drop, but anger still shivered through him. "I don't like cages."

"Me either."

"I'm sorry I hurt those men."

"And Dora Bates?"

Like a caged animal, resigned but looking for an opening, he darted a wild look back and forth between Romeo and me. "Shit. I about shit my pants when I saw her hanging there, upside-down like that." A faraway look displaced the anger in his eyes, like he'd gone back in time to be assaulted by the vision all over again. "God, the look on her face."

Having traveled back with him, I shivered.

Focus returned and reality dawned. "You can't think *I* had anything to do with her murder!"

But he knew the opposite. I could see it in his eyes and the veil of self-preservation that dropped across his face. "Well, let's review the facts. You took the little red ball thingy that we found in your daughter's horse's stall after someone had tried to kill the animal by injecting it with barbiturates. You assaulted the young detective here, and the vet, then stole more of the drug from the doc's van. Next, you were caught on video lurking around Dora Bates's murder scene. One of the red ball thingies was missing from her jacket. You put two and two together, didn't you, Mr. Beckham? You saw the red ball and knew exactly where it had come from, along with the lipstick that had been found at both crime scenes."

He backed away from the bars, putting distance between himself and my version of the truth, which sounded rather damning, even to me.

"The bitch tried to kill my baby's pony." The yowl of an angry, helpless animal.

"Maybe so. I'm not sure of that yet. But that's no reason to kill her."

Beckham snorted. "It's every reason in the world, but I didn't do it. She was dead when I got there."

"You'll have to do better than that. Why don't you start by telling us how you knew she was staying here?"

"I asked around."

"Who told you?"

"I got it from the kids."

The girls. "You headed over here to find Dora Bates after you assaulted Romeo and stole the barbiturates from Doc Latham's van?"

"Yeah, like you said, but I wasn't going to kill her. She needed to know I would fight back, that's all."

"You were mad as hell and weren't going to take it anymore."

"*The Network*," Romeo said under his breath as he leaned

in to me.

"You need a vacation," I whispered back, then turned to Beckham. "If you didn't kill her, who did? Any theories?" Mona always told me answering a question with a question was bad manners, but I'd always found it effective when grilling was involved.

With no ready answer, he appeared not to have thought about that, so I kept the floor. "So far, to hear you tell it, you're the only one who had a beef with her."

The fear returned to his eyes. "You have to believe me. I didn't kill her."

Romeo, who had been lurking behind, now stepped to my shoulder. "You look like a guy who knows the score and you know how this game is played."

Wow, and I thought cops only spoke like that on TV. Thankfully, I kept my snark to myself, but I did feel like the short half of the *Dragnet* team.

Beckham weighed what sounded like an offer but was semantically nothing more than a statement of fact. A few waggles of his head indicated his waffling. The red in his cheeks faded as serious replaced the anger.

"You give me something to catch the killer, and I'll not press charges. I can't speak for Lucky's security guards." Romeo waited, presumably for me to respond.

"I'll suggest they don't press charges, but it's up to them. But you have to deliver a killer."

"Extortion. That's what was going on."

"Pay or your pony dies," I said. I'd suspected that all along. "You can't be the only one." I wasn't going to share what I knew. "Who else?"

"Nobody wanted to talk about it. Everybody was scared. Especially since Reno. One of the horses ended up dead."

"She proved she wasn't bluffing."

"Yeah. After that, the chatter quieted. Turnbull was the only one who stepped up."

"He was helping you?" Romeo paused in his note-taking.

"More like tagging along." As he thought about his friend,

the fight left him. "Should've been me she tried for."

"The predators pull from the back of the pack." The stuff you learn from *National Geographic.* And as predators, humans were the most deadly. I felt for him, really I did. The responsibility for getting a friend killed would be a heavy burden, even for a guy with anger issues...maybe especially for a guy with anger issues. "You think she killed him?"

"Don't know. I was sure it was Dora Bates until someone hung her up. She was just enough of a whack job to do it."

I wanted to give him a lecture on mental illness, but Beckham was on a roll and I knew better than to derail a speeding train. He stepped back to the bars. Grabbing them, he got so close he practically poked his nose through. I resisted an involuntary urge to retreat.

The need to tell us spurred him on and he gained momentum. "She never had any money, always complaining about it. As if any of us was flush. We all struggled for our kids—this is an expensive sport. But every weekend, our teenagers are with us while their friends at home are getting into trouble."

"Hanging with their folks—something they'd never do without the incentive of a horse." The more I learned about rearing kids, the less I wanted to do it.

"Better than paying to get them out of whatever trouble they find." He pushed at the curls that stuck to his forehead. Sweat dripped off him and darkened half-moons in the pits of his shirt.

What exactly made him nervous? Getting out? Getting caught?

All of the above, if it'd been me. Against all my better instincts, I started feeling a bit sympathetic.

What would I do if someone was shaking down someone I loved?

"How much?"

"Always something barely affordable."

"Different amounts for each of you?" That sounded like a play Dora the front office accountant could pull off.

"At each new city, when we'd pick up our competitor packet, if we were to be targeted, a note would be in there. It would state the amount and where to leave it. All cash, of course, and unique to each location."

"Where in Vegas?"

"I don't know. This time I wasn't the target."

"Turnbull?"

"Yeah, he was pissed." His gaze drifted from mine as he looked over my shoulder, scoping the room.

"Looking for someone who'll believe you?"

His eyebrows lowered as he glared at me and rubbed his jaw. "Should've taken care of you when I met you."

Behind me, Romeo chuckled, but wisely let me run with it.

"Maybe, but I'm your best bet right now. Here's how it went down. You were the one who drew the line in the sand, and you convinced Turnbull to help you. He didn't have your balls. That's why they came after your horse."

He chewed on the inside of his mouth as he avoided the truth by staring into the dark behind me.

"Damn fool." Beckham's voice held his pain, putting him on the path to redemption.

So far, he was guilty of stupidity and arrogance and maybe excessive temper, though I couldn't be sure what I'd do in the same position. But Dora Bates still hung out there. The metaphor made me cringe.

"What was Turnbull doing that got him killed?" I thought I knew, but I needed to hear it from the horse's mouth. Pasting on a dispassionate look, I ignored myself and forced my few functioning brain cells to focus.

"I'd told him to go back to the hotel, that I'd wait for whoever was coming. He said he would. Why didn't he?" Beckham's grief rang with truth.

"Maybe he intended to. Did you think the extortionist would strike while the rodeo was just getting going for the evening, while everyone was around and the risk of being seen was greatest?"

"No!" Emotion filled that one word. "That surprised the

hell out of me. We figured the best time would be when everyone had left and the security guard had too much to keep an eye on all at once."

"The sensible time to do it." I would've assumed the same. "But they didn't."

"No."

"Is it possible Turnbull saw something? Surprised them in the act?"

Beckham's eyes widened. "Sure. His kid's horse was just down from my kid's. Before we left for the night, we always checked on them, threw them another flake of hay." His eyes filled with tears. "They're really sweet animals. Not so smart, and so trusting. Who would hurt them?"

"A deranged asshole without a heart." Vehemence punctuated my words, surprising Romeo, who shot me a look. "My pony saved my childhood. I told you that. You never forget."

"Turnbull wasn't a big guy," I said, trying to remember from his lifeless body. Darrin Cole's clown suit was big on him, and Darrin was a good bit smaller than me.

"Small but he was a scrapper," Beckham confirmed.

"So, if he saw someone hurting your horse, he'd jump them, wouldn't he?"

"Totally." Beckham sounded sad. "I shoulda been there."

He'd been drinking in a bar. His burden increased.

"You couldn't have known." A few of the tumblers clicked. "You showed up at the barn about when I did. That was the time you thought the rodeo would be ending and the killer would be ready to do his deed."

"A bit before, actually. Poppy called me, told me what had happened. When I met you, all of it had just hit me."

That was the closest a man like Beckham would come to an apology, especially to a woman.

Although I was earning his respect, albeit grudgingly given, a hint was there. As I did the talking, the postulating, he kept listening.

"And you were furious."

"Worse."

"So, when you saw the red ball thingy and the lipstick..."

"I went ballistic."

"Did you kill Dora Bates?"

"No." As he said it, he looked right in my eyes and never wavered. "I'd heard she was hanging out with the high rollers at your place, then when the lipsticks and the red thingy showed up, I was sure it was her."

"So, you stole the drugs from the doc and headed for my hotel, ready to give her what she had been giving?"

"Your hotel?" He gave a derisive snort. "Knew you were too smart to be a cop."

I didn't hazard a look at Romeo.

"Did you tie the halter rope to the stall?" I explained what I'd seen.

"No, nobody who knows anything about horses would do that."

"Any idea who did?"

"Nobody I know."

I didn't disabuse him of that notion. I felt sure it would end up, in fact, being someone he knew. Instead, I waited for Beckham to finish the story—he was already in so far, I knew he'd give me all of it. "Tell me the rest. Catching who's really behind all of this is your only ticket out of here. And I'm your best chance because I believe you. And I'd be the last person to want to see an innocent man on Death Row."

The reminder of the gravity of his situation took the last of the fight out of him. "My kid's mom took a powder." That fact alone explained a lot. "I've raised Poppy from the time she was barely dry. I'd put the world on my back and give it to her if I could."

Parents and the lengths they were willing to go for their spawn still surprised me. "I'm sorry."

Beckham reared back. "Don't be sorry. The woman did me a huge favor. Best gift ever, actually."

"What did you find when you got to Bungalow Twelve?"

"Door was open." From there, he described the scene

exactly as I'd found it. Of course, the killer would know that, as well as an innocent who stumbled on it.

"And the red ball thingy? Did it come from her jacket?" I held my breath. Curiously, I so wanted him to be innocent.

Beckham shrugged in resignation. "I don't know. She had that weird jacket thing on her, her hands tied up like that." A memory slithered through him, crawling under his skin. "Most of her jacket was under the thing. Only the collar showed, so I couldn't tell."

"What did you do then?"

"Ran." Pink crept into his cheeks.

"Why?"

Angling away from me, he gave me one squinty eye. "Scared the shit out of me."

"Why?" I had a feeling the answer wouldn't be the obvious one.

"Murder's some serious shit." He waffled a bit, then gave us the real reason. "When we were breaking up, the ex accused me of trying to kill her."

"Did you?"

"No. I got mad, sure. Lost control. I pushed her down on the bed, but that was it. Nobody believed me. Did some time for felony assault." He stared down Romeo. "I couldn't have your kind digging that up and leaping to conclusions."

I jumped in before anyone said something they would regret. "Do you think Dora Bates killed Turnbull?"

Beckham pursed his lips. "For sure she was shaking us down—and more than just me and Turnbull. Think about it. Where else would she get the green to stay in that fancy little hut at *your* hotel?"

The guy had a knack for being irritating, but he asked good questions.

"Were you with the rodeo in Reno?"

"Yeah. We joined there."

"Did you know the Browns?"

"The folks whose horse died? No. We hadn't had a chance to meet too many people."

"You're from Oklahoma, right?"

"Lawton."

"Is that near Wichita Falls?"

"A short drive. Why?"

I ignored his question. "Do the names Sara Pickford or Dr. Dean ring a bell?"

"No." He didn't seem surprised at the names.

"What did you do with the evidence you stole?"

"And the drugs," Romeo added just as I was about to.

"Ditched them in one of the bins in the place where all the shops are."

"The Bazaar?"

He shook his head. "I guess. It was close to that place with the drinks."

"Daiquiri Den," I said, turning to Jerry.

He stepped away from the group and talked in hushed tones into his security handset. Depending on timing, we might get lucky.

CHAPTER FOURTEEN

*T*HE night had fallen dark and deep by the time I found myself behind the wheel, the Ferrari growling as if it knew where we were going.

Home.

The spotty traffic thinned further by the time I'd flown through the mousetrap, headed north on the 95, then peeled off on the Summerlin Parkway, and I found myself virtually alone. Vegas changed as the night progressed toward dawn, the frenetic party giving way to the...hangover. I hadn't thought of it quite that way before, but it fit. The Bacchanalian overindulgence giving way to the recovery.

To start again the next day.

But for now, rest.

Romeo's text followed Jerry's. Both confirmed they'd found the evidence where Beckham had said it would be. The vials of barbiturates looked full. The red thingy and the lipsticks were still in the plastic bag, although, since they'd been out of the chain of custody, their usefulness in court was gone. But Romeo had delivered all of it to the Coroner's Office. Maybe his staff would work their magic and give me a thread. I'd find out in the morning.

The girls were asleep at the Babylon with a security detail keeping an eye out. Doc Latham had been released. With Doc Latham unwilling to press charges and Romeo himself ambivalent, he'd booked Beckham on the murder charge, more for his own good than any real chance we had our killer. With his runaway anger, there was no telling what Beckham would do. Keeping him on ice for twenty-four hours wouldn't hurt anyone, and it would give us more time to pull all this together. Twenty-four hours. Not much time.

So, with everyone tucked away and nothing more to chase right now, I planned on curling up with my chef and his promised bottle of wine.

Yes, it was late. But chefing was a late business. In fact, I might even beat him home.

Home.

There was that word again.

Quiet reigned in Summerlin. The city still slept, not yet yawning into a new day. One garbage truck lumbered ahead of me. Thankfully, it continued on as I turned into the subdivision—Eagle Hills, a nice combination of affluence and keeping it real. Out of habit, I reached over my head to punch the button, then realized not in this car. My Porsche had been programmed with the code—part of the old me that had been incinerated.

A borrowed car. A borrowed life?

No, it felt real; it just didn't feel like mine.

Change, not my best thing.

I needn't have worried about not having the clicker—Jean-Charles had beaten me home...and barely; the light was still on. It flicked off as I pulled in and killed the engine.

"I thought I heard you." My man met me at the door, relieving me of my purse, then giving me a kiss warm with the promise of more.

"You left the door up." Not an admonishment, but a question.

"I do every night until I know you aren't coming." He looped an arm around my waist. Conjoined, we walked through the kitchen; spotless, yet the aroma of pizza lingered. "Take out?"

"Chantal, she is tired of cooking at night." His niece, Chantal, a full-fledged teenager, was following in her uncle's footsteps and attending a prestigious cooking school nearby. "I am worried she does not have the calling here." He patted his chest over his heart.

"She's a teenager longing to be an adult but with no clue how much work is involved once you get there."

He deposited me at the couch then peeled off, slipping behind the bar. The wine he'd promised was already chilling. "You are a wise parent."

"No, a terrified one."

"All parents are terrified."

"I don't believe you." With a groan, I sagged into the welcoming softness of overstuffed cushions. After kicking my shoes off, I leaned back, my arms over my head, stretching until every vertebra in my spine crackled and popped, releasing its tension—the very definition of hurts so good.

"Why this?" He pulled the cork, sniffed it, then poured a taste into a glass. After swirling it, he stuffed his nose in the bowl of the glass.

That always struck me as either silly or bad manners, but when it came to wine, I was woefully unsophisticated.

He handed me a glass then took a spot next to me, our bodies touching at the hips and shoulders. In that way he was like a puppy, needing the tactile connection, not that I was averse. "This wine, it is very nice. The grapes, they grow only on Santorini. Have you been?" At the shake of my head, he continued, "It is so peaceful."

"As only sleeping in the caldera of an active volcano can be."

"You are missing my point." Mock petulance—he looked so much like his son...who was five.

"No, I'm playing with you. It amuses me—what can I say? I'm shallow that way."

"Indeed. We must keep the flame of a child inside."

"There you go, sounding all grown up again."

Holding his glass at an angle to the light, he admired the soft golden hints. "It is pretty, no?"

I took a sip. "Yum, dry, acidic, mineraly, but smooth."

"Yes, this." With his eyes closed, he savored the wine.

I'd asked him once why he did that, closed his eyes while sipping wine. He'd told me for the same reason he closed his eyes when he kissed me—taking one sense away focused the others, making the experience so much more.

Yes, falling in love with him had been a given from the get-go.

Done savoring, he opened his eyes, then angled toward me, crossing one leg over mine. He stretched an arm along the couch behind my shoulders, his fingers lightly caressing my neck and shoulder. He smelled of hamburgers, grilled onions, and contentment. "So, why do you not believe all parents are scared?"

"Because none of them look scared."

"If we let the children sense our fear, all will be lost." He said that in all seriousness.

"So, it's a game?" I didn't mean to mock him, but my voice held that tone.

"As is all of life. A game with not so many rules where we all must try not to make mistakes as we go, but knowing we will. The learning comes in the recovery."

As I sipped my wine, I tucked in closer to him—if that was possible—and really thought about what he said. "Compassion is in accepting our fallibility." And I had no idea how the perfectionist inside of me could handle that. But I also knew she had to for me to have a chance at happiness. In my defense, while I held others to a very high standard, I held myself to an even more exacting one.

An explanation that no longer held the comfort of an excuse.

Piercing the veil of my own self-delusion—a start down the path toward self-acceptance. Damn, I hated change.

"I knew you would say it better than me." Jean-Charles pretended to be impressed with my grasp of my native language.

"You're cute, but patronizing doesn't suit you. English is my first language."

"No." He touched my heart. "This is our first language, the one that connects everyone. The rest is just to confuse us."

Turns out he had the best words after all.

I rested my head on his shoulder.

"So, what is this about, how do you say it? Cold feet?"

"Yes, that's how you say it. And it's not so much that as resistance to change. I feel safe in the comfort of sameness—an ordered world."

"This is normal, but it is not the best life."

I put my glass on the floor next to my feet, then I leaned back again, angling my face up for a kiss. As I pulled his head toward me, I murmured against his lips, "No, it's not."

Then I took what I wanted, what my heart knew I'd wanted all along.

I *RAN. My mother behind. So close I could feel her fear. "Run," she gasped. My short legs churned. "Faster." Fear pounded through me. The man behind us. He crashed through the forest. Gray branches stripped bare by winter. They slapped at me—the prodding sting of a whip. Tears, hot and desperate, burned down my cold skin. "Run, Lucky. Don't stop." The voice faded. I turned to look. My mother was gone.*

With a tight shriek, I bolted upright, blinking against the nightmare.

Jean-Charles folded me into a hug, his skin warm, his breath hot against my neck. "It is okay."

Home.

Daylight barely pinked the sky—in our heat we'd neglected to close the shades. The memory of our desperate lovemaking chased away the terror that lingered.

I was safe here.

But why had my mother disappeared? Who had taken her? Was the dream my desperate attempt to justify her abandonment—or something else?

Although the dream was gone, I couldn't shake a lingering, stalking fear.

A soft scratching against the door pushed back into the darkness the last bits of cold. Jean-Charles groaned as he nuzzled my neck, creating waves of warm desire, making me groan in unison.

"Papa?" Christophe, his voice soft yet insistent, conspiratorial in the way of five-year-olds.

"Children," Jean-Charles sighed. "*Oui, mon coeur*?" he said, his voice loud enough to be heard through the slatted door.

"Are a gift," I whispered, using words I'd heard him say many times.

He took my hand, guiding it to where need pulsed, hot and hard. "But their timing is not always so impeccable."

I stroked him a few times before letting go. "Considering how many times he has stopped us as we've started, I'd say his timing is impeccably consistent."

"*Papa?* Please say Lucky is here."

That's all it took. I bounded out of bed, shrugged into a robe, tied it, and threw open the door almost before I was aware of doing so. Bending on knees that croaked their objection, I gathered the boy in a bear hug. Holding him tight, I breathed him in. His arms, tight around my neck, ensnared my heart. "*Voilà, mi corazon.*"

His body echoed with giggles. "That's not French."

"What?" I leaned back to look him in the eye and give him an exaggerated face. "It's not?"

He rewarded me with a cascade of more giggles and another snuggle.

"You must teach me."

"Only if you make happy-face pancakes with lots of chocolate," he whispered against my neck.

Chocolate for breakfast—one vice I'd managed to avoid. Not that I wasn't above inflicting it on others. "Happy-face pancakes, coming right up."

"I will help." A man on a mission, Christophe scrambled

out of my hug, then disappeared through the living room into the kitchen, his legs churning.

Jean-Charles had stepped into a pair of gym shorts. He extended a hand. "I have competition for your heart, I think."

My knees thanked me as I let him pull me to my feet. "You both have it, just different parts."

He gave me an I-told-you-so smile. "I am sorry he awakes when the day is so young."

"We will have to adjust our schedule so we have *us* time. But today it's actually good."

With two dead bodies cooling on his tables, the coroner would start early.

*T*HE Office of the Coroner/Medical Examiner was housed in a low, squat building behind Sunrise Hospital. From the outside, it looked like the rest of Vegas, stucco painted in desert colors. Few would suspect the grim search that went on behind the unassuming façade.

The stench of death and decay hit me the moment I pushed through the doors. Even though somewhat prepared, I fought a gag reflex. Even though I'd resisted lingering in a child's happiness and a father's amusement, the coroner was hard at work when one of his team ushered me inside. A bright overhead light illuminated the body, open and raw. Hunched in concentration, the coroner barely registered my presence. "Working on the second one now."

"Dora Bates."

"Prelim tox screen came back. Both she and Turnbull had lethal levels of barbiturates in their systems."

"Not unexpected." In an effort not to focus on the grisly work, I occupied myself with a pile of photos from the crime scene. "May I?"

"Knock yourself out."

Flipping through them, I reacquainted myself with both

Turnbull's and Dora's deaths.

"Looks like Dora took one hell of a beating."

The safety glasses exaggerated his eyes as the coroner glanced up from his work. "How so?"

"The color of her skin. Looks like a bad bruise."

"Not a bruise—well, not like you mean. Not due to physical trauma. It's lividity. After the heart stops beating, gravity works its magic and the blood pools."

With that tidbit, I returned to the photo. "So, she was dead before she was strung up?"

"Not necessarily. But she'd been dead for some time before you found her."

That got my attention. "How long?"

He pursed his lips. "Time of death is an inexact science at best, but from the state of both the lividity and rigor, I'd say at least six hours, maybe a bit more."

"Really?" My mind whirled. "She died *before* Turnbull?"

"That's the way I see it."

I'd been operating under the assumption that they'd died in the order we'd found them. *Stupid.*

"I've got something else interesting." The coroner peeled off his gloves then took off his safety glasses. "Follow me." He led me into one of the labs filled with all kinds of equipment that I couldn't identify. Technicians bent over scopes and analyzed printouts. He pulled a plastic tray labeled with a case number. "This is the red thread ball you found in the horse's stall."

The ball nestled by itself in the tray. "Looks like it."

He looked at me over the tops of his glasses. "It's the one that was in the plastic bag retrieved from the trash at the Babylon."

"Okay."

He shook the tray until he could see what he wanted me to see. "See here? The thread leading off the ball part?"

Bending over the tray, I squinted.

He thrust a pair of cheaters at me. "Use these."

Donning them brought things into sharper focus. "What am I looking for?"

"The end. See how it looks clean, no threads longer than the others?"

"Yeah."

"It was cut."

Pulling off the cheaters, I raised up. "Like on purpose?" I tried to get my head around what that meant.

"Yes." The coroner waited, letting me get there on my own.

"So, someone cut this off her jacket? It was off her jacket, right?"

He donned another set of gloves, then pulled the jacket from a plastic bag. "From here."

The fabric held the smell of death and fear. The ball had been cut from a place almost hidden by the others around it.

"The killer cut it, then planted it in the stall?"

"That would be my theory."

"Someone set up Dora Bates?"

The coroner shrugged. "Or they were delivering a message."

I let that sink in. "Did you find anything of interest in the doc's van?"

"I assume you know it was registered to Dr. Dean, one of our recently deceased in Reno."

"Yeah, they were friends. Dr. Dean was not feeling well. He let Doc Latham take the van and sub for him here."

"The girl tell you that?"

"Yeah." I went still. "Any reason I shouldn't believe her?"

"Not yet."

"Spoken like a true coroner." My world came back into focus. "How could the police have released the van?"

"They'd gone over it, hadn't found anything that shouldn't be there."

I could tell by the look in his eye something good was coming. "But you did, didn't you?"

"I found three coiled ropes in the back."

"The same rope?"

"Red and blue thread," he said as he nodded. "Only problem is, we can't prove who they belonged to or how they got there. The vet claims innocence."

"Let me guess: he swears he's never seen them before and has no idea how they got there."

"You ought to write for the movies."

"Truth is stranger than fiction, don't you know?"

New clues, yet no closer.

CHAPTER FIFTEEN

"WE need to talk."

The Big Boss. He'd managed to find me tucking into a plate piled high with food I needed but could hardly stomach. The stench of death was so strong it lingered, almost turning into a bilious taste. That thought alone was enough to put me off my feed. Now I regretted my earlier decision to pass on the chocolate happy-face pancakes, opting instead for the feast at Nebuchadnezzar's—Neb's to the staff—the twenty-four-hour buffet at the Babylon.

After the coroner's, and armed with a time of death for Dora Bates, I'd given Jerry a narrow time window to search. I hoped he would find our killer on the security tapes, but I wasn't counting on it. Nothing about this case was coming together.

So, feeling sorry for myself, I'd done what I always do, I'd opted for food. A necessity, or so my body told me.

I speared my father with a scowl. "*Now* you think we need to talk? Why now when I am so far ahead of you in the next move in the Game of Life?" I asked through a mouthful of flaky croissant. "Comfort food," I excused my choice before he had time to criticize. A reflex from decades with my mother.

"No rebuke from me. Eat what you want—tasting of life is important. Besides, it all looks good on you. And, as far as you being ahead of me, most days, frankly."

Was he buttering me up or being the father I needed?

Having seen too much darkness today, I opted to believe the latter. I needed to believe the latter.

Since our paths had last crossed, his paleness had deepened and his worry was palpable. "Are you okay? You don't look good." I tried to hang onto the angry but I couldn't. All of this was getting to me. So much of it seemed so personal. My family in the bull's eye; life as I knew it hanging in the balance. What I would give for a run-of-the-mill drunk-and-disorderly, or even a card counter draining our profits.

He eyed my food like a feral animal. I pushed the plate toward him. "Let's share." I got up, then returned with another setup.

He dug in and his enthusiasm was catching. We powered through half the pile—sushi, fried chicken, something Chinese, marinated cucumbers, a few other vegetables to assuage guilt—before he spoke again. He laid his fork next to his plate, lining it up precisely with the fold of his napkin. Then he placed both of his hands, palms down, on the table. When he spoke, his voice was tired and far away. "No, I'm not okay. Your mother..."

We both reaped the benefit and bore the burden of Mona. If this was half as important as they were leading me to believe, I could only imagine the emotional scenes he had been wrangling with.

"But you have seen the doctor, right?"

"There's just so much they can do, Lucky. I'm old. I'm worried. And a body can take only so much." He shut down my argument with a side-eye. "I won't give up without a fight, so let it be."

I capitulated, for the moment, with a sigh.

"What did Mother have to say about Dora Bates?"

When he looked at me, his face had gone slack, his eyes hard.

"You two know her." Oh shit! They really were hiding something.

He didn't admit or deny, preferring to take the Fifth. "Can you come with me?"

This smoke and mirrors game both alarmed and discouraged me. "What? Now?" My phone dinged. Sitting on the table between us, the thing lit up like Christmas. I flipped it around so I could read the message.

Dane. Something about the rope. "Excuse me," I said to my father and punched up the whole message. He'd tracked down the rope maker in Wichita Falls, well, he'd tracked down the guy's son. The rope maker had died decades ago. The family had donated his inventory to Huntsville State Prison.

Interesting. So, Cole lied.

His source was the killer, or potential killer.

What was that about? Lost in thought, I forgot where I was. I hit Romeo's speed dial. The call rolled to voicemail. I left a message—I tried to be succinct. It was really important. "Pick up Darrin Cole. He may be in danger. Find out who he buys his ropes from—he'll know what you're talking about. Tell him if he lies again I'll personally break his kneecaps. And, no, I'm not kidding."

My father's voice cut through my muddled thoughts. "Does that work?"

"You should know." I ended the call but didn't put my phone away—if Romeo called back, I didn't want to miss it.

"So, can you come with me?"

"What?" I tried to focus, then I remembered. "You want me to leave in the middle of all of...this? A killer on the loose...now Darrin Cole with info that could possibly blow this open?"

"Yes. There's a story you need to hear. I only have part of it; the rest is your mother's to tell, when and if she wants to. But I think I can help you find your killer."

"*Her* story? You're the one who knows where all the bodies are buried."

"That mouth of yours..."

"Is my best weapon, but often too pointed. Sorry. Is Mother coming, too?"

"No, I've left her at home. Strict instructions not to leave the apartment." He held up a hand as I started to argue. "This time, she'll listen. She knows what's at stake."

"Am I the only one who doesn't?" Hurt and anger crept back in. And, this time, real worry. I covered his hand with mine. "Look, I trust your judgment, but you're a bit close to this one. And, not feeling well—you said so yourself. If you'll give me a bit more to go on, I can help."

"You won't want the consequences of knowing, and your mother and I can't afford them. Trust me." He looked like this cost him as much as it did me. I doubted it, but at least it hurt him. "You must believe that keeping you out of this is for your own good."

If he'd stopped before that last bit, I would've been okay. But telling me that sort of thing, using those words, made me feel like a powerless kid again, and I was anything but...well, most days. "Murder. It's the only explanation. Mother, as your wife, can't be forced to testify against you."

"But you can. If you'll trust me, I'll show you. At least part of it. And we'll have our killer."

"Show me?" My heart was pounding. My nightmare came back to me in Technicolor flashes of fear. "Is Mother in danger?"

His lips thinned into a wicked line. "Yes." He held up a hand. "I don't know for sure, but if you'll come with me we can find out."

"Where?"

"Reno."

That one word told me I had to go.

"Your mother thinks I'm crazy. Maybe she's right." He pressed a hand against his chest. With a wince, he rearranged the pain. "She has a point—it's pretty far-fetched. Humor me and we can be certain."

At least he was honest. "You dangling a carrot? Waving the white flag? Going to dazzle me with bullshit, or are you really here to help? We got two dead. Now's not exactly the time to go wild goose hunting."

The air left him and I could see how sick he really was.

I laid a hand on his arm. "This is killing you."

"So then, getting rid of the secret I've carried since I met your mother will help." He brushed off my concern. Even in his condition, he wasn't one to back down, especially when reason wasn't on his side. Just like my mother. They were two-halves of the same heart.

"Your mother's story to tell. The girl is not mine, I can tell you that. But she is important to your mother for reasons that time will make clear." He speared me with a look.

"You know who the killer is?" Wow, I'd always asked for easy answers. Now that one stared me in the face, I was a bit skeptical.

He gave me a lopsided grin that struck me as incongruous. "I need to dig up a body first. You in?"

"You do know how to show a girl a good time. How could I resist?"

*T*HE G-5 waited on the tarmac in front of the FBO at McCarran. The car tooled through the gates and stopped next to the stairs, extended to welcome us, before the whole thing registered. "I'm in the middle of a murder investigation—well, two actually—and you're whisking me away?"

"We won't be gone long."

Paolo's eyes flicked to mine in the rearview as he mashed his chauffer's cap on his head and then stepped outside.

I knew not to say any more. Instead, I followed my father up the stairs, his gait painful and slow. Somehow, I resisted taking his arm to steady him. He had to believe in his strength to get us through. As much as I'd love to force him back in the car to head to the hospital, there were lives at stake here...including his own.

Once the door was buttoned up and the pilots were busy up front, I leaned forward. We were seated in the club seating, my father across from me. "We're going to Reno?"

He nodded.

"To the girl's grandmother's farm?"

"No, we tried everything we could to keep them out of it."

"You know about the doctor who was killed on the farm in addition to Bethany's grandmother?"

My father turned to stare out the window. "He was the only link. We thought so, at least. Then Dora Bates. It's starting to add up to something crazy."

His eyes were red-rimmed when he settled back in his chair and buckled his seat belt.

"So, who's the killer?"

"You wouldn't believe me if I told you."

"Try me."

He ignored me.

A shovel, so new the bar code decal still stuck to the concave face of the long blade, the wood of the handle blond and unsullied, lay across the seats on the other side of the aisle. Closing my eyes, I counted to ten. That didn't work, so I kept counting. When reached one hundred, I gave up. Opening my eyes, I fixed my father with a stare.

"Grave robbing. A first-degree felony?" I should've put Squash Trenton on retainer.

He waggled his eyebrows and gave a bad impression of an impish smile. A man raised in mobbed-up Vegas, my father had toed the line but never fully embraced corporate Vegas. Despite not wanting to know the particulars of his past, right now riding with a guy with that particular experience set was maybe a good thing. And, unfortunately, my father's daughter had an authority issue, so this sort of game got my juices flowing.

I should be bothered by that, but constraint bothered me more, always had. Probably why Mona had seen fit to rid herself of me when I was fifteen. Not an excuse, but perhaps an explanation—one I'd accepted. The guilt of what I must've done resonated at the core of my being. Maybe I'd been trying to make up for whatever it was ever since?

I'd been joking, but the ring of truth reverberated.

How did somebody fix that? How did one erase the sting of

abandonment by the one person who should never, ever abandon them?

What would fix that kind of broken?

And there it was, what I had feared all along—I was a living FUBAR: Fucked Up Beyond All Repair.

*T*HE clouds hung heavy over Reno—somehow appropriate. Our wheels kissed the ground just as we broke through, not that the scenery changed much. Only slight differentiations in the shade of gray distinguished land from sky, tree from dead grass. A short flight and yet we'd landed in a world devoid of the light and color and energy of Vegas. Same state, light-years between the cities—in every way.

Reno—the Biggest Little City in the World. That's how they liked to think of themselves. But really, dwarfed by the legend of Vegas, Reno was the Biggest Little City None Had Ever Heard Of.

My take, but I'm biased.

Reno would always be a wannabe. Not that that was a bad thing—it had its own charm, and I'd always thought they'd be better off sticking with the whole beautiful mountain, gateway to Tahoe thing. But, a city could run pretty well off of gaming revenues, so all Nevadans chased them, with varying degrees of success.

Today, gray gloom snuffed out the Reno charm. The snow lining the streets was days old and now mounded in forlorn brown piles melting slowly into the gutters. Rivulets of water wallowed tunnels under the snow and a thin crust of translucent ice. The low clouds hid the mountains to the west—the mountains that captured Lake Tahoe, one of the most beautiful places I'd ever seen. For years, I tried to get the Big Boss to open even a small property there. Too close to Reno, he'd said, which had made no sense at the time.

But now, I was starting to get a glimmer.

True to his problem-solver personality, my father had

arranged a car from a property owned by one of his friends. Despite corporate consolidation, the old guard still hung on—a few dinosaurs like my father. He'd told me once that if I ever sold to a conglomerate, he would come back and haunt me—a ghost with a baseball bat and an attitude. I believed him.

I checked my phone. No message from Romeo. And here I was on this crazy chase. My father seemed intent on purging his soul. My mother? God knew. "Can't we just catch the killer the old-fashioned way? I'm really not dressed for grave robbing." My silk pants in a stunning royal blue, matching sweater, and kitten-heeled Lou-bous were the perfect uniform for shoveling bullshit, figuratively speaking, but little else.

The driver held the door and pretended not to have heard—that was one of the reasons they got the big bucks. He didn't meet my eye as I leaned in and whispered, "I'm kidding," as I helped my father into the car—he insisted on riding up front.

"Lucky, you drive," my father ordered as I shut the door.

The driver hesitated, but my father had issued the order with a finality we both heard.

"If it's any consolation, he could write a check for this car and not miss it."

"I could lose my job for this."

"Me, too." *Among other things.*

As he rolled the keys through his fingers, he glanced at the shovel I was holding, but, a true pro, he didn't ask. In fact, he was so good his expression didn't even change. Perhaps sensing my good humor was evaporating fast, he relinquished the keys. "How long will you be?"

"As long as it takes. The FBO has hot coffee and warm cookies. They'll take care of you." As a driver for a casino in Reno, he should have intimate knowledge of the perks of waiting at the airport in the Fixed Base Operator's offices. They had lounges and TVs for the pilots, snacks, and non-alcoholic libations. In fact, our pilots had made a hasty retreat inside out of the cold.

"You made the right choice." I palmed the keys and climbed behind the wheel. "You want a job in Vegas?" I asked before I pulled the door closed.

He glanced at the shovel. "Not on your life. You folks push my boundaries."

"Mine, too." I pulled the door shut, leaving him staring through the side window. He looked like he was contemplating a career change.

So was I...as if I had a choice.

Blood, the tie that binds.

So many ways that could be interpreted.

"Very clever how you got rid of all the witnesses but one," I said to my father as I maneuvered the big car out of the enclosure at the FBO. With a sinking feeling, I watched as the driver faded out of sight.

My father was acting really weird, which was uncharted territory.

And he wasn't telling me much other than we were *en route* to commit a felony. Right now, my life was nothing more than the Bermuda Triangle of Bad Shit. The set of my father's jaw told me there was nothing to do but soldier on.

Of course, with the lure of answers hiding in the misty gray, I wouldn't run back now even if I had a choice.

"You know where we're going?" After the Ferrari, the big car took some getting used to.

"Not really."

Now, that was a surprise. "You've not been here before?"

"It's been a long time since I thought about this place." He pulled a few sheets of paper from his inside pocket, then pressed them flat against the dashboard.

The squiggles I could see looked like a map.

"Terrific. A dead-body scavenger hunt," I muttered, mostly to myself since my father was ignoring me. "Could today get any better?"

My father stared out the front window. "It couldn't get much worse." He pointed straight ahead. "Go north until you hit the 80, then head east two miles or so."

As the day slipped away, my father looked worse and worse.

"This date with the past isn't looking too good on you." I kept the tone light but I wasn't feeling at all good about any of this.

"A date with the Devil," he muttered.

"What?" I thought I'd heard him right but couldn't be sure.

He waved my question away. The veins stood out, purple against the white skin of his hand. Old man hands. Since when? "Something your mother said."

"What part does she play in this?" Knowing Mona, she was up to her hairline in this bad business.

"She's at home." A non sequitur as an answer—he was adopting his wife's ways. Not a good thing.

"Did she draw that map?"

"Lucky." He looked so tired and strained.

I let it lie. Forcing answers wouldn't make him any better, nor any of this go away. We'd come to do what he wanted to do—I'd signed on. And that was that.

Not that I liked any of it.

And, while I'd manhandle my mother in this situation, I'd follow my father into any battle, or let him lead any charge. A slavish attitude, misplaced loyalty, a lone lemming...right off the cliff. I tried not to think about it. Instead, I let myself be carried along on a wave of curiosity.

With nothing to say, my father clutched the papers, the shovel across his lap as he stared straight ahead.

The casinos north of the airport slid by. We headed northeast. Occasionally, he'd give me a direction—turn here, straight ahead, that sort of thing—and I did as I was told. The trappings of civilization disappeared behind us. My phone made the out-of-service sound. If this went south, we couldn't even summon the cavalry. And I didn't have my gun—to be honest, I couldn't remember where I'd left it. That was probably a felony, too.

The bleak landscape, caught in the vise of winter, loomed around us. A few pines gave a hint of color, but, for the most part, it was as if each low shrub, each naked tree, the grasses pressed low by the scouring wind, even the sky, had been painted from a bucket of gloom.

I felt a Hitchcock movie coming on.

Why did I feel like laughing as I clutched the wheel and tried not to look at my father? Panic, sheer panic.

"Do the letters S. S. mean anything to you?" I asked the question casually, not expecting a response.

My father focused on me—I caught his intense look out of the corner of my eye.

"Where'd you hear that?" His attention wasn't the only thing that had sharpened—his tone could cut steel.

"They were shaved into the coat of Dora Bates's daughter's horse." I'd touched a nerve and somehow, I felt like I'd missed something, something important.

"Why didn't you tell me this before?"

"The grave-robbing thing derailed logic."

After a moment, he relaxed back in his seat. "Get off here!" He pointed to an exit that was barely makeable at our speed.

I cranked the wheel hard to the right, then turned back into the skid as the rear end broke loose. With a car this heavy, momentum usually won. We slid for the guardrail. But today, I was the lucky one. The wheels regained traction, giving me control. We narrowly missed the railing as we rocketed down the exit, then blew through the stop sign at the bottom. Rural Nevada, no cars, not even a cow to avoid.

My lucky day.

When I'd gotten the car to a full stop, my father said. "Go back. Head north from the last intersection."

I took stock of my surroundings and figured the best way to get where he wanted me to go was to back up the service road. My father white-knuckled it but kept quiet as I arrived back at the intersection almost as fast as I'd passed it.

Manhandling the car felt good—a modicum of control in a life spinning beyond my ability to even hang on, much less direct it.

I'd settled into a slightly excessive speed for the patched and potholed asphalt road. Straight as an arrow, the road to perdition stretched to the horizon.

The flood of adrenaline brought me back. "Could you give me a head's-up next time?"

"I'm doing this from memory."

"An old one and not your own, must be a challenge." Okay, there was a question buried in there that he ignored.

He stared at the map now, studying it, then glancing out the window to his right and occasionally straight ahead. "Landmarks have changed. Trees grow or are cut down. Buildings are erected or razed." We bounced along for another several miles. "Your mother said it was pretty far off the highway. That you'd never know it was there unless you'd been put there or knew someone who had."

Interesting choice of words I didn't quite understand, but I knew now was the time to be quiet. The past pressed in around us. I imagined the whispers of ghosts and I shivered. This whole thing was creeping me out.

A road off to our right came up quickly. It was more of a rutted cow path now that headed east from the hard road. Two columns of stone about three feet high bracketed the turnoff. One of them wore the years better than the other—it tilted precariously. The top half had already succumbed to gravity and lay scattered and broken among the weeds and dead grass.

"I think that's our turn." My father squinted at the drawing as if trying to intimidate it into giving up its secrets.

My reaction time in tatters, I missed it. Maneuvering the big car back around on the narrow blacktop took a minute. Patches of ice kept me from throwing the thing into reverse and doing what I'd done before. This time, I thought it would be better if I had a good view of where my tires were in relation to the road and the ice—the road was barely wider than my axle as it was. Finally, I accelerated back the way we had come, then slowed as my father leaned forward in his seat. I stopped at the turnoff. "Are you sure?"

"No. But it's the only one that's even close. Let's try it."

The ruts were deeper than I'd thought at first. Even still, it looked like they'd been carved a long time ago, then the road had been abandoned. The dirt was unmarred by recent tire tracks. "No one has been down this way since Christ was a corporal."

"Yes, the sanitarium closed right after..."

"Sanitarium?"

"Hmm..." the faraway, pained look told me he wasn't really listening. "Loudon was a bad place. Nothing good happened there."

"Loudon Sanitarium? Like for the mentally ill?"

"Yeah. I guess they tried to make it a nice place, but that's hard to do with folks as sick as the ones housed here. It was a farm, if you will, with animals for the patients to care for or at least interact with. Didn't do much good—most were beyond help. The inmates called it Suicide Shores, an inside joke."

"S. S.," I whispered. "Dora Bates was here at about the same time as your...association?" I raised my voice in question, hoping he answered both.

"Yes. That's what your mother said." He shot me a look—he'd been more open than he intended. "I'm sure this is it. Can you go down the road? It's only a few hundred yards, if I remember correctly. I can walk but I'm not sure how far."

No way was he walking. I eased the car off the paved road, wincing as I did so, but the scraping I expected didn't come. "Barring any potholes, we ought to make it."

The further we inched, the paler he became, his hands fisted around the shovel. Behind a copse of trees that sheltered it from the road, an imposing stone manor house came into view. All the glass had long ago been broken. Torn and tattered curtains wafted in the slight breeze, ghosts shaking their laundry. The double wooden front door remained resolute, closed to those searching for secrets.

I parked on the cracked and crumbling concrete of what had been a circular drive and killed the engine. The quiet amplified the creepy. "I'll try the door, but it looks like we'll have to skinny through a window. You stay here."

"What we're looking for won't be in there." My father's voice held a note of grim reality.

"So you've implied. But it wouldn't hurt to take a look around while we're here."

"What are you hoping to find?"

"Honestly? Courage." I buttoned up my sweater and popped the door. "I'll let you know when I find it." I scanned the front of the building and the part of the side I could see for a window wide enough and close enough to the ground to accommodate my bulk and my age. Only one looked promising, but the lead latticework of a lost stained-glass window barred easy entry.

My father's hand on my arm stopped me. "The building was cleaned out years ago. Anything we could use is long gone." His hand tightened as he turned to stare at the building. "If it was ever here." He let go and buttoned his overcoat, then lifted his chin, indicating something ahead of the car. "The stables were behind the house. But we need to go just beyond the stables, down over that ridge. We need to go that way. Take the car as far as you can, then we'll go the rest of the way on foot. Over the rise, the hill drops down to a small pond next to the stables. What we're looking for is there."

At the top of the hill, I stopped and peered over. What had passed for a road now turned into a goat trail. "We'll have to hoof it from here."

My father carefully folded the sheets of paper and eased them back into his inside pocket. His hand on the handle, he hesitated, then, with a nod, opened the door and eased his legs out.

I left the lights on as I rushed around to help him. Ignoring his attempt to brush my help away, I grasped his hand and elbow and pulled him to his feet. His breath came hard and fast with the effort. His skin was cold and clammy. "I really don't want to do this," he said, surprising me.

"I don't either."

"Turn off the lights. You'll kill the battery."

I glanced at the gray sky. The sun had already dipped below the mountains to the west. A bare hint of pink colored the clouds, but it too would soon be gone.

"We won't be that long anyway." His way of capitulating. As he leaned on me, I could almost feel the extra weight he carried.

"I don't need to remind you this was your idea." The instant I said it, I felt like a schmuck. Nothing like adding to the load that already threatened to break him.

"We have to know." Fear radiated off him—not at all like him. "If your mother is right, we'll know who you're looking for and why."

That was the prod I needed to get over my whine. "I'll carry the shovel." Never letting go of him, I reached back inside and grabbed it. "If we can keep him from killing again, I'll dig up as many bodies as you need."

He let me steady him as we made our way down the path. In the shadows, ice hinted along the edges of the stagnant pond where it had caught the snow, which remained a stark white in the safety of the cold. As a final resting place, this place was right out of Hollywood—Bela Lugosi would feel right at home. Chills chased through me, from the cold or my overactive imagination, I didn't know. Remnants of a barn, the wood graying with time and inattention, the door hanging open, one side missing altogether, leaned away from the wind. A year or a good snowstorm would take it down.

My father stopped a few times to get his bearings. I'd lost him to the past—I let him stay there. The past was where we'd find the answers. "The years have changed this place," he whispered.

"From what you say, any change would be for the better."

On the verge of saying something, he paused, then shook his head. He consulted the map. "Do you see three rocks, large rocks, piled on one another?"

"After all these years? Seriously?"

He ignored me.

I let go of him and we both searched in an increasing radius. I kicked at the leaves littering the ground, wet and wilted. Somehow, I identified with them. I felt awe and terror as I hung on the precipice of my parents' secret—one so awful they still couldn't breathe a word of it.

Would an old murder stop a new one?

Would my father go to jail?

And here I'd thought a new sister wandering into my life was the worst I had to worry about.

One kick, then another. On the next one, my toe connected with rock. Bending down, I brushed back the dirt. One stone, then two more, but not resting on top of one another. "Here."

My father abandoned his search and joined me.

"Are these the stones you remember?"

After consulting the papers then stuffing them back, this time not as carefully, he squatted. His hand shook as he reached for the first rock. He brushed off the dirt, looked at that side, then flipped it over. Not finding what he was looking for, he moved on to the second rock and did the same. On the third, he paused and paled...if that was possible. A flat stone covered with mud and darkened by time. Normally a fastidious man, he was heedless of the mess as he scrubbed at the dirt, wiping it away.

On the rock, someone had carved a set of two initials: MF and LF.

He wiped his hands on his five-hundred-dollar Italian wool slacks. In the past, I'd seen him apoplectic over a small spot. He worked at the dirt covering the carvings a bit more. "I haven't seen this stone in a very long time."

"Are you going to tell me who MF and LF are?"

"Not now." He pursed his lips and shook his head. A slight smile of remembrance played with his lips. He wiped at the rock some more. His smile evaporated.

Scratched below the initials, the lines whiter, the message newer:

Fuck you.

"No need to dig." His hands still shook as he pulled a handkerchief out of his back pocket and pretended to wipe his hands clean. As he stuffed the cloth back where he'd found it, he looked at me, his expression cold, his voice lethal. "I know who we're looking for."

"Who?"

"A dead man."

The news wasn't exactly unexpected—I'd figured there was

a dead guy involved since we were on a grave-robbing expedition. But the news that a ghost was doing the killing was a bit of a surprise. "We need to dig to make sure."

I turned the cold earth as the light to the west disappeared and the night deepened to an inky black.

We found nothing...only ghosts.

ON the drive back, I left my father alone with his ghosts. His lips had moved in silent conversation as he'd thought through whatever it was. Several times, he'd pulled out his phone—I knew he wanted to call Mother, but I knew he didn't want to talk in front of me.

My phone chirped when it picked up coverage again. Then another tone signaling a voicemail. I hit the button to listen. Romeo. Cole had taken a load of ropes off old Dr. Dean.

Interesting.

Back on the plane, I tried everything to warm the Big Boss, but chills racked through him, although the twenty-five-year-old Macallan seemed to help.

"Father, I can help you, but first you need to help me. I need a name to give to Romeo so he can stop all of this and so no one else gets killed." I added the last part in case he'd gotten so caught up in his personal stakes he'd forgotten the real risks.

"I don't think he'll kill anymore. He's got our attention."

"What does he want?"

"It's not what; it's who."

My blood ran cold. "It has to be either you or Mother. That's the way this thing is shaping up, right?"

"Looks that way." He didn't want to believe it any more than I did. "Your mother is safe at the Babylon. I made sure no one would be allowed up to the apartment. Security is on it."

I wasn't sure if he was reassuring himself or me. "I still can't figure out why he killed Turnbull. Any connection that you know of?"

"Not that I've put together, but there were a lot of pieces to the story I didn't have."

He kept saying that. I didn't want to go where that was taking me, but I did. "Mother is the key, not just a target."

"Like I said, part of this is her story." He wrapped his hands around the tumbler of whiskey.

Some of the story could wait, but not all of it. "You have to tell me who you threw in that shallow grave back there." I waited for a response. "Who are we looking for?"

As the pilots buttoned up the door and then worked to bring the engines online, I resisted urging him to hurry.

"A man who deserved it." But he wouldn't meet my eye.

"No doubt. But I'm sure vigilante justice was illegal even back before the earth was cool and you were young."

That didn't even get a disgruntled look.

I held my phone at the ready. "Give me a name."

He shook his head. "I don't know it."

"What?"

"I don't know it. Your mother wouldn't tell me. At first, she didn't want me going after the guy, then after..." He slugged back his Scotch, then poured himself some more.

The engines spooled up and the pilots began to taxi to the runway.

My brain seemed to capture the energy. "So now, whoever it was, has risen from the dead and is seeking revenge." I was being half-flippant, but the stone-cold look on his face told me I'd struck pay dirt.

The engines whined, eager to be in the air and the pilots let them run. Acceleration pressed me back in my seat. "Give me some of that." I motioned to the fancy Scotch. "And don't skimp." I stared out the window without seeing.

"I never thought he'd come back to life, not really," my father said. "I thought maybe it was someone out for revenge. Or out to extort money. Someone who had finally pieced together the story, then confirmed it by checking the grave. I thought, worst case, we'd find the grave disturbed." He slugged back more of the Scotch. "But I never thought we'd find the grave empty."

"Not too many risen-from-the-dead realities." The whole thing seemed surreal.

"If it's him, really him, I wonder why? Why after all this time?"

"Since I don't know who or why, it would be ridiculous for me to speculate."

My father weighed my words as he stared out the window. "The person who tried to kill him? It wasn't me."

My world tilted. "What?"

He took another sip of Scotch as he settled back in his seat. "That's all I'm going to say. There was no murder, so that's off the table."

"Attempted murder?"

"Much easier to defend. Squash knows the particulars. He has a file. He can help."

"That's how you met?" My turn to slug some Scotch.

"He was a total greenhorn, but I could tell he knew how the game was played. He was Mona's attorney—I stayed out of it. I couldn't know. We weren't married, and if any of it came to light, I'd be called as a witness. So, they collected evidence, built the case, on the off chance it would come back to haunt us." When his eyes met mine, they were clear, unclouded by worry. He had a plan; he trusted the plan.

"He still has it all?"

"Of course. There's no statute of limitations on murder."

"Attempted murder," I corrected. And now I was sure that what I'd been desperate to know, was something I didn't want to know at all.

My father held out his hand. "Get your mother on the phone. We can run all this by her." At my look, he added, "I'll make her give us a name."

I had to check my cell for Mona's number before I could log it into the satellite phone—speed dial made remembering numbers a waste of time...until you needed one. I pressed the send button, then handed the phone to my father. Then I settled back with my Scotch—I didn't really like Scotch, but right now I needed the punch it packed. We were close. We'd have the killer in custody soon, and maybe I'd have some answers. Whatever the story was, we'd deal; we always did. I felt myself relax just a little. It felt good. This adrenaline junkie was perilously close to an overdose.

My father's voice broke through my reverie. "She's not answering. The call rolled to voicemail." He held out the phone.

I could hear my mother's voice reciting her message.

Ice shot through my veins. We both knew the phone never left my mother's person—it was her talisman against boredom. A whole world to bother right at her fingertips.

I grabbed the phone. "I'll try the landline."

One of the nurses picked up on the first ring. At the sound of my voice, she dissolved into hysterics. "The babies, they are here. They are safe." She pulled in two ragged breaths that I died through. "But your mother! She is gone!"

Before I could ask any questions, someone wrested the phone from her.

"Lucky?" Jerry! His tone cut through any hope I had. "We've got a problem."

CHAPTER SIXTEEN

*A*T twenty thousand feet, I made phone calls on the satellite phone, and, between them, I tried to keep my father from stroking out. "It's going to be okay."

"I am too old and have seen too much to be comforted by platitudes." My father shifted from Scotch to coffee.

At least he had some fight left.

"Okay, how's this: this time she'd listen? That's what you said, right? Don't you know better by now? You should've..."

"Should've what?" His voice rose. He was looking for a fight.

I knew the need. "Drugged her. Chained her to the bed. You're good at that."

"I beg your pardon?" Squash Trenton answered then swam for shore as he found himself in the eye of the storm. "Chain them to the bed? Do you have that on good authority?"

"Trenton, Lucky here. You know that file you've been holding onto for my father?"

"Is he there?" His voice sharpened.

I held the phone out and gave my father an imploring look. "Talk to her, but use your discretion," my father said loud enough for the lawyer to hear and understand.

I pressed the phone back to my ear and filled Squash in.

He let out a long breath. "Whoa."

"I know, right?" I tried to process. Failing, I banked the

problem and focused on the killer. "We can assume he has Mona. According to Jerry, against orders, Mona came down to the lobby. She met a young girl who I suspect was Bethany." I could totally see how Mother's curiosity got the better of her. And the Babylon was her home; she was safe there.

Until she wasn't.

In so many ways, my mother was like a child.

"The problem here is we're chasing a ghost. I'm narrowing it down—I need one more piece of information." I hoped Jeremy called soon. "In the meantime, I need you to talk to Beckham. Romeo has him."

"No," Squash's voice had lost its hardness. "No, he doesn't. When the coroner established the time of death for Dora Bates, we couldn't establish his alibi—the hotel didn't have a security system, so no way to know if he was swilling booze at the bar or not. But nothing we have put him at the scene of the crime around the time of death—much later, yes, but that's hardly incriminating. Nobody pressed charges on the assaults. He's gone, Lucky."

"And he could be the killer." If we'd had him, then let him go...

*M*Y phone started pinging on final approach. Nothing from Mona. I hoped she was alive so that I could kill her when I found her. "Couldn't she have given us a clue?"

In answer, my father stared at me with tired, worried eyes. He looked like a ghost, fading away. If I didn't find Mona alive, I'd lose both of them.

The first call that had hit my phone while I was airborne was from a number I didn't recognize, so I hit redial.

Bethany answered. "Lucky! Shit, where have you been?"

"Chasing ghosts. Where are you?"

"At the Babylon, in your office. I didn't know where to go or what to do." Her words strung together in a hurried rush.

"Tell me what's going on."

"I was at the hospital with Doc. He was acting all weird. Didn't want to stay. I think the whole thing with Mrs. Bates really bothered him. He told me and Poppy to wait in the waiting room while he got dressed—he was going to check himself out. We did. But Poppy got a phone call from her dad and started acting really weird."

"The doc checked himself out?"

"Yeah."

"Poppy was acting weird? How so?"

"Just like she had something to hide."

"Or someone to protect?"

"Yeah, like that."

Fuck! "Okay, what happened?"

"I followed her here, to the Babylon. Then some lady came down and met her in the lobby. The lady pulled Poppy into a little alcove. I couldn't get close enough to hear what they were talking about without being seen. I assume the woman was Mona? You look like her."

Double fuck! "I don't see the resemblance. What happened next?"

"They left."

"In the limo?" Oh, please, Mother, be that smart.

"No, in a car."

"A cab?"

"No, a pickup."

Triple fuck! "Could you see who was driving?"

"No, but the truck was theirs. It had a longhorn sticker in the back window."

Grand slam fuck! "You didn't follow them?" How I didn't shout, I don't know.

"I don't need to. I know her password to iCloud. I can use Find My iPhone."

I had no idea what she was talking about, but it sounded like a good thing.

"I don't know anything about following people, and I don't

have any money or a car. I can find them when we're ready." Her voice trailed off as her confidence fled. "I hope I did the right thing."

"The perfect thing. Do you know where they are?"

"Let me check. Before you called, I'd been following them around the 215." A moment of silence, then she came back on the line. "Still heading west on the 215. They're at Rainbow Drive."

"Keep watching them. Tell Miss P to have Paolo drive you to the FBO at the airport—tell him there's a C-note in it for him if he breaks our record and delivers you alive. He'll know what I mean. Run, Bethany, run."

"You need to go now." My father used a tone that brooked no argument.

Except it was me he was dealing with and that tone no longer worked. After terminating the call, I stared at my father. "We're taxiing. This would be a bad time. The Feds frown at folks dashing across the runways at their airports." At his look, I was glad there were no weapons readily available. "I need help. And help will be here by the time we get off this bucket of bolts." Stifling my own fear, I tried to imagine his. "I'll hurry, but having some help will better our odds. If Dora Bates is any indication, when it's personal, the killer likes to take his time. I'm assuming this is personal?"

"Very."

"Then have faith."

"I always have."

Now, perhaps, was not the time to tell him it was often misplaced. It also probably wouldn't help to tell him that handling psychopaths was a bit out of my comfort zone, and I was scared, *and* my ability to function normally was gone—which, now that I thought about it, was a good thing, for so many reasons, but right now primarily because I would be required to function abnormally. So, instead, I offered a weak, "Something's bothering me."

"Only one thing?" His deadpan delivery was spot on, but the terrified look in his eyes killed his attempt at humor. "I can't lose her," he whispered.

"I know." I squeezed his hand, then held up a finger. "One more call."

This time I didn't even have to ask. The Beautiful Jeremy Whitlock started right in. "I was just getting ready to phone you." He sounded defeated. "I didn't get a hit cross-checking everyone on the suspect list with the prison database."

"That's terrific!"

"What?"

"None of our suspects had been incarcerated there?"

"No."

"Read me the list of names you searched."

"Homer Beckham, Dr. Walter Latham, Toby Sinclair, Darrin Cole, and I added Trevor Turnbull for good measure."

"No hits."

"Right."

"Awesome. Remind me to tell you to increase your hourly rate, after you bill me, of course."

"Of course." I could hear his smile and his confusion.

"How soon can you get to the FBO at the airport, the northwest corner? We're having a party and wouldn't think of starting without you."

Despite the odd location and the late hour, Jeremy didn't question anything. "Be there in ten."

"Make it five." Now I could return my attention to my father—reinforcements were on their way. "We'll bring her back to you." I knew better than to tell him not to worry.

"So, what's bothering you?" He picked up my former train of thought.

Thankful he'd kept me on track, I sorta smiled at this one and resisted torturing the metaphor with some reference to being derailed. I held up another finger. "Sorry, one more call."

I hit Romeo's speed dial. When he answered, I started in. "How far are you from the FBO at the airport?"

"Northwest corner?"

"Yeah."

"Turning in now. I've been tracking your flight. Somehow I

knew you might want me."

"I always want you." I disconnected before I felt him blush through the phone. Making him blush was great sport, but not now.

I smiled at my father, a tight evil smile. "How I love it when a plan comes together." We'd get Mona back or die trying. I didn't wait for my father to ask me again—the thought train had yet to derail. Getting my bitch on, I worked that in without smiling. "Actually, two things are bothering me. Okay, maybe more. I think it's a whole cascade, but let's start with two. Let's think about how this went down and who the killer is. First off, Turnbull's death."

"He's taken Mona. Why do you care which one it is? You'll know soon enough."

"Are you sure it's only one? If we're doing a Cowboy take on *Murder on the Orient Express*, it'd be nice to know that going in. No one has an alibi for Dora Bates's murder, and they all were at the arena when Turnbull died. Why kill Turnbull?"

"He surprised the killer?"

"No, too many presumptions. He surprised someone trying to hurt Poppy Beckham's horse."

"That's not the killer." It wasn't a question; he was following.

"Bear with me here. I think I know who the killer is. But I want you to walk through my thought process with me. The whole thing was about an extortion plot gone bad. Was mother acting strangely before you left?"

"She was nervous, sure."

"Was she doing that evasive thing she does when she's trying to hide something?"

"No."

I angled a look at him. "Did you get any odd calls?"

"No more than usual."

"Think back. It may have seemed normal at the time."

He winced and a muscle in his cheek bulged as he leaned over to extract his phone from his front pants pocket. He scrolled through slowly, breathing hard against the pain as he did so. "I only see one. Local. I didn't recognize it, so I didn't answer."

I held out my hand for his phone then redialed the number. "How may I direct your call?" I had my answer. "Wrong number, sorry." But, oh, it was so the right number.

My father leaned forward. His hope was almost palpable. "I recognize that look."

"That number came from the Kasbah." We had a system that routed outgoing calls through dummy numbers to protect our clientele from redials, and the operators are instructed not to identify the Kasbah when they answer. I double-checked the time and date. "And it came on the same day Dora Bates was murdered."

"What time?"

"Three p.m."

"So, she was alive until then?"

"Maybe. She didn't leave a message, so we don't know if Dora Bates made that call. But we do know they wanted to talk to you badly enough to have found your private cell number."

"I was her next mark?"

"I'd bet my soul on it. She registered under the Fiorelli name, knowing that meant something to you and Mother. She and her partner discovered the killer's secret—he must've done something really bad for you to have tried to kill him."

My father remained impassive.

Something about how his gaze drifted from mine... "Or mother..." I narrowed my eyes. "She did it, didn't she?"

"Lucky."

"Okay, I can wait. I need one more answer." I texted Flash: *Have you found Dr. Dean's son yet?"*

"Who's the killer?" A low, hard, demand.

"Oh, so you get to ask the questions?" As the pilot opened the door and lowered the stairs, I stood, offering him a hand.

He let me pull him up.

My phone dinged an answer from Flash. *No.*

Bingo.

Seeing his pain, I relented and slid off my high horse. “Come on. Let’s go see if I’m right.”

CHAPTER SEVENTEEN

*A*T this time of night and with New Year's behind us, those who wanted to leave had done so. And with the party over, not too many were flying in, so the FBO was running on a skeleton staff. The kid behind the counter looked far too perky. "Make yourselves at home. You look pretty ragged, if you don't mind me saying so." He took in my father's frailty and the mud-smeared pants. He was wise enough not to overtly include my formerly very nice outfit and righteous shoes. They would never be the same, but neither would I.

Why couldn't I discard my baggage as easily as changing clothes?

As if dressing the outer would redo the inner. A nice idea as long as one's taste was impeccable.

I shook my head—I was losing it, and just when focus was so critical.

Mona needed us.

I slammed my mind closed to the possibilities and I fought with my need to hurry. But I needed Bethany to tell us where to go. And I needed Romeo and Jeremy...and some answers before we went charging off half-cocked. We weren't too far behind them.

With my arm looped through his, I escorted my father down a hall to the pilots' lounge, depositing him in a recliner, then elevating his feet. The strong aroma drew me to a full pot of coffee on the burner—it looked and smelled fresh. I poured a mug for each of us, mine with milk.

"Take me through the rest." Knowing I wasn't leaving without reinforcements and needing distraction as much as I did, my father blew on his coffee as he eyed me. "So, the guy came to the Babylon and killed Mrs. Bates, then—"

Romeo skidded into the room, interrupting my father. One glance between us and he said, "Bring me up to speed."

I did.

"So, one killer. That's consistent with the security video tapes."

"What?" I hadn't seen the tapes from the hotel. "Have you seen the Babylon's tapes?"

"Jerry and I were just going through them. I left him when he got the call about Mona and I came here to find you. We found a hooded figure, just like at the rodeo. He was there around the estimated time of Dora's death."

"What time was that?"

"Time stamp on the tapes was just after three thirty p.m. that afternoon before Turnbull died."

I snagged my father's coffee mug—he'd powered through the brew even though it was barely short of scalding—and stepped to the counter to freshen it. "My father got a call from Bungalow Twelve at around 3 p.m. He didn't pick up and they didn't leave a message. I figure Dora's partner met her there, they called him together, then he killed her. She'd served her usefulness."

"She'd given him what he wanted," Romeo said.

"Yeah, access to Mona."

Romeo didn't seem surprised. "I knew you and your family were in the middle of this."

I started to argue, but that would be a waste of time—time I didn't have right now. I glanced at my watch—everyone should be arriving momentarily. I put my coffee down and buttoned up my sweater.

Romeo's phone rang. He looked at the caller ID. "Beckham? I wonder what he wants?"

"He's going to tell you someone stole his pickup."

"Yeah, right," he huffed. "Mr. Beckham, Detective Romeo here." He listened for a moment, his eyes growing wider as he looked at me.

"Told you so," I mouthed at him.

"I'll get right on it. I think we know where your truck is." He disconnected and stared at me. "How did you know?"

"We gotta go. Let's go get my mother. Times a wasting."

As if on cue, Miss P and Bethany pushed in behind him, with Bethany worming her way to the front.

The outside door dinged open as I turned toward Bethany. "Where are they now?"

She'd been staring at her phone. When she looked up, she looked stricken. "I've lost them."

I pointed to Miss P. "Take Father to the hospital, please." I shifted my glare to my father. Shivers wracked through him; his hands shook. So pale, his skin looked translucent. "No arguing. Do as she says."

"I'm more afraid of her than I am of you."

A lie, but I let him have it. "Good. Jeremy, can you help her?"

"You need my help more."

"No, we got this." Next, I pointed to Romeo. "You, come with me. We have a killer to catch and my mother to rescue."

"What about me?" Bethany asked, the steel returning to her voice.

"You stay with Jerry."

"No."

That killed my momentum. "No?"

She put her hands behind her back. "I won't tell you where they got off of the 215 if you don't let me go."

I knew when I faced a superior hand, so I folded. "Okay, you and Romeo come with me."

"ANYTHING?" I asked for the hundredth time.

Bethany shook her head, which I caught in the rearview. "No."

Romeo hunched over the steering wheel, his nose almost touching it. "Can you see like that?" We were rocketing around the 215—well, as fast as his bucket-of-bolts squad car could go. "What kind of cop car is this? Can't you go any faster?"

"This is a detective's car and I'm flooring it."

Clearly, detectives had no need for speed.

"They got off at Charleston heading west," Bethany shouted as we hurtled toward the exit.

Barely slowing, Romeo steered into the turn.

"Too fast!"

I practically threw myself on top of him, adding bulk to fight centrifugal force. The car rolled onto two wheels. We angled toward the guardrail. Draped across Romeo's lap, I grabbed the steering wheel to keep him from involuntarily tightening the turn. I felt it break and tightened my grip. The car fell back onto four wheels, and I yanked the car around. We brushed up against the guardrail. Romeo let up on the gas. I stomped a foot on top of his. The wheels spun then caught, propelling us due west down Charleston.

"I got it." Romeo's muffled voice came from somewhere near my left boob.

"Right." I let go of the steering wheel and scrambled backward off of him.

His face bright red, he stared straight ahead. "Thanks."

"You lost it when you let up on the gas through the turn. Brake before, then accelerate through the turn."

I glanced in the rearview. No Bethany. Momentarily panicked, I swiveled around and peered over the seat.

The girl was on the floor, reaching under the front seat. "Found it." When she pulled her hand back, her phone was clutched tightly. She had a red welt on her forehead to join the one that had turned blue. "I lost it back there."

"Join the club."

I settled back in the suicide seat, rethinking this whole

have-to-ride-up-front thing of mine—a control issue that could get me killed...especially with Romeo behind the wheel. Clutching at random thoughts kept my mind off Mother.

Worry would only carve a hole in my stomach lining—it wouldn't save her.

That was up to us. I stared into the deepening darkness in front of us as we left the lights of Vegas behind us. They could be anywhere out here. Red Rock State Conservation Area would be closed and gated, not that something so simple would slow down a sociopath. On the south side of the road, opposite and a bit before Red Rock on our right, a barren mountain loomed—a perpetual battleground between developers who want to build houses all over it and the citizens who wanted an unspoiled tract close to town. Heading west, nothingness stretched to the Spring Mountains. A great place to hide a body.

"Anything?" I didn't even try to hide the tightness making my voice twang with fear.

"No. Wait."

I whirled around.

Bethany's face creased into a frown. "I got something, but it doesn't make sense." She held out her phone for me to see. "This says they're right next to us on the left, but that's a mountain."

I smiled. "Take the next exit. It's a dirt road, so be prepared," I said to Romeo. I caught Bethany's eyes in the rearview. "They're on top. That's why Poppy got service again."

Bethany glanced at her phone. "Mine's dead. No service."

"About where you lost Poppy, right?"

"Yeah."

Romeo slowed as he eased the big car off the road. "Once bitten, twice shy, eh?"

"You really are having too much fun," Romeo groused, his nose still almost making contact with the steering wheel.

"You're gonna..."

As I said it, we hit a pothole and he clonked himself good.

"...hit yourself on that wheel."

He didn't hit me and he sat up straighter—double win.

"And I'm really not having any fun at all. I'm just trying to resist the urge to curl into the fetal position and make it all go away. You know the more scared I am, the more inappropriate I am."

He took a deep breath and relaxed. "What's the plan?"

"I'm making this up as I go. We should stop well below the crest—it's pretty steep up there, but we don't want to alert them we're here."

"They'll know. It's not like lots of cars come grinding up here in the middle of the night."

"Then grind quieter."

We decided to kill the engine about two-thirds of the way up. "Leave the car here in the middle of the road—this is the only way up or down."

The full moon helped us navigate a road that hadn't seen a grader in more winters than Bethany had been alive. One of those make-out places when I was in high school, the road up and the top it lead to had been dangerous even then. We'd all been forbidden to come up here, which meant it was the first place we all congregated. Of course, I hadn't been forbidden—I was living by myself in a small room at a hotel in downtown. My mother hadn't had a clue where I was.

But the upside was I knew the place pretty well. "This way." I left the road and scrambled up what amounted to nothing more than a goat path...well, burro path to be exact. Out here there were herds of wild burros—I'd loved them forever. Burros and Mustangs gave the desert a wonderful panache. Hand over hand, finding a foothold, we worked our way up with me leading the way, Romeo bringing up the rear and Bethany between us. The going was slow. With the hardscrabble, I had to test each foothold before I shifted my weight. Every now and then, one gave way. Rock skittered downhill, leaving me clutching for a handhold. Or stabbing my toes in to get a better foothold—Christian Louboutin would never forgive me. Maybe he'd send me a new pair...now, there was a thought.

"Turn your phone off," I whispered back to Bethany after

one more cascade of rocks. We were getting close—the moonlight painted where the dark solid of rock gave way to star-dotted sky.

"But I'll get service at the top," Bethany hissed back.

"We know where they have to be, and the light will attract attention."

I didn't have to check—I knew she'd do as I asked. My fingers found the lip, and I pulled myself up so my eyes cleared it and I could see. We'd come up where I thought we would, in a secluded little carve-out protected by some rocks from the vast expanse of the summit. I worked a foot over, then pulled myself the rest of the way, rolling onto the ground, then crabbing to take shelter against a nearby rock. Turning back, I could just make out Bethany as she eyed my position. I motioned her to join me, which she did far faster than I'd made it. Romeo didn't wait to be motioned over. He, too, was there in a flash, leaving me feeling my decrepitude.

The three of us, our backs to the rocks, caught our breath and made a plan.

"Okay," I whispered. "Romeo, what do you think about working your way around until you're behind where they are?"

"Shouldn't I work my way to the other side and cut them off?"

"There's no escape that way, just a sheer drop. The way out is the way we came in."

"One exit, that makes it easier."

"One *safe* exit," I reminded, putting a reality pin in his bubble of confidence. We all needed to be real. "The rest of this rock is a sheer drop."

"Okay, I'll work my way behind." He paused. "But behind where?"

Bethany reached for her phone, but I stopped her. "My bet is they are at the overlook. From there, you can see all of the Vegas valley. It's spectacular."

"Why would he take her there?"

"Let her see all he's taking away from her? I don't know. It doesn't matter."

"Why is he after Mona?" Bethany asked.

"She knows what he's done." Among other things, but that was speculation, and private, so I left it at that. "Bethany, you come with me. Romeo, you ready?"

He showed me his gun, locked and loaded. Good, someone had thought ahead.

My Glock was where? Last time I remembered having it, I gave it to Romeo. "Do you have my gun?"

"I guess I lost it when Beckham beaned me. It must be in impound. Sorry."

When I'd seen Romeo down like that, the gun had been the least of my worries. "Let's go."

"Are you going to tell me who we're after?" he asked as he checked his gun. "It'd be nice to know who to shoot."

"Our Doc Latham."

Behind me, Bethany gasped.

Romeo accepted my word as gospel, God love him.

I wished I was as confident—oh, I was close to absolutely sure, but with lives on the line... "Can't prove it just yet, but the planets are aligning. We'll see if I'm right. But, if I'm not, shoot whoever looks like he wants to hurt Mona."

Romeo rolled his eyes—well, I couldn't really see that in the pale moonlight, but I could feel it.

Romeo angled off to our right. I watched until the night swallowed him. I put both hands on Bethany's shoulders, steadying her, focusing her. "This is serious stuff. Mona could die. Hell, we all could. The guy is a sociopath. Don't underestimate what he will do."

"Doc?" Bethany's voice was a tortured whisper.

"He's not who you think he is. You have to trust me. Don't be fooled."

"What about Poppy?"

Ah, the wild card. Was Poppy a good witch or a bad witch? "We'll get her, too. How much did she know?"

"She knew about you and Mona."

"Did you tell anyone else?"

She ducked her head. "No."

"I need the truth."

She stared straight into my eyes. "I'm telling the truth."

I believed her, not that it mattered. "Okay. Stay close and do what I tell you to. No arguments, okay?"

She nodded, her face serious.

"And no ad-libbing."

Her agreement to that was less than enthusiastic.

I turned and looked around the rock. All clear. "Follow me."

I followed the line of the ridge—not the safest route but the one that had the most protection. Feeling my way in the half-light of the moon and distant memories, I fought the urge to hurry.

We'd be in time. We had to be.

A calmness settled over me. A coldness. And I knew I could kill.

All that separated me from Doc Latham was motivation.

CHAPTER EIGHTEEN

THE night cocooned around us. With my heart pounding in my ears, it was hard to hear, so I paused several times. On the third pause, I heard them. Actually, I heard him. A male voice, low and menacing, that raised my hackles. But he wouldn't be talking to himself.

Mona was alive.

As if Bethany could sense my next move, she slowed as I did. Care was important now that we were close enough to hear...and be heard. After what seemed like an eternity, I peeked around the last rock and could see them.

Unbound, Mona balanced on the precipice. Latham, gun in hand, stood back twenty feet or so. A bandage still wrapped his head. He stooped a bit, softening his shoulders to cradle his head. I bet it still hurt like a mother. The thought made me happy.

Poppy sat against a rock on the far side. Her hands behind her, she looked as if he'd tied her up, but from here it was hard to tell.

Latham spoke to Mona in a low voice, ugly and filled with menace and anger. "Never expected to see me again, did you?"

Mona didn't give him the satisfaction of showing her fear. Shoulders back, head high, she stared at him. "It's not surprising, really. Even the Devil didn't want you."

Oh, good line, Mother. Keep him talking.

He laughed. "Yeah, he couldn't handle the competition."

The laugh died quickly. "I've been looking for you for years. You were the one loose end. But it was like you'd disappeared off the planet."

"I changed my name. Moved."

He snorted. "Became a hooker after I'd had my way with you."

"I was thirteen when you raped me."

Whoa. I tried not to think about all that, what had happened to my mother. She'd been just a kid. Latham wasn't a lot older than she—he must've been a kid, too. This explained a lot, actually.

"Doc, you have to stop this!" Poppy, her voice wild and afraid, called from the shadows. "You said I was—"

"I know what I said." Latham cut her off, not a hint of warmth.

Okay, a true sociopath. So not good. Since talking him out of the tree wasn't an option, how were we going to immobilize him?

I analyzed the setup, working through my options.

Expecting to see Romeo somewhere behind Latham, I looked but didn't see him. Either he was there or would be soon.

"*Doc!* We can move. Go somewhere she'll never find us."

Wait? What? My skin crawled. What kind of relationship did they have? Latham had raped a child...

Latham prowled. Mona appeared composed—not resigned, just in the moment, which surprised me. She so loved to play the part of the victim.

I reached behind me to pull Bethany closer so I could whisper to her. My hand found nothing but air. I whipped my head around.

The girl was gone.

Fuck!

I scanned the area, waiting for a glimpse of her moving between rocks. Nothing. But I knew where she was going—to her friend. If she passed Romeo, I hope he shot her. Okay, not really, but...

Mona lowered her chin and gave Latham a stare. "I killed you once. This time I'll do it right." That sounded like my brand of bullshit.

He waggled the gun at her. "Give it your best shot." He laughed at an old joke. "Oh, wait. You've already done that. And here I am. Bet I haunted your dreams." He sounded like he liked that idea.

"I'd forgotten you." Those words were the most grievous of all. Mona had to know that—men were her only area of expertise.

Okay, so she was escalating, feeding his anger, hoping he made a mistake. Her words had the ring of truth to them, like she really had forgotten.

I'm a woman. And no woman ever forgets being forced.

"But your sister didn't. Watching me and you made her crazy, didn't it?"

I could see Mona pull herself taller, steeling against the hurt.

"She was the one I really wanted. You know that, don't you? But you fought."

"You found her anyway."

"Yeah, every time I'd come home, I'd look for her and you. You two were the ones who got away. The others didn't. I needed to fix that, but you were hard to find. I found her first."

"When you found my sister, why'd you rape her and leave her like that?"

He shrugged. "I took what I'd always wanted. Couldn't believe it when I saw her. It was like no time had passed. I'd finally found her. And I wanted to make her pay. You remember, don't you?"

"You'd come with your father to the sanitarium. You blew back into town like you always did, fresh from incarceration somewhere. One day, you saw her." Mona was dragging the story out and confirming my guesses. "My sister got crazier and crazier, talking about a man from the past who visited her each night."

"Nobody would believe a crazy woman, right?" He smiled

at the irony.

"But I did."

Latham's grin turned into a snarl. "You put a blade in my chest, then dumped me by the pond behind the stables."

"I should've stabbed you again to make sure. Next time, I will."

He lowered the gun. His finger through the trigger guard, he held it out to her. "You'll have to get the gun away from me, though."

She held her ground for longer than I thought she would. Then she skittered to one side. He darted that way, cutting off her escape. She tried the other side, but he was too fast.

Head held high, staring straight at him, she dug in. As he closed on her, she flinched, then took an involuntary step back in self-preservation.

The ground crumbled from under her foot.

My breath stuck in my throat.

Windmilling her arms, she fought to find a foothold.

Latham lowered his gun, letting his arm hang at his side. With an evil grin, he reached out to give her the final push.

"No!" I rushed from my hiding place, running as if my heart would burst.

Surprise registering, Latham stepped back.

As Mona's leg slipped from beneath her, carrying her over the drop, I leaped.

I grabbed her hand. She held tight.

Falling to my knees, I added my other hand, gripping hard to hers. My arms straight, my toes and knees dug into the scree, I leaned back as her weight hit me with the power of a freight train.

Somehow, I held on.

Me on my knees. My mother hanging over a drop to sure death.

Not good.

Time stopped.

"Lucky," my mother breathed. "Go home."

For some reason, that made me laugh.

"Neither of you is going anywhere."

Holding my balance point against my mother's weight, unable to pull her up, I turned to look at Latham. He pointed the gun at me with an arrogance that gave me hope.

Romeo had overshot his position by a fraction. I could see the moon of his face over Latham's right shoulder, then he disappeared. He needed a better angle for his shot.

Bethany every now and again peeked out from behind Poppy, as she worked on the rope binding her friend. I prayed Poppy wasn't a chip off the old block.

I needed to buy time, but I knew in my gut, I had nothing to barter with.

Nothing but the truth. I hoped Hollywood was right.

"This time when you blew back into town, you and Dora decided it was time to spring the blackmail trap on Mona here, didn't you, Mr. Dean?" I couldn't see his surprise, but I hoped I had his attention. "That's right, I know who you are. You're Doctor Dean's son. But you're not a vet; you're a felon with a long rap sheet. Riding around with your father, you learned just enough to fake it. And then, Dora Bates saw you. She knew what you'd done."

"The bitch was going to rat on me."

Ah, I did have his attention. "So, she bartered with all she had, and to you it was everything. She let you into her scheme. She falsified records to get you the vet gig. But that wasn't enough, was it?" I looked at my mother. My arm was shaking with the effort to hold her. My back screamed, but my strength held.

"The bitch was holding out on me."

"But you convinced her that was unwise." Sweat trickled down, stinging my eyes. I couldn't hold on much longer. *Romeo, hurry!*

"I reminded her who she was dealing with."

"So, she gave you my mother."

"Let go," my mother hissed. "I couldn't bear life without you in it."

I didn't want to remind her that, right now, if I died, she would die too, but I appreciated the sentiment—the most I'd gotten from my mother in I don't know when. "You love me?"

"Of course. Stop playing; this is serious." Distress aged her features.

"Dead serious." I closed my eyes and summoned what strength I had left. Throwing my back into it and my weight against hers, I pulled with everything I had. She inched higher. I gained momentum.

"This is fun," Latham said, sounding the opposite.

I paused to catch my breath. Mother tried to worm her hand from mine. "Don't you dare," I said so only she could hear it. I glanced to my right—Bethany was still working on the ropes. Had the girl heard enough? Had both of them?

"And when Dora was going to spring the trap, you killed her. You had the information you wanted."

"It's my game now."

"And you cut the ball off her jacket and planted it in the stall when you tried to kill Poppy's horse." I pulled in deep lungsful of air. "You set up Beckham, knowing he'd recognize it and come charging to find Dora. But she was already dead."

"You're very clever."

Clever for sure—that's why I found myself holding my mother over an abyss with a gun pointed at my back. But I didn't argue.

I pulled, this time even harder.

"Stop!" Latham ordered, his voice hard, cold.

I didn't look at him. I blinked against the sting of sweat and pulled harder.

A shot split the night. I yowled as the bullet hit my calf. Pain blinded me. My hand slipped...

"Do as he says, Lucky." My mother's voice, strong and sure.

"Not. On. Your. Life." I punctuated each word with a hiss of air in through my teeth. Now the ass had made me mad.

Fighting the white-hot sear of pain, using it, I gave my mother a steely grin and pulled.

She inched higher.

I didn't look behind me. I could feel my mother rising.

"No!" Two voices from my right. The girls.

I turned as I pulled.

Romeo stood, but the girls, long legs flailing, blocked his shot.

Poppy hit Latham high.

A shot rang out.

Pain burned through my shoulder. My vision blurred. My grip weakened. I fought to hold on.

Another shot.

Then the girls skidded in beside me. Bethany looked me in the eye. "We got this."

Their hands joined mine and we pulled.

Then my world spun and went dark.

CHAPTER NINETEEN

I HEARD voices first. Feeling the pull of recognition, I worked toward them. Fog surrounded me. My movement was slow, frustrating me. Finally, I opened my eyes, blinking against the light, working for focus. The voices pulled me.

"Lucky? Come back to me." Jean-Charles. What was he doing here? We were on the ridge, Mona falling.

I bolted upright. "No!" Pain seared through me. And the world cleared.

"Where am I?" I stared into the blue eyes of my chef, my love, and they centered me. I didn't feel danger. My breathing slowed as I leaned back. I clung to his hand, an anchor in the storm of confusion.

Pain. I moved my right shoulder. More pain, so I stopped. My leg was on fire, too. Then I remembered.

"The hospital. You are fine."

I swatted that away. "Everyone else? Mother? The girls?"

They gathered around my bed as they were called. Mother snagged my remaining hand before Bethany could grab it.

I was never so happy to see anyone as to see all of them. I closed my eyes, fighting tears. "And Romeo?"

"Here, but I'm not going to hold your hand and moon over you like a female." Then he said, "Oooff," as Brandy's elbow connected with his ribs.

"Might want to rethink that."

"Latham?"

The energy in the room quieted and I knew. "Who killed him?"

"Romeo," Bethany said, with not a little bit of hero worship. She clung to Mother's arm. Aunt and niece. So much story there.

"Thank you," I said to the young detective.

"I owed you." As close as either of us would get to a "You're welcome." I didn't think that was a good thing. Another line item on the list of things to work on. We were good for each other. We needed to remember that. And I needed to appreciate Romeo for who he'd grown into and not for who he used to be.

He beamed for a moment, then his face fell. "But I let you get shot. I'm sorry for that. I didn't know he'd do that. I was angling for a better shot—from directly behind him I was afraid I'd take you out as well."

"I would've done the same thing. Not to worry. Didn't he have a felony record, though? How'd he get a gun?" A naïve question—anybody who wanted a gun could get one if they knew the right people to ask. Since Latham was blowing through town, I doubted he had those kinds of connections, but he could've.

"It was your gun." Romeo looked a bit sheepish.

"Mine? I was shot with my own gun?" The humiliation!

"I had it when Beckham clocked me. Latham must've taken it then."

"Neither one of us noticed, but you had an excuse." I couldn't decide whether I should be embarrassed or not. It sounded like I should, but I couldn't work myself up to being all hot and bothered by it. I mean, it wasn't like the guy wrestled it away from me, then gut shot me or something. "And Poppy?"

Romeo's face darkened. "Latham had his hooks in her. We're getting her some help. Her father is stepping up. In the end, she did the right thing."

"Just a kid." I didn't voice my opinion as to what should be done to men who preyed on youngsters, but it was ugly and involved lots of pain. I closed my mind to the kids; I had to. I'd need time and probably some help of my own to process it all. Instead, I turned back to something more pleasant. "Shot with my own gun," I muttered.

"A bullet is the only way to slow you down." Jean-Charles, a smile playing on his lips, looked at me but said to Romeo, "I am grateful you killed him before he could do more. And perhaps now I can get her to take a vacation."

There were mutterings of disbelief all around.

"Do I do vacations? My leash is pretty short."

"Oh, I'm sure we can let you out to run a bit," Miss P said. "You must come back, though."

"A vacation." I warmed to the idea. "Would that involve a bucolic place, lots of personal attention, and righteous Champagne?"

"Of course." Jean-Charles had a way of saying that that implied a bit of insult. "I was thinking Provence. My mother, she would like to meet you."

The entire room held its collective breath.

I almost laughed. Then I almost ran—but running was out of the question...for a few reasons. "Parfait."

Everyone pulled in a breath, dropping the oxygen level in the room dramatically. My head swam, then cleared. I could do this.

Meet his mother! Damn.

I wanted to live in my own little bubble where other people, people I didn't know, couldn't throw their weight around and mess up the magic. Would his mother be one of those? That could be a problem. If she was anything like Mona...

I scanned the room once more, this time with clearer vision. "My father?" If Mona was here, I knew he was okay, so I wasn't worried.

"Here any minute," Jean-Charles said. "We could tell you were coming back to us, so we sent for him."

"I'm sure he liked that." No one summoned Albert

Rothstein and lived to tell about it.

Bolstered by a couple of extra pillows that Jean-Charles stuffed behind me, from my new vantage point, I realized everyone was staring at me, as if waiting for me to do something.

Everyone I loved. "You all here to pay your respects?"

Everyone laughed.

"I wasn't joking. You're staring, but my song-and-dance repertoire is limited to a couple of shuffle steps and maybe a ball-change or two."

They still laughed...and still stared.

A nurse, young, blonde with an unctuous attitude, wheeled my father into the room. Thank God. Pink had returned to his cheeks. Without the burden of worry, he looked a decade younger. Everyone turned towards him, flowers following the sun. When the Big Boss was present, he commanded attention.

The audience was complete. Who would be the setup guy?

Romeo stepped up. "How the hell did you figure it was Doc Latham?"

"A few things." Suddenly, a thought dawned. "What day is it?"

"You've lost a day."

I processed that. "At least I got some sleep." That made everyone laugh. And I took the time to think about what I wanted to share. Mona's story was hers. "Really just a few things. First, Latham said he had dinner with Dora, but the kid at the steak stand put them there for a late lunch. Latham was the last to see her alive. Poppy said she saw him at the arena when Turnbull died, but he denied it. The rope in the back of his van—that had come from Huntsville State Prison. I had Jeremy run our list of suspects."

"I thought she was daft when she was happy we didn't get a hit," Jeremy said, getting a chuckle all around.

"Dr. Dean, a vet in Reno who was helping Bethany and her grandmother, had a son, but nobody could find him." I looked at Jeremy. "After this went down, did you happen to run Dean through the prison database?"

"Yep, got a hit. Stuart Dean, the missing son. And then, when Beckham called about his truck, I knew."

"How so?" Mother asked.

"The coroner still had the keys to the van. If Latham/Dean needed a ride he'd have to steal it."

"What about Turnbull?" my father asked.

"Collateral damage. Latham was trying to get Beckham off the warpath. Beckham's scrutiny was threatening Latham's big score. Turnbull stumbled on him trying to kill the pony and he got most of the dose."

"Why the upside-down crucifixion thing?" Romeo asked, clearly still shaken by that. "He did it to the people closest to him—his father, Sara, Dora."

I waited, letting him get there on his own.

"It was personal," the detective said, answering his own question.

"Grasshopper, you just stole the marble from my hand."

Someone told me once that a true psychopath could hide who they were, but not forever. Invariably, something would trigger their need again.

With her promise of Mona and the fact she too knew what he had done, Dora had triggered Latham.

"What about the letters shaved in the horse's coat?" Bethany asked.

"Poppy had to have done it. Doc was in the hospital." I reached out and took her hand. Her skin was cold. "She was protecting someone; you said so yourself."

"But the doc?" She grimaced in revulsion.

"A father figure when her own father was lost in his own selfishness and pain."

Bethany took that in, but I had a feeling it would be a long time before she truly understood. And she had yet to understand that Doc Latham had been her biological father. When the full load of that dropped on her, I planned to be close by.

"Justice was done, I guess," Romeo said.

My mother's look caught my eye.

We weren't done yet.
We had one more slight issue to deal with.
A matter of attempted murder.

CHAPTER TWENTY

"WHAT time is it?" I still had no sense of day or time. Darkness had fallen. Everyone had filtered away—Mona had been the last, leaving Jean-Charles and me alone. He'd crawled into bed with me and pulled the duvet he'd brought from home over us both. His head rested near mine on the pillow, his breath warm on my cheek. Heat burned at each point our skin touched.

He'd curled in on my left—my right shoulder had taken that last bullet. Neither bullet had hit anything the least bit important—the doctor's assessment, not mine. At the moment, it all felt important.

"Early. Just eight o'clock, a bit after."

"What day?"

He kissed my shoulder. "Today."

"Shouldn't you be at the restaurant?" Dinner would be in full swing. The restaurant was new; diners would expect him there.

"No. For one night they will not die without me."

"I believe this is the second night?" I snuggled in as much as I could without moving too much, although I was getting used to the constant sting of the pain.

"Now, this might be a disaster. Are you okay? Do you need something for the pain?"

"Just you."

"But this will help, no?" He reached down beside the bed and came back up with a split of bubbles, really good bubbles. "I don't have any glasses."

"Is it cold?"

"That question offends me." And he sounded like it did, which made me giggle.

I tried not to be disappointed in myself—I'd sworn on the altar of all smart women that I would not be one of those who giggled in the presence of an impressive man. Yeah, right.

He popped the cork—the sound reverberating in the small room.

"Are we supposed to have this in here?"

"No." He handed me the bottle. I took a good solid slug, then handed it to him. "I like your style."

He gave me a one-shoulder shrug. "But, of course. I am French." He tilted the bottle, covering the smile he didn't want me to see, and drank deeply.

"Hey, leave some for me. It's only a split."

He wiped his mouth with the back of his hand, which added a decidedly American *je ne sais quois*.

"Have you been hanging around the cowboys a bit too much?"

The innocent look made me giggle...again.

"Drink. It will help. I will get more."

"You have more?"

"In France, it is bad form to run out of Champagne. I have more."

"Where?" I moved to crawl over him to look. I didn't get far.

"Stay. Tonight, be still, just this once. When you are still and your mind quiets, that's where you meet yourself."

"We probably should be acquainted, or at least visit every now and then, me, myself, and I." I took another pull from the bottle, draining it. "One dead soldier."

"The other bottles are in the nurses' station. They have ice and are keeping it cold for me."

"I'm sure." I know he heard the tone in my voice—his ears turned red. Jean-Charles, like all Frenchman I'd ever known, wore charm like a birthright. I'd get used to it. "Will you have to move?"

"Yes, this would be so."

"Then no, no more Champagne. Not right now."

Contented, we curled into each other, enjoying the nearness.

Teddie found us exactly like that.

"Oh!" He hadn't knocked, but the door was open. In one hand, he held a bouquet of purple and orange tulips—my favorite. Teddie could always do the grand gestures. But he failed to understand that love was in the daily details. "I'm sorry. I can come back."

Jean-Charles stroked my arm, then brushed his lips against my shoulder. "I will go get some more Champagne." He eased out of bed, straightening the comforter around me. "I'll be back in a few minutes. You talk to your friend." Then he walked out of the room without ever acknowledging Teddie, not overtly anyway.

"I think I just got a very classy French brush-off." Teddie grinned from the doorway. "May I come in?"

I motioned to the chair. He pulled it next to the bed, laying the tulips on the windowsill. "I should've brought a vase, too."

"The flowers are lovely, thank you."

He looked like he was trying to find some new footing between us. I let him struggle. Helping him, enabling him, had only hurt both of us.

"Are you okay?" He settled on an obvious opener.

"They say I'll be fine. Right now, I'm a bit tired, but things don't hurt too bad."

"The second day is the worst. Once you get past that, you're good to go." He'd just gotten past that with his own bullet to the thigh.

"You'd think a singer and corporate flunky would be the last people taking bullets; yet here we are."

"Yes, here we are." His hands dangled off the end of the

chair arms, his fingers moving—a silent song only Teddie heard. "Is there any hope of us being who we used to be?"

"We're not those people anymore." I didn't answer the question he asked—there was no answer. The future would bring what it wanted.

"You're going to marry him?"

My breath hitched, then I calmed. "Yes."

He nodded once, then forced a smile. "I'll warn you, Jordan is fit to be tied. They wouldn't let him come up since it's after visiting hours."

"A woman said no to Jordan Marsh?" If I could, I'd go down there and shake her hand.

"A dude. Big guy with hair growing in places it shouldn't."

"I know that guy! How'd you get up here?"

His momentary spark faded. "Mona told them I was family." He gave me the big baby blues.

It didn't work. Oh, maybe a slight flutter, but other than that I was numb to him. And, although I'd been asking my heart for that, I mourned what had been between us.

"They say you saved your mother." He gave me a look that spoke volumes—he'd been witness to much of my recent history with my mother.

It struck me that the saddest part about a breakup was losing your history.

"I'm known to do stupid things every now and then."

That got a smile, melting a bit of the hurt.

Jean-Charles returned with an ice bucket and several bottles of Champagne. "I hope I am interrupting."

"Are we having a party?"

Jordan peeked around the door jamb. "Hell, yes!" His partner, Rudy, appeared around Jordan. "We're going to kill that Champagne and then bust you out of here." Smoldering and dark, Rudy with curls, Jordan with salt-and-pepper, they were two of the most handsome men I'd ever seen. Jean-Charles kept pace and, as much as I didn't want to admit it, Teddie with his boyish blond could hold his own.

Multiple handsome men focused on cheering me up—just

what the doctor ordered.

Corks popped. Laughter ensued.

"Did Teddie tell you the news?" Jordan asked.

My heart sunk a little—typical Teddie. He hadn't, and there would be a reason—one I wouldn't like. "No." I kept the panic out of the one word but I didn't trust myself to do that to any others.

"After our run at your place—and maybe one encore." He flashed the smile that melted hearts around the world. "My agent has booked our show for France. JC tells us you guys might be there around the same time."

Everyone seemed invested in that except me—since I hadn't been consulted. Too tired and sore to be pissed off right now, I tabled it and simply smiled in answer. "Monte Carlo or Deauville?"

Jordan's brows came together and his mouth puckered into a pout. "I'm not sure." Then his face cleared. "But it's France, so who cares?"

Right, who cared?

"JC, pop that cork and let's get this party started," Jordan ordered.

At the sound of the cork, a nurse came running. She skidded into the room, then got a good look. Her eyes bugged as she backed out and ran.

"If I'd known getting shot was this much fun, I would've done it more often."

CHAPTER TWENTY-ONE

BY the third day, I was feeling almost human and more than antsy to get back to life. After the Champagne party, the hospital had given me my marching orders early the next morning. While the administrators were happy to see us go—yes, all the men had stayed for an epic sleepover—a few of the nurses were very sorry to wave goodbye. The thought of all that male pulchritude draped around my room warmed my heart.

Since then, I'd been sentenced to interminable days spent by myself at home. Well, with two kids on varying schedules and Jean-Charles working nights and worrying over me the rest of the time, I wasn't by myself often.

When I'd talked with my parents, they'd been circumspect. All in good time and all of that. I was dealing, but not particularly well.

This was that hair shirt of a problem I couldn't fix.

Bethany was with them. Squash was sorting it all out. Once Mona was free to talk, she would. All very logical, but not the least bit emotionally satisfying.

Worse, sitting on the sidelines waiting for the coach to send me into the game stung like salt in a wound.

When my phone rang, I was happy to see it was Squash. "Please tell me you have some great case for me to get involved in? Some racketeers we can threaten? I have a new Louisville Slugger ready for intimidation training. Or maybe a wayward spouse we can scare straight?" I kept the obvious question to myself—if I didn't ask, I wouldn't be shut out one more time.

"Bored, are we?"

"If the asshole had shot me in my left leg, I'd be outta here."

"You could call the car to come get you."

"Tomorrow. I'm trying to be good and do what I'm told." Frankly, healing sucked me dry.

"Right." He knew but didn't skewer me with the point of my denial. "Are you feeling up to a visit with your parents?"

"Stupid question." My energy surged. "When?"

"Would twenty minutes work?"

Barely. Thankfully, I'd already washed my hair and made myself somewhat presentable. Jean-Charles had just left for work. Chantal would pick up Christophe. "I'll clear you through the gate."

As promised, precisely twenty minutes later, a late model 911 with its patented Porsche growl eased into the curb—a convertible, with the top down, white with a tan interior. Squash extricated himself from behind the wheel and rushed to help me as I hobbled down the steps.

"Still hurt like a mother?" he asked.

When he took my elbow, I let him. "Not too bad," I said through gritted teeth as I landed heavily on my sore leg.

"Easy, these things take time."

"And I have the patience of a hungry puppy."

"And the nip, too." He installed me in the passenger seat, then settled himself in the driver's seat and turned the key. Everything about the car inflamed a need for another Porsche of my own. For the first time in a long while, I felt carefree, happy, and alive.

The cold air caressed my face and leaked in between the collar of my jacket and my neck, as refreshing as a cold washcloth on a hot day. Before I forgot, I texted Jean-Charles and Chantal to let them know where I'd be. That sort of accountability used to grate. Now, it made me feel connected.

And the Porsche made me feel like a kid. "To hell with growing up."

"Highly overrated," Squash said with a grin, knowing exactly what I referred to as he pulled away from the curb.

"You do know it's winter?" I pulled my jacket tighter around me as the wind picked up with his speed.

He flipped the heater to high. "Your point?"

My laughter trailed behind us as we accelerated up the on-ramp to the Summerlin Parkway.

Laughter was indeed the best medicine.

*W*HEN the elevator opened, I peeled myself off the back wall and stepped out into the middle of my parents' great room. Squash stayed near, but sensed I needed to walk back into my life on my own.

"Lucky!" My father sounded happy to see me—I took that as a good sign. His smile split his face wide. His skin was ruddy with health, his hair neatly combed. And he was back in uniform, at least for a casual day: creased slacks, starched shirt, loafers, no socks. No hint of the worry that had recently creased his face remained.

The first sign that life was settling back to normal.

He gave me a gentle hug, avoiding my shoulder.

"How was Reno?" I assumed I'd been summoned for answers, so I asked. For the last two days, my parents had been there with Squash and Bethany. Frankly, with so many things to settle, I was surprised they were back so soon.

"Let me pour you a drink, then we'll talk. Champagne?"

"Sure." With his glow, I didn't mind waiting.

"Squash. Your usual?"

"Yessir."

"Go find your mother," my father said. "You know where she is. Squash and I will be along in a minute."

I wandered through the Great Room, heading for the wall of windows. Before my mother had moved in, I'd loved this room. So many dinners I'd shared here with my father. The paintings by the lesser Masters dotting the leather upholstered walls, the furniture made of mahogany and hides of beasts from continents far away, the burnished wood flooring—the place was a testament to masculine good taste—an oxymoron when describing any man besides my father. The fireplace was mobile, within a certain perimeter, and he would position it for the desired warmth wherever we settled, usually on the couches in front of the wall of windows on the far side of the large room. From there, we could drink in the beating heart of the Vegas strip. I never tired of the view.

Mona had barricaded herself into the corner of one couch, her feet tucked under her, and surrounded by a wall of silk pillows in colors that matched the neon outside. She leaned across and patted the open section. "Come. Sit."

Her dark hair trailed down her back in loose waves. Gray showed at the roots. Her skin was flawless, but I detected a loosening along her jaw I hadn't noticed before. Her lack of sleep showed in shadowed half-moons under her eyes. Her robe was a threadbare, peach fleece number I remembered from my childhood. So, too, the shredded collar of a light blue t-shirt that showed where the robe gapped. Wise in the ways of seduction, she had much better boudoir attire. But now Mona needed comfort clothes—her version of comfort food. The past rushing back like it had left us all reeling.

I moved the pillows so I could snuggle up against her. It'd been years, and we didn't fit together quite as comfortably as the younger me remembered, but we made do. "Tell me about your family."

I stretched my legs out so I could work my hand into my pocket to extract the photo. Sitting up, I turned so I could see Mona's face. The lights of the Strip played a kaleidoscope of color across her features, but I could still see the worry lurking there. Why was she worried? The worst was in the past.

And the wariness. What was it with me today? I should write a speech, "Give me your tired, your worried, your wary..." Or maybe not. Somehow it lacked the gravitas of the original.

Without a word I handed her the tiny bit of paper I'd been secreting since Bethany had given it to me.

She gave me a look, then popped her eyeglasses open with a snap of the wrist and settled them on her nose. A deep breath, a moment of hesitation—she licked her lips.

Angling the paper to catch the light, she stared at it for what seemed an eternity. A softness settled over her features, reminding me how pretty she really was when the stress left and only love remained. "Where?"

"Bethany gave that to me the night we met. Was your sister the other one in that photo?"

Mona took a moment, fussing with her glasses as she took them off, folded them, then stuffed them in a hidden fold in her robe. Finally, she looked at me, her face open, a sadness there. "We were twins. This was her favorite picture." A faraway look gripped her as if she'd walked back in time.

"Twins?" The twins Flash couldn't find. "Sara Pickford was your mother."

"Yes." Mona's life had been built on secrets—secrets that had sheltered us both.

"I'm sorry." I squeezed her hand. "And your sister?"

"She's not well. Hasn't been for a very long time. Something happened. Something bad. When we were just kids, almost thirteen. You heard part of the story."

"She's alive?" I whispered.

She reached an arm out, hovering it over my shoulders until I nodded, then she laid it across me, holding me gently.

"Does Father know?" I settled back into her warmth.

"Of course. He was there for part of it."

And so she began, the story of her life, my life, and how we came to be. "I want to get through this part quickly. I don't want to talk about it, so no questions, okay?"

Typical Mona. I shook my head—I'm sure she felt my response.

"One night, my sister and I were walking down the dirt road to our farm. It was dark. It's funny, but through the years I've tried to remember why we were out late, but I can't—the reason is gone. I don't even know if it was for a good reason. It really should've been for a good reason, not for no reason at all." She choked to a halt. "It had to be for a reason."

The hidden wail of pain in her voice sent chills through me—she wasn't talking about being out after dark anymore.

"There was a boy. Even though he was a few years older, we knew him from school and his father owned the ranch we lived on. I was a fighter, even then. He hit me with a rock, then held me down while he raped me. All I remember is my sister screaming and screaming. She never stopped screaming. Not ever...not really."

I couldn't breathe. "Mom, I never knew."

She stroked my hand, seeking comfort and giving it. The power of connection, where skin and hearts touch. "I know, honey. Mothers don't share their pain with their children."

"I'm not a child."

"And pain has come calling." Mona shivered once, the whisper of horror brushing by her.

"What happened to your sister?"

Mona drew me tighter. "She couldn't deal with what had happened. It's as if something broke inside of her that day. She was never the same. Nothing was ever the same."

"You knew the boy. Why didn't he go to jail?"

"We had no money. His father owned our farm, our home. My father had everything invested in the ranch and was paying it off slowly." She stopped as her voice hitched.

"So, he bartered your virtue and your sister's sanity for the ranch?" Anger and then forgiveness filtered into the tight places, the hidden places in my heart. Anger toward my grandfather. Forgiveness for my mother.

"Every night as I fell asleep, my last thought was that he could still be out there. How many other girls?" Her voice cracked. "But Dr. Dean sent him away, so that was something—he couldn't hurt my sister again."

"Or you."

She ignored me. "I heard he'd come back from time to time, but I was gone by then. I didn't know where he went or why, and I didn't care." Her eyes filled with tears. "Whenever he haunted my dreams, I asked God to kill him."

"A powerless child with no champion, of course you did."

"And he found your sister at the asylum."

She looked at me, confused. "How did you know?"

"The ridge?"

"Oh, yes, right." She pulled the pillows tighter, enveloping us both. "My sister loved the animals. The horses calmed her. When Stuart would come back to town, he'd ride around with his father to see the sick animals."

"And the past came rushing back."

"My sister started babbling to everyone, making no sense about a ghost from the past who visited her at night."

"But you believed her."

"Not at first. She'd really left us. The doctors said she'd retreated because the real world was too painful. But, slowly, I realized something was happening, something real. So, after a visit, I stayed. And I saw him. He was leaving my sister's room, zipping up his pants like he hadn't a care in the world." She shivered.

I rubbed her hand between mine. "It's over now. He can't hurt you anymore."

"The past can always hurt you. It's our job not to let it." Those words went far beyond Mona's story—that subtext was easy to read.

I mulled on her intent as I listened. "You had a knife?"

"Yes. I was afraid someone might hear it if I shot him."

Premeditation. My mother was a warrior.

"I followed him to the stables and buried it in his chest. I don't know how I did it. I was wild—the memories, the fear, the pain. And knowing he was raping my sister every night like he had the right. I snapped."

"I'm so sorry." Words failed. What could I say to ease the pain? There was nothing. It was what it was.

"Your father helped me pull him into that shallow grave." She stared out at the lights of the Strip; her hand tightened around mine. "That's why we couldn't prosecute or do anything like that. I cut off that solution. Stupid, really. Now, this." Her voice dropped to a whisper. "This was my fault."

"You didn't know he was looking for you or that he'd become a killer. Hell, you thought he was dead and you'd buried the past along with him."

"If I'd made a different choice..."

I could see how much this tortured her.

"We all make the best choices we can with the information we have, in the time we're given."

"I know." Her voice was filled with I-told-you-so. "But it's so hard to forgive yourself."

She was singing my song. "Your sister?"

"We moved her. We couldn't tell anyone. Maybe we should have and none of this would have happened. We were scared. Your father's career was just taking off. You were in Vegas and on the cusp of becoming the beautiful, powerful woman you are. Had all this come to light..."

"I understand. You made the best decision you could at the time you made it. Only thing you did wrong was not making sure the asshole was dead."

"We were in such a hurry. There was blood everywhere. It was dark."

"Mother, it's okay. Really, everything is okay now."

"Are you sure?" Her question extended beyond the topic at hand.

"Completely."

"I never abandoned you," she whispered under the hurt. "I just couldn't tell you."

She could've; she knew that. But, again, she made the best choice in an impossible situation.

"If you'd stayed with me, if I'd let you, the same thing would have happened to you. A whorehouse isn't a safe place for a beautiful young woman. I couldn't let that happen...not ever."

I hadn't thought about that. At fifteen, all I knew was her house was my home. Now, in the bright light of perspective, things looked different. "I know." I didn't want to talk about me, or us. I had to either push Mona from my life or accept she had done the best she could, which she had. Were her decisions perfect? Hardly. Was life perfect? Never. Could I live without her? Impossible.

Human frailty, hard to accept and hard to forgive. Especially your own.

"Who put your sister in the asylum?"

"She needed help and understanding, and even with that, she had a questionable path to recovery. She didn't make it. My father couldn't cope. The farm was a bad place for her, but he couldn't leave."

"So, he sent her away."

Mona's hand shook as she plucked at a thread on one of the pillows. "We were told it was best."

"What did you think?"

"Honey, I was only just barely fourteen then, and a girl at that. I wasn't allowed to think."

That punched every button I had, but venting to my mother couldn't fix stupid—stupidities of the past, stupid that still existed today. "Everybody should have a voice, Mom."

"She was most at peace around me. When they sent her away, she was like a wild animal." A tear trickled down Mona's face, catching the light. A neon pink slash.

"And you?"

"It was like carving out the center of my heart." That explained a lot about my mother. Sometimes her actions could be unforgivable, but her motivations were generally selfless—and that made it all forgivable.

She'd given up her sister.

And then she'd given up me.

Both because she had to. Choices came with a price.

"Where is she now?"

"She's in an institution...an asylum...in Minnesota."

"Which you pay for."

She didn't answer. She didn't have to.

"What happened to you?"

Mona drew in a ragged breath. I got the sense this next part hurt almost as much. "My parents, they couldn't forgive me. I was the strong one. I should've protected my sister. They told me that so many times... They couldn't forgive me so I couldn't forgive myself."

"They blamed *you?*" My voice rose on a tidal wave of indignation.

"My sister was their favorite, their golden child. The weaker ones usually are. They couldn't deal with their own fault, their own pain. Of course, I didn't understand that until much later. At the time, I felt they hated me, that I reminded them of what they'd lost, and I'd been the one who had taken her from them."

"So, you ran."

"At fourteen, I was on my own in Vegas. I changed my name and built a life."

I knew the rest of the story, or as much as I needed. "But you visited your sister; that's how you knew he'd come back."

"Dora Bates would call me and tell me when my parents had been there so I could time my trips to avoid them. They didn't come often. Dora had the room across from my sister's."

And the story fell into place.

Mona drew herself up—the pain of the past weighed less after the telling.

"And your niece?"

"She was born in Minnesota. I wasn't there." Mona stared out at the lights, the Vegas magic—a place where fantasy reigned and reality receded. "My mother took the baby."

"Why prostitution?" A question I'd always wanted to ask her.

"I didn't deserve any better. I was guilty, you see..."

"Of what?" Again, my voice rose.

She shushed me and gave a quick glance over her shoulder toward the private area of the apartment where her babies slumbered. Then she turned big eyes on me and pulled the edges of her robe together to cover her legs. "I was the one who survived."

I could only imagine how she felt and had no doubt that fell woefully short.

The window beckoned, and for a moment I paused, drinking in the hope and promise in the blinking lights. My father and I often stood here, shoulder to shoulder, solving the problems of the day. But today's Pandora's Box of problems might not have any solutions...other than hope, left in the bottom.

"Aren't you going to ask my sister's name?" Mona flicked a glance my way.

"No, I already know it." The girl had said she liked my name. "It's Lucky, Lucky Bean."

"Anyone who underestimates you—"

"—is on the right track."

"That wasn't her real name, of course. She was christened Bethany Grace, but she preferred her nickname."

My heart cracked open. Every time my mother called to me or said my name, she remembered her sister. "Where did O'Toole come from? Fiorelli is your family name, right?"

Mona nodded and gave a tight laugh. "You're not going to like it."

"What else is new? Come on, tell me. No more secrets."

Mother brightened a bit. If I didn't know for real, I would strongly suspect she took glee in causing me a bit of consternation...okay, *a lot* of consternation. I braced for impact—I mean, this one was personal—the derivation of a moniker I wore like a second skin.

"Peter O'Toole." Mona actually flinched when she said it, cowering back enough to trigger my kinder instincts.

She rushed on, her words piling on themselves like a flood behind a dam. "He was so dashing and handsome as Lawrence of Arabia." If she'd been standing, she would've swooned.

Okay, now she was milking it.

"I was named after an actor?" I let my voice rise in mock indignation. Drama was in my toolbox as well. After all, it was my birthright and probably etched into my DNA. They say that very terrifying experiences can actually alter your DNA.

Mona changed mine on a daily basis. And who said I wasn't evolving? "And not just any actor. He may have been dashing, Mother, but he was an asshole."

Mona quieted. Her light lessened as the darkness filtered back in. "Seems to me we need a bit of both to get through life, don't you think?" she said in a tiny voice.

I hated it when Mona spouted smart. I liked her better when she was a pain in the ass.

But an *actor!* I shook my head. If Mona was good for anything, it was for surprises—at least she was consistent.

The men, either sensing we'd had our talk or simply tired of waiting, joined us. My father handed me a much-needed libation—he'd forgone the Champagne and poured me three fingers of Scotch, desecrating it with one lone ice cube. My father took his normal place at the window, this time his back to the lights. Squash took the only other spot—the place beside me on the couch.

"What do you have to add to all of this?" I asked the lawyer. "What happened when push came to shove in Reno?"

"Your mother's off any hook they might have tried to hang her on—the guy she allegedly attempted to kill is dead. No witnesses. No admission. We're good."

"I figured. And Bethany? Where is she?"

"I left her in Reno with family friends. We're working out the details on the ranch ownership. She's going to sell it. Cornell is an expensive program. She'll be back in a week or two. I think she wanted to let Mona process everything, then maybe they could go see her mother."

Mona nodded when I gave her a questioning glance.

Family. Yes, it was definitely the Fifth Ring of Purgatory, and I wouldn't have it any other way.

"I'm sure Bethany can keep her farm. Her family can find a way to fund her educational expenses." At my father's smile, I raised my glass. "After all. What is family for?"

Squash joined in the laughter.

It felt good. I felt good, like somehow banishing my mother's demons had fixed the bad between us. "And Poppy?"

"You were right, Latham had hoodwinked her. He told her to shave the letters in the horse's coat. She thought it was a game to lure a bad parent out of hiding so her daughter could find her. Bethany had told her just enough of her story, for Poppy to swallow the lure."

"She's lucky he didn't kill her."

"Both the girls are," my mother added, her voice hard with experience.

Silence stretched as we each dealt with the horror of the could-have-beens.

"Hell of a birthday for you," my father said, apparently settled on a happier topic.

"Your birthday," Squash said. It wasn't a question—he knew it as well as I did—but mischief sparked in his eyes.

Before I could backpedal, my phoned dinged, rescuing me.

A message from Chantal.

When might you come home? Christophe is asking for you, and I could use some time at school to practice for my exams.

I smiled. Family.

On my way.

I looked at my parents. Lifting their worry had restored them, even though Mona looked way behind on sleep. As if that thought awakened them, the babies' wails filled the air and Mona's face fell.

"Albert?" she asked.

Without a moment's hesitation, he handed her his drink and went to fetch the rest of his family.

"Mother, are you ever going to give those girls names?"

"Yes, I think I might have a couple in mind." She gave me an enigmatic smile.

I didn't take the bait. Instead, I tapped Squash on the thigh. "Come on, I need a ride home. Duty calls, and I never leave the party with anyone other than the person who brought me."

CHRISTOPHE launched himself into my arms—the pain almost dropped me to my knees, but the joy chased it away. Chantal flew by me with a wave as she headed out the door. And I was home. Something about letting go of the past, making peace with it had opened my future wide with possibilities.

The boy and I cooked and played, and read...and read. He had a bath and we read some more. We'd fallen asleep in my bed in a sea of books.

Jean-Charles found us that way.

Something awakened me. A sound? Sensing his presence? I opened one eye and saw him standing at the foot of the bed. Weary but filled with the day, he looked at us with such love.

Oh, I hoped his mother didn't put herself between us.

He saw that I was awake and brushed his lips over mine. "I'll be right back. Don't move." He lifted Christophe, who moaned, then smiled, and fell right back to sleep on his father's shoulder.

"I'd take a bullet to the other shoulder to sleep like that," I whispered as I watched him carry the boy out of the room.

When he returned, I opened my arms, inviting him to join me.

"In a minute. I have something to show you. Can you come with me?" He pulled back the duvet, then extended a hand.

"The last man who asked me that wanted me to rob a grave," I half-groused just for the effect.

"Hard to compete with that." He pulled me to my feet once I'd gotten my legs over the side. "Come." He kept hold of my hand, leading me to the front door where he stopped. "I have not given you your birthday present."

"I wasn't expecting one. You gave me my life." Overstating and sappy, I know, but I was feeling emotional—the last bit of life had been one heck of a ride.

He opened the door.

Nestled next to the curb was a car, and not just any car. "A 1953 356 American Roadster." I almost couldn't breathe.

"That's like the rarest Porsche ever built." I couldn't take my eyes off the car.

"For the rarest woman I've ever met." He tossed that line off with ease and got a kiss for it. "I am sorry it is late. They are hard to find, then I had to get it here. She is a beauty, no?"

Silver with a beige top and darker brown interior, if the street light wasn't playing tricks. "The most beautiful thing I've ever seen. Where did you get her?"

"Paris."

"Of course, she would be French."

I rewarded him with another kiss and lost myself.

TO BE CONTINUED...

Thank you for coming along on Lucky's wild ride through Vegas. For more fun reads, please visit www.deborahcoonts.com or drop me a line at debcoonts@aol.com and let me know what you think. And, please leave a review at the outlet of your choice.

Novels in The Lucky Series

WANNA GET LUCKY?
(Book 1)

LUCKY STIFF
(Book 2)

SO DAMN LUCKY
(Book 3)

LUCKY BASTARD
(Book 4)

LUCKY CATCH
(Book 5)

LUCKY BREAK
(Book 6)

LUCKY THE HARD WAY
(Book 7)

LUCKY RIDE
(Book 8)

Lucky Novellas

LUCKY IN LOVE

LUCKY BANG

LUCKY NOW AND THEN
(PARTS 1 AND 2)

LUCKY FLASH

Other books by Deborah Coonts

AFTER ME

DEEP WATER

CRUSHED

Made in the USA
San Bernardino, CA
03 August 2017